BURNING
ASHES

James Bennett

orbit

www.orbitbooks.net

ORBIT

First published in Great Britain in 2018 by Orbit

1 3 5 7 9 10 8 6 4 2

Copyright © 2018 by James Bennett

Excerpt from *Strange Practice* by Vivian Shaw
Copyright © 2017 by Vivian Shaw

The moral right of the author has been asserted.

A CIP catalogue record for this book is available from the British Library.

ISBN 978-0-356-50667-8

Typeset in Plantin by Palimpsest Book Production Limited,
Falkirk, Stirlingshire
Printed and bound in Great Britain by Clays Ltd, Elcograf S.p.A.

Papers used by Orbit are from well-managed
forests and other responsible sources.

MIX
Paper from
responsible sources
FSC® C104740

Orbit
An imprint of
Little, Brown Book Group
Carmelite House
50 Victoria Embankment
London EC4Y 0DZ

An Hachette UK Company
www.hachette.co.uk

www.orbitbooks.net

BURNING ASHES

Ben, who knew the city like the back of his claw, watched as the panic multi̶ ̶ ̶ ̶ ̶ ̶ ̶ ̶ ̶ ̶ring down Westfe̶ ̶ ̶ ̶ ̶ ̶ ̶ ̶ ̶ ̶ked suitcases. Others, youths, went ̶ ̶ ̶ ing and swe̶a̶r̶i̶n̶g̶ by on bicycles, on skateboards, or stumbling on discount store high heels. Over eight long centuries, Ben had seen London grow and spread out from a huddle of houses around the Palace of Westminster – and seen no end of the city's troubles from the Black Death to blitzkrieg bombs – but he had never seen anything like this before . . .

By JAMES BENNETT

This one is for my brother, Benjamin Streets.
I wrote most of it in his house, Kent.

PART ONE

Seven Sleepers

Say, who is he, with summons strong and high,
That bids the charmed sleep of ages fly,
Rolls the long sound through Eildon's caverns vast
While each dark warrior rouses at the blast
His horn, his falchion, grasps with mighty hand,
And peals proud Arthur's march from Fairyland.

Leyden, Scenes of Infancy

ONE

There were giants on the earth in those days. Someone had written that down long ago. *And apparently, in these.*

Snout curling with the thought, Ben Garston veered low over the Thames, one old serpent reflected in another, the September wind rushing through his under-wing gills. A red-scaled dart, his arrowhead tail zipping over power cables, bridges, railways and masts, the one-time Sola Ignis, six months retired, sped in pursuit of a monster. His passing bulk, lizardine, streamlined, left a v-shaped wake in the waters below, waves slapping against the embankments on either shore, a passing storm rattling the jetties and the masts of boats at moorage. The stench of the river, a heady brew of factory fumes, dead fish and diesel, blustered in his nostrils, a pall he'd have gladly avoided if he'd had a choice, preferring the damp of his lair, deep under the charred remains of his townhouse on Barrow Hill Road.

Gold and forgetfulness. The times have denied me the luxury of both.

When rubble had come clattering down from the stalactites, bouncing off the rune-carved pillars and his slumbering snout, Ben had awoken with a roar that embodied his mood. Leaving the sanctuary of his underground cave, he'd made the journey

3

to the city above, his swelling shoulders shoving at the tunnel walls, his curses held behind his teeth. Emerging from the depths of the West Hampstead interchange, ignoring the screams and the stalling traffic (*it's too late for modesty, folks*), he'd launched himself into the sky to investigate, saddling the wind for a decent view.

He didn't get one; the vista only presented the bad news, dark, smoky and to the east of him.

A towering shape rose from the urban sprawl. For all the unorthodox angles and curves of London's skyline he could tell that the newcomer wasn't a skyscraper simply by the fact it was moving. A distant cannonade boomed through the streets from Blackfriars to Belsize Park. The sky cringed with the echoes, the sound of crumbling brickwork, shattering glass and wailing people all too familiar, a dissonance that he'd come to know.

Ben greeted the sight with a grunt.

The devil is loose, all right. You knew it was only a matter of time . . .

Crusty-eyed, horns tipped, he shot after the Sleeper – who, at present, was wide awake and bellowing to deafen England – by force of habit more than anything else. No one but Ben was going to save the panicking masses that were pouring out of doorways and stalled cars, pushing and shoving up, down and across the roads in their urge to escape, some of them falling in the flood, never to emerge. The screams and shouts made a harsh accompaniment to the calamity, the echoes shuddering over Limehouse. The sound pricked his shame, his heart going out to the humans.

Always playing the hero. That's what Von Hart had said, all those months ago in China. *But there is only one thing I need from you here. You're too late for anything else.*

4

As things stood Ben knew that he'd been making a pig's ear of heroism of late, sinking up to his neck in chaos, bitterness and guilt. In the past two years, the city below had seen more than her fair share of trouble, including an African goddess, an undead priest, Texan witches, a vengeful knight, a battle dragon, a shit-stirring vampire, a holy assassin and a murderous saint cult, not to mention a treacherous fairy. The resulting damage to London landmarks, to London scepticism . . . well, it was beyond belief.

And that didn't touch on the turmoil caused by the breaking of the harp. Six months ago, far from here – far from anywhere, really, in the depths of the nether – the *Cwyth*, the mnemonic harp, had shattered, torn apart by the envoy extraordinary Blaise Von Hart. Like a fool, Ben had believed the warrior monk Jia Jing when she'd described the Ghost Emperor as an otherworldly menace hell-bent on forcing its way into Creation. In truth, Von Hart had summoned the giant Lurker himself, empowering the thing with spells and his fragment of the harp, drawing destruction to the door of the world. Beyond that door, the gate of the Eight Hand Mirror, the tragedy had played out. The Ghost Emperor – or as it happened, Von Hart – had stretched out a tentacle and wrenched Jia's fragments from her grasp, reforging the artefact anew.

And then ripping the harp apart. The following explosion had sent the *sin-you* tumbling to her doom, lost to the blackest eternity. Ben had managed to escape with the envoy, although "escape" probably wasn't the right word for it.

What do you call it when you jump from one shitstorm into another? Oh yeah. Life . . .

In that blinding moment of truth, the Long Sleep had come undone, the enchantment of centuries violently broken. Of

5

course, the repercussions followed. The Remnants, long ago lulled and lured, slumbering, buried beneath the earth, were slowly waking up.

And of course, Ben thought with the same old sneer, *I'm the one left cleaning up the mess . . .*

Somehow, he'd survived all that, his bullshit "happy ending". But not without certain breakages himself, in his mind, his body and soul. He had lost so much. The love of his life, for one. His trust in his friend, for another. And his faith in the Pact. By the skin of his teeth, and like the butt of some cruel god's joke, he was alive and kicking.

The giant on the skyline, however, could easily put an end to that. Put an end to all of them, perhaps. The situation was scaling into a crisis of cataclysmic proportions. The Pact was undone. The Lore was over. Exploding oil refineries, butchery in Beijing – these events had not gone unnoticed. Some had started to seriously question the slew of shaky camera footage and the wild reports of monstrous creatures around the globe. In the past six months, the frequency and detail of these reports had surpassed the level of mass hysteria and, according to the news, the military was on high alert. Intelligence agencies were investigating the sightings from the Sahara to the South China Sea. Rumours abounded, whispers about strange discoveries, scales the size of dinner plates that didn't conform to any known DNA. Inexplicably shattered museum roofs. Massive craters on Hampstead Heath . . .

More than likely, the *National Enquirer* and the *Fortean Times* were facing bankruptcy, forced to compete with the mainstream media now that the paranormal and the unexplained flickered across the TV screen in the daily headline news. World religions, of course, all screamed Armageddon, heralding an imminent

Day of Reckoning – Doomsday, Ragnarok, you name it – with a renewed and palpable delight.

At street level, it was getting harder for the humans to shrug off these reports as hallucinations, photoshopped fakes and suchlike, when the damage was plain for all to see, from claw marks in an aeroplane's fuselage to a derailed bullet train. A little video analysis from internet geeks suggested that some of the clips could even be real. *Dragons* were fucking real! And with no Guild of the Broken Lance, no Whispering Chapter in place, the carefully constructed wall between the Remnant and the human world was crumbling. In short, there was no longer anyone available to explain away these events, put them down to earthquakes, tidal waves, visions inspired by gas leaks and potent street drugs.

In the Middle Ages, we spread tales and songs, the more unlikely the better. Throughout the Enlightenment, we cast doubt on your existence, put it all down to superstition, ignorant reactions to storms, comets, the aurora borealis . . .

Yeah. Sir Maurice Bardolfe had told him about the Guild's "tireless work", all right. Explaining him and the few others like him out of the world . . .

And even now, that world rumbled on, although humanity's blindness, he believed, was currently due to mass denial rather than outright scepticism. Even as a giant crashed his way through the city, people had got up, brushed their teeth and caught the train to work. Some, he imagined, had switched off the morning news. Or shaken their heads at the footage of smoke rising from the heart of the city.

He envied them. Bleary-eyed, half regretting the bottles of Jack that he'd chugged the night before, Ben soared onwards, following the curve of the Thames. His quarry rose directly ahead, and he was drawing ever closer, close enough for the giant's shadow to fall across him, rendering him a mere red-winged bird in comparison. Dwarfed, helpless, he flapped through the clouds towards the giant's shoulders, a barricade of brawn that was currently smashing a cascade of steel and glass from Canary Wharf as he waded further downstream.

Cormoran. He's Cormoran. Shuddering, Ben put a name to his dread. *Bane of the Summer Country. Town Crusher. Or, to put it another way, a two-hundred-foot-tall pain in the arse.*

Ben recognised the giant from his past, rather than legend. The building of St Michael's Mount and the hurled rocks that had formed the Scilly Isles had happened long before his time, back in the Old Lands. But he remembered the giant who'd lumbered his way to the Remnant gathering at White Horse Hill, Uffington, in 1215, the night he'd signed the Pact. Like the other creatures who had trembled in that moonlit vale, the giant, one of the last *Gog-men* of Albion, had come to discuss his place in the grand scheme of things, to find some way to resist the relentless march of civilisation, the onslaught of knights that craved his territories and treasures for their own.

But, of course, it had been too late. A matter that even now made Ben uncomfortable, because the offered reconciliation, the dangling olive branch from the humans, had drawn a desperate rabble into the valley that distant midsummer night. And only to bring them within the ambit of the *Cwyth*, the spreading music of the mnemonic harp. The lullaby had sent giant and all down, down into the ground. Into the dark. Into memory.

Until now.

Ben, an unwelcome guest that night (to say the least), had tried to tell them, the gathered Remnants. *We cannot fight time nor tide. It's a matter of survival.* Some had listened. Some had turned away. And even as the ink from his quill was drying on the scroll and the music came spilling into the valley, most had cursed him, spitting words like *traitor* and *coward* and *milk-drinker*. To most of the gathering, he had simply been a royal pet, a wyrm in cahoots with humans. *A snake among apes* and therefore not to be trusted. He'd found himself unable to reassure his fellow Remnants. And in the end, he was wrong. King John, in typical fashion, had shown no compassion for the "fiends" standing in his way. He had deemed giants too big and too dangerous (not to mention the odd one or two having a taste for the blood of Englishmen) for the Pact to spare them, to let even one such creature remain awake and unfettered in the world. And so, Cormoran, and every last one of the *Gog-men* across the land, had gone into the Sleep, slumbering under hill and dale, the grass growing over their temporary graves.

Airborne, slowing, Ben took in the giant's earrings, each copper pendant about the width of an Underground tunnel. He took in his topknot of hair and his dreadlocks, as tangled and grubby as a thicket in Epping Forest. Cormoran's loincloth, made up of innumerable pelts, covered the hairy humps of his buttocks, sparing the people gawking in the surrounding office buildings at least that terrible sight. Ben saw the club in the giant's fist too, a yacht-sized chunk of wood studded with rocks, the weapon swinging back and forth, tossing up silt and foam as it lashed the surface of the water.

What hole had Cormoran crawled out of? Ben knew exactly. Rousing, he'd have shrugged off an Oxfordshire hillside, rising from some black-as-pitch cavern hollowed out of music and molten rock eight hundred years ago – a cave recently made molten again by the breaking of the harp. The giant's awakening, however, had come as a surprise. It wasn't in the schedule. Or rather, in the prophecy, spoken centuries ago, or so the story went, by the Lady Nimue, the Queen of the Fay, upon her departure from Earth.

Yes. It was in all the old books, wasn't it? The Queen's Troth, ringing in his skull these past few months along with the echoes of the alien music.

One shining day, when Remnants and humans learn to live in peace, and magic blossoms anew in the world, then shall the Fay return and commence a new golden age.

Well, nothing about the present situation looked golden to him.

The return of the Fay was meant to signal the fulfilment of the Pact and the end of the Long Sleep – an event that Ben had come to see as far-fetched, to put it mildly, a fairy tale cooked up out of Remnant hope and King John's coercion. Miles and months away in China, Von Hart had told him, in a wide-eyed, breathless fashion that could've been shock or could've been triumph, that the Fay were coming back. It was a strange thought and an alarming one. All his life, Ben had believed that the long-vanished masters, the creators of all the Remnants, remained aeons away in the nether. A memory. Ancient history. Gone. It struck him as both ironic and cruel to now discover that he *hoped* so.

I should be cheering at the news of their return. Not shitting myself.

The only word that fitted the knot in his guts was "dread". It was an old story and an old score. Prophecies and fancy words aside, the Fay, known in the oldest of tales as fickle, had abandoned the Remnants, leaving their magical children to crawl on their bellies through the shadows of the ages. Besides, Von Hart's double dealing had hardly convinced him of Fay benevolence. He had no reason to trust the creatures at all, let alone their promises.

But he had learnt to trust his instincts. Wasn't the giant ahead of him stark proof of the trouble to come?

10

Cormoran loomed. Christ, he could smell the fucker, an earthy fetor that put the city's pollution to shame. It was the stink of an ancient bed, unkempt, magical and rank, sour as all the spells were sour these days, in these End Times of enchantment. The giant was up to his knees in the river, his massive boots sinking into metres of junk and filth, the wreckage of countless centuries. Ships, bridges, *dragon bones* . . .

The width of the Thames allowed Cormoran free passage through London, and Ben, having surveyed the damage caused by the giant's feet through Clerkenwell, could only feel grateful that he'd chosen this route. Foot-shaped craters peppered Fleet Street and Ludgate Hill, the shops, pubs and offices crushed as if they belonged in a model village, pulverised by the passage of mammoth boots. At the top of the hill, the giant's club had cracked the dome of St Paul's Cathedral as though it was a boiled egg, the giant grumbling and turning, stamping down on Queen Victoria Street, a tower of sinew heading for the river.

The road had cracked like a liquorice stick, buses and trucks ramming into a descending foot. A church steeple went tumbling through the air, splintering apart on Mansion House tube station, blocks of stone choking the entrance, burying commuters. Trees shook, shedding branches and birds. Pigeons, squawking, fluttered through the invaded sky. A furrow of rubble – most of it smouldering, sparking or aflame – marked the course of Cormoran's journey, a broad thoroughfare of ruin. The Monument to the Great Fire had toppled in his wake, the Doric column thumping down on the adjacent buildings, its golden crown shattering, riddling the crowds with debris. HMS *Belfast*, the navy museum battleship, had capsized at moorage as the giant's boot splashed down in the Thames.

Tower Bridge now rose snapped and crumbling behind the

brute, and several barges and boats had run aground, hurled by the displaced tide. Lightermen and tourists milled on the shore, bedraggled, shell-shocked, but alive. Ben didn't want to think about the people in the city, how they'd fared under the march of leather soles with who knew how many tons behind them. With a familiar twist in his guts, he knew that he wouldn't be able to save everyone. As ever, this was a game of damage limitation.

And you're losing ground. You've been losing ground ever since the breach in the Lore . . .

Somehow, he had to draw the giant away from London, lure him further downriver into the marshes, into the deepest mud, let the estuary tides close over his head . . .

Wishful thinking. The only kind you know.

Still, he had to try. The giant shrugged off Canary Wharf in splinters and crashed onwards past Millwall, the river flooding Surrey Docks Farm and Sir John McDougall Gardens. Mud and trash went washing into the Isle of Dogs, wrecked boats, stunned seagulls, fishing nets, dislodged crates and shopping trolleys swirling down the streets towards the inner docks.

With eyes as keen as a hawk's, Ben watched as people below wrenched open their front doors, Sunday papers in hand, to see what all the fuss was about. Men in boxers and women in nighties looked up at the sky. Teenagers dropped their mobile phones. Children squealed and pointed. On the corner, a bearded gent clutched his turban and hurried inside to lock his shop door, as if that was any defence against the huge and impossible creature barging its way into the day.

Ben, who knew the city like the back of his claw, watched as the panic multiplied throughout the Docklands, hordes hurrying down Westferry Road, some of them clutching badly packed suitcases. Others, youths, went shouting and swearing by on bicycles, on skateboards, or stumbling on discount store high heels. Over eight long centuries, Ben had seen London grow and spread out from a huddle of houses around the Palace of Westminster – and seen no end of the city's troubles from the Black Death to blitzkrieg bombs – but he had never seen anything like this before, the populace screaming, running scared from a monster.

The usual empathy, reluctant, foolhardy as it was, tugged at him. Down there, the human medley of ages and cultures for which the capital was famous had become united in terror. And, in the shadow of the giant striding down the river ahead, Ben couldn't deny that he was part of the threat, a red-scaled, leather-winged freak that *should not be*, that belonged in fairy tales and big-budget movies, not in the skies above modern-day London.

A buzzing in his ears, mechanical and way too close, reminded Ben that his concerns for secrecy were pointless. The helicopter was an example of the dangerous state of play. Flanks emblazoned with the logo of a popular and utterly bullshit national tabloid, the chopper swooped in alongside Ben like a mosquito, the whirling rotors and humming engine as annoying as any sting. He spared the craft a weary glance. In the cockpit, a slack-jawed pilot took in the behemoth ahead, Cormoran's wading bulk currently making a sewer of Deptford. In the cabin, a journalist was alternately taking snapshots of the giant and the dragon coasting beside them, although the wind and his trembling hands made the chance of decent photographs unlikely.

Say cheese. Ben gave the pilot a glimpse of his fangs, warning him to keep his distance as he climbed for greater altitude, racing after the giant. The press, in typical fashion, ignored him, the increased whine of the chopper's engine informing him that it meant to stay glued to his tail.

Fine. It's your funeral.

Despite his cynicism, Ben knew that this wasn't good. The press he could handle. He didn't give a shit about his five minutes of fame – it was much too late for that – but an airborne craft would soon bring others. Perhaps Royal Air Force jets armed to the teeth with machine guns and missiles, if experience was anything to go by. And maybe Tornadoes could even stop the giant. Maybe not. Maybe Cormoran would bat them out of the sky, King Kong style. All the same, Ben was sure that the pilots wouldn't draw a distinction between the giant and himself. A monster was a monster, after all. A threat was a threat. Besides, where the hell were they? The military response was tardy, to say the least. Every step the giant took meant more trampled and drowned people, more casualties, more structural damage. He had to act fast or forget this latest, ill-advised attempt at heroism.

He zipped upward, venting flame, trying to catch Cormoran's attention. Comparatively bird-sized as he was, he might as well have pecked at a statue's head. What the hell did the giant want? Eight hundred years underground hadn't left him rested and in a good mood, that was for sure. And no wonder. Judging by the shambling mountain before him, his shaggy head and shuddering groans, Ben reckoned that Cormoran was more dazed and confused than anything; the needling harp song – a melody that Ben recalled with a cramp in his balls and an ache in his skull – must've been a rude awakening. And that didn't even begin to account for the giant's arrival in modern times.

Giants weren't exactly known for their brains. Nevertheless, on the whole, they'd been smart enough to steer clear of King

John's new cities and towns, preferring the open reaches of the countryside, the Cornish moors, the Cumbrian hills and the Scottish Highlands. Back then, London would've been a smoking huddle of huts on the horizon, two or three spires pointing at the sky, most of them long since crumbled or sunken into the shadow of tower blocks, their weathervanes outstripped by satellite dishes and radio masts.

The modern city must strike the giant as a vision of hell, surely. A festering, stinking bed of industry, a sea of clamour and smoke. Cormoran was angry and confused, clearly. A lumbering oaf at the best of times, he must've climbed from his bed with what amounted to a raging hangover. Had he realised that someone had stolen eight hundred years from him? That people had fooled him, forced him into slumber? Did the sickening song still ring in his skull? It was only a matter of time until his club started swinging this way and that, crashing down on an unsuspecting Greenwich, his shadow falling over the historic district as he trudged further downriver. Water, black and foul with the ceaseless river traffic, gurgled and slopped up the tributaries of creek and canal, a steadily rising wall of destruction that went crashing over houses, roads and railway tracks, prompting a fresh chorus of screams.

Ben made his move. Wings folded, he navigated the giant's head, shooting over crusty ringlets of hair and emerging above his sloping brow, his coarse skin glistening with scars and runnels of sweat. From the giant's temples, faded tattoos curled down to his jawline, which Ben recognised as markings from the Old Lands, back when such tribal symbols mattered. Giants were as old as the hills and just as hardy. Had Cormoran fought at Camlann, the ancient, legendary battle that had seen the fall of King Arthur? His brands appeared to suggest so, but whether he'd sided with the Pendragon or the Usurper, Ben couldn't say.

Unhappy with the sight, an echo of a war that wasn't lost on him, Ben set his gaze on Cormoran's eyebrows several feet below him, a briar sprinkled with the frost of age. Snapping out his tail, he dived directly downwards, all four claws naked and splayed. Roaring a challenge, he raked his way down the giant's face, leaving a scattering wake of blood.

Big mistake.

Cormoran bellowed, but with the thunder of outrage rather than pain. As Ben pushed himself off the giant's nose, Cormoran turned his cliff of a head, looking around for the source of the attack. Air, hot and rank, came blasting from the giant's lungs, slamming into Ben like a battering ram, flinging him wheeling out into space, his wings flailing. The ground spun below, a kaleidoscope of buildings and streets. Then a hand, a wall of meat, came up to grab him.

With a grimace, Ben slipped through the giant's fingers, the ridge of his spine scoring a vast and scabrous palm, missing a crushing end by inches. Fighting for calm, he let gravity drag him towards the earth, the wind ironing out his wings and tail, untangling him from his nosedive.

The sky shook as Cormoran lunged. The river crashed over the south bank and smashed down on Greenwich Pier, chasing screaming tourists before it, some snatched up by the squall. Up on the quay, a helter-skelter ride became a sudden island, the waters gushing around its stripy conical tower. Falling fast, Ben watched as the *Cutty Sark*, the famous clipper moored near the National Maritime Museum, budged and shifted in the barrelling tide. Her masts swayed, her rigging creaking in the gusting wind. The deluge cracked the framework securing her hull to the wharf, her cage of tessellated glass twisting and shifting, the vessel breaking free. The ship – named after, of all things, a dancing witch – hadn't been at sea since the Opium Wars and she seemed oddly buoyant as the waves took her, bearing her aloft – and then ending her brief and final voyage in black smithereens against the walls of the Royal Naval College.

Ben looked away. Rolling in the air, tail lashing, he again steered himself for the heights. He slipped around the knoll of Cormoran's knee, shooting over the jungle of the giant's loincloth, his belly fat and pale enough to rival the Millennium Dome in the distance. Drawing level with the planes taking off from London City Airport, Ben could see the eastern limits of the capital, a living toy town about to get crushed. So many lives trampled underfoot. One way or another, he had to grab Cormoran's attention, speak sense into him if possible, get him to head back to the hills.

Or find a way to kill him.

Such notions shattered as flames flowered around him, an explosion smacking him about the head, shuddering through his bones. Jags of metal came whistling past as he made his ascent, the debris bouncing off his horns and rump, startling, but unable to burn him. Peering through the smoke, he made out the helicopter – now missing its tail boom and rotor – wheeling across the sky, the pilot punching at the controls.

Well, you got your scoop. Hope it was worth it.

The chopper spun, rudderless, towards the earth. For a moment, Ben looked on, thrown off his battle charge. Then, with a grunt that carried a weight of reluctance, he turned and dived after the craft, his snout wrinkling at the stench of kerosene, his claws stretching out. In the cabin, the journalist watched him approach with bulging eyes. Even as the man vented a wail, he wrapped one of his arms in a seatbelt, clutching onto his camera for dear life. Impending crash or no, he didn't want to lose his snaps.

In a snarl of metal and a belch of smoke, dragon and chopper thumped into Island Gardens, a park on the north bank. Debris clattered down, scorching the surrounding grass. Trees shook, wild with leaves. Hedges burst into flame. A quick scan of the area told Ben that the park was thankfully empty, the people scattering at the sight of the giant booming his way down the river. *Small mercies.* With no time to waste, he unfurled himself from the crumpled craft, a seven-ton length of crimson flesh having shielded pilot and passenger from certain death. Exhaling in a smoky plume, he watched the men clamber from the wreckage and crawl as quickly as possible away from him without so much as a backward glance, let alone a thank you.

Humans.

With a sigh, Ben turned away from the crash site. His tail swept up a storm of leaves and his wings rattled the swings in the nearby playground. Nostrils trailing smoke, he pointed his snout back at the sky, back up at the towering menace. The sun shone overhead, beaming through the scudding clouds, but he felt a chill creep into his bones nonetheless. He was standing in the shadow of a two-hundred-foot-tall mountain of muscle, framed by the steel-blue sky.

The screams, though distant, were louder now, an odd stillness falling over the day. Gradually, the Thames was returning to calm, her waters slopping at the embankment. The faint roar of collapsing buildings and the wail of sirens filtered to Ben's ears, faraway and dreamlike. A tingle went through him, goosebumps prickling from his snout to the tip of his tail.

Cormoran, Bane of the Summer Country, was looking down at him.

Whether distracted by the crashed chopper or dragon fire, the giant had stopped dead in his tracks, his rampage interrupted. He was peering down at Island Gardens – what must've looked like a little ring of scorched grass to him, with a small red bird cringing in the middle. The giant's face was in shadow, but Ben felt eyeballs bigger than boulders taking him in all the same. Swallowing a lump in his throat, he found a sudden reason to regret his attention-seeking.

If there'd ever been a good time for diplomacy, this was it. There were certain codes among Remnants, certain ways of doing things. Calls to parley. Invitations to battle. Sure, bloodshed and terror had a funny way of following the formalities, but before all that, there was a kind of etiquette. *Honour among fiends.* Could he rely on that here? He could try.

Ben roared a challenge, calling for the giant to desist. This was the dragon city, after all, and Ben had made it his business to protect it. *Sworn* to protect it as he had sworn to protect all humans by upholding the Lore. The Lore might be over, but old habits died hard. Besides, it was home. Scratch Mordiford, far away in the Welsh Marches; London was the only home he knew, the one he'd chosen. In a growl of *wyrm tongue* that he hoped Cormoran could understand (and hiding the tremble in his voice), he demanded a moment to parley.

What do you say, big guy?

Cormoran bent, stretching out the rolls of flab that passed for his neck as he leant down for a closer look. His head blocked out the sun, granting Ben the unwelcome sight of his beard, flecked as it was with broken branches, struggling birds and the remains of sheep and cows – no doubt snaffled from some field or other on his way here. His face split in a grin that seemed as wide and as crooked as the river he presently stood in. Gobbets of drool splashed down on the park, each one forming a wide, viscous pool. Cormoran's breath, an opened sack of a hundred farts, gusted all around Ben, ruffling his wings and flattening his tail as the giant spoke.

"Benjurigan. Backstabber. *Snake.*"

"It's been a while," Ben spoke through his fangs, hoping the giant would take them for a disarming smile, "but I see you remember me."

"Cormoran never forgets a face." The giant tapped his chest with a pillar of a finger, the echoes shaking the ground under Ben's claws. "And I remember both of yours."

"Wait a minute. I—"

It was no good. With that, their parley was over. Ben's smile shrivelled up as a mighty arm came swinging down, aiming to squash him like a bug. Thrusting his haunches, he bounded out of the way, clods of earth and jags of machinery exploding all around him as several tons of ham-hock fist went slamming into the ground.

The smart thing, of course, was to make himself a smaller target. First to shrink were his wings, the leathery membranes folding up like umbrellas, his metacarpals merging with the rack of his flanks and spine, both dwindling in size. His arrowhead tail rippled towards his retracting snout and somewhere in the middle, his transformation met in the shape of a man. A flash of will, a gentle push, and impossibly, magically, the dragon coiled up inside new hominid dimensions.

Ben landed on the turf, a flame-haired, broad-shouldered man stumbling across the shuddering ground. Recovering himself, he headed west, sprinting across the park. Through the giant's legs, he could see the twin domes of the Old Royal Naval College across the river, the classical façade, the pillared porticoes, trimmed lawns and statues stretching beside the Thames.

Between ornate golden weathervanes, the Grand Square had become an escape route for tourists, the last of the crowds haem-orrhaging through the gates onto Romney Road. Ben surveyed the area with gleaming eyes, the crush of faces striking him as all too familiar, a blur of dread and desperation. Of spent disbelief. He had seen these expressions a lot lately, from London to Cairo to Hong Kong, a mosaic that he'd put together to work out their revelatory sum: the old order had shaken and fallen. The Lore, like the damned harp, like the Eight Hand Mirror, had shattered into pieces. The events of the last two years amounted to a disaster. All of them, Remnant and human alike, were standing on the edge of a new era, a new age – and things didn't look too pretty.

Legs pumping across the grass, Ben tried to ignore the looming presence at his back, the imagined pendulum of fists about to come crashing down on him, or maybe a boot, grinding him face-first into the dirt, leaving a crimson puddle. He took in his surroundings in short, breathless flashes, searching for an escape route, some kind of solution.

Think, damn it. Think.

Half a mile to the south, the Royal Observatory stood on a hill overlooking the broad sweep of parkland where the Greenwich Palace had once stood, the birthplace of Tudor queens and the favourite haunt of kings. Ben reflected as he ran, remembering simpler, happier times, when he hadn't had to deal with battle dragons and angry giants, the detritus of his unravelling world. Not that he hadn't faced his fair share of trouble back then. History was like that, he supposed. The glow of nostalgia. The rose-tinted past. And if he didn't get the hell out of here, he was about to become a part of it.

He did a double take as he spied the chimneys further up the south bank, the old building an eyesore of yellow brickwork rising over the rows of riverside houses. At once, his mind blazed with desperate inspiration, his eyes narrowing on the four angular smokestacks. It was a long shot, but it would have to do.

Panting hard, he skidded in that direction, darting towards the squat round building with the glazed dome that stood at the edge of the park, mere yards from the Thames. With a voluble slurp, Cormoran raised one boot from the river, trailing muck and fish and trash, and stamped down on the offending bank, trying to crush the little snake who'd dared to dicker with him. With the impact of his boot, the ground became a trampoline of thrown-up trees and earth. Ben didn't hang around, waiting for a premature burial. Knocked off his feet, he let the tremors carry him into the domed building he'd been heading for, making a graceless entrance into the Greenwich foot tunnel. Bricks and glass showered down around him as he tumbled forward, his skull, spine and backside bouncing off the steps of a broad spiral staircase, down into the murk.

An ordinary man would've found himself sprawled at the bottom in a heap of broken bones, unable to move. Ben only had to wait a minute or so for his limbs to straighten, his bruises to fade, restored by the magic in his physique. Wincing, he sprang to his feet, a hand held out to the shuddering wall, the light fixtures flickering over his head. Often, his deep knowledge of the city, a shifting map of streets imprinted on his mind, came in handy. For example, when one had to flee from rampaging giants. In the early twentieth century, the foot tunnel had replaced an unreliable ferry service to ensure that labourers could reach the docks and shipyards on time – anything in the name of industry – and a similar expedience would work for Ben here. Peering into the gloom, he understood the risk he was taking. Bearing such a tremendous weight, the river bed was shifting, punching pipes, bridges, banks and perhaps tunnels out of true. But if he could make it safely to the other side, emerge behind Cormoran unexpected, he might just stand a chance . . .

He was pounding down the remaining steps before he'd finished making the decision. At the bottom of the staircase, he found himself looking down a long, round, white-tiled tunnel, the passage sloping slightly in the middle. Cracks had appeared in the walls, rank black water, grit and mud frothing through the fissures, breaches caused by the giant's feet. Cricking his neck, Ben made his way forward, wading as fast as he could through the slop, his inner heat, retained even in human form, resisting the flooding cold.

By the time he'd reached the halfway point, he was up to his knees, his bare feet thumping on the concrete under him. A few yards further on and the water was boiling around his waist, the scales of his suit wet and slick. The lights overhead gave up the ghost, plunging him into darkness. He was near the staircase on the opposite bank when the waters rushed over the *wyrm tongue* sigil on his chest – the envoy's symbol months redundant – then the flood was covering his chin, his nose and eyes. The tunnel was buckling, caving in.

Lungs aching, Ben thrashed in a swirl of bricks and filth, his hands splayed, blindly thrusting himself forward. Brackish water filled his nose and throat; the metropolitan river was anything but fresh. Mentally, he toasted himself for his smart move, with an imagined glass of *Château d'Yuck*. A creature of the sky, death by drowning was probably the worst thing that could happen to him. Sure, his kind found the proximity of water soothing, some long-lost primal echo, but that wouldn't serve him here. Here, the deluge would simply extinguish him, snuff him out.

With a roar that only he could hear, Ben spun in the chaos, the water pushing him halfway up the staircase at the end of the tunnel, his skull and shoulder cracking against the wall. Gasping, he broke the surface, sucking air into his lungs. Coughing, cursing, he swept his sodden fringe from his face and climbed the steps hand over hand, trying to drag himself out of the muck. It was no good. Shaped as an ordinary man – one stupid enough to take this route – there was no way he'd escape the collapsing foot tunnel, the daylight filtering through the dome above a false beacon of hope.

Ordinary. Please.

Seconds later, Ben burst from the entrance to the foot tunnel, emerging on the opposite bank in a scatter of bricks. Wings shaking off glass, tail dripping filth, he hurled himself upwards in full dragon form, regaining the advantage of the heights.

A quick glance down revealed the state of the stricken wharf, the decimated *Cutty Sark* and the gushing market, the stalls carried off by the flood like brightly striped, ridiculous boats. The thoroughfare of the Royal Naval College had become a swirling morass of debris, of toppled statues, litter and the odd boat that had snapped free of its moorings. And there were bodies. Floating bodies. The grand old building was no longer a museum; it was a mausoleum. A dog shivered on a half-submerged plinth, whining for its owner. In the distance, the survivors clambered in droves up the slope of Greenwich Park, but considering the scale of the threat, the landscape of brawn and forest of beard above, no hilltop was going to offer a safe haven.

Snarling between his fangs, Ben soared up the two-hundred-foot cliff of legs, loincloth and back to the hirsute horizon of

Cormoran's shoulders. He snapped out his wings to slow his ascent, coming up behind the giant's formidable head. The giant turned away from him, scanning the Thames for the red-scaled nuisance, his grunts and breaths – breaths that stripped leaves from the trees below– revealing his annoyance.

Before Cormoran grew bored and returned to his stampede through London, Ben made his move. Levelling his wings, he caught an air current that swung him around the giant's skull and vented a roar of his own into his cavernous ear.

"Give it up, ugly. I don't see a beanstalk around here, do you? The only place you're going is *down*."

The insult had the desired effect. Bellowing, the giant turned in the river, waves thrashing around his shins. He pummelled the sky with his fists, forcing Ben to make a manoeuvre worthy of the Red Arrows as he zipped through the gap between the giant's elbow and torso. The London skyline smeared across the horizon, the Shard glittering in the sun, a sword rising from a lake of industry. Upside down, Ben crested the crown of the giant's head, riding gravity as he fell back towards his intended destination, the yellow brick smokestacks below him.

Greenwich Power Station rose from the bank of the Thames, its four chimneys pointing at the sky. Despite the weatherworn look of the building, Ben knew that a fire still rumbled in its belly. Once, the place had been a boiler house and an engine room, housing great steam engines that had pumped power to the newly electrified London Underground. Generators had long since replaced the antiquated machinery, fuelling the Tube as the trains rattled through the veins of the city. Ben had never found the building below attractive, the massive brick warehouse designed as functional rather than architectural. All the same, the power station appealed today, representing as it did his last and only chance.

Glancing over his shoulder, it relieved him to find that Cormoran had followed him, the giant wading through the river, his face a moon of grinding teeth. Ben coasted further inland, over the riddle of streets that sprawled around the power station. He only hoped that the people in the houses below had caught the morning news and, taking the hint, run for the hills. It was too late to turn back now. It was a question of survival. Fight or flight.

Ben intended to do both.

With a crunch that shuddered through the borough, Cormoran dragged himself out of the river and stamped down on the power station, the roof caving in. Nearby, the spire of Trinity Hospital and the Star and Garter pub exploded in brick dust, plaster and glass under the giant's boot. Standing in the crater where the warehouse had stood but moments before, Cormoran swung his club, taking out three of the station's chimneys in one fell swoop. Like skittles, the smokestacks toppled, a smouldering blanket of debris and dust billowing into the surrounding streets. Parked cars flipped over like toys. Trees thrashed and lampposts snapped.

Rubble ricocheted off Ben's snout, thumping on his horns and breast. He paid it no mind, dismissing the pain. His nostrils flared, smoking and twitching, picking up the bitter, sulphuric smell that was wafting its way into the day. The breath of the earth, raw and foul, mixed with some chemical compound. *Gas. Natural gas.* With the fall of a mighty boot, Cormoran had ruptured the huge turbines and the tanks inside the shell of the building, reducing them to crackling, hissing jags of steel.

Bullseye.

With no time to spare, Ben swooped in low over the collapsing roof, his wings spread. He breathed in deep, then exhaled in a plume of fire. Flame blustered from his belly, venting from the chambers in his guts and sparked by his back teeth. Speeding through the gauntlet of the shattered building, he strafed the machinery under him, licking the wreckage with heat. Reaching the far wall, he skated upwards on a blazing cloak, past the tip of the giant's club and out over the Thames.

The next second, the sky throbbed, the air above the power station drawing in tight, a fleeting moment of compression. Ben heard Cormoran grunt, the giant puzzled by the bonfire flaring between his legs. He lifted a boot, intending to stamp it out, when—

The world shattered. The ruptured gas tanks welcomed the untold heat of dragon fire, and Greenwich Power Station – foundations, walls, chimneys and all – took to the sky.

The explosion slammed into Ben, the fire overtaking him, a blast like a kick in the rump. Wings buckling, tail over snout, he went tumbling out over the river, the London skyline lost in the heat haze, the Shard rippling in the distance. Fighting for consciousness, he let the impact carry him and sailed over the Isle of Dogs, Canary Wharf shimmering at his back. The moment he slowed, he snapped out his wings, his neck twisting towards Greenwich.

Cormoran, Bane of the Summer Country, was burning. In a pillar of flame, he stood, caught in the shattered bowels of the power station. Echoes smacked against the sky; the giant was howling to bring down the sun. His boots had become great stubs of ember and ash, indistinguishable from the blaze around him. His loincloth and hair, having kept out centuries of subterranean cold, had gone up like haystacks in a bushfire. Blisters, red and weeping, spread in angry pools across his skin. With a whoosh, the giant's beard went up, his howl scaling into a deafening scream.

Head a burning crown, Cormoran managed to crash his way

out of the ruins of the power station. Ben wanted to look away, but looking away was a privilege he couldn't afford. He was hypnotised by the fire, riding on the winds of destruction and observing his handiwork. An idol towered over Greenwich Park, old as the hills, two hundred feet high. Cormoran had become an effigy, a blazing wicker man of flesh and bone. The giant berated the sky, his flailing arms stirring up thunder and smoke, setting fire to the bushes and the trees below. A scorched ring of grass, the width of a football pitch, spread out from the giant's feet. Burning ashes shrouded the sky, a curtain falling on an age of secrets.

The power station had done its work. High overhead, Ben could see that Cormoran wouldn't survive.

He wished he could say he was sorry.

Fee fi fo fum, motherfucker.

With a boom to shatter the earth, Cormoran fell. The giant dropped to his knees and then slumped face forward, collapsing across Greenwich Park.

TWO

"Home sweet home."

The echoes scattered along with Ben's sarcasm as he entered his lair. Well, the cavern next to his lair. With an innate sense of covetousness, he'd decided that he'd rather face the adjoining caves than let his prisoner into his treasure trove. But it was more than that, he recognised. He was also afraid, wary of the power he'd caged. And these tunnels and grottoes comprised more than just caverns. No, the whole place was a barrow, long sunken under the earth. In truth, a *mausoleum*. As uncomfortable as the thought made him – he hadn't had much luck when it came to tombs – it was best to confront the reality. He'd been telling himself fairy tales for years. If he'd learnt anything from the events in China, it was that the time for comforting lies was over.

Deep, deep in the earth, the chamber, with its smooth alabaster walls and floor, was unmistakably a crypt. Crystalline spindles loomed in the gloom, some of the stalactites and stalagmites joining in the middle. The rock around him held a faint and inexplicable glimmer, illuminating a broad and airy cage that always made Ben think of the bones of a whale, buried half a mile underground. For all its splendour, Ben knew that he stood in a barrow for the alien dead, a forgotten crypt of the Fay.

The tombs, vast, pale, soared up into the shadowed vaults. Magic had touched this space, hollowing out the raw rock, bleaching the earth into white stone, polishing it like glass. Time had touched the cavern too, the imposing sepulchres around him not quite as grand as he imagined they once were, the edifices corroded by the endless drip of water, worn away by dust and cracked by the shifting of the earth. Earth that grew ever more restless, he knew that too. Soon the tombs might crumble completely or fall into some chasm or other, carrying down the last traces of their eldritch design.

Each tomb resembled a miniature castle, oriel, portcullis and spire rising from the carved foundations of seas and clouds, great orchards of stone that bore fat and unidentifiable fruit. The twining sculptures knew no modesty. Satyrs and nymphs frolicked naked in marble cascades. Men-who-were-not-men and women-who-were-not-women lay brazenly locked in carnal pleasure. The crypt, he thought, had to be the most indecent of resting places, devoid of gravitas, brimming with debauch. Here, the dead slept not, but fondled and fucked each other, copulating beyond death in an architectural mockery of life.

The sight made Ben ache, his bruises tingling as they healed, though his pangs for the most part remained a mix of loss and revulsion. As a Remnant, Ben felt little sympathy for the Fay. But he realised that they must have suffered too. Forever sensing that they had a higher purpose, belonged to a higher plane of existence, yet finding themselves brought low, left to wade through a world of blood, sweat and shit. To watch mortal after mortal wither and die as their pale flesh remained untouched, their eyes undimmed by time. To see oceans rise and forests fall. To witness war after war.

"Is that why you fucked with the humans?' Ben wondered aloud, muttering to limit the echoes. "So you got to act like gods again?"

It was one reason, that was for sure. One murmured among Remnants. Because once upon a time the Fay *had* been gods, some said, or as good as gods. Millenia ago, an unrecorded cataclysm had seen the First-Born become the Fallen Ones, the Fay. Legend claimed that those early fairies had lain down the circles of protection, great spells branded in the earth to shield Creation from the nether, hold the dark at bay and thus allow the High House of Avalon their golden age, the Old Lands, King Arthur – all of it. One could be forgiven for thinking that the Fay had wanted to re-establish themselves as deities, as overlords, however diminished and earthbound.

Well, that went well. Long-lived or no, the Fay sure as hell weren't immortal; for all their otherworldly arts, those first pioneers had withered and died. Shit, looking around at the marble debauchery, Ben realised that he could even be standing on their graves.

Who knew? Nor could he say why they'd spawned the fabulous beings and beasts (himself included) that still haunted the earth; foreign, unnatural, yet primal creatures who these days only endured as survivors, magical refugees, since the alien race had departed.

Ancient history . . .

Like all Remnants, Ben knew the story well. Unable to prevent a catastrophic war, the Fay had left the Earth in disgust from Camlann Field, the last battle of the legendary King Arthur. That battle hadn't just seen the end of a golden age, but a schism in history, a severing of worlds. The Great Example had failed and peace on earth was not possible. Between men. Between monsters. The Fay had returned to the nether, leaving their lost children to their fate.

And that's where the trouble had started. That's where the battle truly began.

Abandoned, adrift, it soon became clear that there was no place for Remnants in the tireless drive for human advancement. In the Fay's absence, magic was on the wane, no longer the pure and shining stream of cosmic energy that threaded through all things, but a stain, an unknown quantity, a power, a danger, something to be feared.

Ben snorted, remembering his history. The *real* history. Come the reign of King John, magic had become a constant source of irritation – and sometimes more than that, bubbling up into bloody chaos and unrest. The Remnants, forsaken and feared, were, for the most part, throwing a tantrum of historic proportions. Trolls smashed bridges. Giants trampled crops. Witches beguiled queens. And dragons . . . well, dragons, of course, reduced entire towns to ash.

In turn, humans were trying to stamp out the monsters in their midst, dispatching knight after knight to dragon's cave. To goblin's mine and griffin's nest. It soon became painfully clear that the progress of civilisation was facing something of an uphill struggle. For every city wall built, one crumbled and fell. For every new road, a spellbound marsh sprang up to swallow travellers. For every new invention, there was one superseded or warped by magic.

Something had to give.

Under pressure from Rome, King John founded the Curia Occultus, a great council set up with the intention of ending the long war between Remnants and humans. One day in London, the king issued a momentous decree. An envoy had come to him with an extraordinary harp, a broken relic of the long-vanished Fay. Reforged, the envoy claimed that the harp held the power to lure and lull all of the Remnants to sleep, conjuring a song that would circle the globe from Westminster Palace to the distant walls of Xanadu. Every fabulous being and beast who heard the music would fall into an enchanted slumber, sinking into caverns deep under the earth, there to rest until the Fay prophecy came to pass. Some of the Remnants had even believed in the prophecy, the Queen's Troth – spoken in whispers, in long sighs – that one day the Fay would return, arriving in some shining, sorcerous Second Coming when Remnants and humans had learned to live in peace. *La la de la*. Others, however, had not. Either way, the envoy had strummed his little harp and the Remnants – most of them, anyway – had fallen into the Long Sleep.

As with all fairy gifts, there was but one condition. A great compromise.

This was the Pact. John's secret charter of 1215.

With the goodwill of his Majesty and all future monarchs, and to secure the peace, but one of each Remnant may endure, awake and unfettered under the Lore, governed, protected and guided by the Guild of the Broken Lance, hereby appointed wardship of this bond for all the time to come·

In short, as long as no fabulous being or beast should breed, make known their presence, employ magic or otherwise interfere in the progress of civilisation, then the king would permit one leader of each Remnant group to remain, alive and unharmed, upon the earth.

This was the Lore under which they all lived.

"Or had." Ben spat the words and damn the echoes. "Gods help us. Except there are no gods left."

Gods. Prophecies. Promises and Pacts.

Bloody fools, the lot of us.

Cut to today. The Lore was broken. The Long Sleep undone. This morning's bout of fisticuffs over the Thames had made that fact painfully clear. And what, Ben wondered with the opposite of relish, did he have to look forward to now? A resurrected goddess and a battle dragon had been bad enough. Was he honestly facing the rousing of *all* Remnants? If so, he was staring down the barrel of another war. The Big One. Because most of the Sleepers weren't going to be happy when they came to learn of their imprisonment. Most of them, he expected, would blame the humans. They'd blame Von Hart, the envoy extraordinary.

And him. There'd be no sense in pointing fingers. Ben had been wrapped up in this from the start. Once upon a time, Von Hart had put a dragon to sleep in the Zhoukoudian Hills, China. Ben had been there at the time, their failure to slay the beast fermenting ages of enmity. Earlier this year, the fairy had woken the dragon up, unleashing terror and destruction on an unsuspecting world. Ben, of course, had been the one to face Mauntgraul down, to put an end to the venom and the screams that followed in his wake. Later, Von Hart had gone on to destroy the harp completely, breaking the enchantment of centuries. There were some, Ben reckoned, who might thank the envoy for releasing them into this brave new world of smog and selfie sticks and melting ice caps, where the human population had swollen to disastrous levels and millions starved. Where Remnants had become no more than a myth, a tale that grew ever less frightening in the face of reality: a future so grim it was hard to compete with.

Most would not.

Why? Why had the envoy done this?

The Fay are coming!

Yeah. That's what Von Hart had said, minutes after they'd escaped from the nether, tumbling onto the southernmost tip of the Fan Lau peninsula, below the smouldering ruins of the temple. Those had been his last words, before he'd slumped, unconscious, in Ben's arms.

Ben looked at his palms, discomforted, as he recalled the triumph in the envoy's voice. Von Hart's betrayal, Jia's bogus mission, well, they'd made him question the truth of everything. Had it all been wishful thinking? Denial? The Remnants' refusal to accept their abandonment? Was the prophecy, the Queen's Troth, simply a myth, an ember stoked by King John to ensure the suppression of the "devils" in his kingdom, the banishment of Remnants from the world?

Take a wild guess.

Over the centuries, Ben's hope had rotted, of course, leaving bitter seeds. Seeds that curdled and burned in the belly. Seeds that he'd finally spat out. The price of that was the loss of comfort. The loss of his trust in his friends. Because in the end, it turned out that the Lore was a lie.

As for Jia Jing, the Remnant who had brought him to this stark revelation? Well, it had cost Jia her life.

You couldn't catch her. Save her from herself.

Standing here in the cavern, in the bosom of his vanished creators, Ben wanted to feel something other than shame, just for a change. He didn't like it down here. Didn't like the reminder. The last time he'd come here, he'd led Jia into the crypt on reluctant feet, pretending that the place was his lair, for all the good it did him. True to her kind, she'd seen right through him and he'd opened up his home to her, his sanctuary. It didn't last. Thanks to the Sister, an assassin of the Whispering Chapter, his home was a sanctuary no more. His treasure trove might still be secure, but the townhouse above it remained a heap of blackened bricks.

It wasn't as if he was *fond* of the place. In its own way, 9 Barrow Hill Road had been a tomb too. Half-heartedly, he'd shelled out for some scaffolding and tarpaulin to cover the shattered Victorian façade, creating the semblance of restoration. He'd blamed the explosion on a dodgy boiler to a sceptical police force and two or three nosy parker neighbours. Delvin Blain of the Blain Trust, his dwarf accountant in Belgrave, had posed as his insurance company, answering all enquiries in his usual cantankerous manner. Investigations were ongoing, and it was obvious that nobody really believed him. Terrorist attacks in the capital had long since wiped out the benefit of the doubt (plus even an idiot could see that the explosion had occurred from the street *inwards*, not the basement out). But bigger problems than a dodgy boiler and a dodgier story had taken up the news channels since then. Like two-hundred-foot giants, say. In the rising panic, it was easy to forget the man going by the name of Ben Garston.

Suits me.

It didn't matter. He was too vexed to feel relief. Who knew what remained of the Chapter, what ragged band of disciples still roamed Britain and the Continent, clinging to righteous scraps of power? He didn't even know if the Cardinal, Evangelista de Gori, had survived the collapse of the Alpine monastery. All he knew was that the Lore was over.

So here he stood in the decadent crypt, forced to confront the silence of the Fay, the long rejection of his kind.

And the silence of Blaise Von Hart, his prisoner.

"Is this meant to be funny?" Ben strode across the gleaming

floor to the foot of one of the tombs, an orgiastic eyesore stretching up into the gloom. A hooded statue peered down from the monument, gigantic marble arms emerging from the folds of an exquisitely carved robe. Cupped by a pair of polished stone hands, the fingers laced at the level of Ben's chest, Von Hart, the envoy extraordinary, lay cold and comatose. *Chained.* Ben had bound him in heavy iron, the chains rifled from Ben's hoard and threaded through the writhing sculptures on the tomb. Fairies, he'd read, weren't big fans of iron. He didn't know whether the stories were true, coming as they did down the tangled vine of folklore, and he doubted that the earthly metal would have the same effect on the Fay as *lunewrought* had on him, but he needed all the help he could get. Still, heavy chains were heavy chains. Von Hart wasn't going to vanish so easily next time. His chest, a pale lattice of bone, rose and fell with his shallow breaths, a faint frost misting his lips like a memory of the nether. "Thanks to you, the whole damn world is waking up." Ben jabbed a thumb at the cavern roof. "Meanwhile, you go and take a six-month nap."

Frustration informed all these one-way conversations with the envoy. Not to mention a quiet rage. Ben, a creature of passion, had lost count of the times he'd had to turn away, fists clenched and shaking, from the fairy's recumbent form. From his peaceful, blissfully ignorant face. Von Hart might be safely locked up, but his lips remained locked too, denying Ben his secrets, a confession of his (no doubt long and intricate) plan that had seen Jia Jing, a supposed champion of truth and justice, betray her very nature to steal the fragments of the harp. In silver, in fire, Von Hart had reforged the artefact only to break it, finally showing his hand. His treachery. In the depths of the nether, the fairy had damned them all . . .

37

James Bennett

A sad necessity. A choice of evils.

What choice? Extinction or war? Did Ben honestly believe that? He breathed in, trying to quell the flames inside. Sure, the Long Sleep was coming undone, the enchantment dispelled and unravelling, but so far, the consequences had been thankfully slow. It shouldn't have surprised him; spells, for all their magic, cleaved to certain rules like all equations. Eight hundred years ago, the lullaby had spilled out from Westminster Palace and gradually circled the globe – a process, as Ben understood it, that had taken nigh on a century . . .

Another faint hope. A two-hundred-foot-tall giant in the Thames . . . well, it kind of implied that the breaking of the harp had a sporadic influence, rather than a localised one, considering that Cormoran had risen from an English bed, not somewhere near Hong Kong. He guessed that some creatures slept more deeply than others . . . Or was it down to the souring magic, he wondered, the souring song? The harp had shattered beyond the world. It made sense that its echoes should scatter in kind, like shards of glass from a broken—

Ben snorted again, this time at himself. He could examine the disaster as much as he liked; there was no way to undo it. Even if Von Hart somehow miraculously woke up, a Sleeping Beauty he'd love to kiss with a punch, it was unlikely that the fairy would restore the spell or even help him if he could. Besides, he wasn't that lucky.

It struck him now that the coming of Queen Atiya and Mauntgraul last year had been mere holes in the dam, the Lore shaking, the floodgates about to burst. The best he could hope for now was damage limitation. But that would grow old soon enough. He couldn't take on every last Remnant single-handedly.

"How long have we got?" he asked the unconscious fairy. "A

year? A decade? You've started a war, you bloodless bastard. I'll be damned if I'm going to let you sleep through it."

But threats aside, what could he do? He turned away, his jaw clenched. The damp air filled his lungs, the mildew and dust of despair. Helplessly, he crossed his arms, gripping himself. The subterranean chill couldn't touch him, but fear could. A six-foot-tall, broad-shouldered figure of a man, he shuddered in the shadow of the tombs, his crimson hair a torch, guttering in the dark. Had he ever felt more alone?

And by sundown, the city will be empty.

He knew it was true. Apart from the cautious presence of the British Army, perhaps a handful of tanks and the odd surveillance drone, no one was going to stick around in the city after this morning. OK, so he only had monster movies to go by, but he could imagine the fallout easily enough. Barricades placed across the main arteries of the metropolis, the M1, A2, M4 and A10. All the planes at Heathrow grounded. The Eurostar suspended. Waterloo, Victoria, Paddington and Charing Cross stretching abandoned and silent. Cars and trucks crawling along the roads through hastily erected checkpoints, men in white vans cursing and thumping the horn as all the vehicles sat bumper to bumper in their rush to escape. Even access to the internet might be limited, the networks down, the phone lines jammed. Then the National Grid would switch everything off come midnight, plunging London into darkness. Roll down the shutters. Leave the key under the mat. Game over. Thanks for playing.

No one in their right mind was going to stay in the capital when a giant could come along and crush them underfoot at any moment. Or a dragon like the one on the Beijing news, swooping down from the sky and scooping up clawfuls of shoppers. No thanks. In the past two years, reluctantly, painfully, the breaches in the Lore had woken Ben up too, each one seismic, shattering his world. And now these events went tremoring across the human world, unbelievable, undeniable. And unstoppable.

There is no going back.

The military, presumably on red alert, would find itself swamped by refugees. The government, true to form, would have decamped already, leaving the Houses of Parliament to the statues and the pigeons. The Royal Family wouldn't sit and cower behind the gates of Buckingham Palace either, taking to this or that countryside estate. Ben could see it now. The populace heading out into the country, thousands of people on foot, lines that stretched from Westminster to Watford, from Camberwell to Crawley and beyond, seeking the safety of the Chilterns and the Downs. Wailing babies. Hobbling pensioners. Slinking dogs. Ben felt for them, these imagined denizens of London, all of them huddled together, clutching the few possessions they could carry, rucksacks stuffed with food and blankets, the old family clock. The market stall holder from Portobello Road. The imam from the Regent's Park mosque. The Jews of Stamford Hill. The Afro-Caribbean folk from Brixton. The Polish students. The American tourists. The gentry and the tramps. The multitude all one in their terror, with the great city smouldering at their back, dark and deserted.

Come nightfall, London, the dragon city, would be his and his alone. But for how long, exactly? Ben shook off the thought, focusing on practical matters instead. By now, the Prime Minister must've declared a State of Emergency, surely. He had no radio down here and it wouldn't work even if he did, deep as he was in the earth.

With a shake of his head and a funny sound in his throat, Ben accepted that he'd failed them, the people of London. The

Lone Fire standing guard? Watching the gates? Right. Those gates, seven of them, were nothing much to look at these days. Aldgate, Bishopsgate, Moorgate, Cripplegate, Aldersgate, Newgate and Ludgate, all of which had sported the heads of countless traitors, were little more than tarmac and pavement lost in the urban sprawl. Today, the people he'd sworn to protect swarmed and jostled over their memory, running for the hills. Nor could he guarantee their safety in the lands beyond. Who knew what was waiting out there? Strange marsh lights and hungry goblins? Men who inexplicably turned into wolves? Trees with eyes and weaving branches? Witches, ogres and headless ghosts? Who knew which Sleepers were stirring . . . ?

He swore, finding no comfort in practical matters either.

"Jia died because of you." Reining in his temper, Ben muttered at the envoy over his shoulder. "I want to know why."

There was no answer in the edifices soaring around him, in the spiralling towers of marble. Bestial figures brayed down at him, laughing, screaming as spread-legged sprites filled their chalices with wine. Nor could he find comfort in his memories; the *sin-you* and he hadn't exactly been friends. Allies, perhaps, and that was a push. Lost in grief and indecision, he'd been too late to stop her, turn her back from her quest to see the harp reforged, to awaken the Remnants.

I can save them, she'd told him. *Don't you see? I can save them all!*

Leaping through the Eight Hand Mirror, out on the very brink of existence, Ben had faced the Ghost Emperor, the architect of rebellion, and he had watched Jia Jing fall. Even now, standing in the shadow of the eldritch tombs, he couldn't say for sure whether he disagreed with her or not, her longing to liberate Remnants, to reveal the truth of Creation, that Remnants

41

lived and breathed among humans. For all that, he'd dreaded the consequences, the catastrophe awaiting them all. Freedom, he knew, would come at a price.

"And she paid it, didn't she? She paid it for you."

We must all make sacrifices.

Scowling, he realised that he was talking to rock, nothing more. The fairy couldn't answer him. Heat flared under his skin, tiny scales rippling up and down his suit, black blushing to red. Blood pulsed, hot, at his temples. This always seemed like a good time to leave Von Hart and go outside, make a flyby of the city, check that will-o'-the-wisps weren't luring lines of refugees into a bog or that dwarves weren't plundering the Crown Jewels. Regardless of his failings, he was watching over them still.

He'd taken three steps when he noticed his shadow on the cavern floor, lengthening out before him. The line of his shoulders, bubbling with impatient horns, cast a silhouette as grotesque as the tombs around him. The earth tremored, rumbling. A growing illumination, he realised, a cold, crystalline blue, was filling the subterranean space. The radiance, eerie in the dark, slid like satin over buttock, hoof and tail, the sculptures writhing in a distorted embrace, a clinch of shadow and stone. The light rose from the chamber floor to challenge the vaults above, its progress slow yet deliberate, before rippling out, its source withdrawing, defeated by the enfolding darkness.

Ben couldn't see that source. After recent adventures, he could guess that the light wasn't coming from anywhere earthly. Looking up, his mouth wide, he heard a whisper of music the second that the light began to fade, a tinkle of bells that caused his balls to draw in close to his body and vomit to rise in his throat.

The lullaby . . .

Or what was left of it. He spun on his heel, chasing the echoes
– and found Von Hart spasming on the cupped stone hands, his
chains clanking around him. His eyes remained shut, darting
back and forth behind their lids, tracing the progress of some
nightmare or other. Froth bubbling on his lips, limbs beating
on stone, Von Hart struggled in his sleep, his brow creased with
anguish. Or *hope*. A frantic mutter issued from the envoy's throat
and Ben had to draw closer across the shuddering floor to make
out the words.

"She comes," he was saying in a ragged whisper. "She comes.
She comes . . ."

Ben didn't like the sound of that. Not one bit. He reached
forward, meaning to shake the envoy awake, but he didn't get
the chance. With a rush of displaced air, a great black cloud
came bursting from the tunnel mouth behind him, flurrying
through the entrance to the crypt. The echoes exploded, a mighty
ricochet causing him to flinch, an arm held over his head. Turning
from the tomb, he bellowed in shock as darkness poured into
the chamber, a wave crashing over the sombre peace, gyring
around the stalactites and scattering across the cavern roof. At
first, he took the creatures for bats – Lord knew there were
enough of them down here – but the next minute, the croaking
and squawking gave them away.

They were birds. A flock of birds. Birds half a mile underground, a hundred or more.

"What the—?"

His next question, directed inward, was as cold and as sharp
as a sword point. What the hell had driven them here? What had
driven the birds, blind and fluttering, into these depths?

Something in the world above. Something bad.

This was no accident. He was past giving that notion the time of day. The flock had come here deliberately, seeking his lair.

Or more likely the fairy.

Yeah. Von Hart was the hub in all this, the last son of Avalon on earth, a focal point of all that was magic and strange. *And the cause of all the trouble* . . . Ben had seen it before, of course, how the phantoms in the nether had pressed against the fabric of things, hungry for the essence of Creation. It made a weird kind of sense that the natural world would respond, panicking over the ever-fraying skein between reality and elsewhere, if that's what he was seeing. He had good reason to think so.

Magic. *Hocus pocus.* He could smell its stink on the air.

Witches . . . ? A slice of shock went through him, served cold. But for all the blackness of their wings, these birds weren't crows. Not exactly. He had his extraordinary eyesight to thank for the insight, his shoulders falling in relief. *Not witches. No.* The Coven Royal had fallen. The Three were dead. If other witches were to come – and he had no reason to doubt it – they'd have to find him first. These birds had come for the envoy, surely.

Get in line.

Spine straightening, he stood up, searching the feathery fracas above him for an answer. As if his attention was a cue, the flock blustered as one around the crypt, a slick black wave washing over stone, and shot back into the entrance to the cavern, sucked into the tunnel mouth like oil down a plughole.

In a matter of seconds, the birds were gone. Ben cocked his head, alarmed and puzzled, listening to their retreating cries.

The echoes sounded oddly like a summons.

Or a warning.

Mount Snowdon, Wales

Fifteen hundred years had passed and the ravens still circled
the summit of Snowdon, the highest mountain in Wales. The
black-winged birds cawed above the tumulus, the great peak
snow-draped and white, heralding this crisp October morning.
The sun slanted through the teeth of the range, these grey guardians of the northern coast, refracting in rainbows and mist on
the surface of the tarns that glimmered like mirrors in their laps.
Pine trees creaked and sighed in the wind, the echoes carried
down gullies like the tick of some huge, invisible clock, measuring
out the slumbering centuries. Somewhere, bells tinkled – or
perhaps it was harpsong – a lullaby whispering between the
rocks, between the trees. Between the past and the future. Both
met here in this breath, this moment, to break the chains of
time with the ghost of a melody.

At the sound, the ravens, cawing, fluttered away, mere dots
in the haze, leaving the mountain behind. The song was over.
The task, having passed down countless black-winged generations,
done.

The days grew short as they drew close to Samhain, the pagan

45

festival of old. Long ago, the tribes of Logres had lit fires and danced naked around them to celebrate the end of the harvest, the coming of the dark half of the year, on a night that folks now called All Hallows' Eve. And others, more devout, had burned a virgin or two in the pyre, hoping to stave off the omens of plague, famine and war. These days, those who observed the ancient date did so as a passing curio. The ravens of Snowdon were in sharp decline and most had smoke and tar in their wings, the residue of urban pollution. Logres was now called Britain, the United Kingdom, and most would agree that quite a lot had happened in fifteen hundred years. These were no longer the Old Lands.

But the bones remained. And deep in the mountain, in the heart of Yr Wyddfa, some said those bones still wore flesh.

On the eastern flank of Snowdon, craggy and sheer, there stood an unseen door. There was also a ledge, of sorts, no more remarkable than the surrounding rock face, but no handle, keyhole, knocker or bell betrayed an entrance of any kind. A long time ago, according to folklore, a man had once come calling and found a secret cavern behind the door. Sometimes, depending on who was telling the tale, the man was a herdsman and sometimes a thief, but never a knight or a prince. And sometimes, this lowborn man found an empty cave and sometimes he found one filled with gold. Sometimes the herdsman stole a cup or a crown (and if he did, both later served to prove that his tale wasn't a dream), but mostly he just ran away. He ran away from the people he found sleeping in the cavern, and in particular, he ran away from the man with the beard that had grown so long it trailed down between his boots, who would always wake up and ask, bleary yet hopeful, whether the ravens still circled the mountaintop. The herdsman, thief, or sometimes even a mysterious voice, would reply, "Yes, the ravens still circle the mountaintop." Then the man with the unfeasibly long beard would grow angry and shout, "Begone! Begone! For my time has not yet come!"

Folklore is given to change and unreliable, full of fancy and wild ideas.

But there has always been a king in the mountain.

He slept here still, this ancient thane of Logres. Behind the door, down a tunnel, in a large and echoing cavern. The chamber, roughly circular and domed, stretched out from a raised rectangular plinth in the middle of the floor. A tomb, of sorts, or a stone bed, its single occupant lying upon it in regal repose. In full armour, a jewelled sword positioned beside him and a shield upon his chest, the king slept. He slept as he had always slept, since the Lady came stepping out of the lake, turning back from her farewell at the battle, and bade her servants bear his body here, into this waiting place.

Fade not, but sleep, she'd told him, stroking a hand over his cold face, her long brown fingers coming away wet with blood. *When the ravens no longer circle the mountaintop, when Logres has need of you again, you will awake. Awake and reclaim your destiny.*

That was fifteen hundred years ago. The Battle of Camlann Field had ended in blood, fire and tears. And a schism, a severing of worlds. The end of a golden age. The king, however, recalled from death to linger here for centuries on the doorstep, had not aged a day. His hair fell around his face in thick grey curls, framing a nose that spoke of both Roman and Celt. His beard, shot with silver, straggled down to the middle of his chest (and not to his boots as some liked to claim). Wrinkles and scars crisscrossed his brow, relating the trials of a glorious life, of maidens won and giants bested. Of lost love and pain. Yet his features still held a trace of the boy, a gangling squire who'd dropped plates in the castle kitchens and fallen headfirst out of trees. Both man and boy – the One True King – slumbered on in silence, his dreams unknowable, his presence long sunken into myth. The Lady's servants had cleansed the blood from him and his skin was white, white as snow in the not-quite darkness, the soft blue glow emanating from the plinth on which he lay, creeping into the cavern.

The light, somewhere between sapphire and frost, rippled out into the cavern greater, illuminating a circle of other tombs placed around the king. The ground shuddered, rock dust raining down, and many a sword and gauntlet clanked, many a helmet rang on stone as the tremors ran through the chamber. The knights on the tombs around the king, heroes all, numbered six. Aside from Lancelot, the White Knight, who had not been interred here, these warriors were the best of them, the champions of the Round Table that the Lady had shaped this circle to portray.

There was Gawain, who had once lopped off a green knight's head. There was Bors the Younger, who had slain three dragons with a single stroke. And Kay the Seneschal, who had bossed the king about as a boy and then served him as a man. Tristan, the greatest archer in the realm and, some said, the greatest lover. Fierce Bedwyr, the only woman in the company, who had cradled her king at the last and thrown his sword, Caliburn, into the waters of Llyn Llydaw. And there was Galahad in his blood-red armour, who had once gone in search of a holy cup and perhaps even found it.

Six knights and their king, Arthur. Arthur, son of Uther. Arthur Pendragon, the Bear of Logres, who stood with his feet planted firmly in two worlds, that of history and that of myth. Arthur, the Once and Future King.

And this day, at this hour, as the ravens fled, and the bells tinkled, and the cavern shook, that future had arrived.

The first sign of movement was the hounds, Caval and Gast, that curled at the foot of the great king's tomb. The beasts twitched in the brightening light, an ear flicking, a muffled whine, a paw stretching out. The next sign was the sword, dislodged from its place on the plinth and clattering to the floor in a flash of silver and gems.

"Fuck," said a voice. "Not again."

The tremors met the cavern wall, dispersing with a boom. Not far away, there was a loud crack, the unseen door sundering, stale air and a plume of grit billowing from the mountainside. The sunlight in the cavern winked out, the shaft swallowed up by the murky light, a radiance that pooled and shone in the king's eyes as, slowly, he sat up.

Arthur's shield slid off his chest as he did so, revealing his gilded horn, carved from the tusk of the monstrous boar, Twrch Trwyth, he of the poisonous bristles, that legend claimed had long ago been a prince of Powys. The king blinked, the blue light trailing from his head, and looked down at his hands. Then he looked up, wonderingly, facing his knights, who also sat, drowsy and confused, yet awaiting his command.

"How long . . . ?" Arthur managed, but then his words became a meaningless croak.

He watched, his eyes blazing with frost, as a shadow fell over the knights around him. It was as though a vast wing passed over the cavern, although the seven of them were deep underground. A breath, a whisper, eddied through the air, carrying the hint of a woman's voice, familiar and soft, husky as autumn leaves, sonorous as a forest well. In a heartbeat, it was clear what magic touched the cavern, this ancient waiting place. A spell of awakening, faded, yes, and tainted by the touch of a more powerful force.

Time.

Gawain crumbled first, a hale-looking man in his early forties reduced to a pile of dust. Bors the Younger had never looked older, his face shrivelling to resemble a dried fig, his grimace of shock caving inward along with the rest of his skull, the insides pouring out in a steady stream of grit. Kay the Seneschal slumped, one of his arms – rendered skeletal in a matter of seconds – falling from his shoulder and rattling to the floor, the rest of his body sinking inside his breastplate like a crab withdrawing into a shell. Tristan simply exploded in a shower of bones, a grey cap of hair left spinning on his tomb.

Bedwyr cried out, her short-cropped hair bleaching to white, her eyes sinking into her skull. Teeth dropped out of her mouth like pegs and her hands withered to bony claws, and yet she somehow maintained her form, sitting upright in the cavern. Likewise, Galahad, wormy and decayed in his blood-red armour, sat ravaged but whole, the blight of time reeling in, its hungry touch checked by the spell, the charmed suspension reasserted. As one, the two knights looked up from their stalled deterioration, tendons creaking, to attend to their king.

Arthur greeted them with a grin through his bearded skull. In his hollow eye sockets, the light raged, washing away every trace of his character, replacing it with a cold intent, as bright as it was fierce.

His two remaining knights, as enthralled, as wasted as he, followed the king as he slid off his bed of stone, his boots thumping on the cavern floor. With a wheeze of escaping gas, Bedwyr raised her mace, silently swearing fealty. Galahad lifted his double-headed axe, his tongue twisting in a habitual oath

– his brain was rotten, devoid of thought – but he only succeeded in dislodging maggots between his teeth.

In turn, Arthur reached for his sword. The fabled Caliburn, lying on stone.

"I don't think so," the sword said.

There was a flash – perhaps of sunlight on silver, perhaps not – and the king in the mountain retracted his hand, his gauntlet crunching with brittle bones. For a moment, he glared at the fabulous weapon, as though recalling some distant memory. His tongue, dry and grey, wormed in his mouth, trying to form the words once carved into rock.

Whoso Pulleth Out this Sword of this Stone is Rightwise King Born of all England.

But no, the Old Lands were over. That destiny done. He was Arthur of Logres and yet he was not. He was something else, a corpse king, a foul echo, animated by a mouldering spell and steered by another's will. And thus, Caliburn spurned his touch.

Hissing between blackened teeth, the king turned away, shuffling towards the unseen door and the future promised to him.

The hounds, frost-eyed and skeletal, growled and clacked across stone to his side.

The dead knights followed.

THREE

A long time ago, according to folklore, a man had come calling to the mountain. Sometimes the man was a herdsman and sometimes a thief, but never a knight or a prince. And certainly, never a dragon.

Wings spread to catch the wind, Red Ben Garston soared above the English plain, chasing a flock of birds. Ravens, to be precise. He'd burst from the Hampstead railway tunnel and banked over the cowed city, trying to ignore the flattened buildings and the spirals of smoke rising from Shoreditch and Greenwich, the evidence of fires still burning below. Pools, grimy, glimmered along the Thames, the foundations of the London Eye, Cleopatra's Needle and the Globe all submerged in the displaced water and muck. In the still, he could make out the distant wail of fire engines and the honk of cars, line upon line of vehicles choking the motorways out of London, grim proof of his fears.

The people were abandoning the city. To what, he found hard to think about.

Tail weaving, its arrowhead tip slicing the bellies of the autumn clouds, he made sure to keep a low altitude, the black riddle of birds flapping ahead. The air through his underwing gills was cool and slow as he kept pace with the flock, which, if pressed, he could easily outdistance. Cruising at a thousand feet, the birds led his snout northwest, soaring over Oxfordshire and the Cotswolds, and into the Marches beyond. The land below, a patchwork of fields and farms, scattered towns, rivers and roads, related his own story as he went. Down there, in the Vale of the White Horse, he'd first signed the secret charter, the Pact, that had secured the peace between Remnants and humans. Down there, in a border village, he had fallen in love with a maiden called Maud and walked into history and legend. Or rather, into centuries of pain . . .

It occurred to him then that for all his travels, he was as bound to this country as if he'd been chained to it. From forest tavern to underground cave, he'd found himself in every corner of Britain, its greatest secret and, at times, its keeper. Hadn't the Curia Occultus charged him with the task, back in 1215? To protect the humans from the Remnant world. To police his own kind as the Sola Ignis, the Lone Fire, Guardian of the West. And he had done so – reluctantly, granted – but faithfully. Well, up to a point. His affairs with humans hadn't exactly been Loreful (breeding, particularly so) and his transformations into dragon form weren't either. What could he do? He was himself, guided and ruled by his nature. Rose McBriar, his long-suffering ex-girlfriend, and the child she carried – *his* child – had made it clear that he was out of their lives. *Wherever they are . . .* That aside, surely the cost of his long service, the sacrifices he'd made and the trials he'd faced, outweighed the rest of his misdemeanours. He had plunged an old wyrm into the Thames and incinerated a troll in the name of the Lore. Witches, a mummy, a goddess, another dragon and yes, a *sin-you* – all had come to a sticky end on his watch, not that he felt a shred of regret about anyone other than Jia.

But all that was over now. He was the Sola Ignis no longer.

He had failed the humans. So many had died. Many more faced certain doom. And he knew in his heart of hearts that he wasn't following the birds into Wales out of a lingering sense of duty either, but simply one of shame.

You'll die protecting them. And they won't even know . . .

The sun was setting by the time that Ben drew near the mountain, the flock of ravens spiralling around its distant peak. Perhaps it was the half-light that dragged his gaze to the earth, his nostrils flaring as he noticed the radiance there, fainter than when he'd seen it before, over the North Sea and the Pearl River. The great arc ran under the earth like a vein, a mile wide or more, curving from the south through the hills ahead of him, across the forests of Gwydir, under the tarns and over the rock-bound slopes. The Fay circle of protection – by now, Ben understood what he was looking at – shimmered and gleamed with indecipherable runes, the arcane sigils of the long-vanished race who had branded these wards deep in the earth. The circles were vast, spanning continents, and Ben wondered if this was part of the same ring that he'd seen before, the one stretching east into the Netherlands a few months ago. Judging from the size of the thing, its radius must encompass the Scottish Lowlands, the Irish Sea and North Wales. Perhaps London too, threading through the caverns that he'd chosen for his lair, the forgotten barrows of the Fay. That would make sense, wouldn't it? The reason for the disturbance earlier today, the strange radiance in the crypt and the coming of the birds, spurred by some event further along the circle. The notion didn't bode well. The enormous brands served to shield the earth from the nether, the ravenous ghosts of the outer dark. Jia had told him as much.

The magic of the Fay is growing old. The circles of protection are souring.

Gods only knew what the failing wards might attract. Six months ago, the Lurkers had gathered at the door to Creation. Von Hart had managed to head them off by using himself as bait, a "living source of magic", according to the fairy. In doing so, he had turned the phantoms to his own ends. The harp, of course, had shattered into pieces and Ben had seen the menace fly apart, the Ghost Emperor scattered – but he didn't know if that had bought him any time. What was to stop the Lurkers returning, hungrier than ever? He didn't know how long they had. Not much, if his luck was anything to go by.

Looking down, he watched as the shimmering circle faded. Could he see the brands because he'd touched the fragments of the harp, forever stained by *lunewrought*? He thought so. *That shit kind of sticks.* The Fay metal, the ore of Avalon, was both perilous and rare, able to summon Remnants, to bind them in human form and limit their abilities. Had any slivers of the alien metal survived the destruction of the harp? Somehow, he doubted it. But how strange that the *lunewrought* should change him too, granting him this heightened vision. Well, it was a gift that gave him no ease, the sight of these immense sigils, the borders of the spell corroding, flickering out. It only confirmed the fact that he was up to his neck in it.

Thinking this, he turned his attention to the mountain ahead, rising from the arc of the dimming circle. The ravens, cawing louder than before, circled the peak in a great black gyre, once, twice, three times, before scattering off in all directions, released by the dregs of some binding spell, or so Ben reckoned. *A spell to bring someone to the mountain.* The creatures swept down into the valley, heading for the forests and the sea. Just ordinary birds, as far as he could tell. *Someone. But not anyone, surely.*

Despite his inner heat, a chill crept into his bones as he tried to connect the dots. The harp, the circles . . . well, all of it was Fay business, wasn't it? As uncomfortable as the thought made him, he could only assume that he wasn't the mountain's visitor of choice. *Would the ravens have flown all the way to London to summon a washed-up dragon in a cave?* Even if the flock was following the arc of the circle, why enter the barrows? *Don't flatter yourself.* If *lunewrought* spoke to *lunewrought*, as he'd learnt, then it followed that Fay spoke to Fay. And there was only one creature who went by such a description on this side of the nether. Had he come here on another's journey, fulfilling some unknown task? The task of the envoy Blaise Von Hart . . . ?

Hmm. Well, he's out to lunch right now. You'll have to make do with me.

The summit of Snowdon shone pink in the deepening dusk, as old and as mystical-looking as the surrounding countryside, a maze of velveteen valleys dotted with bracken and gorse, adorned with rivers and lakes, silvery in the sunlight. Here, he could detect the vestiges of the Old Lands, untouched by urbanisation, the wilds holding dominance yet over the looping roads and the march of pylons, the smoke coiling from the occasional hostel and the Day-Glo flash of hikers' jackets, sparse on the paths at this hour. This, the golden hour, where the sun slipped between the gates of night and nothing looked quite solid or sure. Snowdon, Yr Wyddfa, loomed like a giant spindle of myth, an axis between the now and then, drawing Ben down to its snow-dusted slopes.

At first, he saw nothing out of sorts, scanning the rock face with keen eyes. Then, some residual glow, a familiar shade of blue, drew his gaze to the eastern precipice, the narrow ledge and the small dark crack in the rock face there. He didn't need to squint too hard to recognise it as a door of some kind and he dropped towards it even as he shrivelled, his tail coiling up into his spine, his wings folding, his snout retracting into his skull. Human-shaped and grim-faced, he landed on the ledge with a thump, dust and scree showering from his bare feet down into the valley below.

"Hello? If you're gonna jump me, make it quick. I've got a war to attend."

Echoes alone answered him. Cautiously, in the faint light that illuminated the roughly hewn tunnel beyond the door, Ben took a few steps forward. He could see well enough, his extraordinary senses on high alert. The hand he trailed along the wall was to steady his nerves rather than his feet. He paused when his fingers ran over a series of ridges and he peered at the wall on his right, seeing the symbol etched there.

It was old, but human in design. Pictish, he thought. The Picts remained shadowy, enigmatic figures. Down through the winding vines of history, people had come to see the ancient race as half mythical, even fairies themselves. Ben, long-lived and half mythical himself, knew that wasn't entirely untrue, according to the stories anyway. The Picts were one of the earliest tribes of Britain, a Celtic people that hailed from the Iron Age. Back in the Old Lands, the tales claimed that the tribe had been the result of the Fay interbreeding with humans, investing them with power, a power that eventually led to their decline, as magic had a nasty habit of doing. Some claimed that a line had survived and continued, however, culminating in the birth of Arthur Pendragon, the storied king of the Britons, who was half Celt and half Roman by the most credible accounts. But, of course, all legend.

Ben had seen the symbol on the wall before. It was a spiral, representing a labyrinth. The pictograph symbolised life, if he remembered correctly, the path that one took from birth and out into the unknown, out into the cosmos. Into death. With a shiver, he recalled that in occult mysticism, the reverse might also be true, that the spirit might return, reborn from darkness, reincarnated in flesh. Or resurrected.

Ben knew just how much fun the latter could be.

The symbol reminded him of another myth, another legend linked to this place.

Of course . . .

"And the harp," he muttered under his breath, picturing the cobwebbed paintings that had hung in du Sang's tomb under Paris. The faded legends that all Remnants knew. "The Lady tried to give it to you, didn't she? At the Battle of Camlann, she wanted you to put Mordred's armies to sleep. The *Cwyth* was known as yours."

He was speculating, still connecting the dots, mustering his courage as he traipsed further down the tunnel. The Pact and the Sleep had all started with the fairy. Now the envoy's words rang in his skull, as stark, as shocking as when he'd first heard them, months ago in the nether.

I made a mistake. Times change. So do hearts. I have found another way.

As Ben made his way through the gloom, drawn to the faint

blue radiance at the end of the tunnel, he swallowed a lump in his throat as another revelation struck him. This hadn't started with Von Hart at all. It went further back, back into the hazy days of myth. Back into the Old Lands. It had started with a battle and a shattered harp. It had started with the departure of the Fay, a severing of worlds, a schism between history and myth.

It had started with a king.

"Arthur . . ."

Ben entered the cavern with the name upon his lips, a breath that felt somehow sacred even as it confirmed his suspicions. Slack-jawed, he took in the circle of tombs, the shields and the runes on the walls, all lit by the weird radiance. Hairs bristled on the nape of his neck, but the sight of the domed space shouldn't have surprised him. Because this was all part of the same tale, wasn't it? A tale that had spanned fifteen hundred years, springing from that last legendary battle and a desperate fairy gift. Arthur, or so the story went, had lifted his magical sword, Caliburn, and brought it down upon the harp, shattering the relic, and with it, the hope of peace. In return, Queen Nimue, Our Lady of the Barrow, had spurned humanity for its weakness, its unshakeable folly and greed. She had led her court from the earth and damned them all in the process. Damned the humans to a world devoid of magic, to a world ravaged by unchecked ambition and technological advancement. And damned the Remnants to ages of abandonment, centuries of oppression and strife until the coming of the compromise, the founding of the Pact.

Arthur had been centuries in his grave . . .

"'Yet some say in parts of England that the king is not dead, but had by the will of our Lady into another place,'" Ben frowned, summoning up the timeworn words, "'and some say that he shall come again, when the realm faces its direst threat . . .'"

Any hope, any longing that Ben might've felt at this evidence of awakening, the seven tombs empty and bare, shrivelled up in his breast at the smell. The dry, sour and faintly sweet stench of rot hung in the air along with the dust. Recently, he had grown too familiar with the scent to mistake it. It was death. It was darkness. Whatever had risen here, it hadn't been in the best of health. Again, he experienced the same pang of misgiving he'd felt last year, wondering why this apparent end to the Pact, this chance of freedom, should make him so afraid. Wasn't it what the Remnants wanted? The Queen's Troth coming true? The Long Sleep over? The chance of peace restored?

Something is wrong. I can feel it in my balls.

A flash of silver caught his eye. He made his way through the ring of tombs, heading towards the central plinth in the middle of the chamber. As he went, he noticed the piles of rusted armour and the bones heaped on a couple of the tombs. He wiped a hand through the dust and wrinkled his nose, wondering whose remains he touched. The tattered banners on the walls, washed out and unidentifiable, were only serving to cement his fears. The carved crest of a stag, bordered by leaves, took up the flank of one tomb. And the stone dragon that coiled on the ceiling, its scales circling out to make up the walls – all of these things related the regal function of the chamber. Yeah. He remembered the legend, all right. What Remnant wouldn't? Nimue, the Lady of the Lake, weaving one last enchantment before stepping into the nether, that being the return of a certain magic sword and the internment of Arthur and his knights deep in the mountain, slumbering for centuries on the threshold of death.

Sounds familiar . . .

The last nail in the coffin – and curse him for thinking such a phrase in this dusty place – came when he reached the central tomb and bent to read the inscription carved on its side.

HIC JACET ARTURUS, QUONDAM
REX QUE FUTURUS

Here lies Arthur, the once and future king.

"Well, I'll be damned," Ben breathed.

He said this, then started as someone, not too far away, answered him.

"You took your time."

He scuttled in retreat, away from the tomb. Scales, slick and hand-sized, flickered up and down his suit, black to red. Then his back met the ring of stone around him, dislodging the bones heaped on the slab with a rattle and a cloud of dust. Coughing, his eyes flared, golden beams spearing the haze as he searched the chamber for the intruder.

"Who the fuck is that? Show yourself!"

"Are you blind? I'm right here." There was a tut, hollow in the gloom. And then, after a pause, the voice said, "You're not the envoy."

"I guess you're not blind either," Ben growled, straightening up. He peered into the shadows, detecting no entrance to the chamber other than the tunnel he'd taken, the one that led to the mountainside outside. There were no archways, no alcoves, no stairs, only the curving walls. Even the shadows weren't particularly deep, shrunken as they were by the strange spectral light. Whoever was in here with him was either hiding behind a tomb or invisible. "What are you? A ghost?" He'd read that sometimes a spirit would guard an old tomb, attending the

61

ancient dead. Or a *wight*. Not a pleasant thought. "Dead or not, it won't stop me from kicking your—"

"Please." The voice was cold, male and sounded educated, cutting in its confidence. "Let's not waste time on bravado. Tell me, where is the envoy? After all, he was the one that the Lady appointed to attend this place in the event of the king's . . ." a cough, "revival."

"I'll bet. But it's news to me, sweetheart. And I'm not giving you a thing until you step out and face me."

"Impossible, I'm afraid. You see, for all my gifts, I lack even the most basic motor skills."

"Dead then. Hey, it's nothing to be ashamed of."

"Oh, I assure you I'm very much alive. Forged in *lunewrought* and star-studded, tempered in the ice of Avalon and spun across worlds to the hand of a king. And I'm right in front of you, numbskull."

Ben let the insult pass, his eyes growing wide as realisation dawned. The flash of silver that he'd noticed before originated here by the tomb, sparkling in the uncanny glow. Propped up by the foundations of the plinth, a sword rested against the stone. But not just any sword. An idiot could see that. And Ben knew *lunewrought* when he saw it too, having seen the fragments of the harp and their eventual destruction. Besides, he'd felt the touch of the Fay metal for himself, an encounter that was too close for comfort, a collar locked around his throat.

The sword bore a resemblance to the harp, all liquid, shimmering silver. The blade was broad, a mirrorlike length of sharpened metal tapering towards the business end. Glyphs, indecipherable, ran along the fuller – the groove in the middle of the blade – perhaps etched by an alien hand. Thick leather straps bound the grip, but that was the only mundane part of the weapon. The pommel echoed the sculpture on the ceiling, moulded to look like a dragon's head, its fangs wide, leaving Ben in no doubt about the sword's ownership. At either end, the crossguard bulged out in gem-studded balls, tiny diamonds and mounted pearls bordering the two large and gleaming sapphires set there.

To Ben, the jewels looked very much like eyes.

"You've got to be kidding me," he said. "You're—"

"Yes. And you're not the envoy, Lord Blaise of the Leaping White Hart."

Ben took a step forward, tipping his head. "The who?" He spoke slowly, distractedly, his voice thick with awe. Then he snorted. "He'd find that a little old-fashioned these days."

"Where is the envoy?" the sword asked again. "Why isn't he here? As I said, he was the one charged with the task."

"What task?"

"Why, to welcome the return of the king, of course. Or rather, the return of the Fay, imminent as it is. To prepare these lands for a new golden age. Is it just me? I thought there was only one fairy left in this world. And therefore, only one who could receive the ravens. Instead—"

"You got me," Ben said, disliking the sword's tone. Disliking that it *had* a tone. At the same time, a lead weight sank in his belly, the sword confirming what should've come as a relief to him, a delight even, but only seemed to sum up his fears.

The return of the Fay . . .

"And who are you, exactly? If I'm going to get out of here, I'd at least like to know who bears me."

"Bears . . . ?" Ben came to a halt, his feet scudding in the dust. He hadn't even noticed his hand stretching out, reaching for the pommel beside the tomb. Those sapphires. So pretty. So *watchful.* "I thought . . . I thought that Arthur alone could . . . you know."

"Yes. Well. Needs must and all that," the sword said. "It wouldn't be the first time either. Gawain carried me once, that proud defender of maidens." A steely chuckle in the gloom. "And Bedwyr, most faithful of the knights of the Round Table." The sword gave a sigh. "I suppose you'll just have to do."

Ben retracted his hand, stung by his own curiosity.

"Oh no you don't," he said. "I know your game. You can cut that luring shit out for starters. I'll keep my freedom, if it's all the same to you."

"Don't be an ass," the sword said. "In case you hadn't noticed, things have . . . changed. Arthur and his knights shuffled out of this chamber hours ago. At least, something that *passes* for them. And why do you think I'm still here? You can't really be that stupid, can you? If you're here, then you must have a shred of wits about you. Not that I'm seeing any evidence of that, but—"

"Shut up." Ben sneered, shrugging off his entrancement. "Did your king put up with that lip?"

"I'm a sword, not a subject. What was he going to do? Throw me in a lake?"

"You're hilarious, you know that? Personally, I don't see anything to joke about."

"Neither do I, which is why I'll ask you again – politely – to stop standing there like a rusty mallet and take me up. Time is of the essence."

Rusty? Despite himself, Ben's hand climbed to his ruffled head.

He scowled, remembering. "Fairy gifts tend to come with a price. A high one."

"Do I look like a gift to you? Some yuletide token lying under a tree? At this point, I'm not even a choice."

"That's what you say," Ben said with a grunt. "You know, I didn't hatch yesterday. *Lunewrought* and me . . . well, we don't mix well. Pick you up and I'll find myself stuck in human form. Won't I?"

"So you're of the bestiary." The sword sounded vaguely sad. Ben didn't need to ask why. "The *erlscion.*"

"The what now? Is that French? You're not making any sense."

"Beastkind. The children of the Fay."

"Oh. Yeah. That." Ben rubbed the back of his neck. "I'm . . . Ben Garston. Red Ben, to my friends. If I had any. I'm the Sola Ignis. Or I was."

"The what?"

"Never mind."

"Anyway," the sword said. "Rest assured. All *lunewrought* is one metal, true, but binding was never my purpose. All the same, I wouldn't advise holding me by the blade, that's if you're fond of fingers." The sword coughed again, aiming for an encouraging tone. "But there are certain perks. For one thing, I'm unbreakable. For another, I can slice through most things as if they were paper." The sword sniffed. "It's such a shame that Morgan threw my scabbard away. It bestowed swift healing to the gravest of wounds."

Ben grunted. "Trust me. I've got that."

"You're beginning to get on my nerves." The sword shone a little brighter, obviously piqued. "Do I have to spell it out for you? Arthur has awoken. Except that he isn't Arthur, not in the truest sense of the word. The magic is sour, corroded. I heard the song ringing through the cavern, the echoes of a great enchantment, recently broken and fading. But I'm not the one to blame this time."

Ben nodded, catching the thread. "The mnemonic harp."

"Excuse me?"

"The *Cwyth*. You'll know it as the *Cwyth*," Ben said. "If you're Caliburn, then the king used you to shatter the harp in the first place, all those centuries ago. Hate to break it to you, but your precious *Lord Blaise* went and reforged the blasted thing."

Silence. Then:

"That wasn't very bright."

"And then he dismantled it. This was centuries ago, after . . . after Camlann. And then he reforged it again, recently. Then he destroyed it completely. Out in the nether." Ben puffed out his cheeks. "It's kind of a long story. You know, a lot has happened in fifteen hundred years."

"Oh dear. Well, that explains it. I can't see the High House taking the news of his meddling very well. I imagine that's what caught their attention."

Ben pictured Von Hart lying in his arms outside the temple on the Fan Lau peninsula, his voice weary, but holding satisfaction.

Time enough for the echoes to travel through the nether. My work here is done.

Since that dark, disastrous day, Ben had been putting the pieces together, closing in on the thrust of the envoy's plan. The sword before him sliced through the last of his doubt. Because *attention* was exactly what the fairy had wanted.

He swallowed. "The Fay. You mean the Fay, don't you?"

"The harp was of their making, as am I," the sword told him, not without pride. "The song may be over, but I'm afraid that our king dances to a different tune. Something is wrong. You know it and I know it. Whatever sat up and stretched on this tomb wasn't exactly *wholesome*, if you take my meaning. Maybe

I'm reaching here, but I'm guessing our best bet is to try and stop him."

Ben rolled his shoulders, bristling at the sword's acid-sweet tone.

"And I suppose you're going to tell me what happens if we don't?"

The sword whined, its hilt clanking against stone.

"Why isn't the envoy here? Look what I have to work with." Before Ben could protest or utter a retort, the sword, lofty and cold, continued. "Do you honestly think you can face this alone? A single beast against the horde? Listen to me. The corpse that shuffled out of this cavern thinks he's the One True King. What would you do in his position, hmm? He's going to raise himself an army. He's heading to London to reclaim the throne."

FOUR

Worlds. Spinning. A shining necklace of worlds scattered across the cosmos. As Ben gripped the hilt of the sword, the vision exploded in his skull, even as a familiar frost crept through his palm and into his bones. White fire shuddered through him, as bright, as burning as when he'd gripped the mnemonic harp, rendering his mind naked, his soul bare. Was he back in the nether? The darkness wheeled around him, depthless, cold, but neither silent nor empty. Time roared, monstrous in his ears. He heard the grinding of stars, a ceaseless beat that echoed his heart. Adrift, unmoored from flesh, he found himself soaring above a cracked moon, the shrapnel of rock and dust forming rings around it. Squinting, he looked down, saw the silver spilling from the moon's molten core, tendrils weaving into the gulf. The blazing rivers met and fused, spiralling out in a vast web, a mesh that he somehow grasped went stretching out, bright, infinite, joining world to world. Lost highways. Uncharted roads. Silver leys riddling the nether. The Dark Frontier.

At the heart of the web, the leys met in a knot like a star, a braided world of helixes, spirals and threads. Arcs of light speared through the riddle, each beam miles wide and strewn with symbols, arcane glyphs beyond his understanding. And in among the thousandfold layers, the twists and turns of the blazing knot-world, Ben made out the glint of mountains and fields, green, gold and grey, cloaked in flowers unlike any he'd known. He saw rivers cascading over impossible edges, a spray of diamonds washing out into eternity. He saw deserts of bone sweep to the horizon, the terrain curving like a giant wheel, descending into the light or looping over his head. He saw oceans glimmer in the maze, the waters rolling as red as blood, and winged ships flying over the waves, their keels throwing up spume. Islands dotted the weave, seemingly afloat on the radiance. Storms flashed in the purple bellies of the clouds.

He peered into the warp and weft, his dreaming gaze lifting from the glittering roots – and he realised then that was exactly what he was looking at: the roots of a tremendous tree, gnarled, burnished and spectral, all pulsating with power. The roots drank from the moon, he saw, sucking up the shining ore, the source of the pervasive light. *Lunewrought*, surely. A closer look revealed skiffs, borne aloft by balloons and strange engines, laden with the luminous rock. *Lunewrought, yes*. Factories, spindly and black, peppered the rim of the chasm, rippling in the argent haze.

Ben traced the roots to the trunk that rose above the shattered moon. As he took in the branches, leafless and silver, he grasped the vast scale of the tree, growing here for countless epochs in the fathomless dark.

Far above, in the upper reaches, he saw a palace perched on the highest branch. Every battlement, turret and buttress rose as though carved from a single block of crystal. The foundations of the structure overhung the branch – which must have been a hundred feet in breadth, if not more – like spindles of melted wax, bulbous and tapering. Resting upon this massive bole, the palace stood. A moat surrounded the edifice, swans trailing across the polished surface. A drawbridge ran under the central keep, a tongue sliding into the face of the building, all high white walls, windows of sunset pink, parapets and pinnacles with silken flags. Here and there, Ben spied the hint of courtyards and follies, patches of lawn for reflection and games. There was a dome, which he took for a chapel, though what gods the denizens of such a place worshipped he found hard to imagine. The palace loomed, a medley of glass shot with blue, a spear thrust into the dark. This was the spindle on which the worlds spun, Ben knew, his senses stretched beyond earthly comprehension, his heart leaping at the sight. Bodiless, breathless, he took in the High House of Avalon, built aeons upon aeons ago in the uppermost branches of the Great Tree, which legend knew as the Isle of the Apples, the Font of All Worlds. Its roots went sprawling out into the cosmos, silver veins weaving through the darkness, across an ocean of unformed space. Of possibility.

At least one of those veins, Ben suspected, still reached the Earth. A bridge, or so he'd thought at the time, as he'd leapt from the nameless temple in China and into the nether. In truth, it was a road. He got that now. A road that stretched to the Eight Hand Mirror. A door into Creation.

But the bridge fell with the breaking of the harp, didn't it? Evaporated in sparks and mist . . .

Ben grasped at this hope, wondering why this proof of the Fay's endurance should only fill him with dread. He was a creature of instinct; his guts had been his guide for many a year. And when his gaze fell once more on the palace, his heart shrank with a nameless fear.

Up there, on a balcony, a woman stood. Dark, she was, both in skin and mystery. She wore a gown of pale blue silk, gossamer-sheer, the fabric moulded to her bosom and hips, her limbs left slender and bare. Her hair, as white as the palace walls, resembled a serpent coiled high on her head. Below her piled braid, her face was noble and proud, cut by angles of bone that fitted together in beauty despite their severity – or perhaps because of it. Her lips, brown and full, seemed forever poised on the verge of a kiss. Her nose was the dive of a hawk and her eyes, a soft yet penetrating violet, fixed on him in evident surprise.

Then she frowned, a thin shadow slashed in her brow. He caught the flash of teeth, tiny pearls, and then the woman cast out a hand, a swift, sharp motion in the gulf.

A *dismissal*.

Ben found himself tumbling head over heels, into the nether. The palace, the tree, the cracked, bleeding moon all fell away from him, a shooting star. Dizziness claimed him, the emptiness filling his eyes. There was a sudden weight in his hands, an anchor bearing him down, but it was nothing compared to the weight of his heart. It was laden by the hope of thousands, tugging at a hilt embedded in stone. It was the lust of battle, of singing steel and severed flesh. It was a sigh of sorrow, the surface of a lake closing over his head.

And in the end, it was darkness. The darkness that comes at the end of all dreams.

He came to himself leaning against the wall of the tunnel, the last minutes of daylight winking up ahead. In his hand, the legendary sword, Caliburn.

"What . . . what did I just see?"

The blade glinted in the half-light. "Oh, I think you know."

Ben hawked up, spat and curled his lip. "I saw a painting once. The Lady . . ."

He'd heard stories too. Stories beyond number. The painting in du Sang's tomb had only confirmed an image that he'd held in his mind, a precious secret, a jewel. But he knew he probably

71

shared that sense of wonder with all Remnantkind. Even the thought of it made him jealous, his covetous nature coiling around the memory. Still, he was afraid.

"Yes. Nimue. Our Lady of the Barrow," the sword said. "She looks out from the High House, searching the leys for the source of the disturbance."

My work here is done . . .

"Yeah. And I'm guessing she wasn't expecting me." Ben growled down at the sword. "Don't ever do that again."

"What should I do? Turn the volume down from 'king' level? I'm afraid it doesn't work like that. We are all the creations of the Fay, Mr Ignis. And we must answer as such."

Great.

"Don't call me that either." He shook his head, then vented a sigh at the fading vision. "She looked . . ." He swallowed. "She looked like a goddess."

As far as gods were concerned, he wasn't exactly a fan.

The sword made a snorting sound. "Once, perhaps. The First-Born had their day. Now she is merely a queen."

"Even better."

With this, he lifted the blade and staggered up the tunnel, navigating the rubble of the door to clamber out onto the narrow ledge. Grit trickled into the valley below. Windows flickered, fireflies in the distance. He leant against the rock face and breathed, sucking the evening into his lungs. There wasn't time to gawp at the first stars, twinkling in the darkening blue. Somehow, he had to find something to wrap the sword in. He'd seen the effects of *lunewrought* up close and personal, a crazed light in a battle dragon's eyes. He wasn't about to bear the blade in his claws all the way back to London. Again, he was keenly aware that he was standing here in borrowed shoes. The cavern, the sword, the Lady – all of these things had been meant for Von Hart, the envoy extraordinary. The Lord of the Leaping White Stag, whatever. The sword had said so. Instead, the task rested on his shoulders, that for all their shame also bore a weight of cynicism. He'd hate to break it to Caliburn, but under the circumstances, the chance of a *new golden age* looked pretty slim. So where to start his latest bungling attempt at heroism this time? Face down a dead king with a magical sword? Or shake the fairy awake?

As ideas went, he kind of preferred the latter.

He was thinking this, shoving himself off the rocks and starting to make his way down the track, when a figure leapt from a boulder above him, a sword swinging out. In the gloom, Ben made out the sheen of a leather jacket, ripped jeans and a helmet of some kind. His eyes grew wide as his fist came up – he didn't think to use Caliburn – and his assailant's weapon clanged against his thickening scales, parried by his forearm.

As his serpentine vision kicked in, Ben took in the figure staggering back, arms wheeling, desperately clutching the sword. That sword, broad-bladed, was instantly recognisable as a claymore, the edge notched like the teeth of a saw. It was also burnt, he noticed, fifty-five familiar inches of charred black steel, toasted a couple of years back in an underground car park in London. And recovered, no doubt, from the equally charred ruins of an oil refinery in Cairo.

Not this again.

The slayer was dressed in black too. *Typical.* Black leather jacket. Black motorcycle boots. Black helmet – the visor, he noted, charred like the sword. Evil-looking spikes covered the helmet from its crest to its vulturine beak. Ben laughed, a humourless bark. The scrap pointing up at him belonged to the Lambton

armour, of course, the antique vessel that had delivered the
Guild's downfall, the death of the chairman Bardolfe and Ben's
initial suspicion of Von Hart. The last time he'd seen the helmet
– miles, oceans away from here – it'd been rolling across a factory
floor with a decapitated head inside it.

"You guys need to get a new act," Ben said.

The Black Knight recovered his footing, gripping the claymore
with both hands and swinging it out before him.

"Red Ben Garston." The slayer's voice sounded hollow and
tinny encased in metal. "I have some business with you!"

Ben was busy counting his fingers, his free hand raised before
his face.

"So you're what? Fulk Fitzwarren CDXIII?" He spat out the
Roman numerals. "Is that right? I forget."

"Yield, knave!" Caliburn cried.

"It's OK, really," Ben told the sword. "I've got this."

The Black Knight yelled, "Milk-drinker! Snake! Prepare to
meet your doom!"

The narrow track made a headlong charge difficult, but the
slayer gave it a shot. Holding the claymore out before him like
a lance, he came at Ben, obviously intending to run him through.
Nice. Caliburn thrummed in Ben's grip, eager to engage, but
he held the sword point downward, sending a silent message
of restraint.

When the claymore was inches from him, Ben swung out his
arm, simply batting the blade away. This time, he couldn't detect
any charms around the antique, and besides, the person holding
it, for all his apparent skill, didn't have much in the way of
room. The assault was clumsy, guided by temper, and quite
rightfully, the claymore flew into the air, clanging off the rock
face and spinning down into the valley. Boots skidding on grit,

the knight hollered and tried to veer away, abandon the attack. Ben's hand snapped into a claw, grabbing the man as he fell, his talons closing around his throat.

Feet wriggling, the Black Knight gasped and spluttered as Ben lifted him up off the ground.

"'Prepare to meet your doom.' Seriously?" He jutted out his jaw, glaring up at the absurdly spiked helmet. "How did you find me?" he asked. "I'm halfway up a bloody Welsh mountain."

"The prophet . . ." the knight croaked, struggling. "The prophet came to us . . . at the Last Pavilion. Told us . . . to follow . . ."

The Last Pavilion. He'd heard of the place, naturally. Or rather, unfortunately. The knight was talking about the Fitzwarren stronghold, a ramshackle mansion somewhere in Shropshire where the family elders, the patriarchs, had trained generation upon generation of Fulks for a singular and violent purpose: to chop off Ben Garston's head and win back the deeds to their ancient seat, the crumbling ruin of Whittington Castle. He recalled the house motto with a sneer.

Spei est Vindicta. Hope is Vengeance.

Well. About that . . .

"Don't you people watch the news?"

But *prophet*, he'd said? He didn't know what to make of that, but he knew that it sounded religious. Something to do with the Chapter, had to be. That led to another idea, just as unpleasant as the first.

"*Lunewrought.* You've got one of those damn manacles, haven't you?" He rattled the slayer in his grip as if to shake loose the suspected restraint. "Come on. Out with it. Or I'll chuck you down there after your sword."

Truth be told, he wasn't sure whether he was going to do that anyway. These encounters, ancient, tedious as they were, tended to wind up with a dead Fulk at the end of them. Nevertheless, if the knight did have *lunewrought* in his possession, Ben would happily take it from him. It didn't surprise him that the Whispering Chapter was still hot on his heels, tracking him down with the alien metal. In the Cardinal's eyes, he was guilty of breaking the Lore on several counts and he didn't think that the destruction of the harp, not to mention the Chapter's plan to annihilate all Remnants in the Long Sleep, would've changed matters. Fanaticism was fanaticism, after all. If House Fitzwarren had thrown in with the CROWS a couple of years ago, then what was to stop them jumping into bed with the Chapter? These days, nothing surprised him.

Seems I'm more popular than ever.

With a trembling hand, the Black Knight fumbled in the pocket of his jacket and brought out the manacle in question, a thin silver circlet sparkling under the stars.

Ben grunted and lifted Caliburn, nodding at the Fulk in his grip. Fulk, choking, obliged him, sliding the manacle over the tip of the sword. Like a game of ring toss, the manacle spun down the length of the blade, tinkling against the jewelled hilt and then liquidising in the air, silvery beads dancing around the crossguard, slowly melting into the sword. All *lunewrought* was one metal, or so folks said. And to *lunewrought* the manacle returned.

"Toothsome," the sword said.

"Now," Ben said, ignoring it. "Get out of my face."

Without ceremony, he released Fulk, dropping him onto the track. The knight's helmet fell off with the impact, bouncing off a rock and over the cliff edge, joining his fallen sword. Mindless of the spikes, Fulk cried out and made a lunge for it, his finger-tips missing the helmet by inches. Ben might've gone after him,

delivered a swift kick to his butt, if surprise hadn't arrested him.
Eyebrows raised, he took in the slayer's scrawny figure and bobbed
black hair, cropped short in an evidently rough and hurried
fashion. A smooth, unscarred face shot in his direction, dark
eyes aflame.

Just a . . . boy?

"You bastard! Have you any idea what they'll do to me for
that?"

"Who? Your patriarchs?" Ben said. "They should've known
better. Antiques like that belong in display cases. Admittedly,
that piece of junk doesn't come with a 'keep away from children'
sticker."

"I'm not a child. The dragon slaying was mine by right. Mine!"

Ben laughed. "Is House Fitzwarren so desperate these days
that they're sending kids out on the hunt? You know, there's an
old saying. Play with fire and . . ."

He left the phrase hanging, a threat in the air.

The girl crouching on the track – and she *was* a girl, he saw,
with a snort – screwed up her face. Even in the gloom, he could
make out her light brown skin and dark lashes, revealing a trace
of Asian blood. Indian, he thought, mixed with English, like
many of the immigrants that had sailed to these shores – that
had *always* sailed to these shores, for as long as he could remember
– enriching the country's culture with their own. Sensing his
scrutiny, the girl looked away, down at the ground.

Ben read something telling in the gesture.

"Wait a minute. No one sent you, did they? The vendetta for
the Mordiford Shame falls to Fitzwarren *sons*, as far as I'm
aware. And I'm pretty well versed in the custom, trust me." He
crunched over to where the girl sat, growling down at her. "You
fancied a shot at the cherry, right? You're what – all of sixteen?"

"Seventeen." The girl exhaled, letting him know that this was a common and incredibly boring mistake. "So what?"

The sword gave a chiding tut.

"And you're no Fulk, that's for sure." He made it sound like an insult, but it wasn't. Not really. "What's your real name? Tell me and I might even let you walk out of here."

"Annis," she said through her teeth, proud all the same. "Annis Cade."

"Wrong. You're raw meat. Only one thing to do with raw meat."

Ben drew himself up, his suit rippling, his chest and limbs expanding in a shield of scales. Horns danced up on his shoulders, yellow and curved. He conjured the furnace in his belly into his eyes, and when he opened his mouth to speak again, fangs glistened behind his lips.

He only meant to scare the girl, send her running down the mountainside and, hopefully, back home. But unlike her attack, she caught him off guard, leaping to her feet and facing him with a snarl.

"Kill me if you want," she spat. "Your doom is upon you either way, snake." Then she dropped the traditional scorn, seething at him with typically teenage vitriol. "You don't know what it was like. The chance, taken from me. And why? Arlen drowned and I should've taken his place. Father should've sent *me* out on the hunt. Your head should've been mine! So instead I stole the helmet. So what? I took Fulk's sword and the manacle from the chapel. I was going to show them." She took a breath and, despite her position, corrected herself. "I'm *going* to show them all."

Ben rolled his eyes.

This is turning out to be a very long day.

78

Growling, he grabbed the girl's shoulder.

"I don't have time for this shit," he said.

An hour later, sixty miles to the east, Ben swept over the border into England. In full dragon form, he flew over the hills and fields, horses and sheep fleeing below, leaping paddock gates or bleating in briars. Dogs barked, straining at the limits of chains. The odd car wound through the Marches, headlights beaming, unaware of his presence. Trees thrashed in his wake.

In his front claw, he gripped Caliburn. Gently. Despite its assurances, he'd wrapped the sword in a leather jacket, the arms tied tightly over the blade. For one thing, he didn't want to find himself forcibly transformed into human shape three hundred feet over Shropshire. For another, he reckoned that he had enough scars.

In his other claw, he held the would-be Black Knight, Annis Cade. At first, she had struggled, punching and kicking against the scales around her. But she'd soon worn herself out, settling into a sulky silence for the rest of the journey. Part of him, while vexed by the delay, admired her spirit, not that it was going to stop him teaching her a lesson.

Down below, a village spread out, the streetlights illuminating the tiny houses, the odd pub and the fish and chip shop. Water glittered in the sodium glow, a narrow lake running beside the main road. On the shore, a castle stood, the restored ruins of a thirteenth-century gatehouse and bailey, a relic of tumbledown stone with an inner and outer wall. Trees sprouted from the place where the hall had once stood, the courtyard a trimly mowed lawn. There was a booth beside the drawbridge, closed at this hour, to sell tickets to tourists.

"Whittington Castle," Ben said, naming their location. "Back in the day, King John snatched the deeds to the place, keeping hold of them until your house managed to meet a certain provision. That being, that as long as this head sits on these shoulders, the castle will remain in trust, in the care of the Guild of the Broken Lance. Sure, things got complicated when the Pact came along in 1215, protecting the Remnant leaders from harm, including yours truly. Not that it stopped a shedload of Fulks from having a go."

Since one tragic day in Mordiford, the Black Knight had tried – and failed – for over eight centuries.

Annis said something, muffled and hot.

"Maybe it's time that your lot woke up," Ben told her. "No Guild, no Pact. No Pact, no provision. Whittington Castle is all yours."

Fifty feet above the village, Ben released the girl. Screaming, sans jacket, she tumbled through the sky and splashed down into the moat.

"And you're welcome to it," Ben said and flew on into the night.

FIVE

Through wisps of cloud, Ben doubled back, sweeping west towards Snowdonia. The Black Knight niggled him, however. The old grudge was a minor inconvenience and one he'd grown used to; it should've been easy to put it out of his mind. Had he honestly thought that the Fitzwarrens would leave him alone after Cairo? After the Pact went up in smoke? Maybe. Even so, it seemed yet another generation was after his head.

They're getting younger every time. Or I'm getting older.

Eight hundred and sixty-two years old, to be precise. His birthday had passed in April, unmarked as usual (there wasn't really anyone who'd celebrate his continued existence). *Shit. I feel it.* Eight hundred and sixty-two years since he'd hatched under a girl's bed in Mordiford and drank his first saucer of milk. He'd seen so many things, from the signing of Magna Carta (and its no less important, but secret, twin) to the "discovery" of America to the dropping of the atomic bomb. In modern times, these seismic events gave him the impression of time speeding up: space travel, the internet, the Twin Towers and global warming. There was less and less room for creatures like him, rare and unique as they were. In a shower of mobile phones and selfie sticks, the human race was about to plunge over the edge of a waterfall, civilisation shattering on the rocks.

Shattering just like the harp. And taking the Remnants with them . . .

Shooting over the darkened hills, he wished he could believe that his view was down to pessimism, a doom-and-gloom outlook born from centuries of loneliness and the resulting cynicism. It was the fire that tears couldn't quench, his pain soused by bottles of Jack. Still, the end was coming. That was a fact. *The bitterest truth.* Shuddering, he focused on the matter at hand.

How far a dead king and a handful of knights could travel on foot at night in the mountains was anyone's guess, but he was guessing it wasn't far. In this, it turned out that he was wrong. And he should've known better. The elements at play, ominous, perplexing as they were, were far from earthly. According to Caliburn – and judging from his vision – the Fay had a hand in all this, the warped awakening, the coming of the king. It didn't take a genius to realise that the shockwave of the harp's destruction was more than just musical; somewhere, alarm bells were ringing, likely to bring about consequences. Ben didn't know what Arthur's return to London would mean for either Remnants or humans, but experience told him he shouldn't expect a party.

Seven tons of red-scaled flesh rushed through the air into Denbighshire, or Edeyrnion, as he'd once known it, the commote of medieval Wales. His wingspan, forty feet of slender metacarpals supporting a web of leathery skin, flowed over the fields and farms, the moon casting his shadow on lands that hadn't much changed, a fact that gave him a little comfort. In a creak of trees and a howl of dogs, all sixty feet of him was gone, horned snout to the tip of his tail vanishing into the dark. Into the ancient hills.

As Ben made to veer north, retracing his steps to the mountain, Caliburn thrummed in his claw, an icy shiver running up

his foreleg. When the sword spoke, he could hear its voice clearly
through the wind, informing him that its words echoed in his
skull, rather than his ears. A revelation he didn't like. He was
sick to the back teeth of magic.

"Whoa. You'll want to keep flying west. I can sense the king
up ahead. Ten miles or so."

Whoa? Ben bristled, fighting the urge to drop the sword,
hopefully into a bog below. Instead, he drew in a breath and
replied between his fangs.

"Did Arthur steal a car? There's no way he could reach
Penmelesmere this quickly."

Penmelesmere – or Lake Bala, on a modern map – spread
out below, a four-mile-long body of water stretching smooth and
black between the hills. It was as though someone had poured
the night into the valley, the moon and the stars glimmering on
the surface. The sight prompted Ben to recall the old legend,
how Bald Tegid, the husband of the sorceress Ceridwen, had
once held court here back in the Old Lands. Tegid, or so the
story went, had been a wicked prince, visiting many a cruelty
upon the villagers who lived around his palace. One night, a
harper, pale and pointy-eared, came to the court, and after one
thing and another, the entire palace sank into a lake, a fitting
fairy punishment. On moonlit nights like this one, some said
that one could still see the lights of the drowned palace shining
under the waves.

Thoughts of fairies didn't allay Ben's unease, dousing the
romance of the tale. People had died here. Lots of them. This
kind of wanton slaughter tended to happen a lot when the Fay
were involved, it seemed. February in Beijing hadn't been any
different . . .

We must all make sacrifices . . .

Ben curled his lip, the moonlight glinting on his teeth. Only a fool would trust the Fay. He'd learnt that at his peril.

Caliburn was talking again. ". . . think he'd get here by earthly means, you oaf? He bears the horn of summoning. Look!"

Horn of . . . well, that sounds perfect.

Ben scowled. The sword's tone was bad enough, but he liked the sight below even less. Halfway down the road on the north side of the lake, Arthur and his knights were riding through the gloom. Besides the king, there were two knights, Ben saw, sat high in the saddle. He recalled the bones and the dust in the mountain tomb, realising that some of the Sleepers hadn't made it. Rotten spells and all that. As he drew closer, the faint blue glow, cold and somehow rancid-looking, resolved into the figure of the bearded, skeletal king of old, a golden crown, dragon-shaped, upon his head. His armour shone with magic and moonlight, while his knights, no more than corpses in breastplates and greaves, rode a pace or two behind him. Their hollow eye sockets burned with the strange, revivifying light, scouring the darkness ahead. Ben caught the glint of an axe, the gleam of a mace. A couple of hounds, frost-eyed and stripped of flesh, clacked at speed alongside them. The ghoulish troop was galloping down the road, dry crests and white hair waving, shields clanging against desiccated flesh and naked bone. Their mounts were comprised only of darkness, tendrils of smoke wafting from their manes and hooves, the latter striking the tarmac of the A494 with a weird, whispering rumble.

"Shagfoal," Ben muttered.

"I beg your pardon?" said the sword.

"Never mind." He wasn't in the mood to explain the phantom horses to a weapon, of all things, however magical it was. The vaporous beasts had frightened many a traveller back in the day, haunting the byways of Britain. If the shagfoal galloped here, that could only mean one thing. *Christ.* "He's dragged them out of the Sleep."

"Oh, the Remnants are stirring anyway," Caliburn said. "Arthur merely hurries them along, summoning them to his cause."

"Now tell me the bad news."

"Well, he's only summoning the Remnants that will serve his purpose. I'm sure he'll leave the nymphs, fauns and brownies to wake up in their own time. No doubt he'll want Mordred's brood, judging by the state of him. You know, Remnants with a mind to violence. Destruction, pillage and murder. That kind of thing."

"Wonderful. Forget I asked."

Ben dropped down from the heights, shrinking in size as he approached a gorse-clad hillside on the south side of the lake. The night air hushed as he slowed, sending ripples across the lake. He landed with a thump on soft earth, rolling through the tangled bushes, thorns snapping against his suit. Then, spitting out a clump of moss, he crawled on his belly to a nearby rock, peering down for a closer look.

It wasn't good. Arthur held up a hand – no more than a twisted, mortified claw – and, in silence, his knights obeyed, their features pale and withered masks, their spectral mounts drawing to a halt. As they did so, Ben noticed the shadowed forms scrabbling down the road several yards behind them, a mass of horned helmets, clubs and mallets bristling under the moon. With a sharp intake of breath, he made out the broken teeth in the swamp-green faces, each one covered in warts. He made out the rags that hung from their small and sinewy limbs, and their slitted eyes hunting the dark, their hunger unmistakable.

Goblins. I'd know that smell anywhere . . .

85

Larger shapes rose from the mass, bull-shouldered and hunched. Here, at least, he could see that some of the creatures had made an effort in terms of appearance. Richly furred cloaks that dragged along the ground, striped tunics and silken hose, all tailored to grotesque size. Despite the powdered faces, fake beauty spots and braided wigs, nothing could disguise the drooping lips that revealed their stubby fangs. Under beetling brows, their piggy eyes squinted down the road, glinting with the promise of a hundred evils. Ben counted three or four of the ogres in the mob, and ogres, he knew, weren't known for their kindness. He spared a thought for Bala, the town at the eastern end of the lake. Somehow he had to warn them, before half the population wound up in a pie.

He was making a move to do so when Arthur blew his horn. The echoes, sonorous in the dark, shuddered up and down the length of the valley. On his horse, the king sat, the gilded ivory instrument pressed to his peeled and permanent grin. He was staring at the lake, Ben realised, the reverberations of the horn travelling across it, the surface alive with ripples and bubbles, something stirring beneath. His Adam's apple rose in his throat as he saw a limb, long-fingered, hook-nailed, emerge from the waters to clutch at the bank. Others followed, reaching from the weeds and anchoring on land, dragging their boil-ridden bodies behind them. As one, the hags rose from the lake, their long green hair straggling in their faces, unable to hide their hideousness. Bent spines supported birdcage backs and bony shoulders, the hags looking slick and amphibian in the gloom. There must've been thirty or more of the creatures; Remnants that Ben knew as *greenteeth*, river hags, as cruel and as cannibalistic as the rest of the summoned throng. Marsh lights danced between their legs, illuminating sagging bosoms and bellies as the greenteeth joined with the goblins and the ogres, gathering behind the king.

Half swollen to dragon size, Ben faltered as the echoes rang off the hillside behind him and the ground shook under his feet. Boulders came rolling down the slope, one shattering apart on his shoulder, others, larger, thundering downward and splashing into the lake. With a snarl, he could see that the disturbance had drawn the king's attention, his ensorcelled gaze scanning the valley across the lake. Heart frozen, he thought that Arthur was staring directly at him, but the next moment a roar of sundering threw him from his feet and into the gorse. Caliburn flew out of his claw, a jewelled Catherine wheel spinning to land point-first in the earth, the blade shuddering. He made a lunge to reclaim the weapon, the ground buckling under him in great clods of turf, rendered molten by the sounding of the horn. The scene struck him as horribly familiar. Was the instrument picking up the strains of the lullaby, he wondered, amplifying the wake of the broken enchantment, focusing the spell on this specific point? A reluctant expert on the subject, he reckoned so, because the ground under him was slowly parting, the maw growing wider, and even in the darkness, he could see the tell-tale glimmer of obsidian, the sheen of some subterranean cavern like an egg sunken into the earth, now rising to the troubled surface.

Something – someone – was breaking free.

Ben yelled, rolling and covering his head. In an explosion of rocks and dirt, a large shape burst from the hillside, roaring into the moonlight. The beast landed, claws splayed, further down the slope, the impact sending a tremor through the earth. Grimacing at the stench issuing from the chasm, the pall of eight centuries' sleep, Ben clambered to his feet, looking down at the Remnant below him.

The night didn't spare him the sight of her, her crimson-furred flanks markedly feline, her four paws planted on the earth, claws unsheathed. Any resemblance to a lion ended with her size, however, which easily doubled that of a rhino. The muscles sliding under her pelt revealed a greater agility, promising danger and death. A pair of bat-like wings protruded from her spine, flapping in apparent confusion as she took in her surroundings, drawing her first breath of fresh air in eight hundred years. Smaller than his as they were, her wings looked nimble and strong, more than able to get her airborne for battle, and that didn't bode well. Nor did her tail, which swished back and forth, hissing with more than displaced air. Her tail, in fact, was a snake, a living threat affixed by some perversion of nature to the beast's rump. One bite and he'd find himself paralysed, at the mercy of a monster who had no reason to show him any.

We're all monsters here, honey.

His blood cooled with an unwanted realisation. There was no way he could face down the horde single-handedly. Even a battle-hardened dragon like himself would be up against it, considering the beast on the hillside below him, the mob of goblins and ogres and the hags beside the lake, not to mention the corpse king and his knights and whatever sorcery they happened to conjure up. He couldn't suppress a surge of excitement at the sight, some warped sense of liberation, despite his sense of doom. How strange it was to see more than one creature of the same kind after all these years. There were what – a hundred-odd Remnants down there? Perhaps not the world's greatest army, true, but his heart sank as he remembered that this war had never been a numbers game. Humans might remain the earth's dominant species. Lord knows, populations had risen to hazardous levels since the rabble below him had gone into the Long Sleep and Remnants had been dwindling even then, facing eventual extinction. *Or so the envoy said.* In this case, discretion really was the better part of valour. His mind took a quick, panicked series of snapshots, saving them for later reference as he contemplated his next move.

Fight or flight? I think the sword already answered that one.

He had to get out of here. Recover Caliburn and warn the town, make the residents of Bala take to the hills. Then back to London, take the sword to Von Hart, try to shake the envoy out of his coma. He was in way over his head – this time by leagues – and if nothing else, he'd make the fairy pay for his deceit before the end.

For Jia . . .

Under this, a doubt nagged him. His aggression was a mask, he knew, hiding a deeper, uncomfortable truth. In the past, he'd always had the envoy to turn to when matters got out of hand, a regrettable but necessary ally. That was over now, any sham of a friendship gone up in smoke. *In shattered lunewrought.* It pained him to acknowledge the fact. Even though the times had drastically changed, the age-old requirement hadn't. When it came down to confronting an undead king and an army of Remnants, Von Hart was his first and only hope. He needed help. And fast.

Keeping low, his dragon form coiling within, Ben made to leave, creeping across the hillside. The snake, alerted by the movement, reared up on the beast's rump, noticing him. Hood flaring, fangs bared, it hissed, ready to strike. Whatever signal passed from the tail to the Remnant's mind, Ben couldn't know, but he froze in the spotlight of her yellow eyes as she spun around and saw him.

"Benjurigan," the manticore said, a hiss between her fangs. Then, "Turncoat."

"Hello, Jinx," Ben said. "It's been a long time."

He hadn't expected any other kind of greeting. Any other greeting would've been strange.

Jinx, the manticore, glowered up at him. Apart from her shaggy mane and her teeth, her face was human, resembling a woman with high cheekbones and full lips. He might've found her attractive if not for the mess surrounding it, the claws, the bat wings and deadly tail. Manticores were hostile creatures, given to cruelty and violence, with a penchant for taunting and playing with their prey. Back in the Old Lands, many a traveller had never returned from the mountains where the creatures liked to roam, their flayed hides later found by family and friends, sometimes hanging in a tree, fluttering like a flag. And often on the rocks nearby, a poem would accompany these finds, describing the flavour of the victim, scrawled in human blood. There were solid reasons why the Pact hadn't spared a manticore the Sleep, not that the beast below him was likely to agree with them.

Her tail reared up again, peering over her shoulder as she lowered her body, preparing to pounce.

"Too long," she said.

In a shower of stones and shrubs, dragon and manticore tumbled down the hillside. Her tail darted back and forth, snapping at his body, but the scales of his suit prevented her teeth from sinking home, from spiking venom into his veins. Likewise, her claws, ripping at him, scoring his crimson carapace, so recently shaped from his thoughts, the trick he'd learnt from Jia. *Saving my bacon yet again* . . . As he locked a hand around the manticore's throat – a hand swelling into a plated claw – Jinx laughed, a not-quite-sane burst of amusement, causing him to doubt her reasons for taking him on. Overconfident or no, it wasn't exactly advisable. She'd only just woken up, hadn't she? And, in an avalanche of meat, wings and fangs thundering down the slope, his newly fledged dragon form rendered her half his size.

There was no way that she could win this fight. Unlike her, he'd been walking the earth for the duration of her sleep, confronting a host of enemies, from vengeful knights to battle dragons. *Stupid beast.* Did she even *want* to win? Or simply ensure her own ending? Oh, he could see the same old glint in her eyes, all right. The confusion, the hate – and the madness bubbling under it. Most of the Remnants had already had a screw loose long before the envoy strummed his little harp, striking up the lullaby and binding them all in enchantment. If Jinx had gone to her temporary grave as a half-crazed thing, she had clearly risen as an outright maniac. He didn't feel too bad about landing a heavy punch on her skull.

More Remnant blood on your hands. But who's counting, right?

Locked, growling, the beasts struck off the hill and took to the air, their wings thrashing, their passage carving a v of froth across the surface of the lake. Distantly, Ben could hear the racket of the horde, the dead king leading the rabble on towards Bala, but whether the creatures roared and cried at his appearance or not, he couldn't say. Blood pounded in his skull. In his ears, the manticore squealed and hissed, her claws scrabbling for his belly, unable to reach the softer parts of him. Still, she was a handful, slippery in his grip – and fast, just as he remembered. If he released her, he'd be facing a time-consuming and tiring chase over half of Wales. God knows the damage she'd do on the way, not to mention Arthur, riding on into the interior.

No. Better make this quick.

Despite her recent rousing, the manticore was horribly strong, and her wings, small yet nippy, were managing to throw him off course, his intention to slam her into the opposite bank, break her on the rocks. Grimacing, he tried to lift her to his jaws. Maybe he could bite off her head and spit it out into the water. Or roast it, turn her glee into gobbets of melted flesh and ash. But she thrashed in his grip, a sleek, wild thing. Slowly but surely, she was dragging him towards the town, determined to force him into chaos, into harm. All he could do was vent a bellow, a resounding warning through the night, loud enough to rattle the windows and the streetlights. A few seconds later, a chorus of screams and shouts rose from the buildings below. Lights flicked on. Doors slammed open. As he descended, Ben watched the people run, abandoning dinners and computers and TV shows to take to the night, a pale-faced mess spilling in all directions through the adjacent streets. Some stared up at the sky, frozen by the horrors roaring out of the moonlight. The knowledge made him groan, a weight pressing down on him, squeezing his heart. He was drowning in a sea of failure, help-less against the turning tide. The times hurled him towards Bala like driftwood in a deluge.

Jinx, perhaps sensing his despair, went limp in his grasp. He might've taken this as defeat if not for the chuckle in her throat, her wings snapping in, surrendering to gravity, pulling him down. Too weary to carry her further, he closed his eyes and turned his snout, bracing for impact. The next moment, roof tiles went flying around him, the houses shattering (he only hoped that the tenants had managed to get clear; couldn't think about that now), and in a cloud of bricks and glass, dragon and manticore rolled, booming, snarling, along the high street.

Car alarms went off, silenced a moment later in a crunch of flattened metal. Tarmac cracked and shopfronts exploded, decimated by Ben's flailing tail. A pub sign fell, the image of a ship breaking apart on the shuddering ground. As his breath flew from his lungs, Jinx flew from his grip, rolling away from him up the road. With a crash, the manticore came to a halt by the entrance to a supermarket, a mangled security mesh and a display of cut-price goods collapsing around her.

Wincing at his cuts and bruises, Ben shrugged off the wreckage and rose to his feet. Through the smoke and the dust, the wail of alarms, he could hear Jinx laughing, laughing fit to burst. But moving towards her, his fangs parted, a claw outstretched, he realised his mistake, his talons closing like a wilting rose. She kept her face turned from him, her body sprawled in the debris, her breaths misting the air. Still, he could hear the tears in her voice.

"Kill me, then," she said. "Even if you tear me limb from limb, it will seem quick in comparison."

To the Sleep? He cocked his head, surprised by her outburst, her grief leaden between them. In that moment, even his own shadow struck him as unfair, looming over her broken, huddled shape, her shoulders, trembling, letting him know that this battle was over. Was there some way to reason with her? No. He doubted that. Bind her, perhaps? Chain her up somewhere? Unlikely. A memory of flayed skin and bloody poems suggested otherwise . . .

The fact that he was staring coldblooded murder in the face doused his fire somewhat. A flicker of will, a burst of his breath. That's all it would take, he knew. Like he'd done for Gard, for a handful of other Remnants in the past. *Lord, I'm tired . . .* Before he knew it, he was man-shaped again, tousle-haired and striding towards her through the rubble.

"I'm not some monster," he said, then snorted at the irony. "I swore to protect them. I'm damage limitation, that's all. You know how this has to end."

"End?" she said, sniffing. "It's already over. You made your choice. The Remnants are dying because of it."

"The Remnants are asleep." *Or they were.* "I did what I had to—"

"Fool! You may have shut us up in a prison, nice and safe, but you cannot stop the flood that seeps through the walls. Poison, it is. Dark and sour. You can taste it even here, in these blasted hills."

Ben swallowed, then spat out blood, the bitterness she spoke of. He took a step closer, shuffling through guilt. He wished he could refute what she was saying, but he'd seen the truth for himself.

"Dodge. Ruse. Gambit. All dead," she told him. "My entire family, rotting under the earth." She struggled to hold back a sob. "Asleep, you say, Benjurigan? No. You mean *buried.*"

That hurt him. It hurt him far more than her claws had, scratching at his scales. *Damn her.* He came up around her rump, a finger pointed at the back of her head.

"The Lore—"

"Spare me," she spat at him. Then, softer, "Yet don't." She sighed, her head bowed. "Do what you must. I am finished."

He hesitated. Under his skin, muscles slid and throbbed, yearning for transformation, to bloom to draconic proportions and get this over with. *Fire and ash.* But she'd asked him to consider the blood on his hands, the death all around him, and although such a beast, with all her cruelty, could never say anything to stay his hand, the sight of her in the rubble brought home the awfulness of his position. That the ages had made a killer of him. That he'd lost even the luxury of mercy. And self-pity. It was his choice.

He didn't bother to invoke the Pact. No *By the grace of God.*

The gods were over. No *King's wish and command.* The king in question was long dead. And he no longer held any authority, no official role. This would be a death at his own discretion. For the good of the—

As he took another step, he sensed movement behind him, a flicker in the smoke. He spun on his heel, but it was too late. Too late to prevent the trap into which he'd fallen. *Damn fool.* Distracted by the manticore's grief, he'd forgotten all about her tail, its serpentine menace shooting up now, fangs bared and dripping, to snap at his neck.

Pain, sharp and bright, went racing through his system. As his nerves exploded, so did his bulk, his shadow dwarfing Jinx on the ground, his wings covering her like a shroud. Any empathy he'd felt burned up in the oven of his jaws, incinerated by a torrent of fire.

The manticore screamed, a brief, shrill peal of agony, carrying, Ben thought, a trace of relief.

He had no time to savour the sound. The serpent's teeth, sharp as steel, had managed to pierce his humanoid flesh, pouring mud and then stone into his veins. Blearily, he looked down, grimacing at the blackened patch on the ground before him, the cracked tarmac, the melted shopfront, all that remained of Jinx.

Then the weight of the venom bore him down and he rolled, crashing onto his back. He lay there staring, golden-eyed and rigid, up at the passionless stars.

SIX

Daybreak. Ben came to in the rosy-grey light creeping into the valley, rays slipping through the trees. Wind played across the lake, but the surface stretched otherwise undisturbed, its murky denizens either stirring in the deeps or prematurely risen, following their king. A cheery waking thought. Somewhere, he heard the trill of a bird, but no lowing of cattle, no bleating of sheep. Even the farm dogs hereabouts had fallen silent. The people, of course, had fled hours ago.

He lay on his back in the rubble, a broad ring of shattered brick, collapsed timber and broken glass that he foggily recalled as a row of shops along the high street. A litter of goods, tinned food, vegetables and crushed shopping trolleys, told him as much. Above him leaned a streetlight, bent out of true, its bulb fizzling out. Parked cars, crushed beneath him, bit into his spine. Further vehicles lay strewn along the road, most on their sides or with wheels in the air like dead mechanical dogs. Smoke wreathed the morning mist, bringing to mind the fight that had rocked the town during the night, ending in a blast of dragon fire. He heard no sirens. No planes overhead. The heavy silence told him that he'd made the area a no-go zone.

He sprawled, wings spread in the debris, tail snaking down the road, in the middle of the town. The last of his cuts and bruises were healing, restored by his inherent magic, but the pain inside him lingered.

Ouch.

Shame hauled him back to consciousness, a chain around his neck. As if skulking from his part in the destruction, having crushed chimney pots and toppled trees, he pulled himself back into human form like a thief throwing on a cloak. His wings drew in, great red fans zigzagging closed. His tail went wriggling through the wreckage, dislodging bricks and gouging gardens. His snout melted inward, forming a face that held tears behind emerald eyes. Alone in the ruins, he turned his gaze to the road beside the lake, empty now, the reefs of mist wafting across the valley. The lack of noise struck him like a harbinger, a battle drum of absence. A promise of death.

"Fuck," he said.

He rubbed his neck, the muscles cramped and sore. Despite his aches and pains, he realised that his paralysis had probably saved him. The king, the horde, had taken him for dead, marching past his vast, recumbent body without so much as a backward glance. Unblinking, barely breathing, he'd watched them go, the cadaverous Arthur and his knights on their shadowy steeds. The goblins in their dented helmets. The preening ogres and the greenteeth. A cackling, revelling mass snaking off into the hills. Rigid, he'd focused on the horn that hung around the king's neck, a gilded ivory relic that nudged at his memory, prompting an image of some bristly beast or other . . . No. It was gone. The horn blared on in his skull, the remembered echoes eclipsing his thoughts. *And to think I used to love music . . .* Then the horde was gone, leaving him to unconsciousness, a thankful absence of dreams.

He had no such comfort now. Hours had passed. How many

miles had the army marched in that time? What foul things had the king summoned from the earth, ushering on the broken enchantment, the scattered echoes of the lullaby? It didn't bear thinking about, but he forced himself to, dragging himself to his feet.

People had died here. In flames, in screams. He'd lost the right to look away.

He found the sword where he'd left it, sticking point-first in the ground.

"We have to get back to London," he said, his fingers closing around the hilt. Any admiration of the jewels left him at once, a familiar tingle running up his arm, the icy touch of *lunewrought*. A threat of visions making him tense. "Much as I hate to admit it, we need to wake up Von Hart."

Caliburn sniffed. "Is there no end to your wisdom? Are you quite sure you can't face this on your own? After all, it's only a Remnant army and—"

"Shut up," he growled between his teeth. "I'm not in the mood."

"Well, excuse me. I wasn't in the mood to spend the night covered in mud. You know, I'm a legendary sword, Benjurigan. Not a toothpick. There are better ways of doing things."

"What's that supposed to mean?"

Now its pommel, gem-studded, appeared to regard him in disbelief.

"It means, halfwit, that you might want to think about using me next time. You know, to hurry things along."

Smoke coiled from Ben's nostrils in a sardonic snort.

"I've managed just fine up to now."

The sword barked a laugh. "Oh, do tell."

Ben glowered, but considering the current state of affairs, the broken Lore and the shattered Sleep, he didn't really have grounds to argue. And that didn't take into account the mess below him, the sight of the ruined town. Bala met the morning sun with tendrils of smoke like reaching arms, begging for mercy. The entire place was little more than a circle of rubble. Wincing, he thought about all the cities, towns and villages lying between here and the capital. Shrewsbury. Birmingham. Oxford. The roads, choked with traffic. By now, the panic in London would've spread across the nation, surely. Could he count on that? A media storm of red alerts and warnings, shaky camera clips that no one could deny, that no one would try to – perhaps even a declaration of war. Because it *was* a war, he knew that beyond a shadow of a doubt. The disaster he'd tried so hard to prevent was upon them, a clear and present danger. As of yesterday, the human race had become united in its fate. Every living person was now a refugee.

"When . . ." The words rose raw in his throat, scraping on smoke and grief. "When is it going to end?"

The sword, when it answered, sounded oddly subdued. But blunt, all the same.

"Once upon a time, you stood a chance. The Example failed, Benjurigan. Perhaps war is inevitable."

"I don't want to believe that. I can't."

Otherwise I couldn't go on, he thought, but didn't say. The idea that the Pact had only held off an inescapable doom, and endangered the Remnants along the way, filled him with a despair so deep . . . well, he couldn't face it.

"Hope too, granted," Caliburn said, as if reading his mind. "In the end, it's all we have."

Ben grunted, then gave a melancholy nod. All he could do

was return to the city, try to rouse the damn fairy. If anyone could avert this disaster, stand against the dead king's army, then it was Von Hart. *Or at least he can explain himself* . . . The thought made him sick to his stomach, the necessity to turn to his old acquaintance, a known traitor who'd cost him so dearly. And cost Jia Jing her life. Nevertheless, his choices were thin on the ground.

Yes. He'd get back to London and he'd fly low. The time for hiding was over; it wouldn't serve any purpose now. Let the people below see him. Let them look up and see. Let the age-old fear take them, a primal chill in their hearts. And once they'd seen him, let them flee. Into the hills. The forest. The night.

Just like the old days.

How small his hope had become.

Like a squire in a cathedral square, long ago and far from here, Ben pulled the sword free.

It was time to go home.

SEVEN

"The Fay are returning. I felt her . . . hand, cool on my brow."

Ben had waited so long (*six months!*) for Von Hart to wake up that when he came marching into the crypt, the sight of the envoy muttering in the cupped stone hands only served to fill him with shock. He halted in the gloom, his feet scudding on polished stone, the sword in his grip drooping, scraping on the ground. It only lasted a moment. He flinched as the echoes skittered around the chamber, off the monstrous tombs. Goosebumps prickled up on his skin.

Not so long ago, a strange blue light had crept into this chamber, the earth shuddering, shaking the stalactites. That had been the omen of awakening, the precursor to the ravens, the flock of birds blustering into the cavern to find the envoy, to warn him, Ben reckoned, wherever he might be. *An unkindness. A conspiracy. Isn't that the collective noun for those birds? Both belong in this place.* He'd seen the same eerie radiance in Arthur's tomb, hadn't he? The glow of magic, responding to some unseen hand, an ancient spell of summoning. Why shouldn't the light rouse the fairy too? In the mountain, Caliburn had been expecting him, the envoy meant to arrive to attend on Arthur – the *real* Arthur – restored, no doubt, to the peak of health to aid Britain in her darkest hour.

Ben curled his lip, recalling the myth. The darkest hour had arrived all right. But the magic had gone to seed. The spell unravelling. Whoever was pulling on this particular thread (and he had an idea who, much as the thought rattled him), Von Hart was as tangled up in it as the cadaverous king.

Shit, he's probably the spindle. After all, every Remnant has pricked a finger on him . . .

Confusion and loss, Ben realised then, had offered him a kind of refuge, a place to hide from the truth. From the consequences, anyway. With all his rotten luck lately, he honestly hadn't expected the envoy to wake up at all, bracing himself for mass destruction in the world above while the fairy held his silence. And a minute after Von Hart spoke, Ben dearly wished that he had.

Chains clanking, the envoy sat up, apparently untroubled by his bonds. Could cold iron even hold him? Ben wasn't sure. That was the trouble with folklore; you couldn't rely on it. Von Hart looked gaunt all the same, weakened by his ordeal, despite the grin that lit his fine-boned features, the flash of his violet eyes. For all his imprisonment, he was obviously jubilant. Delirious with joy.

"It worked!" he crowed. "The harp's unmaking echoed across the nether. I have drawn the eyes of Avalon. She comes! She comes!"

And how much did Ben like the sound of that? Not much.

Six months ago, Ben had finally managed to make Jia see that there was more to the fairy's plan than simply reforging the *Cwyth*, the mnemonic harp. He had made her see the danger, the threat of a coming war.

But the lesson hadn't come cheap.

"Why?" Swallowing the embers in his throat, he struggled to remain calm. His lips trembled around the question that had sat locked behind them for months. "Why Jia? Why her?"

Von Hart blinked, as if seeing Ben for the first time. Then he frowned and cocked his head, clearly considering the question as an odd, even obvious one. He sighed, regaining his composure, and seemed happy to explain.

"Jia Jing was the last wakeful *sin-you*," he said. "Able to perceive the truth from illusion, though I admit that it took her longer than expected. Centuries, in fact. I never knew myself capable of such patience, but in the end, I was rewarded. My choosing all those years ago in Xanadu justified." He smiled to himself, as if recalling some pleasant memory. "Right from the start, she saw the strength in me."

"I don't understand you," Ben said. He spoke in no more than a hot breath, a strained whisper.

"No? Then let me explain. My people bound the doors to the nether with complex spells. When the Fay departed this world, all but one door was destroyed. The remaining door was locked, then forgotten, a relic of the ages. Over time, the door grew black with filth, hiding the depths that lurked behind it, equally black and endless. You've been there yourself, haven't you? Into the Dark Frontier . . ."

Ben gritted his teeth. Even the memory of the gulf couldn't cool him.

Von Hart didn't appear to care for an answer.

"If one drew close to the door – its surface a substance much like glass, but infinitely stronger – one would observe one's heart's desire, an illusion reflecting one's deepest hope. That's fairy magic for you. A way to . . . hide the true nature of the thing. Only a creature able to see through the illusion could shatter the glass. *Verstehen Sie?* Even I, tutor to Merlin and guardian of the ages, wasn't able to break the charms of such an ancient barrier. But I could look for it and find it. And I could fashion myself a key. Jia alone could open the Eight Hand Mirror."

Ben's knuckles whitened around the hilt of the sword. He knew the rest, of course, or could guess at it. Jia had longed to see her parents again, slumbering for centuries under the earth, and, over time, her longing had got the better of her. But the mirror, the door, had opened onto a road that led through the nether. Von Hart had wanted access to that road, a bridge from which to summon the Lurkers, distract them from invading the Earth by letting them sup on him instead, feeding off his magical essence. Perhaps this parasitical leeching had weakened the harp as well, enabling the envoy to shatter the fragments that Jia had brought to him, a thief in the night. Under the ghostly tentacles of the Ghost Emperor, she had found herself betrayed. *Used.* Von Hart might've wanted to wake up the Remnants, as he'd claimed, but that wasn't his primary motive. He'd reforged the *Cwyth* simply to break it, sending a signal into the dark . . .

For all that, Ben hadn't asked for an explanation. That wasn't what he'd meant by *I don't understand.*

With a roar, he lunged forward, grabbing the envoy. He wrenched him, chains and all, from his perch on the tomb. The links snapped in the force of Ben's fury, chips flying from the statues to which he'd fastened them, a cloud of alabaster billowing around him. The envoy gave a wail as he found himself transported through the air and dumped onto the cavern floor, the onetime Sola Ignis – who might or might not have been a onetime friend – looming over him, his fists clenched.

"She died, you son of a bitch." Flames blazed in Ben's eyes, his hair crackling with heat. "She wasn't a fucking *key*. She lived and breathed. She had hopes and dreams. And she died because of you."

But that wasn't the half of it. Jia had fallen, cast from the evaporated ley and down into the depths of the nether. And she was probably falling still, starved and frozen in the bottomless dark. Falling, falling. Or perhaps she'd been eaten by a Lurker, devoured by ghosts . . . Since that terrible, desperate day, he'd run the possible scenarios through his mind over and over again. Whatever had happened, her death wouldn't have been quick. He had Von Hart to thank for that.

It didn't give him the slightest satisfaction to see the envoy's triumph fade, his head bowing, his white-gold fringe hanging in his face. Apart from the chains dangling around him, he was naked, his star-spangled robes burned away in the nether, in the converging mass of ghosts that had formed the Ghost Emperor.

"Yes. She died." Von Hart looked up at him. "I asked you to catch her. To let me fall. Was it so—?"

Ben punched the envoy in the face. The crack of flesh on bone rang between the stalactites, rebounding around the crystal cave. In a clatter of chains, the fairy slumped to the floor, his bound hands unable to prevent his fall, his forehead striking rock. Still, he remained conscious. He shut his eyes, tightly enough to draw wrinkles on his otherwise smooth skin, and Ben saw the tears trickling down his cheeks. The sight surprised him, spiking through his rage. In all his years, he'd never seen the envoy look sorry about anything, not in a way that he'd taken as sincere. All the same, he didn't feel too bad when the fairy spat out blood, a splotch like a payment on the white marble floor.

When Von Hart opened his eyes, he stared across the chamber, unable, unwilling to look at his assailant.

"It was her choice, Ben." His voice was so faint, it barely stirred the dust. "I know you don't want to hear it, but please believe that I offered her one, a million moons ago."

"I don't know whether to let you keep talking," Ben stood panting over the envoy, his knuckles crackling, "or to shut you up forever."

Von Hart raised his eyebrows at the threat. Even now, bound and bleeding half a mile under London, he was far from as shaken as Ben would've liked. He held the same casual, fatalistic air as he'd had in Club Zauber a year ago, as if they were discussing a regrettable spillage of choice champagne rather than Remnant blood. One thing he didn't really seem was afraid. And that, in turn, clamped a claw of ice around Ben's heart, holding his fire in check.

"You want answers, naturally," Von Hart said. "I don't blame you. And really, it's simple. Didn't I try to tell you before? We are exiles in our own land. We live in a time of change. You've seen for yourself that magic is souring. The circles are breaking, leaving this world at the mercy of phantoms. You of all people understand the risk we face. How some in the darkness long to be gods . . ."

"You've told me lies, that's all. Riddles. Bullshit. When I came to you for help in Berlin, you pretended that you didn't know anything." Without realising, his fist had wound back to his shoulder again. He was leaning over the envoy, breathing hard. "The Lambton armour. Winlock's tomb. It was all down to you, wasn't it? You wanted to cause a breach in the Lore. To stir up rebellion. And in the resulting chaos, you woke up Mauntgraul and had your *key* steal the fragments of the harp. *Didn't you?*"

Von Hart's hair blew about his face with the force of Ben's roar. Like a spider, he shrank closer to the floor, his chains spooling around him. He spoke to the ground with bloody lips, as if the dust could hear the reason in his voice and absolve him, not that he sounded remotely ashamed.

"The world is dying, Ben. Ever since the Fay left the Earth, the Remnants have been living on borrowed time. I told you that I made a mistake. Well, the Pact was my mistake. The Sleep . . ." He sighed, his shoulders trembling, a motion that Ben read as genuine pain, though whether from his blow or his memories was hard to tell. "In my desperation, I didn't realise the danger of the compromise. Long ago, in the dawn of the Old Lands, the Fay branded their circles of protection in the earth, guarding Creation from the nether. And when the Fay left this world, every door, every road closed behind them, cutting magic off from its source. But some remained – a reserve, I suppose. In the Remnants, of course, and also in human hearts. In the widespread acceptance of magic. With the signing of the Pact, however, we suppressed what little magic was left, seeking to bury it under the ages. Under forgetfulness. Disbelief . . . Too late, I realised my error. And soon enough, the circles began to weaken, to rot. Don't you see? It's their decay, the stench of it, that draws the Lurkers to the earth. That threatens the safety of the Sleep. Hidden, banished, forced underground, magic grows sour and will eventually die. We'll snuff out the soul of the world. All will fall into darkness. It's already falling into darkness. For us. For them." *Remnants and humans.* "You've seen the state of affairs, *mein Freund.* Can you stand there and deny it?"

Ben snarled, his teeth locked. But he found that he couldn't.

"And you say that I play the hero. Sounds like nobody needed your help."

"At first," the envoy flinched, but went on, "I had but the faintest suspicion, an inkling of the fading circles. It dogged my heels from Westminster Palace, haunting me across Byzantium, across the deserts and into China. Fortunately, I acted upon it.

Don't think for a second that I underestimate Jia's sacrifice. I . . ." He caught his breath. "She was very dear to me."

"Sacrifice," Ben said. "Why do I get the feeling she was yours?"

The envoy winced but let that slide. Von Hart spoke of darkness and change. This Ben could understand. Someone had told him once that change was the only constant, and no creature who'd seen humanity drag itself out of the Dark Ages and into the dubious light of modern day could really argue with that. As for himself, he wasn't the same dragon who'd come to the Great Forest, heartbroken and green, all those centuries ago. Once upon a time, he'd believed in the Lore. He'd believed in love. Time had chipped away at him and lately . . . well, this past year or so had seen his faith tested to the limit, his old allegiances shifting, his loyalty eventually renounced. The codes and beliefs that had formed the foundations of his world, giving him structure, a reason to go on, had all collapsed and crumbled away. Been *ripped* away. Standing here over the envoy, it stunned him to learn that all the chaos around him, the danger he'd faced, came down to the simplest change of all. A change of heart.

"As I said, it worked," Von Hart told him. "The way is open. The harp shattered. The High House has heard."

"Yeah, they heard you loud and clear, *Blaise*." So saying, Ben brought up the sword, slammed the point down in front of Von Hart, an inch from the tip of his nose. "But I don't think they're dancing to your tune."

The envoy recoiled, perhaps shocked by his reflection in the blade. A bruise was swelling around his eye, as violet as his iris, stark against his enervated skin. Whatever pain he might feel was forgotten, however, as he took in the gleaming length of *lunewrought*, his gaze sliding up to the dragon-shaped hilt and the diamond-bright jewels on either end of the crossguard, looking down at him with steely regard. Then, tentatively, he reached out, his fingers trembling, for the sword.

"Is that . . . Are you . . . ?"

"Caliburn," the sword said. "Has it really been that long?"

"Caliburn. The Sword of Albion," the envoy breathed, as if the sword hadn't spoken. "World-cleaver. Demon-slayer. Harp-breaker."

"Indeed. I hear that we share the last in common. You've been busy, *hexenmeister*."

Von Hart dropped his hand, wonderingly, a trace of his former passion gripping him.

"Then the time has truly come. But . . ."

Like chips of amethyst, the envoy turned his gaze up to Ben.

Ben snorted. "Do I look like a king to you?"

Von Hart didn't bother to spare his feelings. "*Nein*," he said, shaking his head. "No one could accuse you of that."

"The king has risen," Caliburn said, its impatience plain. "You reforged the *Cwyth*, broken centuries ago at the Battle of Camlann when Arthur refused the queen's gift. And with the harp, I understand that you lulled the Remnants to Sleep for eight hundred years, seeking to preserve them."

On the way here, Ben had done his best to explain, bring the sword up to speed. Inform him of the envoy's treachery. The crisis was bad enough, the city a smouldering mess. No one should go into it blind.

"After a fashion," Von Hart replied. "The prophecy . . ."

"Ah, yes. Who doesn't love a prophecy?" And the sword intoned, "*One shining day, when Remnants and humans learn to live in peace, and magic blossoms anew in the world, then shall the Fay return and commence a new golden age. Isn't that how it goes?*"

"Yes." But the envoy sounded uncertain, even a touch anxious. "That is the Queen's Troth."

"Yet you grew impatient, did you not? You thought to quicken her steps, bring about the prophecy yourself. As if anyone should take her word as bond. There's an old saying: Never trust the—"

Ben laughed, a sharp but nonetheless hollow sound in the cavern.

"I did what was necessary," Von Hart snapped, visibly nettled. "What better way to save us than to reunite with the Fay? Surely, the High House can restore the failing magic and salvage this world. Haven't we suffered enough? The Example failed and so did the Pact. Yes, I destroyed the harp. And Nimue, our queen, has seen my beacon, heard my song through the dark. She whispered in my dreams, speaking of her return. The king has awoken, hasn't he? *Ja*. As a vanguard. A champion. To prepare the way."

Again, this should've been music to Ben's ears, the prophecy come true, the long years of waiting over. Instead, his guts churned, a lump rising in his throat. There was a tone in the envoy's voice that he'd heard before, a hint of desperation that reminded him of the Cardinal, de Gori, standing high in her lectern and greeting a dragon as if he were a visiting angel. The light in Von Hart's eyes, a reflection of *lunewrought*, belonged entirely to the White Dog, however. Another breed of madness.

"The king has awoken," Caliburn said, confirming the matter. "Arthur and his knights march upon London, intending to reclaim the throne."

"Then what are we waiting for?" Von Hart looked up then, his face igniting with a mix of wonder and glee, sickening to see. "Let's climb from this hole and greet our thane on our knees. Oh, how I've longed for this day. How I've paid for it in blood and tears. The walls of Camelot might have fallen, but their shadow stretches long even so. No more. No more will we quail in fear, crawling on our bellies in the dark. Arthur comes to deliver us. All begins anew. At last, the golden age has come!"

Ben rubbed the back of his neck. "Yeah. About that . . ."

Von Hart wasn't listening to him. "Don't just stand there," he said. "We must ready ourselves at once. If the king marches to London, then the queen will be on her way. The bridge has fallen. Don't you remember? The breaking of the harp severed the ley. We can't afford a second. We must fly to China and recover the Eight Hand Mirror. Somehow, we must rebuild the bridge. Guide the Lady to Earth . . ."

Head cocked, Ben took a step back. He couldn't quite believe what he was hearing.

"You've lost it," he said. "After Jia? After your lies? I'm not going anywhere with you."

"Don't be a fool. There's no time. You can punish me all you like later."

Ben felt the heat flushing back into his face. His fingers closed into a claw.

"Let me put this another way," he said. "*You're* not going anywhere. I get that you've bought the propaganda, all glorious kings, salvation and that, but I think you're out of touch. I've been to the mountain, Von Hart." He tapped his chest, the *wyrm tongue* sigil there, asserting some shred of authority. "I've seen your precious king." *And your queen. The look she gave me.* "He didn't look up for saving shit. There's an army—"

"But this is my duty. The reason I—"

"– of Remnants out there. And I don't mean the fluffy kind. Goblins, ogres, a manticore. You name it." He shuddered to think what else by now, what creatures Arthur had summoned

111

from the Sleep, his horn pressed to his lipless teeth. "Something is wrong. Something stinks. By the look of Arthur, I'm guessing it's your souring magic, because he wasn't exactly in the best shape. Maybe we should take a rain check on the whole prophecy thing, yeah? The country is in a state of panic. Shit, probably the world. I can't see the military greeting Arthur with open arms. Can you?"

"He is the Once and Future King," Von Hart said. "It's his birthright to rule these lands. He was born to save them."

"Once, maybe," Ben said. "Now? I wouldn't hold your breath."

Enough was enough. Ben reached down and dragged the envoy to his feet, the chains clanking around him, a ragged iron robe.

"This is what you wanted, isn't it? The war you planned. And fuck anyone who gets in your way."

"If we must fight a war in order to survive, then so be it."

"That worked out brilliantly before. Damn. It's almost as if the Pact didn't happen." He shook the fairy, the chains rattling. "Everything you touch turns to shit, Von Hart. Except, funnily enough, never for you."

Von Hart pursed his lips, but he didn't try to deny it. Instead, he sighed, fixing Ben with his strange violet eyes. There was pity there, Ben saw, soft and not unkind. Compassion for a beast, perhaps. No more than that.

He spoke gently, in the face of Ben's sneer.

"Ben, Ben. You should be glad. Think of all those years, eight long centuries of waiting. Think of the ones you've loved and lost while living under the Lore. Well, now the Fay are coming. The Lady returns to lift the burden from your shoulders. This . . . this is your happy ending."

"Oh yeah? Then how come it tastes like shit?"

The envoy offered him a thin smile. "Come. Come with me now," he said. "We'll fly to China like in the old days. Remember? When we fought and defeated the White Dog, you and I. Come with me to the temple. I could use your strength to lift all that stone, dig out the Eight Hand Mirror. Then, together, we'll go into the dark. We'll follow the road into the nether. We'll be the first to welcome them home."

Ben set the envoy down. Von Hart staggered a little, the weight of his chains dragging on him. Then he steadied himself, straightening his neck, determined, unbowed. His eyes never left Ben's face, searching for agreement, Ben thought, for some shred of alliance. Or simply a sign of his abating anger. And he found himself drawing in a breath, fatigue washing over him, water on coals. The fairy's words were bittersweet, conjuring memories of lost joy, of a forest maiden who'd choked on poison, and a Brooklyn waitress, stolen and scarred, a sacrifice for the gods . . .

But Ben knew magic when he smelled it.

"Nice try," he said. "Think you'll find I'm not the same *dummkopf* you left on the sands in Cairo. I'm not that wyrm any more." And he wasn't, he knew. Saying it made it true. "You used Jia. You used her and you threw her away. And I'm guessing that you've got plans for me too. That's why you saved me, isn't it? In the underground car park. At the refinery. You *need* me. So what it's to be? What do you want? You might as well tell me. Someone to lug an old mirror around for you? Or maybe just a free ride."

The envoy looked at the floor, giving up his murmured spell, his attempt at mesmerism.

"Oh, Benjurigan. You know that our friendship means more to me than—"

"Save it. What was it you said? Months ago in the nether?

113

'There is only one thing I need from you.' That's it." Ben squared his shoulders, his muscles tense. "Now we have that in common. The only thing you're gonna do is help me kick that crowned corpse back into the tomb where he belongs. And you can forget your welcoming party. Seems to me that some doors stay shut for a reason. When I get my claws on your blasted mirror, it's going straight in a volcano or to the bottom of the sea. Maybe Caliburn can turn it into firewood. I haven't decided yet."

Von Hart frowned. He made as if to argue, but appeared to catch himself, his mouth closing. Ben glowered, stern as stone. How could the envoy doubt his threat after the events of last winter? Ben watched his shoulders fall, his chains rattling. Looking beyond his scruffy-haired captor, the fairy gazed up at the tombs, a sad expression on his face, thoughtful, considering. *Regretful.*

Ben didn't like that look. He liked it even less when Von Hart put his feelings into words.

"It's up to you," he said. "At least, in regard to whether you're willing or not. I also told you that a decent master looks after his pets. You, one of the bound bestiary, a Remnant under my care. Well, the opposite is also true, *liebling.* A good pet obeys his master."

With this, Von Hart shrugged off his bonds. One moment, he stood in the broken iron lengths. The next, his chains were coiling on the floor. Before the last link had fallen, the echoes scattering like glass, he spread his hands, his cords cut by conjuration. The envoy muttered under his breath, a stream of symbols spilling from his lips, faint and rainbow-hued. Naked, he stood before Ben, as pale, as sculpted as the tombs around them. Whatever compassion had shone in his eyes had vanished, evaporated by violet intent.

114

Ben snarled and made to leap forward, his hands swelling into claws. He stumbled, stymied, finding himself glued to the spot. Talons sprouted from his fingertips, yellow and sharp, but his muscles bulged against a surface as hard as concrete, a shell encasing him, restricting his movements. Roaring, he glared at the envoy, his fiery gaze demanding an answer.

The envoy pursed his lips.

"Forgive me. Our Lady awaits. You'll unearth the Eight Hand Mirror and bear me to greet her through the dark."

"Bastard . . . fairy. What are you doing?"

But he could guess. It was the suit. The damn suit. Back in Berlin, Von Hart had given him the outfit as a gift. Extra armour, he'd said, a way for Ben to protect his modesty. It had hung in the alcove in Club Zauber, looking much like a wetsuit, only one stitched with charred black scales and bearing the *wyrm tongue* symbol on its chest, emblazoned in red, circled by yellow.

He could remember the envoy's exact words.

It took some effort to synthesise the scales into a fabric, weave their substance into this. Nevertheless, I think you'll find it as tough as your flesh. I mean, it is your flesh. A second skin.

Or a cage.

He cursed, directing most of his ire at himself. Last year, Von Hart had caught him off guard. He'd been half asleep on the job, thrown into peril after decades of dormancy. Working for crooks, living underground, he'd somehow believed that he'd kept his edge. A resurrected goddess had proved otherwise. His love for Rose had made him soft. But he'd woken up since and Jia had hardened him, shown him his duty – or rather the lie of it and the danger of fairy gifts. The thought made him bare his fangs, anger grinding deep in his throat. He'd never have accepted the suit if he'd known. Never in a million years.

Hindsight. It's always 20/20 . . .

Murmuring, Von Hart raised a hand, his fingers twisting. Like a puppet on a string, Ben found himself lurching towards him, his bare feet dragging across the cavern floor. A flame-haired marionette, his limbs twitched, mechanical, as he tried to resist the pull of the suit. It was a scaly glove around him, flexible, cold, yet hard as steel. Grimacing, he forced his will into his muscles, urging them to swell, to take on draconic proportions, but he met a wall there too, a barrier in his mind forbidding transformation. And he knew that it would do him no good, anyway. The suit was a part of him, sealed to the innate magic of his flesh. With a few muttered words, Von Hart's gift had become a kind of ball and chain, binding him to the envoy. His will was no longer his own.

His own words, distant, but no less mocking, came back to haunt him.

I'm telling you that there is always a price . . .

And here he was, paying for his mistake.

Just how many cards did the fairy have up his sleeve? It felt like he had a whole pack. Ben twisted his wrists, straining against the suit. His toes sought purchase on smooth rock, trying to slow his approach. Growling, he shook his head from side to side, but it was no use. His head, hands and feet, free of the suit, could do nothing to help him. Von Hart stretched out his alabaster hand and Ben was in the palm of it.

"Don't fight me," the envoy said. "In time, you'll come to see that I'm right."

"Fuck you. Fuck you to hell."

Von Hart smiled and crooked a finger under Ben's nose. Again, Ben saw the sheen in his eyes, determination, and under it, madness. The sickening need. Against his wishes, he turned, spinning ninety degrees, twisting him away before he reached the envoy. Denying him the chance of a head butt. Or to spit in his face.

He strained to speak over his shoulder, echoes of urgent despair.

"Von Hart, listen to me. Listen, damn you. Whatever woke up in the mountain isn't your king. And whatever you believe, the Queen's Troth has gone to shit. You must listen to me! I . . . I *need* you. Britain needs you. The world . . ." He grunted, running out of breath, losing grip on his last-ditch effort. He stole a growl from the musty air. "Get your head out of your skinny white arse and *listen*."

In return, Von Hart said, "A new golden age, Ben. Think of it."

It was no good. As Ben, neck tendons bulging, began to jerk towards the entrance of the tunnel, dragged by his scaly restraint, he could hear the fever in the envoy's voice. He'd tried to argue with this kind of conviction before, this kind of faith, blind and as deep as a scar. Jia had died for it.

The truth doesn't matter any more. He wants *to believe. And he'll let the lot of us die for it too . . .*

"You're . . . making a big mistake . . ."

Sweat ran into his eyes, the suit choking him, strangling his

117

words. How long until exhaustion claimed him? Until he simply gave in, let the envoy steer him? Would Von Hart work him to the bone, he wondered, making him dig through the ruins of the temple? And what would he do with him once he was through, once he'd served his purpose? Leave him to die? Abandon him in the dark like Jia . . . ?

Five steps, six, and he vented a roar, an echoing howl of frustration, shaking the stalactites above.

In his grip, the sword hilt tingled, *lunewrought* reaching for flesh.

Grunting, Ben peered down at the blade, sweat from his brow peppering the ground.

"Use me," Caliburn said, low and fierce, his voice piercing Ben's skull. "Use me, you dolt."

The sword didn't need to tell him twice. Gasping, he swivelled his wrist, snapping the blade to the side of his leg, its razor thin edge crossing his shin. The motion wasn't sharp, restricted as he was, but the blade itself was a different story. Fire and frost went blazing through him, and he cried out, the weapon slicing into his flesh, blood splattering marble. Wincing, he could see that the sword had managed to cut through the suit, the scales around his knee hanging tattered and torn, a peeled section of skin.

There are certain perks. In his agony, he remembered Caliburn, boasting in the mountain. *For one thing, I'm unbreakable. For another, I can slice through most things as if they were paper.*

Including spellbound scales, it seemed. Even as Von Hart yelled, realising his error, Ben was turning his wrist again, bringing the sword up, its edge bearing against his belly, slicing across his thigh. The effect was immediate, as sharp as the pain. Like a burst zipper, the scales across his stomach sprang apart, a

118

scatter of tiny scales at his feet. And blood. Flowers of blood.
His tattered suit dripped with the stuff, and as he manoeuvred
the blade up to touch his left arm, watching the living fabric
split apart in charred black beads, he grasped that the sword
had another power too. But he wouldn't exactly call it a perk.

My wounds. They're not healing . . .

The thought made him dizzy, the truth evident in the blood
seeping from his gut, slicking his groin and legs, pooling on the
floor around him. Pain shivered through him, an unfamiliar
coldness, a *deeper* coldness, spreading through his body, his limbs.
The usual prickle of mending flesh, knitting veins and skin, was
gone, replaced by all too mortal injuries.

"Damn you, sword. You could've . . . said . . ."

"Oops," said the sword.

Head swimming, Ben sank to his knees. Come what may, he
couldn't let his weakness stop him, couldn't let the envoy claim
him, body, if not soul. Through the rising fog, he could sense
the suit loosening, the torn shreds allowing him a little movement. Breathing hard, he dropped the sword and clawed at the
suit, talons sprouting from his fingers – sprouting, retracting –
struggling against the binding spell.

"*No!*" The envoy reached him and grabbed his shoulder, his
lips working, trying to recover the slipping rope of his magic.
Picking his moment, Ben growled. With an effort of will, he
vented a roar as the shreds of the suit exploded around him,
flying apart like windblown leaves. With a degree of pleasure,
he watched as the blast hurled Von Hart away from him, his
naked form rolling to a standstill on the cold stone floor. At
once, the envoy drew in his limbs, cringing in the shadow of a
dragon unleashed. Up Ben reared, his plated neck stretching to
the cavern roof, his horns rivalling the stalagmites. His wings

119

folded out, great red pinions brushing the surrounding monuments, rubble and dust showering down from carved buttock and sculpted breast. With a thump, his tail hit the chamber wall, the arrowhead tip slamming over the tunnel entrance like a door.

Fire coiled in his throat. His jaws parted, a sheaf of knives. Like platters of gold, his eyes flared, narrowing on the small figure lying between his splayed claws, an arm thrown up over his head. Next to his other claw, Caliburn rested, a dropped silver needle. If either the fairy or the sword spoke, their words were lost in his roar.

But Ben was bleeding too. Wounds in humanoid flesh had become gashes in dragon hide, several feet long and weeping, crimson and red. Blood loss was taking its toll. The scene rippled, his vision blurring. Bewilderment sang in his skull.

Not now. Not . . . now . . .

With a teeth-rattling boom, his horns collided with the cavern roof. Dislodged rock pounded down on him, bouncing off his spine and rump. Dazed, he swayed, an entranced serpent in the dust. Then he exhaled and collapsed with a crash, a plume of smoke following him down to the chamber floor.

For a long, measureless time, he knew only darkness and silence.

When he opened his eyes, Von Hart was gone.

PART TWO

Siege Perilous

By fairy hands their knell is rung;
By forms unseen their dirge is sung.

                    Collins, *How Sleep the Brave*

Hampstead Heath, London

There were many who'd dreamt of this moment. The king had returned to London.

Since one day on Camlann Field, one dark and wicked day, the course of history had cracked. Time had split into two streams. One of the streams ran narrow and slow, a trickle through an overgrown forest, so tangled in the briar of myth that few would even know it was there. The other ran deep and wide, a stream become a rapids that bubbled and seethed through towering cities, flooding her banks with smoke and industry. Both streams ran red with blood, the price of a million tomorrows.

Here, at this hour, Arthur, the Once and Future King, looked out on the place where the rivers met. From the bluff of Parliament Hill, the city spread out before him, her skyline glinting through the morning mist.

This had always been his purpose. He stood on the edge of reality and dream, a bridge born in flesh and blood. Half human, half Fay, he had ruled over a mighty realm from the white walls of Camelot, riding out with the Knights of the Round Table to uphold all that was good and just and true in the land. With giants, he'd wrestled. To damsels, he'd pledged. On dragons, he'd ridden. Arthur was of the land and in the land. The Old Lands. The green lawns of Logres, stretching through blossom-filled orchards and hollow hills and on to the emerald sea, all shining under a sun of hope. Arthur, the Bear of Briton. An Example of Unity. Of peace.

Once.

Clouds had gathered. The green lawns of Logres had run red. Arthur had fallen, betrayed. In disgust, the Fay had turned their backs on the earth, retreating forever into the nether. Or, some said, until a golden day came, bright and new.

A day much like this one, maggots aside. This morning, the king had returned.

Where had he been, this renowned scion of a golden age? Through battles beyond count. When swords had clashed on bloody French fields. When ships had fired cannons off Cape Trafalgar. When the Luftwaffe roared high above London, there were some who had taken up the cry. "Oh where, oh where is Arthur? Where is the king in our darkest hour?" And others had answered. "Asleep, deep in a mountain. In Cadbury Hill. In Dinas Rock. In Glastonbury Tor. In Alderley Edge. In the Eildon Hills. In St Michael's Mount. Beneath the Castle of Sewingshields. Under a lake. In a hundred caves. In the body of a red-clawed crow. In the Otherworld. In Avalon, waiting." And thus, Arthur endured on living tongues, threaded in memory throughout his lands.

A few paces in front of his flanking knights, the corpse king sat astride his shagfoal steed, shadows wreathing from its mane, its eyes burning, the embers of an unleashed hell. Sunlight winked on Arthur's crown, but no sweat glistened on his brow nor tears on his cheeks from the toil and speed of his journey. On black hooves, the dead king had crossed the border into England and galloped through the Malvern Hills, the Cotswolds and the Chilterns overnight, a journey that, by earthly means, should have taken seven days' ride. But no one who'd laid eyes on Arthur had taken his coming for earthly.

The shadows of the horses had stretched long, a cloak weaving from their manes and tails and trailing into the night, fanning out low to the ground in a swirling cloud of darkness. In Arthur's wake, the wretched rabble, goblin and ogre marching still, the greenteeth loping along, yet all sliding as one through the valleys, the forests and housing estates as though on a rug across a polished floor. Disturbed by the noise, the clatter of weapons, the cackles and cries, the roar of the stampede, children had looked out from bedroom windows and screamed their parents awake. Outside Birmingham, the traffic on the M5 had skidded into a pile-up as the horde raced over the motorway, leaping from Dodford into Bromsgrove. In Stratford-upon-Avon, those lucky enough to have seen the news at that hour were already making for the hills, pouring out of the pubs, stuffing suitcases into the backs of cars or hiding, trembling, under the stairs. Arthur went galloping through the villages and towns and the horde followed, a black wave crashing over the buildings, the churches, the houses and shops.

Outside Bicester, the king had halted and blown his horn. The horde had hunkered in a pall of gloom that rose like fog from the land. Others had joined them. Black shucks had crept from the lych gates of churches to answer the sonorous echoes. The ghostly dogs, once haunting the graveyards of erstwhile Britain, had fallen in with the fray, sucked into the billowing storm, their tongues lolling, hackles bristling. Bugbears had followed them, the former as shaggy and ursine as the name suggested, their maws shaped like an owl's beak and their wide round eyes a sickly yellow. Ghouls had come after, pushing off tomb lids and abandoning the bones they gnawed upon, their ragged bodies, damp, bald and grey, merging with the waiting battalion. And after them came still others. The grims and the gargoyles. The shugs and the shellycoats. The moon hares, wyverns and sooterkin.

As one, the horde moved off again, heading for the dawn and the capital. Behind them, terror. Panic. Tears. England invaded. Reclaimed.

Arthur had never been an earthly king and less so now, his body a vessel for blue fire, his purpose steered by another. *Thus, we take back our sovereignty.* He looked out from Parliament Hill, the black cloud churning behind him, eager to meet the spiralling smoke on the skyline. And there were more than monsters in the rabble now, more than strange beings and beasts dragged from their broken beds. As the horde had charged across the Home Counties, people had found themselves snatched up in the cloud, grabbed by passing hook-nailed hands, by questing lassos and whips. Humans, swept along in the enchanted torrent that bore the king and his ghastly knights, stumbled and wept in the brume. Men, women and children, too late or too slow to run away or simply caught in the king's path like rabbits in the headlights, trudged roped and bound together, a thousand or more, their numbers swelling by the hour. Well, an army had to eat. Even as he lingered here, surveying the gates of his kingdom, Arthur's riders galloped out, dispatched to circle the smouldering city and intercept the ones who fled, the choked lines of traffic and the straggling refugees, with the purpose of driving the crowds back to London. There was no escape from destiny. One by one, the people would kneel. One by one, they would honour their One True King.

At Arthur's chest, his horn rested, dormant, silent for now.

Soon enough, he would call them. Soon the great ones would rise. Dragons. Giants. Bound to his will. He grinned at the city – the *dragon* city – but his withered walnut of a heart did not blossom at the sight. The flames in his eye sockets flared no higher, even after fifteen centuries' absence. A worm slipped between his teeth, climbing from the bed of rot in his bowels, as he regarded London with a hunger not his own.

Eventually, his eyes settled on the Shard, the tallest of the towers rising from the skyline. How the building glittered and shone, much like the walls of Camelot! How the sight resembled a sword rising from a lake! Yes! There, Arthur would drag his prisoners, punish the ones who dared to defy him. There, his subjects would bow to the throne. And in the greatest square, he'd raise a fire like the land had never seen. A glorious hecatomb of flesh and blood. A beacon for the Fay, a chorus of souls to shatter the sky and welcome the return of the Fallen Ones. Let no one living, Remnant or human, doubt the power of the one who came. Let no one doubt her rule. The High House of Avalon would suffer no resistance.

This was the coming of the king. Once, as now, he remained the harbinger of an otherworldly queen.

A harbinger of the future.

EIGHT

Dragon dreams, deep and dark as they are, seemed less and less like dreams to Red Ben Garston. In a pool of blood, he lay sprawled on the cavern floor deep under London, the tombs looming around him like mourners at a grave. He didn't remember shrinking back into human form, lying naked and flat on his stomach, his scars growing as pale as the chamber walls, his hair slick with the mess that had poured like wine from his beast-sized veins, dark and just as red. Nor could he recall a pain like this, a pain that lingered, refusing to recede, carrying him down into darkness. It was the darkness he fought against, his brain foggy and slow. At the same time, part of him wanted to sink into its embrace, accept its comfort, an end to his troubles. *Yes* . . . He was dying. At least he was doing so next to his lair, he thought, in an idling, remote fashion. At least he'd sliced off the envoy's suit. Caliburn, the Sword of Albion, had seen to that, even if his flesh couldn't heal the wounds that the blade had inflicted. At least he was dying free . . .

Benjurigan . . .

Who said that? Who was down here? he wondered. The envoy had vanished and it wasn't the sword, that was for sure. The sword could never manage a tone like that, all syrup and rustling leaves. Sunlight through branches, that was what went through his mind. Flashing silver on his face. The light was cold, however. Cold as frost.

Garston. It's a strange name you chose for yourself. "Gar", meaning "great" in the gallic tongue. And stone meaning stone, of course. There you lie, too. As heavy and as old as one.

"I'm . . . kind of busy," Ben muttered, his breath stirring ripples in the blood. "Dying . . ."

Yes. But no one will mourn you, wyrm. You've outlived your purpose by centuries. Console yourself with that.

"Thanks. I will."

Laughter, somewhere in the cavern, a high, bright sound. Like music. Like bells.

Scowling – couldn't he get a minute's peace even at his funeral? – he opened his eyes. Somehow, he found himself looking at the sword. Fallen against a rock, Caliburn lay at a shallow angle on the cavern floor, the blade turned towards him. Was that the source of the light on his face? He thought so. In the glow, he made out a pair of eyes watching him, leaf-shaped and violet. Amused, perhaps, but not really. Not really amused. The woman inside the sword – looking out at him *from* the sword – couldn't hide her displeasure so easily.

"Come," she said.

And everything changed. One moment he was lying face down on the ground, the next, he found himself slipping towards the blade, a bloody mote, magnetised by a word. He caught a brief impression of rushing stars, a rainbow smeared across an infinite darkness (*the nether*), and an emptiness booming in his skull. The next he was lifting his head from the earth and spitting out clumps of grass.

What the fuck?

"Drink," the woman said.

129

He couldn't see her, but he took her advice, dragging himself across the turf to the little brook that was gabbling a few feet in front of him. Jesus, his throat felt raw. He tried to ignore the fact that the brook ran out not far from where he lay, the waters trickling over the edge of the land and scattering into darkness, diamonds on oil. It was as though the idea of *earth*, the grassy verge overhanging the gulf, ran out. He'd seen that somewhere before, hadn't he? As he scooped and guzzled water, a balm to his throat, he could feel his wounds tingling at last, responding to the magic in his flesh. By degrees, the pain faded, the cold, sweet water hissing on the coals in his breast, his anger at Von Hart coiling into the steam of weariness. He was alive. He was healing. The *why* of it still escaped him.

He froze, water cupped to his mouth, when he noticed the feet on the opposite bank. A woman was standing there. But she wasn't the same one, he realised, the dark-skinned stranger who'd peered out from the sword. Slowly, he followed the shape of her legs up to her hips. Up to her breasts, her face. She stood there as naked as he was, pale, slender and blonde. But this woman wasn't looking at him; her eyes were empty and blank. With a gasp, his heart shrivelled up in his chest, flinching from an inner punch. Forcing out a name.

"Rose?"

She didn't answer him.

How can this be?

Ben was on his feet at once, up and leaping across the brook, his arms parting in embrace. As he approached her, he slowed, a misgiving tugging at him. It wasn't just the way that she ignored him, her face, expressionless, betraying no sign that she knew he was there. Drawing nearer, he could see the smoothness of her skin, her body and limbs, unscarred by the glyphs that the

130

priest had carved into her flesh, a year ago in Cairo. He wasn't likely to forget them, her occult mutilation, because he'd been too stupid to protect her, and ultimately to save her. As he drew closer still, he could see that there was something wrong, a weird, waxy sheen to her skin. Thinking this, the lines and whorls became clear to him, bringing to mind a sculpture, a carving in wood, either aspen or oak. A couple of yards away, he halted, breathing hard. The simulacrum had fooled him, all right. A clever lattice of leaves, each one an autumn gold, comprised the figure's hair, tumbling down her polished back. The artist had embedded flakes of jasper to resemble her eyes, a depiction of the way she'd looked at him once upon a time, one day by an obelisk in Central Park. And later, when she'd loved and feared him in equal measure. Doubted him.

Was that bergamot drifting on the air? His nose twitched, a tear slipping over his lip, falling to the grass. He missed her so much. He missed the comfort of pretending, the sweet bliss of ignorance. Time had stripped all that from him now. Stripped it from him with witches and fate and a shattered fairy harp, leaving him with nothing . . .

Despite himself, his hand reached out, reached for her belly, the polished bole symbolising pregnancy. He choked, realising that this was as close as he'd ever get to his child, the son or the daughter that Rose McBriar bore. A year had passed. She would've given birth by now, surely.

Stay away. From me. From us. I don't even know who you are any more.

Did he even know? The memory of those words held all the weight of a judge announcing a life sentence. When she'd left him, turned her back on the desert sands, his draconic seed had been growing inside her and, Lore aside, he had no way of

131

knowing what pain, what danger that might bring. On top of this, the Whispering Chapter had revealed that they knew all about his "depraved coupling" with a human, his love affair with Rose. To him, the affair remained a brief oasis of joy in centuries of loneliness. He didn't know if the Chapter had learnt of her whereabouts or not, or if it mattered now that the Chapter had fallen. It was hard to think about, knowing that in the real world, he had no way to reach her, no way to find her, that he didn't even know where to start looking.

Still lying to yourself, old wyrm?

An image of the Vicomte Lambert du Sang crept into his mind, crawling across the web of memory, echoing from the tunnels under Paris.

The whereabouts of a Brooklyn waitress, recently spellbound and scarred . . . ?

Ben blinked away tears, angry at himself and afraid. His concern for Rose wasn't simply down to his personal failings: he feared for her life. For the life of his child. But this was just a stupid statue, a joke designed to tug at his heartstrings, remind him of his shortcomings. Mock him . . .

Before his fingers connected with wood, Rose burst into flame. With a cry, he watched dark rings spread out from the sculpture's belly, chased by embers in the grain. The next moment, the inferno took hold, the fire licking up around her limbs, her hair a whoosh of cinders and smoke. When he fell, sobbing, to his knees, he found that he was only clutching branches, burning fragments hot against his chest, his scales forming as if to shield his heart. Swiftly, the sculpture crumbled, charred chunks and ashes filtering through his arms, drifting into the dark like stars, swirling and winking out.

There was no time to grieve. He heard the laughter again, a

light clarion, coming from across the brook. Glowering, his head snapped in that direction.

"What the hell is this? Stop fucking about."

"Is that how you greet your queen?" Nimue said. "At least you have the good grace to kneel."

Ben climbed to his feet. Scales rippled, thick and red, across his flesh. Horns protruded from his shoulders. His face remained human, his unkempt hair symbolising the fire in his breast. Through his rage, it occurred to him then that he didn't need the envoy's suit, after all. Perhaps he'd never needed it. Last winter, Jia had told him that she'd conjured up her own suit via meditation, some kind of mental focus, retaining enough of her bestial form for the purpose. *We don't all need a nursemaid,* she'd said. That had smarted at the time, but he'd been thinking about it ever since. Standing here, he tried to apply the same level of concentration, breathing in and seeking control, preventing himself from changing fully into dragon form or from dwindling back into human shape. To his surprise, his flesh wavered between these states, a fairground organ of rippling scales, bulging muscles and undulating horns. If he could *think* his scales into resembling a suit, let them shrink and wrap around his humanoid proportions . . . *A new trick.* He could see how it was done. But it was going to take some practice.

The distraction stopped him from jumping across the water and clawing the Lady apart.

"That was cruel," he told her.

The Lady cocked her head, the snow-white coils of her hair rising to a tightly bound point atop it.

"Oh? Then you deny that you saw your woman as an object? Don't scowl at us so, Benjurigan. We merely plucked the vision from your skull, here in this garden of dreams. As for her fate, that was always her own affair."

More Fay bullshit.

The Lady stood across from him, looking much the same as when he'd seen her before, his hand closing around the pommel of the sword, sparking wondrous yet unwanted visions. And she was a vision, no doubt about that. A gown of sheer blue silk wove around her limbs as if she'd reached out a hand, snagged a passing zephyr and wrapped it around her. Up close, he noticed that her features, somehow alluring despite their severity, matched the sharpness of her ears, the helices tapering into thin brown points. A delicate tiara, a *lunewrought* lattice, glimmered upon her stacked braids. Under the laced branches of the trees, she regarded him with violet eyes, her gaze somewhere between distant and amused.

"She's in danger, isn't she?" he asked. "I—"

"She is human," Nimue replied, as if that was an answer. "At least, she was . . ."

"You're in no position to judge me. You lot aren't exactly saints."

"We were gods, once," she sighed, unmoved. "Alas, we are not what we were."

You're the Fallen Ones, he thought, but didn't say. *Fallen and fucked off into the nether.*

"Yeah? Well, join the club," he said. "You might say that some of us got burned. No thanks to you. Now if you'll excuse me, I don't really have time for this out-of-body, dream-sequence shit. A dead king marches on London, the envoy has run away and I guess that you're looking to play homecoming queen. Considering the stink of your magic, none of that gives me the warm fuzzies. If it's all the same to you, I'd like to wake up now."

He sounded ungrateful, churlish even, but he didn't care. If the Lady had healed him, if the dreaming brook had undone the sword's lacerations, then it stood to reason that she wanted something from him. He didn't need a near-death experience to wise up to the fact. Again, he had that uncomfortable feeling of standing here in Von Hart's shoes, dragged in over his head, an unwanted but necessary pawn. Probably an expendable one.

"Plus Rose is in trouble," he added, in a gruff, awkward tone, as if it was an afterthought and not the thrust of his worries.

"How sweet. You think we've given you an excuse to see her," the Lady said. "Not that she ever needed your help."

His eyes narrowed into slits as Nimue laughed again. "Don't trouble yourself so. Here in the Orchard of Worlds time moves differently than on the terrestrial plane, if it moves at all," she told him. "Still, we retain some arts as an oracle. You'll never see Rose McBriar again. Not while you live."

That hit him like a hammer, a blow to his guts, and he stopped himself from sinking to his knees, the scene spinning around him. He looked up, fighting for balance, but there were no stars overhead to fix him, help him get his bearings. Only an endless darkness, the darkness of the nether. Familiar, empty and cold.

Ahead of him, beyond the Lady, he took in the trees, their tangled, blossom-clad branches resolving into the strict rows of a plantation. Petals, sweet-smelling and white, drifted on the breeze. The trees went right up to the palace, the walls crystalline and soaring, the tallest turrets spearing the black. The sight steadied him, awe freezing his feet to the ground, his location, dreamt up or not, dawning on him. When he'd first lifted Caliburn, in the depths of Snowdon, he'd seen a lot more than the Lady. If he dared to turn around and look over the precipice, he somehow knew that he'd see the same labyrinthine coils of light, the golden skiffs flying about them and silver veins riddling the dark. The thought made him giddy. He stood in the grounds of the palace that hung in the uppermost branches of the Great Tree. The Isle of the Apples.

He had dreamt his way into Avalon, the mythical homeland of the Fay.

Fay, he reminded himself. *Get a grip on yourself. You can't trust a word she says.*

"Why . . ." He gathered his breath, sucking in air or whatever passed for it in this place. "Why am I here?"

"A strange question," the Lady said. "One of our greatest creations. The glorious dragon. Creature of fire and flight. The wonder of a thousand stories and more."

Ben grunted. "It's been said."

"You're the spawn of Jynnyflamme, are you not? Jynnyflamme, who hatched from the egg of Pennydrake, the legendary mount of King Arthur himself. You're as tangled up in this tale as anyone."

"Don't I know it. But that isn't exactly an answer."

The Lady held out her arm, as slender as a willow branch.

"Come. Tarry with us awhile."

Ben rolled his shoulders and then jumped across the brook, moving away from the precipice and the scorched ring of grass, a scar like the one in his heart. This kind of taunt, this disregard for compassion in the name of amusement, wasn't exactly new to him. Long had he railed against Von Hart's mockery and games, so it didn't surprise him to encounter the same penchant here, in the shadow of the palace walls. The sculpture, clearly intended to prick at his failings, only served to remind him that for all their apparent playfulness, the Fay weren't known for their benevolence. At least not any more. There was usually a price for their help, and their games seemed to share one thing in common – people tended to get hurt. The Fay were like sweet-scented flowers, enticing innocent prey in the forest, the petals hiding a sticky and noxious prison. Only recently, he'd found himself caught up in fairy machinations, the envoy's treachery and his breaking of the harp. And he'd seen the state of Arthur and the army that followed him, a dangerous rabble if ever there was one. *Flowers. Right.* It was enough to remind him who he was dealing with; he'd had his fingers pricked by the thorns.

All the same, curiosity got the better of him. With a caution that he tried to mask as shyness, he sidled up beside the Lady, peering down into her face. Her beauty arrested him despite himself and he coughed, looking away. Nimue didn't appear to notice, however, or if she did, the effect she had on others wasn't new to her. She merely slipped her arm through his, her skin soft on his scales, and proceeded to lead him down a row between the trees, under the blossoming boughs.

"Long ago, when the world was young, we foretold a coming darkness," she said, with the clear and candid air of royalty. "For time out of mind, our people had graced the earth, guiding humanity to wisdom. But it was only with a union of magic and mortal flesh that we perceived a chance of glory. A child born of both worlds, who could lead mankind to the greatest heights of evolution. A king to walk the land like a god."

"Arthur," Ben said. "You mean Arthur. The Pendragon."

"The Example, yes. With this in mind, the High House declared a great golden age. Against the darkness, we set our swords. Indeed, it was with a sword that the test began. In *lunewrought*, in star fire, our smiths forged a mighty weapon. With our spells and the hope in our hearts, we bound the fate of your world to the blade."

Caliburn, Ben thought. *It'd love to hear you say that.*

The Lady slowed, shaking her head at some inner rebuke, a faint shiver of bells.

"Perhaps we're getting ahead of ourselves. There are many worlds, Benjurigan. Worlds beyond number, all dangling like fruit on a vine, spiralling through the orchards of the cosmos. Look."

Ben looked, following her outstretched arms to the trees around them. There was fruit up there, yes, hanging from the branches, but unlike any he had seen. Some, he noticed, hung in clusters of buds, unformed, small and hard. Others looked fat and ripe, weighing down the sheltering boughs. Each one held a different shape and a different shade, swirling with colours at their core, red, gold, blue and green, a myriad of shifting hues. More than likely, the Lady was showing him a vision, a conjured metaphor to illustrate her words. He was getting used to this nonsense too. Was the ground even solid beneath his feet? Was the palace simply his idea of one, what he expected to see? The Fay, he knew, were famous for their glamour, for illusions and fugues. Last winter, he'd seen one shatter for himself – not only in the glass of the Eight Hand Mirror, but in Jia Jing's eyes.

The thought made him sneer.

"So we're nothing special. Is that why you left?"

He hated the tone that crept into his voice, the petulance of a child. What could he say to impress on her the time passed, forever wasted? The impact of her absence on the Remnants, her forgotten children? He found that he lacked the words.

"Please. Have patience," Nimue said, turning back to him. "All worlds are special, Ben. All worlds hold the power, the potential to become something more. More than simply blood and dust. But Creation is vast. As vast as the nether that holds them. Gods, long forgotten, seeded this orchard. Seeded even the Fay. Once, the light held sway, igniting every corner of the cosmos, bringing wisdom and joy. Bringing peace. Alas, it did not last."

"I know this part," Ben said, remembering. "There was a cataclysm, right? No one seems to know the gory details. In a nutshell, the gods went the way of the dodo. Or went mad. Became dreams." He shuddered, feeling the chill of the encompassing darkness. "Dreams that can take on flesh, if we're unlucky enough."

In his mind, a goddess on a mountainside, telling him that the world was dying. But he hadn't wanted to listen then.

"The First-Born became the Fallen," the Lady said, wrenching him back to the here and now. She spoke in the same light tone, but he could sense the sorrow under it. "In our decline, we took up the ancient duty, travelling the leys of Creation, silver in the dark. Throughout the ages, we've tended to the scattered worlds. Each one forsaken, adrift in the wake of extinct gods. Yours was one such world. A world that we longed to heal and advance, cultivating paradise. A mirror of Avalon. Heaven on Earth."

"I know this part too," Ben told her. The knowledge, so vast in scope, so numinous, dazzled and frightened him. He preferred to keep things simple. "Things didn't end well."

The Lady looked down at her feet, the hem of her gown flowing over the grass. Was she hiding a tear? He couldn't tell. But her sadness was apparent now, a sombre music in her voice.

"The Example failed," she said. "Humans, alas, had no flair for ascension. Our magic shone like sunlight through the trees, potent, plentiful, but only the purest of souls could see it. That is the nature of belief. After a fashion, we tried to . . . dramatise the matter, making use of certain props. Artefacts, tools. We shaped a sword and bound it to an earthly destiny. We made a cup and filled it with the stuff of innocence, asking all to drink. And in the end, we forged a harp, begging a king to stay the turning tide. It was no use. Greed, pride and hatred were a thousand thorns, strangling our hope. And the king fell, a mortal echo of our own debasement. The sword lay buried under rock until this, the tolling of the darkest hour. One alone saw the cup, the greatest of knights, and then the grail vanished forever. The harp . . . well, I'm sure you know all about the harp, yes? And of late, the harp has summoned us hence once again. Or rather, its undoing."

Ben stopped, the Lady halting beside him. Under the trees, the branches fruiting with countless worlds, he faced her with a scowl.

"You abandoned us." His tone was an axe, chopping through her fancy speech. "Were you planning on coming back? If Jia hadn't stolen the harp, I mean. If Von Hart hadn't destroyed it . . ." His ire ran out, the language confounding him, a thickness in his throat. "Scratch all that. It's too late now. You can't take it back." *Later. I'll deal with this later.* "Looks to me like we've got bigger problems. You said that you're not what you were. Well, neither is your king."

"No. You speak true."

The Lady released him, reclaiming her arm. Without a sound, she drifted over to the nearest tree and placed her hand on the trunk. For a moment, Ben thought she was weeping and he resented the surge of guilt in his breast. Why should he feel sympathy for her after all that the Fay had done, turning their backs on the world, on the Remnants, leaving them all to struggle through the ages? Leaving them all to die . . .

When she looked up again, up into the branches, he followed

her gaze to a large fruit hanging a few feet above him. Even from a distance, the markings on its flesh struck him as familiar. The frayed edges of continents. The blue immensity of seas. White streaks here and there that he took for clouds. Its perfect shape, fat and round. A single fruit on a narrow branch, lonely against the darkness.

Earth. That's the Earth.

"How long does the fruit stay ripe when cut from the branch?" she asked him. "We couldn't know what our departure would cost us. We were in grief. Traumatised by the failed Example, the end of our golden age. In our pain, we did not see. We left your world to its fate, burying the sword with the king. One by one, we destroyed the gates, closing the roads through the nether. One alone, we left intact, although locked and bound by a charm, because . . ." She frowned, some private concern stirring the smooth waters of her face. "We didn't have the heart," she said and fell silent.

The heart for what? Ben wondered. *To abandon us forever?*

He got the impression that she'd been about to say something else, but he let it slide, caught up in the spell of her admission as she went on. "And alas, we have come to learn that the circles of protection crumble and decay when cut off from their immortal source. The earth sours much the same. In your world, magic dies. Phantoms gather, drawn to the stench. Through the darkness, we heard the echoes of the harp, catching our attention. *Reminding* us. A great enchantment has come undone. A certain failsafe, a certain spell, has triggered to signal our return. Arthur, the Once and Future King, has risen." She swallowed, glancing at Ben, then away into the trees. He couldn't mistake the fear in her eyes, the shadow of an ancient shame. "Or . . . a corrupted version of him. Ever was he linked to the health of the land, a living symbol of nature. Now he has . . . *soured*. Arthur has become a tyrant of death. A bringer of war. An omen of the end."

Ben clapped his hands together.

"Terrific," he said.

The Lady wheeled on him, her face distraught.

"What would you have us do?" she said, in a bladed breath. "For all our arts, we cannot turn back time. All we can do is open the way again, the last silver road. Let your world drink from the font, the eternal source of magic. Even as we speak, a company of Fay rides across the nether, bound for the gate to your world. The envoy will meet us there, Benjurigan."

"Sounds like you've got things all sewn up," he said, though he wished that even news of the cavalry didn't sound like trouble. "I'll ask you again. What the hell do you want from me?"

Because until your company gets here, I'm facing an army on my own.

A wind was coming up, rattling the branches of the trees. The fruit, dangling, was swaying above him, a soft clarion of bells. The noise, musical and sweet as it was, set his teeth on edge. It sounded like an alarm, telling him that his time in the orchard was short. This wasn't just a dream. He was under a spell, surely. His draconic flesh, while resistant to magic, couldn't withstand the workings of the Fay, the erstwhile masters. At least not for long. Nimue, Our Lady of the Barrows, had drawn him here from a pool of blood on a cavern floor to attend to her need. All the same, these kinds of spells had a shelf life, he knew. Somewhere, healed of his wounds, he guessed that he was waking up, shaking off the fugue.

He leant towards her, keen to hear her reply before he did so.

"Arthur's awakening has failed," she said. "And in the wake of the chaos, Von Hart lacks something." Nimue, her words tinkling, cried through the storm of thrown-up blossoms and leaves, her gown whipping around her. "Something vital. Something he left behind. The sword, Caliburn, should have fallen into his keeping. Instead, I sense it in yours."

"Yeah. Well, one of us wasn't taking a nap," he said, thinking of the sword in the mountain, its steely disdain. *You'll just have to do.* "Someone had to—"

"If only I could reach out, across this gulf, and take it," she said, in a way that let him know she wasn't entirely speaking to him, her regret plain, verging on bitterness. "The walls of your world yet hold, Benjurigan, and the road to the gate is long. Do you grasp what the High House asks of you?"

"You might want to elaborate."

Again, she sighed, her disappointment echoing the sword. "In this dire pass, the envoy would have brought us the blade. One cannot underestimate its power. The earth and its fate are one. Alas, Lord Blaise will come to the gate empty-handed. And we are running out of time."

Now he remembered Von Hart in the cavern, his urgency. His need.

We must fly to China and recover the Eight Hand Mirror. We must somehow rebuild the bridge.

He had no way of knowing if the gate remained on Lantau Island, buried under rubble on the southernmost tip of the Fan Lau peninsula. It was a lead, of sorts. But a long way to go if he was wrong . . .

As if reading his mind, the Lady said, "Find the gate. Find the envoy."

"Oh, I'll find him," Ben told her, with a fierce nod. *We haven't finished our conversation.* "I'll find him and break his neck. If it's the last thing I do."

The Lady frowned, disliking the sound of this.

"Bring us . . ." she pressed her insistence through the swirling petals, "bring the envoy the sword."

He wanted to ask why. Why was the weapon so damn important? In what way were the earth and the sword linked? He was tired of all these guessing games, the truth veiled, always just out of sight. But before he could stop her, she stepped towards him and grabbed his face, her hands cool on his cheeks. Violet urgency searched his eyes, even as his nostrils filled with the scent of her, honeysuckle and fresh sap, swimming in his skull. He was aware of her breasts, an inch from his chest, and his eyes grew wide as she pressed her lips to his, a soft yet firm entreaty.

She broke the kiss. Released, he staggered away from her, a hand to his mouth as though stung.

"Do you love your queen?" she asked him. "Will you refuse us in our darkest hour?"

He gave her a wounded look. What had she plucked from him? Memories, pain, and now a taste of his loneliness, the warmth of her creeping into his bones, sunlight falling on ice. He felt blood rush into his cheeks, his legs weak, even as the flesh between them took on a hardness, twitching with helpless desire.

Curse you, fairy. No . . .

Before he could speak, object to her boldness, the Lady said, "Bring the sword to the gate, Benjurigan. Bring us Caliburn, the World-cleaver. It's the reason why we have spared you."

Then the gale picked him up as if he was a leaf and flung him out into darkness.

NINE

Midnight. Tower Bridge. Ben sat atop the remaining turret looking out over the Thames. The streetlights on both banks shimmered on the water, the moon rippling round and full. For the most part, the buildings around him lay dark, monoliths shadowed in the depths, peppered by the odd reflection of a neon sign or an office block window, blinking on an automated circuit. In the distance, the cracked dome of St Paul's Cathedral hunkered over the wreckage as if mourning the shambles of Ludgate and Fleet Street. The fires were dwindling now, the smoke drifting away, leaving darkness to shroud the ruins. No trains rumbled along the tracks. No taxi honked nor rickshaw rattled. No crowds chattered outside restaurants and clubs. No planes flew overhead, but to the west, he swore he could make out the whirr of choppers, somewhere near the city boundary.

The silence doused his thrill of being outdoors again, free of the underground vaults where he'd woken an hour before, lying naked and healed in a drying pool of blood. Recovering the sword, he'd made his way through the dark, stumbling and grunting away from the sordid sepulchres, until flowering into a red-winged beast that shot from the mouth of a tunnel on the West Hampstead interchange. Caliburn in claw (he had no fear of the *lunewrought* now, the blade had done its worst), he'd swept over the darkened city, taking in the streets below with growing unease. Regent's Park lay silent, a black expanse edged by abandoned buses and cars. Soho sprawled in noiseless neon, litter dancing down Old Compton Street instead of partygoers. Further on, the Gherkin rose over the pickle of buildings that had once comprised the City, Bank station, Cannon Street and Leadenhall Market all trampled by a giant's boot.

It was here that his rage petered out, cooling into something deeper and sharper. As he'd veered for Tower Bridge, her broken back silhouetted below, he could no longer ignore the fact that there were people down there, from Camden to Clerkenwell, residents of London in the ruins. On Sandwich Street, he'd seen an old man hanging out washing in his backyard. At King's Cross, a woman in a burka was rattling her keys in a roll shutter lock, opening her shop for the evening. Tents had appeared in Inner Temple Gardens, the squalid stretch of tarpaulin suggesting that the city's homeless had banded together, huddling around small fires, seeking strength in numbers. These sights shocked and impressed him as he flew, making him realise that despite the terror that must've been blaring from every TV and radio station in the land, despite the knowledge of monsters abroad, blowing up power stations and flooding parks, there were some in the city who hadn't fled. Perhaps there was nowhere for them to go. Perhaps they didn't quite believe what they were seeing, couldn't accept the danger. More likely, Ben surmised with a twinge in his heart, the ones who remained simply had an extra dose of London pluck. If the city burned, then by George, they'd burn too. No one would take that away from them.

There were pigeons too, he noticed. Still pigeons. Pigeons carried on about their business in Trafalgar Square, pecking at the pavement in Holborn, decorating the statues of princes and dukes. And rats. Rats scurried through the bins, revelling in the feast with all the glee of vultures picking at a corpse. There was life here, after a fashion. Perched high on the bridge, Ben tried to console himself with the notion. It didn't do him much good.

Not all of London was dark. There was another reason he'd landed here, travelling from one place to another. Less than a mile away, the Shard rose from the south bank in pyramidal splendour. A thousand feet of steel and polished glass, the blade of the building skewered the night. The top of the Shard stood open to the air, her walls culminating in latticed leaves that almost, but not quite, kissed, a marvel of modern architecture. Light swirled around the pointed spire, the uppermost floors of the sky deck blazing with spectral radiance, as blue and as cold as frost. Ben knew that light. He'd seen it before and recently, creeping through an alien crypt. Glittering in a corroded circle. Burning in a dead king's eyes.

Yeah. And shimmering in the Lady's gown.

From a distance, the cavorting brilliance brought to mind a crown, a blazing symbol of tyranny presiding over London. The light flickered, wheeling shapes caught in the glow. A flight of wyverns, twenty or more, were shrieking and circling around the spire. From a distance, the slender, two-legged serpents – he couldn't think of them as dragons, poor cousins as they were – looked too small to present much of a threat, but Ben didn't kid himself. He couldn't take them all on alone.

Arthur was up there. Arthur and his knights. The king had chosen his throne room.

Down below, in the streets around the Shard, Ben could hear the roar of the horde. Judging by the scattered fires, Arthur's army had encamped in a loose circle that encompassed St Thomas Street and London Bridge station. Presumably, whatever hideous captains commanded the king's rabble, they had made good use of the buildings hereabouts, turning the abandoned spaces into makeshift headquarters. Ben could picture the scene easily enough, much as it pained him. Ogres guzzling from the taps in the Bunch of Grapes. Goblins playing dice in the post office. The little wyverns squawking and shitting on the railway tracks. The Remnant battalions at ease.

But for how long? he wondered. *This invasion won't go unchallenged . . .*

He knew it was true. Arthur might've enjoyed the element of surprise, putting the city to flight, but human shock and incredulity wouldn't last forever. Ben knew that from bitter experience. And he had the scars to prove it. How long before one of those choppers ventured out on a recce over Westminster and jets arrived to strafe the streets with bombs? How long before a submarine slid up the Thames, loaded with nuclear missiles? Because in among the noise, the drunken cries, roars, hisses and grunts of Remnant triumph, Ben could hear the screams too, faint but unmistakably human. And for all his draconic bulk, all his fury and fire, there was nothing he could do about it. Not here. Not now.

You're outnumbered. Outfanged. And you can't even trust the cavalry.

Ben gripped the stonework under him, threatening to crush it to dust in his claws. He had lost the city. He'd failed. The Lore was over. The Guild and the Chapter had collapsed. The Long Sleep had come undone. And Von Hart, the instigator of all these things, had betrayed him. Regardless of the fairy's intention, summoning the Fay to save the world from destruction – or so he *said* – the envoy had neglected to tell Ben the truth. As a result, Ben had nearly lost his life and he hadn't been the only one to pay the price. Wherever she was, Rose would always bear her scars. Jia had tumbled into the nether. Hundreds of humans had died. And Von Hart had started a war.

Find him . . . will you refuse us in our darkest hour?

That was the question, wasn't it? And Ben had made up his mind.

The sword, of course, didn't like the idea.

"Of all the thick-headed, ill-advised, self-serving, perilous plans," it said, thrumming in his grip. "The Lady charged you to find Von Hart and bring me to the gate. Are you honestly going to defy her?"

Ben scowled. It hadn't been an easy decision. He was tired of feeling like the dice in a game of craps, thrown up the table to land wherever Von Hart wanted him. It was time to take a gamble of his own.

"I've been listening to fairies for years. Guess where it got me." *Nowhere fast.* "You saw the look on Von Hart's face. Like a puppy awaiting its mistress. And you've seen the state of Arthur." He shuddered, and not from the October wind. "That's down to *Fay* magic, sword. Let's just say that your Lady didn't exactly fill me with confidence."

"But—"

"Look. She told me that the breaking of the harp had reminded her. Of the earth. Us . . ." He trailed off, unable to put his dejection into words, the understanding that for all the Remnants' hope, their faith in a dubious prophecy, the Lady had confessed that she'd forgotten all about them. "That says something. Something bad."

"You don't trust her."

"You weren't lying when you said you were sharp," Ben said, and he heard the sword *tsk* softly below him.

The truth was he didn't trust Nimue any more than he trusted Von Hart. Loath as he was to let the Fay come through the Eight Hand Mirror on the envoy's terms, he was less enamoured of the thought of chasing him down, perhaps making the same mistake twice. Not after Jia. No way. It was clear that the envoy was using him too. If he'd fashioned the *sin-you* as a throwaway tool, then why not a down-at-heel dragon? Was Ben finally seeing a pattern here? Could he predict the envoy's next move? Von Hart liked to make others do his dirty work for him. Like rousing Ben to shut down rebellious witches, neatly covering his tracks. And dispatching Jia to steal the fragments of the harp, the *sin-you* serving as a key to the road through the nether. Shit, finding the fairy would probably play right into his lily-white hands. He guessed that Von Hart had gone to Lantau Island to recover the mirror and repair the bridge for the Fay. Did the envoy expect him to follow? Ben reckoned so. And he thought he knew why.

Together, we'll go into the dark.

It was the sword, wasn't it? In his elation, Von Hart had forgotten the sword. *Elation. Madness. What's the difference?* Ben recalled the way that the envoy's face had lit up in the cavern, the way he'd reached out for Caliburn, his fingers trembling . . .

The Lady, of course, had been more forthright.

"Why are you so damn important?" he asked, growling down at the blade. "Why does she want you so badly?" *If only I could reach out, across this gulf, and take it,* she'd said. Her admission told him that while she may have access to his dreaming self, her reach remained incorporeal, limited, much like the reach of the Ghost Emperor. Nimue might have healed him, using whatever spells she could, and doubtless understanding the fabric of him, Remnant as he was. But the Lady herself stood beyond the world, behind the *walls*, he guessed, of reality. This stuff was becoming familiar now, not that the knowledge eased him much. She could reach him, beseech him, sure, but she couldn't *steer* him, that much was clear. And she couldn't reach the sword on the material plane either, prise it out of his happenstance hands. When Von Hart had neglected the sword, he'd placed the task squarely on Ben's shoulders. Now, Ben wondered at that, in the same way he wondered at Nimue's offhand comment about his position. She needed him. For all her fancy words, and in typical Fay fashion, she'd let that slip too. He was a means to an end, nothing more. "She more or less said I'd be toast without you."

"I wish I knew," Caliburn said. "Aside from being a magnificent example of a magical weapon, famed in countless legends and essentially determining the fate of this country, if not the world, I cannot fathom her plans. The Lady charged Von Hart with the task of attending the king should he ever awaken. Presumably, to await her return, bring me to her. After all, Nimue has played custodian before." The sword gave a tut. "Beyond that, I haven't a clue. I must have missed that particular meeting."

Deep in Ben's chest, fire rumbled. Rubble skittered between his claws. The sense of mysteries just out of reach grated on him. He was getting tired of waiting for answers. Meanwhile, the world around him was burning.

"It's the same old game," he said. "The only difference is I'm not playing blind. Not any more. And it seems to me I've got the world's biggest bargaining chip."

If the Lady bound the fate of the earth to the sword, then I guess that it rests in my hands now. You can't do a worse job than the envoy. Can you . . . ?

Caliburn buzzed. "Excuse me? Bargaining chip? Need I remind you that I was forged in *lunewrought* and star-studded, tempered in the ice of Avalon and spun across—"

"Why should the envoy hold all the cards?" Ben cut the sword off, muttering to himself. "I'm sick of him yanking my chain as if I'm some . . . some glorified guard dog. Well, maybe it's time I acted like one."

"Guard what, exactly? In case you hadn't noticed, there's nothing left to guard."

"Whichever way I turn, there's trouble," Ben went on. "I'm not about to just hand the Fay what they want. If the Lady wants her 'World-cleaver', then she can bloody well come and get it."

"You're going to rebel against the High House of Avalon," the sword said. "And I thought you were merely a dunce. You've got a death wish as well."

"Why the hell not?" Ben spoke more fiercely than intended, flames fluttering between his fangs. "The Fay turned their backs on us and we've been dying ever since. The Lore turned out to be a lie. Von Hart's big mistake. Don't you see? All of this shit starts and ends with fucking fairies. Well, enough is enough. Sometimes you have to stand on your own two feet." *Or four. Whatever.* "I can't do any worse than them."

Caliburn sighed. When the sword spoke again, it sounded softer, choosing its words with care.

"Come now. That's not the whole truth, is it?"

Ben exhaled, hanging his head. The fire in his belly dwindled to embers, a white-hot shame at his core.

"I can't leave them like this," he said. "The humans. I swore to protect them. That was my purpose, the whole point of . . . of everything." He swallowed, tasting ash in his throat. *The old oath has to count for something. Or what was it worth?* "I won't abandon them now."

For a moment, the sword fell silent. Ben closed his eyes, thinking of Maud, of Jia and Rose. The Pact might've gone up in smoke, his world torn to shreds, but the dragon who'd made a promise, back in Uffington, in 1215, was still here. He hadn't forgotten the reasons he'd made it either. *To preserve the Remnants. To protect the humans.* And in the end, his word was all he had, the only rock left to cling to. If he was to die, then he wouldn't go down chasing fairies, a pawn in some ancient game. He'd die with honour, for what he believed in. The choice that he'd made. Hope of atonement hung in the air, an unspoken need behind his every word.

Then Caliburn told him, "There's an army out there. A thousand strong and growing by the hour. You might be a dragon and I might be a legendary sword, but there's still only two of us. You won't vanquish Arthur with a valiant speech."

"There are other Remnants," Ben said, more boldly than he felt. Up there, around the tip of the Shard, the blue light flickered and danced. "A handful of us left . . ."

It sounded foolish and he knew it. But not every Remnant was a hateful creature, hungry for human flesh and dominion. They were out there, all right, all around the world, hiding in forest and cavern and lake. In pub cellars and penthouses. In supermarkets and saunas. In tower blocks and tombs. The Lore had broken. The times had thrust the Remnants out of the shadows, blinking in the harsh light of day. A war was coming. And perched upon the broken bridge, Ben knew that it was the same war, the same old struggle between the Old Lands and the new. The war had never ended. Not really. It had only . . . waited.

If he could somehow reach them. Rouse them. Rally them to his cause . . .

Caliburn sniffed.

"This is folly. The Remnants are far and wide. You don't even know where to find them."

"True," Ben said, spreading his wings. "But I know where to start looking."

TEN

Paris

In under an hour, Ben had crossed the English Channel and swept down into the tree-lined avenues of Père Lachaise Cemetery. As he dwindled into human form, he frowned, concentrating, once again recalling Jia's trick with the suit, visualising a thin, crimson layer of scales encasing his limbs, as tight and slick as neoprene. At first, the notion wavered, uncertain, his bestial self resisting the image of the hominid attire. Then the illusion, modern as it was, took hold, his magical flesh simulating the memory of the envoy's suit, albeit one as red as his scales and sans the *wyrm tongue* sigil. Once fixed in mind, the suit settled around him, a new skill, learned from necessity and sparing the world the sight of his arse.

Hey presto!

Without ceremony, he landed before the Monument Aux Morts, sword in claw translating to sword in hand. Statues toppled in his wake, urns splintering on gravel, scattering dried flowers and dust. Unlike the last time he'd come here, Ben paid no mind to the mess. The dragon was out of the bag now. Who knew what monsters roamed the City of Light? Or, for that matter, this city of tombs? Time was short. And discretion was a ball and chain that he happily shook off.

In the darkness, the pale, naked sculptures of the man and the woman edged the rhomboid entrance to the tomb. Ben had learnt that this was in fact a tunnel that led down into the catacombs under the city. Into the lair of a supposed Vicomte and his eight-legged army of spies.

Back for more punishment, mon ami . . .

Ben wasn't sure if the thought was a threat to the Remnant or himself. The truth was he had little to fear from the *vampyr*, for all du Sang's taste for dragon blood. A pair of fangs, however long, weren't much cop against rock-hard scales. It was the memory of du Sang's desolation and thirst for *fire* that made Ben feel like an ant before the grand mastaba, the faux Egyptian tomb. Because the Vicomte had been right.

A stain in the fabric of things, spreading, growing sour . . .

Du Sang had warned him that the Remnants were done for, that the Lore under which they all lived was nothing more than a boot, crushing them out like used cigarettes. He'd told him that there was nothing left to live for, no reason to go on. To accept that was death, surely. It was the bitter truth that had driven Jia into its maw, made desperate and mad, like so many of the Remnants, by time, longing and loss.

And as for me? Am I mad too? Lord knows I've touched my fair share of lunewrought.

The Fay metal had changed him, that was certain. For one thing, it had granted him the insight to see the circles of protection, see their widespread decay. For another, the breaking of the harp had taken his world along with it, throwing his whole purpose into chaos. *Lunewrought* had a habit of bringing a Remnant's pain to the surface, he'd found, amplifying desperation to a maniacal pitch. But Lambert du Sang hadn't needed any help on that score and he reckoned that there were others like him, the old fabulous beings and beasts that Ben was skipping off to meet, a hulking Red Riding Hood with a blade made from the stuff.

Caliburn was different from the *Cwyth*, however. *Binding was never my purpose,* the sword had said, and Ben had yet to find reason to doubt it. Whatever otherworldly smiths had forged the weapon had obviously designed it for another purpose, that being slicing and dicing. Still, he couldn't help but wonder if the ache in his chest, stoking the rage that had pushed him into this hare-brained course, wasn't due to his contact with the alien ore.

On either side of the wall before him, a bas-relief ascended to the tomb entrance. In the moonlight, he picked out the carved stone figures. A man crouching in grief. A kneeling woman with arms crossed, hiding her face. Other figures, stumbling, kissing and weeping, formed the marble tableau, all drawn towards that black, inevitable door. The monument, a memorial to those fallen in some war or other, portrayed the fragility of man, the pain and the preciousness of life. Too precious to squander on fighting, Ben reckoned. On prejudice and violence. Why did bloodshed thread through the course of history like barbed wire through mud, entwining Remnant and human alike in mindless and mundane horror? Was the nature of life inherently destructive, as the Lady had suggested? *His* life had been a battle from the moment he'd hatched, birthing vendettas and powder keg comprises. Could any of them hope for something better, something more?

Once upon a time, perhaps. The Example had failed, she'd told him. Humanity couldn't overcome its primal urges, evolve into . . . Into what? The notion troubled him, in a way that he couldn't quite put his finger on. He frowned at the sculptures above him, up at that shadowed mouth. When all was said and done, when the last city had fallen, when the last child had choked under skies of ash, was a cataclysm on a global scale the only way to put an end to war?

I don't have the answer to that. I don't think I want one.

The tomb plucked at his sorrow, a reminder that the last time he'd come here, he'd yet to meet the *sin-you* or learn of the envoy's treachery. On some level, he was mourning the loss of his ignorance too – and with it the greater part of his hope. So much had changed in the past year. Standing here, with death all around him, it had never been plainer to him that he wasn't the same dragon.

He stole a breath, steeling himself against the gloom ahead (the memory of spiders and skulls running ice up his spine), and leapt up onto the ledge. He took in the mangled gate, the etched symbol of the Five Families on the wall next to it, but again, he gave no thought to the ancient custom, entering uninvited with a snarl. Last winter, *someone* had told the White Dog the whereabouts of the Invisible Church and Ben could only think of one Remnant with access to that kind of knowledge. Wasn't that the reason he was here? If there hadn't been time for manners before, then there sure as hell wasn't now.

You'll tell me what I want to know. And then, maybe, I'll kill you . . .

Ben traipsed through archways and down stairs and entered the gallery, the cobwebbed paintings lit by the moonlight spilling through embrasures in the vaults above. He paused by the last painting, staring at the portrayal of the Fay departing the earth at the Battle of Camlann. Rendered in faded paint, the ghostly figures in gowns and cloaks were walking up a wintery hillside, leaving no footprints in the snow. On the rise, a broad black circle yawned like a solar eclipse, the Fay vanishing into the nether . . . Yeah, Ben recognised the circle now. After all, he'd leapt through the damn thing, hadn't he? Months ago, in China. It was the portal, the last gate. Legend had come to know it as the Eight Hand Mirror, the doorway framed in wood by some unknown hand, the spellbound surface begrimed with age, resembling the blackest glass.

In a corner of the painting, Von Hart stood in his star-spangled robes, the silk like blood on the snow. His white-gold hair tumbled between his shoulder blades, both slumped with the weight of a silent burden. At his feet lay the fragments of the harp. Ben rubbed his neck, swallowing an unbidden lump in his throat, something that tasted oddly like sympathy. Having learnt of the Fay's abandonment second-hand, a tale passed down through Remnant generations, he could only imagine what it must've felt like to witness it in person, Von Hart watching his people depart. He alone had remained, appointed by the High House of Avalon to serve as an ambassador, an envoy between the Remnant and the human world. *Well, he did a lot more than that.* Ben could understand the fairy's pain, festering over the long years, even if he couldn't forgive his methods, his riddles and manipulations, the conspiracy that had cost him so dearly, unleashing witches and mummies and dragons. *Breaking the Lore.* The painting depicted the spark that had lit the fuse to all of Ben's troubles, and as he turned his back, he only wished he could do the same on the war blazing around him.

I hope it was worth it. He sent a silent message to the envoy, who probably stood before the gate as he lingered here, preparing the way for the Fay. A darker thought followed this one, the memory of the dead king's eyes, that strange, sour blue light. Ben would never forget it. *You should be careful what you wish for.*

At last Ben reached the staircase that spiralled down into the depths of the tomb. Skulls filled the nooks and crannies around him, forming a wall of a thousand grins, a thousand hollow eyes. But the well between them was empty, a shadowed mouth screaming absence.

There was no sign of du Sang.

Ben let out his breath, his shoulders falling. He realised then that he hadn't honestly expected the Vicomte to greet him, all open arms and fangs. His luck had never been that good. The truth was du Sang could be anywhere – that's if he still lived. *Lived. Right.* The thought had crossed his mind that perhaps Mauntgraul had given the Remnant what he was looking for, a swift and fiery end. If that was the case, then the Vicomte's absence was more than unlucky. It was tragic. Ben swore, the fact sinking in. No du Sang, no information. No information and he was facing King Arthur's army on his own.

Caliburn, hearing him sigh, chose that moment to pipe up.

"I told you this was—"

"Really? You're saying that now?" Ben raised the blade, glaring at the jewels on the pommel. "See that well? I'm not even sure if there's a bottom."

The sword appeared to decide that the argument wasn't worth it. It shone a little brighter, but fell silent.

It was only when Ben lowered the weapon, squaring his shoulders for the long march back to the world above, that he heard a soft snapping sound and noticed the faint glimmer in the gloom. In the brief time he'd stood here, spiders had gathered, emerging soundlessly from socket and jaw, spinning silvery tendrils back and forth. By chance, Caliburn had cut through the strands, his magical radiance picking out the gossamer web that the bugs were currently weaving around him.

159

No. Not around him. From the wall at his back to the wall opposite, the web stretched over the mouth of the well. Even as he watched, the strands met and grew thicker, the spiders clicking and rustling along the fast-expanding web. In the space of a minute, a frayed fan of silk spanned the drop, reminding Ben – with no small degree of discomfort – of the strings of a harp.

But du Sang liked a different kind of music. The whispers of whispers, their desire and design . . . Isn't that what he'd said?

The thought prompted Ben to picture the Vicomte, a memory of the last time he'd come here. Usually resembling a nineteen-year-old boy (though he was obviously much older, with nothing youthful or innocent about him), du Sang had looked terrible, a sack of mismatched bones and rags, a hunger in his rubylike eyes. He remembered du Sang crawling over the web in the middle of the well and plucking at the strands, bending his ear to listen.

The spiders had retreated, bristling on the walls. Ben bristled too, goosebumps sliding under his scales. Every eye in the chamber seemed fixed on him, an expected audience of millions. Were the bugs trying to tell him something?

Don't mind my little spies. It is in their nature to gossip . . .

Ben snorted, uncomfortable. Hadn't he learnt a damn thing? Carefully, he reached out a hand and strummed the taut mass of fibres that stretched beside his head. The web gave a twang, reverberating across the drop below him.

"What is it?" the sword asked, alert in the gloom.

"Shut up and I might find out."

With a wince, Ben lowered his head to the web.

At once, he heard voices. Voices in his skull. A man speaking.

Poor Lambert. Did you honestly think you could hide from us? Your treachery stinks as much as your pit!

Next, he heard du Sang, a velvet knife in the shadows.

Pardonne-moi, sweet Bernat. I did all I could to ensure our survival.

The one called Bernat didn't sound convinced.

You deceived us, amigo. His accent was deep, a rich Spanish drawl. *Consorting with humans behind our backs. Six nights ago, on the night of our rising, we learnt of your Pact. Your bargain with the English devil.*

And du Sang replied. *Then it must fall to the Five Families to judge me, non? I see only one here, the don of House Artigas. What a pity. That the weakest should throw off their coffin lids first.* He gave a chuckle. *The blood blooms in your cheeks, brother. It was always such a handsome face, even in your rage.*

The creature called Bernat hissed.

We will serve till the others awaken. I cannot see the Five chastising us. There came an echo of clapped hands. *Ignasi, Lucia, grab him. Let us take this wretch to the castle. There he will answer for his crimes.*

The web hummed. Ben heard a scuffle, hisses and laughter in the dark. Then the strand fell still, returning to silence, the spiders as watchful as before. *Waiting.* But not before Ben had caught the impression, independent of sound, that the encounter had taken place on this very spot – and mere hours ago – du Sang snatched rudely from his web. Not before he'd heard the curse of the one called Bernat, cold and faint, betraying where he meant to take the Vicomte.

Paris was a dead end. In more ways than one.

Time, as ever, was short.

ELEVEN

Barcelona

Barcelona. The Great Enchantress.

Ben flew south, a tailwind speeding him through the night, skimming the teeth of the Pyrenees. The great crags rose shrouded and dark, a majestic wall between France and Spain that tore at the straggling clouds. Coasting at a low altitude, he saw the flash of rivers in the moonlight, the flicker of campfires below. In a rush of wind, he was over the Andorran heights before he knew it, swooping down into Catalonia and racing for the sea. Hilltop villas and farms went by in a blur beneath him, his tail straight, an arrow slicing over the land. By the time he laid eyes on his destination, he judged the hour at around 5 a.m. In the distance, a jewelled labyrinth blazed with light, luring him on.

Barcelona, the ancient city, spread out from the summit of Tibidabo, the tallest mountain in the Serra de Collserola. Crowning the highest church, Christ spread his arms to bless the glittering vista, the famous grid of streets that stretched, narrow and rolling, to the edge of the Balearic Sea. From above, Ben made out the spires of La Sagrada Familia, Gaudi's monstrous vision of Gothic and Art Nouveau, rising over the district like an ornate cake or a giant spider, depending on one's

162

point of view. A warmth filled him at the sight of the surrounding alleyways, the soft green glow of absinthe bars and rustling trees, shadowed in the wind. In years gone by, he had taken his pleasure in these dark and winding streets, in *taberna* and *bordel*, soothed and entranced by the city's Romanesque chic. He hadn't been here since the end of the Civil War and he greeted Barcelona with a sigh that the locals might call *enyoranca*, a longing for a more peaceful, happier time.

That had been eighty years ago. Barcelona was a faded place, yet her glory lingered, a trace of magic in the soil. In her tall, shuttered facades, her leafy courtyards and broad boulevards, she wore her history with pride. Always a dark city, a maze where lovers kissed in hidden gardens and under archways, there was something that struck Ben as odd as he swooped down from the heights, alighting on the rocky outcrop of Mount Carmel. From the crumbling bunkers, he had a clear view of the city below, and when he closed his wings and held his breath, the wind confirmed his impression.

"Silence," he muttered, keen to break it.

He left the word hanging, an ominous note in the gloom as he drank in the view. This was far from a quiet city. From the rattle of trams to the honking traffic to the music pumping from the all-night clubs, Barcelona threw her revelry into the sky, unashamed of her splendour. *Usually.* Tonight, her streets lay under a strange calm, a stillness that held anything but peace. There was death in the wind too, Ben thought. Death and something else, a flat, metallic sweetness that made him wrinkle his snout and growl. Even the faintest trace of blood at this distance spoke of plenty spilled in the streets below, reminding Ben what he was dealing with, even before the sword piped up.

"Remnants have taken the city," Caliburn said. "Vampires, to be precise. Just like London, everyone has fled."

As if drawing himself in for comfort, Ben rippled and changed, his wings, tail and snout melting into the shape of a man standing on the ledge, his legs parted, the silver blade clutched in his hand. *Vampires. What next?* Such creatures, he knew, possessed eyesight to rival his own and he wasn't about to broadcast the news of his arrival for fear of risking the safety of the one he'd come for. Du Sang was down there somewhere, in the clutches of House Artigas, one of the Five Families. And like it or not, the Vicomte was his only hope of finding out the location of the other Remnants. The Wakeful, like himself, and any others that might've risen from their ancient beds. The matter at hand would take speed and stealth, if he hoped to get out alive. Or – he shuddered at the thought – uninfected. Nobody needed a seven-ton undead dragon feasting on the panicked masses right now; humanity had it bad enough as it was. He had no way of knowing how many *vampyri* infested the city or what that might mean for the residents, but his extraordinary senses had given him an insight as sharp as the sword. And he didn't like the smell of it.

"No," he said. "Some people are still here. Fear like that is strong enough to bottle."

With that, Ben leapt off the ledge. Like a fallen angel, he made his way down into the city, his wings carrying him in half-human form over the rooftops below. He dodged aerials and weathervanes, steering himself against the wind. Rooftiles, plant pots and washing lines scattered in his wake, but no lights came on in windows, no one cursed or shouted, and even the whine and hiss of pets sounded muted to his ears. There were people inside the buildings, however. Hiding. The tang of dread never left his nostrils.

And garlic. Entering the city proper, crouching on the roof of a bank that overlooked the Plaça de Catalunya, the odour mingled with the blood, drawing his eyes to the surrounding buildings. All the windows were dark, every shutter closed, but even from a distance he could make out the strings of bulbs hanging from every ledge, along with a veritable armoury of crucifixes, candles and saintly icons. He imagined that the sight would repeat itself all the way down La Rambla, the long, leafy thoroughfare plunging into darkness to the south of him, a city in hiding.

Judging by the splotches that peppered the plaza below, broad and empty under the streetlights, Ben assumed that the locals knew exactly what creatures had come to the city – or they had soon found out. *Myths come to life, bringing death* . . . But the old tales had served as a warning, at least. That was the best he could hope for. He snarled, trying to dispel the thought of human terror, a sudden shift in the world they knew knocking them from the top of the food chain. The *vampyri* might be few, but the creatures had a funny way of reproducing themselves, tainting the chosen with undeath. With a grunt, Ben accepted it as a threat that the Lore could no longer prevent. In the past, the humans had found ways to protect themselves, with crosses, with holy water and fire, but the memory gave him no comfort. Soon enough, other cities like this one would fall, a realisation he loathed, but couldn't deny. Sea monsters would attack New York. Tokeloshe run riot in Johannesburg. Rusalki rise from the river in Moscow, red-haired and pale, luring men to their deaths by drowning . . . And around the world, would the Remnant leaders, the guardians of the Lore, find themselves as unprepared, as besieged as he was? The thought made sense, for all the threadbare hope it offered him.

If I can somehow reach them . . . It was too late to restore the Sleep. That ship had sailed. All he could do was find a way to resist, to fight back. Despite the coming terror and destruction, it was a battle he could understand, at least. The old scores rising to the surface. The old war resumed.

Thinking this, he focused on the task at hand. The blood glittered in the plaza, not quite dry, and Ben reckoned that this invasion was recent; it had happened a couple of days ago at most. A police car parked askew by a statue, its doors open, its sirens flashing, told him that there had been the expected armed response. He saw further police cars down the Ronda de Sant Pere, one of them wheels-up in the road. The carnage implied that he was looking at the scene of some clash or other and he could only hope, as he tarried here, that the army was already mobilising, preparing a raid on the city. He'd sensed the same atmosphere back in London, the air of a coiled spring. When the humans struck back – as he knew they would – everything would go to hell in a handbasket.

The Remnants were few, granted, but among the risen were things long dead. Things that magically healed and things with untold strength. Dark things. Giant things. Things that the humans only recognised as fiction, bogeymen from storybooks, far from a threat in the "real world". And here, with the presence of House Artigas, Ben had witnessed the first Sleepers to rise *without* the aid of Arthur's horn, a fact that hadn't escaped him. Nor did it surprise him that the *vampyri*, ruled by sunset and sunrise, should be the first to throw off the long enchantment, roused by the echoes of the shattered harp. Scant consolation, too, that only one house had risen, indicating that his suspicions were correct, that the Sleep would unravel slowly. Perhaps as slowly as it had taken to come about, the creeping song of a hundred years . . .

He bit his lip, chewing on misplaced optimism. What did it matter anyway? Most of the Remnants had gone kicking and screaming into the Sleep, or at least unaware of the spell that bound them. Better to expect them to emerge the same way, desperate and wrathful, seeking revenge. Best to prepare for the worst. In the meantime, the humans had grown idle and soft. These days, few carried weapons in Europe, no swords and flintlock pistols on the road. Fighting was expressly a military affair. For the most part, capitalism had bred a society of pampered fools, leaving the poor to scrabble in the dirt, ignored and defenceless. The times had exposed every man, woman and child to a great and terrible truth. Disbelief was no armour at all.

He closed his eyes, suppressing unease. He didn't hold out much hope for them.

It was then that he heard the chanting, a sonorous chorus rising from the tangle of streets to the east of him, deep in the heart of the Gothic Quarter. The dirge of many voices – not one of them living, he presumed – seemed to encapsulate his fear, and sweat prickled on his skin, even as he strained to trace the source of the sound. On silent wings, he bounded over hotel sign and rooftop café, leaping the deep and narrow streets that cut the ranks of new and medieval houses. From the crumbling crenellations of the old Roman wall, Ben peered down into the Placita de la Seu, scanning the cathedral square with wide golden eyes.

The procession emerged from the alleyway under him, passing under a restored arch and filing out into the open. Six abreast and at least fifty long, the train of creatures flowed across the square, each pale face raised to the moon in song. Ben grimaced to hear them, the rude mix of Latin and Spanish offering up the odd legible word of justice and awakening and fathomless thirst. All in the throng wore rags, the dusty leavings of velvet and silk from once-noble finery, all eaten away by the grave. That's where the unholy mob had climbed from, of course, creeping and crawling from some forgotten cemetery or crypt, long buried by layers of Renaissance mansions, Castilian forts and modern-day stadiums. Each glowing ruby eye must've blinked in the shadows of a new age, then grown wide in the sight of a swollen population and the promise of a banquet of blood. A strange mist wove around every pair of marching feet, bearing the crowd in a smoky cloud across the flagstones, past the darkened shops and the abandoned market stalls, under the ornate spires and the leering gargoyles of the cathedral.

From above, the parade resembled a line of insects. *Parasites.* That's what these creatures were, Ben knew. He was thinking how good it would feel to dive from the wall and turn the plaza into a gauntlet of fire, see the dry flesh and brittle bones go up like kindling, when he caught sight of the figure at the head of the crowd.

Du Sang!

Borne aloft by the chanting throng, the Vicomte had been bound by the *vampyri* to a large wooden cross, its hooked, broken arms reminding Ben of the symbol etched outside the boy's tomb in Paris. If he could call du Sang a boy. The creature had endured for nine hundred years, crawling into the modern age like the spiders that he employed as spies, surviving on a diet of rats and God knew what else in the darkness. He had only grown colder and harder with time, as was his nature, eventually able to withstand sunlight and grievous wounds. But handy as that was, Ben didn't think that du Sang would survive this. If anyone knew how to kill him, then it was his kin.

As a Remnant, Ben found it hard to shake off the sympathy nudging his heart. Du Sang had been his friend once, back in a debauched and dissolute time, but those days were long gone. Where Ben had chosen honour and to uphold the Lore, others, like the Vicomte, had merely chosen to suffer it, suppressing a natural inclination to conspiracy and carnage under threat of death. With the collapse of the Curia Occultus, of course, there was no one left to punish him. Duped, betrayed, House Artigas had stepped in to fill the gap.

Stripped to the waist, his alabaster flesh exposed to the night, the Vicomte's body was riddled with stakes. A dozen or more stuck out of his chest, his neck, his arms and legs, the rough jags of wood seeping with blood, staining the ropes around him. Du Sang's wounds belied the withered state of him, his limbs hanging like twigs at his side, his ribcage stark, his cheeks drawn. Even his forelock of hair had crumbled, leaving his head a raw skull, his eyes glowing deep and dull in their sockets. The Vicomte didn't struggle or cry out, seemingly resigned to his fate. With a hawk's gaze, Ben could see the garlic bulb stuffed in his mouth, presumably keeping him weak, unable to vanish in mist or turn into a bat and fly away, if one credited such tales.

Thanking his stars that he'd arrived in time, Ben still didn't fancy his chances against a ravenous nest of three-hundred-odd *vampyri*. Fangs might not be able to pierce his scales, but given time, the creatures would probably wear him down, find the softer parts of him . . . it wasn't was a risk he was willing to take. In any case, such a mob could easily overwhelm him and he couldn't employ fire here either, for fear of setting the old, closely packed buildings alight, consuming the humans along with the leeches in an inferno of his own making. Likewise, the streets of the Gothic Quarter were too narrow to accommodate his full draconic bulk, not unless he wanted to smash through a hundred shops, scattering shoes, postcards, food, pottery, bikes and selfie sticks, reducing the historic district to rubble.

Maybe not. He was going to have to face this in human shape, with added scales for armour. Time was running out, he could feel it in his bones. Dawn could only be an hour or so away at most. Was that why House Artigas had chosen this moment for its little parade? Leading the procession, Ben picked out a tall figure in a tattered cloak, his hair and beard black and lustrous with the signs of a recent feed, his lips and cheeks red and full, his skin otherwise ashen. Was this Bernat, the man that Ben had heard in his head under Paris? The woman beside him, all brunette curls and fangs, was she the one called Lucia? And the brawny-looking man marching alongside them, a hunched and drooling beast of the dark, must surely be Ignasi, no doubt the muscle in this scenario. Their eyes shone with triumph, but filth and decay clung to them, a pall like an open sewer that crept into Ben's nostrils, stinging his eyes. For all the grace of their movements, the grave hadn't done them any favours.

Bernat, the don of House Artigas, led the procession across the square. Ben watched them go, many in the throng hissing and spitting as they passed the cathedral, cursing the arched façade and the statues of the saints, the glory of a god who had long since turned his face from them. In swirls of mist, with an echoing requiem, Bernat strode back into the labyrinthine streets, swallowed by the night.

Clutching the sword, Ben dropped down from the wall and followed, a man, to all intents and purposes, covered in thick red scales.

As he crossed Via Laietana and entered the alleyways again, passing a Starbucks on the corner and an old Roman well, Ben noticed the symbol on the wall, a territorial stamp scrawled in blood. The image, dripping as it was, resembled a hooked crescent, the emblem of the House that he currently pursued. Over this, someone had spray-painted DIABLES CREMATS in Day-Glo green, but Ben knew that it would take more than graffiti to incinerate the devils ahead of him. Keeping close to the wall, Caliburn thrumming, he slipped down the street, heading roughly northeast. For all his size, his feet barely brushed the paving stones. When he turned the corner, however, emerging onto Carrer de la Princesa, it was clear that some in the procession had noticed him. A few feet above him, horizontal to the street – an impossible angle – the woman called Lucia stood with her feet planted against the brickwork, her copper curls and tattered dress hanging down in disorientating shreds. She glared at him with wine-dark eyes, indignation wrestling with her hunger.

"*Buenas noches,*" she said. "But this one is your last, I think."

"I came for the Vicomte," Ben replied, raising the sword. "I don't mind toasting the lot of you fuckers in order to do so."

"You are one man against . . . " Her smile slipped, uncertain, and she paused to sniff the air. He watched her eyebrows spring into arches. "My. You are no man at all. Well, I didn't think it too late for a midnight snack, but instead you bring us a feast."

Ben cricked his neck, crooking a finger up at her.

"Come and get it."

Lucia came, dropping to all fours on the wall and loping

171

towards him, her lips parting in a wolfish grin. Before she leapt, he realised she'd wrong-footed him, distracting him with a direct attack. Too late, he heard the snarl at his back and a cold slab of brawn smacked into him. The impact sent him sprawling into the road.

"Bugger," Caliburn said, the sword flying from Ben's grip, clanging away from him.

Ben's chin struck the ground. Bright spots swirled in his skull and a couple of his teeth went skittering across the tarmac. When he looked up, clutching his jaw and groaning, he had a second to register the woman crouching in the road, her limbs at an angle that no human's should be. Without taking her eyes off him, she lowered her lips to lap at the blood on the ground. Wincing, he stuck his tongue in the hole in his gums, already tingling with warmth, his flesh healing, a new tooth forming. He had no time to savour the sensation. A coldness clamped the back of his neck, dragging him upright and slamming him face first into the wall. Above him, a bar sign swung around its pole with the blow. Glass in a nearby storefront cracked along with the bones in his cheek.

Dazed, he managed to swing out an arm as his attacker wrenched him around, Ignasi's dead, oafish face before him, leering through the fog. It was like being drunk, apart from the fun bit. His fist skimmed off ossified flesh, the bloodsucker dodging the blow, then straightening, his lips peeling back from his fangs. The creature wasn't going to win any beauty contests.

"A Remnant," Ignasi said, sounding vaguely impressed. "But what kind of—?"

Ben showed him. His jaw hung loose, partly shattered, but he managed a grin all the same. *Fangs. Two can play at that game.*

His neck grew longer, a snake weaving up to the first-floor window. Wings blossomed at his shoulders. The leathery membranes rippled over the walls, covering roll shutters, snapping cables and shattering light bulbs. Even as his chest bulged, his expanding scales shoving Ignasi away from him, fire came blasting from his throat. Ignasi screamed, stumbling back into the road, his head going up like a Roman candle.

Lucia climbed to her feet. Wiping her mouth, a smear of red on snow-white flesh, she watched her cohort twist and burn, the flames dancing in her eyes. Ignasi fell to his knees, his limbs smoking, and then he slumped and crumbled against the wall, reduced to ash. Lucia squealed, but Ben couldn't decide if it was dread or delight. When she looked at him, her intoxication was plain, her eyes threatening to burst from her head like overripe tomatoes. Veins slithered and pulsed through her flesh, jumping like cables at her breast and neck, her cheeks flushed and filling out, her skin darkening . . .

It's the blood. Dragon blood. She's jacked on the stuff.

Throwing back her head, Lucia gave a screech, and then she was coming at him again, her hands stretching out, extending into claws. As she drew near, he watched her transform, her pale, human shape giving way to something larger and fouler. *Bestial.* Her rags fell away, her face turning black, bristles of hair covering her skin. Ears sprouted on either side of her head, ridiculously large and cupped. Coals took the place of her eyes, reflecting Ben's alarm. He'd barely recovered his wits as two tons of bat barrelled into him, the impact wrenching him into the air.

In a tangle of tails and claws, Ben and Lucia rose from the alleyway, bashing into the bordering walls. A section of guttering raked across the brickwork, showering sparks. A balcony, all elegant scrollwork and roses, twisted into jags of black metal. Flowers and glass rained down.

Ben roared, smoke pouring from his throat. Even swollen to twice the size of a human, the she-bat was tiny in comparison to him, a hairy little beast squeaking and thrashing against his chest, drunk on the stuff in his veins. Lucia meant to drag him into the sky, but what she intended to do with him there was anyone's guess. Nibble on his wings? She was no manticore, that was for sure. As though pecking at fruit, her head darted back and forth, unable to make a dent in his scales. Still, he was flameless at present, the gases in his belly expelled, and he could do little more than endure her frenzy with gritted teeth.

Tiles scattered as she tried to pull him over the rooftops. Finally, his patience ran out. With a grunt, he simply relaxed, his half-formed bulk sagging under her. He heard Lucia screech again, his weight tugging at her, carrying the both of them down. With a crash, dragon and bat smashed into the road, the tarmac cracking, dust billowing out.

For a stunned second, Ben lay wedged in the alley, his wings trapped by the brickwork. Then Lucia was on him, squeaking and scratching, her bloodlust lending her strength. He found that he couldn't move, couldn't lower his snout enough to blast her off his chest or reach her with his claws. If he remained in dragon form, she'd dig her way through his scales sooner or later, scrabbling for his heart. This presented him with a problem. If he changed back into human shape, then he'd hand the she-bat the battle on a plate, her prey shrinking under her.

Damn it. The thought pricked his ego. *After a dragon, a giant and a manticore, you're going to get your arse kicked by a flying mouse?*

He shook his head, mustering rage, and caught a twinkle in

the corner of his eye. Caliburn, lying flat and discarded in the road. Its pommel stared up the sky, the gems hard and bright, yet somehow long-suffering.

"Don't mind me," the sword said. "I could lie here all day."

Seeing his chance, Ben reached out, his straining arm shrinking in size along with his body. Lucia screeched, flapping her wings, thrown off balance by her diminishing prey. With a grunt, his human-shaped fist closed around the hilt of the sword. The she-bat redoubled her efforts, pressing upon him with claws splayed, but the *vampyr* had run out of time. With a cry, Ben swung the sword up, thrusting the blade at her belly.

There was a flash of light, silver and bright. A whine accompanied the sweep of the sword, distorted like a song heard underwater, but Ben couldn't mistake the tinkle of bells, reminding him of the mnemonic harp. With the thought, *lunewrought* bit into flesh and the air around him shuddered with power.

In his skull, a series of images went whipping by. *A sword flying into a lake, flashing in the moonlight. A hand reaching from the surface to catch it, graceful, sure and brown.* The Lady! *Then he saw the weapon – Caliburn – thrust into stone, sparks showering. The blade penetrated some rock face or other, twisting like a key, a door opening. Snowdon. The slopes of Snowdon. Light, silver, exploded in his mind, dancing over the imagined precipice, igniting a band of indecipherable symbols that arched down into the valley below* . . .

It was only a moment, only a glimpse into the past, the blade awakened by battle. He had seen a Fay circle of protection emanating out from the sword, the great glyphs and the border that edged them aglow with argent health. And he had seen this light before, hadn't he? It was the light of the harp, *lunewrought* shining in the darkness, shining with the last dregs of enchantment.

The magic – it struck him with a surge of nausea in his guts – it was all connected, all one. Light. *Souring. Turning blue.* He didn't know what that meant right now, but he could sense that he was onto something. Another unpleasant truth, knowing his luck.

As the sword slipped under Lucia's ribcage, Ben caught an afterimage on the walls around him, a silvery riddle of glyphs, fading like the echoes of the she-bat's scream. The next thing he knew, he was sitting up in the road, his ears ringing. *Bells. Bloody bells.* Flakes of ash drifted through the air, settling on his cheeks and hair.

Lucia was nowhere to be seen.

In his hand, Caliburn throbbed, a cold, steady rhythm, unmistakably triumphant.

Or smug.

"What the . . . " Ben searched for the words. "Why didn't you say—?"

"Pray, do not venture there," Caliburn told him.

Ben was on his feet in a second, the sword held out before him.

"Come on."

By the time he stumbled into the Parc de la Ciutadella, the broad gardens on the edge of the Gothic Quarter, the vampiric procession was swarming at the foot of its destination. In the western corner of the park, the Castell del Tres Dragons rose from a fringe of palm trees. Ceramic shields hung in a row around the top of the building, following the faux line of battlements. Built for the 1888 Universal Exposition, the square structure of apricot-coloured brick overlooked the park from four grand towers. The north tower rose above the others in a crenellated decagon, a baroque turret of small peaked roofs, each

176

one facing a compass point. Above that, the turret grew slimmer still, a belfry of sapphire glass sporting a crown of elaborate ironwork, the spire culminating in a decorative weathervane.

The Castle was Ben's favourite building in the city. Admittedly, a difficult choice with such an embarrassment of riches. He vaguely recalled courting some widow or other here back in the war, swanning through the leafy surrounds, past the duck ponds and the golden cascade, arm in arm under the Mediterranean sun. A dull ache spread across his chest at the sight of the *vampyri* climbing the building, and as he drew closer, ducking behind bushes and statues, he did so with a feeling that bordered on *offended*. Any reverie evaporated as the pallid creatures scuttled up the sheer walls with all the ease of scaling a ladder, a busying line of ants against the brickwork. Looking up, Ben could see Bernat on the battlements directing his underlings, urging them to caution as, hand over hand, the creatures hauled du Sang on his broken cross up to the heights.

From a distance, the Vicomte resembled a porcupine with the array of stakes bristling from his body. Bernat, on the other hand, appeared to be enjoying himself. Clearly, the don of House Artigas had dispatched his cronies to finish off a presumably *human* pursuit, judging by his arrogant stance and gestures, his cloak fluttering in the wind. *Such theatrics.* Ben gave a sour grin in the dark, knowing that the don was in for a dragon-sized surprise. He watched, counting the moments, as the nest of *vampyri* gathered on the battlements, a handful climbing up to the belfry to rest du Sang's cross gently against it.

"Any famous last words?" Bernat asked, calling up to his prisoner. And when du Sang looked down, the garlic bulb stuffed in his mouth, Ben could picture his expression. "I thought not," the don said with a chuckle. "And so you pay the price for your betrayal."

With that, the creatures were retreating, converging along the top of the wall in a dishevelled line, each moon of a face turned to the belfry. A minute passed, maybe two, and then a silent signal passed between them. The *vampyri* turned and began descending the walls, leaving Bernat alone on the battlements.

As the eastern sky blushed a lighter shade of blue, the fate awaiting the Vicomte became clear. Old as he was, cold and hardened by time, Ben doubted that du Sang could withstand the full blast of the Spanish sun for longer than an hour, particularly when pressed against glass, magnifying its intensity. *You wait for the dawn and the sun gives you blisters, soon healing in the dark . . .* That's what he'd said last winter, a confession that betrayed his vulnerability despite his age. Add garlic and wooden stakes to the sunlight and well . . . things didn't look good. House Artigas seemed to think this a fitting execution, anyway, and that convinced Ben of the danger. Folklore must play a part, after all; he guessed that du Sang would eventually burn, his dry, dead flesh going up like a tinderstick. And with it, Ben's last hope.

The time had come to act. The treetops hissed and creaked as Ben bounded into the sky, the rest of his hominid form unravelling in the sky, lengthening and reddening from snout to tail, the Castle of the Three Dragons joined by a fourth.

Looking up at the disturbance, Bernat swallowed his smile, the shadow of wings falling over him. Cloak flying in the wind, he choked back a cry, the throng of *vampyri* arrested by the noise, glancing back from where they clung ragged on the wall. As one, the creatures released a piercing shriek as Ben came swooping down from the darkness, closing a claw around the broken cross and plucking du Sang from the belfry.

Ben circled the battlements, his tail lashing back and forth. He narrowed his gaze on the tall, handsome and utterly deceased figure that stood under the north turret. For a moment, rage appeared to consume the don of House Artigas and he flung a string of profanity up at the sky, his fists shaking. Then light bloomed across his face, thrown by a radiance behind locked and airborne fangs, descending towards him.

Lights go up. Crowd roars. No time for an encore . . .

Closing his eyes, Ben vented a rush of fire. Below, he heard curses turn into screams, lost in the thundering flames. The battlements rippled in the heat, the turret and the belfry a charred spindle of cracked glass and bursting brick. The ornate crown shrivelled and sagged, a rain of melting iron. Atop the spire, the weathervane spun in the blast, each arrow of the compass pointing at hell.

The inferno spurred the throng to flee. The *vámpyri* scattered, skittering down the castle walls, heading for the shelter of the bordering trees, the cool safety of darkness.

Ben didn't give them the chance. Despite his appreciation of the building below, the park was out in the open, far enough away from the district greater, and he wouldn't miss his opportunity to burn. Filling his lungs, his inner gases flaring, he ushered in the dawn. A pink line broke the horizon, the first rays of the sun touching the sea, but the Castell del Tres Dragons was already aglow. Round and round Ben wheeled, a swift, roaring blur of red, strafing the walls with his fury. A great billow of flame engulfed the building, devouring all in its path. The creatures below danced and shrieked, and when at last he dared to look down, he shivered in satisfaction at the sight of the incinerated nest. Ancient rags went up like paper, not to mention flesh and bone that should've rotted centuries ago, all exploding in cinders and sparks. He watched the creatures cringe against the building, their sheltering arms dwindling to matchsticks, their eyeballs popping from scorched skulls, muck hissing on the ground. On his final circle, he could only see rivers of smoke and fire. The shrieks and screams were echoing into silence. All was ash, scattered by the wind.

Then, with Caliburn in one claw and du Sang in the other, Ben turned his back on the pyre and flew off into the night.

TWELVE

And minutes later, the expected gratitude:

"*Connard!* Imbecile!" The moment that du Sang spat the garlic bulb from his mouth, he had quite a lot to say. "You refuse me dragon fire and now this? You pluck me at whim from certain doom. What have I ever done to you?"

"Well . . . " Ben left the thought hanging.

Du Sang wailed, clutching himself with withered arms, his prune of a face wet with tears. "How long must this go on?" He was asking the night, it seemed, and not his unwelcome rescuer. "Another century? Five? All I want to do is die."

The two of them were standing atop the Arc de Triomf, the huge gate of red brick that loomed over the broad, tree-lined mall leading to the park. Even from a quarter-mile away, the flames lit the sculptures adorning the arch, the noble bats and the angels with their wreaths of victory, but Ben was feeling less than triumphant.

"I heard you the first time," he growled, and he had, months ago under Paris. He didn't have the time or the breath for sympathy. "Is that why you pointed Mauntgraul to the Invisible Church?"

The Vicomte stared at him, his eyes glinting with malachite scorn. Then he seemed to remember who he was talking to. He straightened, lifting his chin with a soft yet audible creak. The motion confirmed Ben's suspicion before the boy spoke.

"*Oui*," he said, without a trace of apology. "With all this anarchy loosed upon the world – your fault, I might add, not mine – *someone* was going to give me what I want. Who better than the White Dog? Dragons, it appears, are like buses. And Mauntgraul was quite, quite mad. The harp had stripped away most of his mind and what he had left was . . . well, *malleable,* to say the least. The fragment in his keeping did the rest, leading us from England to Italy, a bargain I thought beneficial at the time." He smiled, never a pleasant sight. "Nothing personal."

"It felt kind of personal when half the monastery landed on my head," Ben said.

He ignored the Vicomte's accusation, near the knuckle as it was. *My fault* . . . The Sola Ignis, Guardian of the West, hadn't turned out to be much of one. He couldn't argue with that. But that didn't mean he had to admit it, especially not to the sorry bag of bones before him.

Du Sang shrugged. "Like me, you have a bad habit of sticking around." The Vicomte turned to look at the fire, a sigh rattling through him. "No matter. It was all a waste of time. Even dragon fire wasn't enough, *quelle surprise*. Down there, that whole performance." He indicated the building in the distance, blazing merrily, with a flick of his hand. "Knowing my luck, I'd have probably survived it."

"You need a helpline," Ben told him. "And a surgeon."

With a tut, du Sang looked down at the stakes protruding from his body. As Ben watched, the Vicomte began to pull them out, the faint sound of wood scraping against bone making him wince. One by one, the boy dropped the stakes to the ground in a black and sticky-looking pool of blood. Venting the odd grunt here and there, he continued speaking as he did so.

"So the harp shattered, according to my spies. Something

about an old Fay portal and a fiesta of phantoms. You can't have come all this way to ask me for news, Monsieur Garston. The fallout is hardly a secret at this point. So tell me, what *do* you want?"

Ben opened his mouth to speak, but du Sang went on in his usual tone, velvet over thorns. "You'll be looking for your friend the envoy, I'll wager. Has he really got you chasing after him again? *Mon dieu.* People will talk."

"I know where he is. And he isn't my friend."

"Oh? Do you imagine he'll be waiting around on that godforsaken island? Simply for you to try to stop him? No. He's gone, Benjurigan. Into the north. Into ice . . . "

"Sounds like you've had an ear to the ground despite your recent trouble."

"You're always within three feet of a spider," du Sang told him, by way of explanation. "Even up there."

Up there. Spiders could get just about anywhere, Ben knew, and the creature before him had the command of a million of them, whispering along the strands of his web.

But Von Hart would have to wait.

"Something that looks like King Arthur has invaded London," he said, after a breath. "There's a whole army of the fuckers dragged from the Sleep. Or what's left of the Sleep. Arthur's using some kind of . . . magical accelerant. A horn of ivory and gold. A fancy-looking ball-ache if ever I've seen one."

"It's the Horn of the Twrch Trwyth," du Sang told him. He pronounced the old Welsh name "*torc trew-eth*", which was close enough. "I'm sure you're familiar with the myth. After all, it's one of yours."

Ben nodded. *Of course.* He knew the tale, all right. It had been at the back of his mind as he'd lain half-conscious in the ruins of Bala. He was hardly one to sniff at fairy tales, but the story of the boar went way back, back to the earliest days of the Old Lands. The ferocious beast, a cursed prince of Powys, had ravaged the lands between Porth Mawr and the Black Mountains in the once-wilderness of South Wales. After a long and arduous hunt, King Arthur had slain the boar and fashioned himself a hunting horn. Presumably a feast had followed, complete with mead and bacon.

"Yeah, well, thanks to the horn I'm outnumbered. I'd like to call in some back-up."

"But the envoy—"

"The envoy will keep." *I hope.* "I'm not going to leave the humans to die."

"Bold words," du Sang said. With a care that betrayed his affection, the Vicomte raised a hand to his face and Ben could see the spider dangling there, the little creature spinning a thread between his fingers. "I wonder how you intend to go about that. It seems that your One True King has been far from idle. My friend here whispers of a pyre in a grand public square. People in chains, dragged back to the city. Arthur intends to make a great hecatomb, you see. A sacrifice to the Lady. A thousand screams to welcome her return. With fire, with fear, he prepares a throne for Nimue, the Queen of the Fay."

We are not what we were . . .

Nimue's sadness breezed across Ben's mind, the memory making him shiver. Was she sending the cavalry or not? He didn't know what to think, and dreams . . . well, dreams weren't exactly reliable. He was almost too embarrassed to share his insight.

"I had . . . a vision." He shook his head as if to clear it, dispel the memory of the Orchard of Worlds and its strange, celestial fruit. The truth was that the visitation had been no dream, not in the ordinary sense. "The Lady told me that she was coming to help us, to restore the world somehow." *Let your world drink from the font, the eternal source of magic,* she'd said. "Just like the Troth promised us."

"Ah, when *magic blossoms anew in the world.* That old story." Du Sang chuckled, the spider weaving back and forth under his hollow gaze. "Then it comes down to a simple question. Who do you believe? A dead king bent on dominion or a vanished queen offering salvation."

That was easy. "Neither," Ben said. And he meant it. "The Lady reckons that the king woke up because she's opened the way again, the Silver Ley leading to Earth. But Arthur has gone rogue, or so she said, the old spell turned sour. That's why he's doing the whole 'dark side' business. But I'm guessing that's not the whole story."

Never, ever trust the Fay.

"I see. Then you've chosen your path. The path of rebellion. Of war." Du Sang grinned. "*Vive la mort!*"

The light in the Vicomte's eyes, catching both the fire in the distance and the dawn, told Ben that he found the idea rather exciting.

"I didn't choose it," he replied. *That was down to Jia.* "But I'll play the hand I've been dealt."

"Oh? With what? A bad attitude and an antique – *sacre bleu!*"

Ben stepped closer to du Sang. The Vicomte had been staring at the inferno, the smoke billowing into the sky. There was light growing on the horizon, pushing back the night, but the boy didn't seem particularly alarmed by it. Not half as alarmed as he was when Ben raised the sword, the blade flashing.

Du Sang hissed. "*Lunewrought.*"

"Caliburn, actually," the sword replied, all glittering pommel and blade. "The Sword of Albion. And as for *antique*, I think you'll find that I was forged in—"

"One strike." Du Sang cut the weapon off, a hand stretching out, his fingers trembling. "One strike and you'd turn me to dust. End this nightmare. The Fay metal has ever been a bane to our kind."

"Charmed." Caliburn gave a modest cough. "I must confess, there aren't many who can withstand my legendary might. For one thing, I'm unbreakable. For another, I can slice through most things as if—"

"Oh no, you don't." Ben took a step in retreat, raising the sword over his shoulder, safely out of the boy's reach. He'd seen what the sword could do, down there in the Gothic Quarter, and he didn't fancy watching a repeat here. Not yet, at any rate. "I've got a job for you, du Sang. Help me out and later – maybe – we'll talk about it."

The Vicomte hissed again, but he sank back into himself, a bundle of shadows and rags. Ben couldn't help but notice the dawn light spilling across the horizon, twinkling off the sea to the east. Nor could he fail to see the smoke coiling off du Sang, faint tendrils of mist rising from his head and shoulders, his undead flesh responding to the kiss of the sun. He didn't know how long the *vampyr* could stand out here catching a tan and anxiety plucked at him, urging him to leave.

The Vicomte retained his composure, however, wearily accustomed to the break of day.

"You want me to find the Remnants, isn't that so?" he asked, unable to hide his incredulity. "You want me to lead you to the lairs of the Remnant leaders in the hope that they'll come to your aid. Let me see now . . . " A touch theatrically, he brought the spider up before his face again, his lips twitching. "We could've flown to Norway, 'East of the Sun and West of the Moon', but I'm afraid that Jordsønn burned out a couple of years ago. Then again, there's always a tomb in Somalia where you could summon a goddess to fight by your side – that's if you don't mind her possessing a child first. *Problematic.* How about your accountant in London? Is he as handy with an axe as he is with his secretaries? China is out of the question, of course. The Guardian of the East isn't taking any calls."

Before he could stop himself, Ben lunged forward. With a growl, he grabbed the boy around his throat, sweeping him up off the ground. He swung him around as if he was a broom, his feet, skeletal, dangling over the edge of the arch.

"You *will* help me, du Sang. One way or another."

"Be my guest, Benjurigan." The boy shook in his grip, his body wracked by laughter. "If you think dropping me a hundred feet will make you feel any better. You can't blame me for the delicate matter of your, ah . . . *reputation.* Even if I lead you from Mexico to India and back again, you won't receive a warm welcome from a Remnant. The nagual will simply change into a puma and slink off into the hills. The Timingila would sooner drown than rise from her bed in the Bay of Bengal. Besides, how long do you have? Such a journey would take weeks. Months. Arthur will start roasting your precious humans a day or two from now."

Ben swore and let go of the Vicomte, dropping the creature on the roof of the arch. As much as it pained him, he knew that he was telling the truth. Considering the breaches in the Lore, the collapse of the Curia Occultus and the breaking of the harp, it was unlikely that anyone would think of him as Mr Popularity and he imagined that the Remnant leaders had their own shit to deal with, such as cities, countries under siege like his own. There was no point taking it out on du Sang.

187

He looked down at Caliburn, weighing the blade in his hand. "What the fuck am I gonna do?"

"You were never the sharpest tool in the box," du Sang said, a mutter at his back. "There is another way, all the same. I can't say it'll be easy, but . . . "

Ben turned and cocked his head.

"Spill."

"First you have to make me a promise. If I come with you. If I help . . . "

He didn't have to speak further. Ben exhaled and rubbed the back of his neck. Then he raised the sword again, the blade rejecting the Vicomte's reflection, the flames dancing in unsullied silver.

"Seeing as we're haggling, there's one more thing," he said. "When the time comes, when this is over, I'll ask you where I can find Von Hart. Then, and only then, I'll give you what you want." He screwed up his nose, peering down it at the creature on the ground. "I'm not shaking on it."

Du Sang appeared to consider for a moment. Then he gave a tut and nodded.

"Very well," he said. "Then listen closely. I mentioned the Horn of Twrch Trwyth and it's the horn that you want, you fool. The Long Sleep is over, but the awakening will take some time. Years, even. The horn will summon and bind the Remnants to your cause. If you plan to reclaim London, then you'll need to raise an army of your own."

Ben looked up at the sky, faintly embarrassed. Back in Bala, he'd seen Arthur blow the horn for himself, summoning greenteeth from the lake and the manticore from the hillside. In all the chaos since Arthur's awakening, it hadn't occurred to him that he could turn the relic's power to his own ends. Under this, he realised that he hadn't *wanted* to see it. What du Sang proposed was madness, a flight into the heart of darkness, one dragon against a corpse king and an entire battalion of Remnants.

On the other hand, it didn't surprise him that the Vicomte had proposed a suicide mission.

What else is there? You've got nothing left . . .

"Then we'd better get going," he said to the smouldering huddle of bones before him. "Hang around and I might see sense."

Du Sang gasped, a fleshless hand to his chest.

"But look at me, *mon ami*. I am broken. I'm weak. I need time to rest and feed . . . "

Ben's face split in a grin, as cold as the creature before him.

"How do you feel about goblin blood?" he said.

London

A thousand feet above Southwark, King Arthur gazed out over the city, a cold blue light in his eyes. The viewing platform on Level 72 stood partially open to the air, the pinnacle of the Shard rising to a point above him, yet he felt no chill, his flesh cooled by death. The wind stirred his beard, a grizzled rime of hair straggling to his chest, whistling through gaps in the window before him, a slope of reinforced glass supported by outriggers that knifed at the sky. All Hallows' Eve had dawned bright and clear, with only a few shredded clouds. As the sun rose higher, the shadow of the skyscraper slipped across the streets below, across cathedral and museum and bridge, a clock hand counting the hours until dusk. The sunlight gleamed on the horn around his neck, an ancient tusk of carved sigils and gold, silent for now.

With a satisfaction that wasn't his own, Arthur nodded at the thought of his army encamped around the foot of this, his chosen watchtower. Down there, Bedwyr and Galahad, his knights, presided over the ranks of Remnants as the creatures made busy sharpening weapons, tending fires and gnawing on bones . . .

So far, no one from the lands beyond the city had come to challenge him, but the smoke to the west didn't bode well. Nor did the strange metal birds that had shuddered through the sky yesterday at noon, some with blades chopping at the air, a quiver of others shooting past his throne room at speed, close enough to make the glass shudder. In response, Arthur had decided to ride out with his knights and a small phalanx of goblins to quash the manoeuvres on St James's Park, the hustle and bustle there reported as the raising of some makeshift human barracks or other. He'd never been one to hide in a tower, behind ramparts and palace walls. The stairway to the spire was open and he was ready to fight.

But first, he'd make sure to strengthen his defences.

The magic at work in the Shard was aglow, the radiance spilling from beyond the world to ignite the tower like a beacon. Even in daylight, the light flickered and danced, announcing the return of the Once and Future King, drawing enemies like moths to his sleepless flame. The shadow of wings, the wyverns gyring around the spire, slipped and fluttered across his skinless face as he considered the coming battle. Humans. Gathering their nerve. The flying machines had made a pass to survey the damage, weigh up the level of threat. Gargoyles, deployed as scouts, had returned to croak about submerged vessels by the flood barriers to the east, black steel ships that bobbed to the surface, creeping ever closer up the Thames. Machines were rumbling onto Hampstead Heath too, a second contingent churning up dust and smoke. The hour was almost at hand.

Spectral fingers, questing for knowledge, plucked at Arthur's mind, judging the army at the gates. London was a city invaded and soon enough the people would answer, their shock resolving into vengeance. He had a day, two at most, before the vanguard sallied forth, trying its luck. An attack would've happened sooner if not for his wisdom in seizing the people, forbidding them to flee. He may have lost his sword, but his warrior instincts remained sharp. The preservation of London's landmarks aside, few would sit idly by as the last of the lines stumbled into the city, the captives chained and caged. No doubt a litter of viscera and bones painted the main roads into the capital, men, women and children devoured by the horde before they could reach his sacred pyre, his tribute to the Lady and the dark half of the year. The great structure rose from the square as he stood here, readying for battle. Built by the hands of ogres, Taranis, the god of thunder, waited for the dusk.

First, it was time to tip the scales, prepare the battleground in his favour. Having come so far, through rock, through death, the king wouldn't leave his throne undefended. The power that drove him, a spur of unearthly will, intended to buy itself time, and to that end, to make retaliation difficult, human or otherwise.

Machines were one thing. Magic another.

Arthur opened his fist. In his palm lay a sprig, snapped from a tree in a park at his command and brought to him earlier, the returning goblin bowing so low that his wart-ridden nose scraped the floor. The hawthorn, devoid of blossoms in this late season, had grown hard and sharp in the shadow of winter. When he opened his hand, he saw that the thorns had pricked his skin, drawing blood as cold and as black as the twig he held. A small libation, congealed, but royal nonetheless, would fuel the ritual and the spell it sought to weave. The king raised the sprig to his hollow eyes, the western skyline framing the thorns. A voice that did not belong to him echoed from his throat, the charm intoned on a worm-eaten tongue.

> By oak, ash and thorn,
> Nazarene crowned, Merlin mourned,
> Come, come roots with teeth,
> Blood-fed, black and earth born.

For a moment, only the wind whined in answer. Then the platform lurched, a pulse of energy shuddering up the latticed panes before him, the light flaring around the tip of the Shard. A tall, stiff figure, Arthur stood his ground, watching the radiance ripple through the air, a faint circle of sigils spreading over the urban panorama. Deep in the mush of his putrefied brain, he envisioned the spell as his words took hold, seeds of magic sprouting across the city.

To the north, a tremor rumbled under Shoreditch Park, splitting a fountain in two, swallowing a row of benches and scattering pigeons in flight. A tramp rolled out from under a bush, swearing and clutching his papers around him. Time to find a new place to sleep.

To the east, Westferry Circus exploded in a shower of concrete and chunks of earth, the roundabout that had rested upon it splashing down into the Thames.

To the south, Camberwell College of Arts, a grand nineteenth-century building of red brickwork and chimneys, collapsed with a crunch of masonry and shattered glass. Cats and dogs fled together through the haze, barking and hissing. Curious bedfellows in the chaos.

To the west, Nelson's Column, the 170-foot-high monument to the erstwhile admiral, shuddered as the chasm jagged across Pall Mall, circling the edge of Trafalgar Square. Shorn through the middle, the roof of the National Gallery caved inwards, burying Turner's *Fighting Temeraire*, along with millions of pounds' worth of classical art.

Between these points, the great trench ran, rumbling and roaring across London in relentless arcs, each quarter eventually joining to form a circle. Through Mile End and Limehouse, terraces of houses slumped and fell as the streets shifted and sagged. The damage continued across Bermondsey and through Vauxhall, swallowing bus, train, car, lamppost, road sign, statue, shop, garden and tavern. The Thames thrashed as the trench shot across the river into Victoria, swamping both embankments. Lambeth Bridge cracked and fell under the barrage of water, dislodged by the sundering ground. On and on the trench plunged, jagging across Westminster and Soho. Big Ben trembled out an untimely gong. Shops along Tottenham Court Road folded into the spreading fissure, racks of clothes, mobile phones, televisions and foodstuff crashing into the maw. Bloomsbury, Clerkenwell and Angel all found themselves torn apart, bisected by the ambit of the chasm, devouring all in its path.

When the circle finally closed in Shoreditch, a great cloud of smoke and dust rose from the capital, smearing the face of the sun. Birds wheeled across the sky, mired and squawking. A chorus of burglar alarms, barks and cries echoed through the brume, measuring out a breathless minute.

Then, after the seeding, came the roots. At first, the growth was slick and green, new-born tendrils pouring from the trench, a knotted bundle dripping with sap. In no time at all, a hedge was creeping along the route of the trench, travelling from north to south for miles, flowing in an ever-joining wave of vegetation. As the hedge strengthened, rising to riddle through cracks in the ground and writhe up shifted and broken walls, the roots turned grey and then, spearing above lamppost and rooftop, a sleek and tarry black. The twisting stems swelled into branches, coiling from the spell-ploughed furrow. In minutes, the tangled mass had grown as thick as tree trunks, thrusting upwards into the sky.

The Thames, choked by roots, thrashed and seethed, her flow checked. The briar, snaking from the water, lifted boats and snapped jetties, bearing them aloft like lost toys caught in a net. On either bank, random pieces of furniture joined them, as did uprooted toilets and baths, unmade beds and dinner tables, parked cars and the odd train carriage. A telephone box on the corner of Russell Square rode the vegetation up to the heavens, the leaflets stuck to it fluttering down. The briar tore the Union Jack bunting from Piccadilly, the plastic flags punctured and limp. Here and there, people hung in the snarl, some struggling, others not.

With the thicket came thorns, a million, million thorns, each one as large as a tusk, as sharp as a shark's tooth, black in the morning sun. The briar wove across the Oval cricket ground, the famous arena shrinking into shadow. Then it devoured Westminster Abbey, wrapping around the Gothic towers and rising further still. The British Museum, its roof only recently repaired, succumbed to the barrier, as did all the buildings along its path.

Five miles in diameter, a quarter mile thick and five hundred feet high, the thorns encircled the city. The London Eye cowered under its uppermost reaches, the looming barricade at last slowing, the charm fulfilled. *Roots with teeth, blood-fed, black and earth-born.* A dense, impenetrable wall had imprisoned London, a barbed maze of countless corridors where none would dare venture. Where none could enter and live.

King Arthur gazed upon his works, the light of triumph in his eyes. The sky, he knew, remained an open field, but the sky he could watch. The wyverns circled the spire of the Shard, hissing and shrieking, hungry for war. The machines beyond the wall would never force their way through, surely. Not in days. Not in weeks. With a joy that wasn't his own, the corpse king again turned his mind to the great hecatomb constructed in the square below, a stamp of his authority and might. A warning to all who would challenge him.

The Lady was drawing ever closer, approaching her conquered realm.

And the sky would sing with screams to welcome her.

THIRTEEN

Two hundred feet above Bromley, Red Ben Garston hovered in the air, flapping his wings in shock. A shedload of plans had been running through his head, all of them ending in dead ends, except for one slender and dangerous notion. He had an idea to sneak back to his lair, find some way to reach the Remnant leaders that might remain in or around London, come up with a distraction, a way to lure the king into a trap. It was all he had. According to myth, the tales that surrounded him, the Fay had spawned his kind (the *erlscion*, isn't that what the sword had called him?) to serve as protection, as watchdogs or muscle when needed, the rest of the time veiling the truth of their monstrous presence in human form. He hadn't exactly been born as the brains of the operation. Nor was he going to win any medals for military strategy. If all else failed, he thought, then he'd simply have to ram headlong into the Shard, shatter the spire and see what fell out . . .

The wall of thorns gave him pause. Someone – someone with a major skin condition and a golden crown, he suspected – had managed to barricade the city. He couldn't believe the scale of it, the barrier of bramble that snarled from New Cross into the distance, a rough, thick ring rising to challenge the shattered heights of Canary Wharf. From the hub of the thorn wall rose the Shard, aglow with sunlight and the cavorting blue light, although the wyverns around the spire had gone, he noted. He drank in the scene through slitted eyes, his diving-bell heart thudding in his breast. Never a fan of mumbo jumbo, the sight of such a glut of the stuff couldn't fail to perturb him. Such magic belonged to the Old Lands, the age of Merlin and the masters, not modern-day Britain. The panorama afforded him the grim understanding that things had gone south much further and faster than he'd feared. Coupled to this was a deeper wisdom, born from bitter experience. Where were the Lurkers? With all this excess of spell-craft, this blazing beacon before him and the decaying circles, the phantoms, the grey ghosts, should've been ripping the sky apart. Despite his fear of the spectral menace, he didn't read anything good into their absence.

One cannot reignite such magic without understanding the cost, Von Hart had told him, months ago and deep in the nether. *I turned the Lurkers' eyes from the earth. I summoned them here, to feed on a living source of magic . . .*

Ben swallowed a lump in his throat. Was the same thing happening as he tarried here, stalled by the horror below? Had the envoy offered himself as bait again? He'd made off with the Eight Hand Mirror, that was for sure, no doubt digging it from the rubble on Lantau Island. What was he up to this time? If what had happened to London wasn't enough to draw the Lurkers, if the sword in his grip had gone unnoticed, it pained him to think what *was* drawing their ravenous attention.

Du Sang, his desiccated passenger, had his own take on matters.

"*Merde*. Your city is in dire need of a gardener." The Vicomte sat high up in Ben's withers, clutching a fan of horns. "At least a little topiary, no? Perhaps an obelisk here. A unicorn there."

The wind carried off his sarcasm, but not soon enough.

"Shut up. I'm trying to think," Ben growled.

"Oh, so *that's* what it is," Caliburn said, tingling in his claw. "I thought I could hear rocks grinding together."

Du Sang chuckled, making Ben grit his teeth.

"It's a long way down, chaps."

If either retorted, Ben didn't hear them. His nostrils were flaring, catching a familiar scent. Smoke. Smoke on the horizon, drawing his eyes to the west. A thin black spiral stained the sky, rising from beyond the wall of thorns, somewhere out towards Vauxhall or Westminster. Squinting, he made out shapes in the distance, closer to him and airborne, their swamp-green wings spread to catch the wind, carry them over the barricade.

I spy with my little eye, something beginning with "fuck".

Focusing, he counted twenty or more wyverns, the scaly, two-legged beasts weaving through the air like eels, squawking with dumb and vicious hunger. Wyverns weren't fire-breathers like the bona fide *draco* breed and the lesser genus didn't spit venom or gas either. Nevertheless, the beasts had teeth like knives, with claws and tails to match. At three tons apiece, a flock of them could cause a lot of damage, particularly against a human target. Wyverns also lacked the ability to change into human form, hence their absence from these lands for eight hundred years. Back in the Middle Ages, they'd been much like vultures or carrion crows, choosing to peck at the edges of battles rather than launch a direct assault. He'd never seen wyverns move with such coordinated intent before. The sight brought home the fact that the corpse king had bound the creatures in enchantment, chaining them to his will with the Horn of Twrch Trwyth.

Fear crept under Ben's scales, his heart beating faster as he noticed the wyvern riders.

Goblins occupied six of the mounts, a small contingent sitting low in the saddle, short swords across their knees and crossbows slung over their backs. Ahead of them rode the two dead knights, the smaller skeletal one and the big rancid one in the red armour. Both commandeered their own mounts and bore mace and axe respectively. Leading the flock was King Arthur himself, his ragged cloak flying out behind him, his perpetual grin and hollow eyes fixed on his destination. Trailing blue light, as cold as winter and death, the flock sailed over the wall of thorns, heading for the smoke beyond.

"Perhaps we should come up with a better—" du Sang said, but the wind whipped his words away as Ben snapped out his wings, drew in his claws and gave chase.

His objectives were clear. This would be a smash-and-grab job. Loath as he was to give up the cover of the thorn wall, an attack from below wouldn't give him a bead on his target. If the wyverns were anything like him, they were likely to smell him as he approached, so staying downwind was his best bet. That meant climbing for altitude, positioning himself above the king and hoping that no one looked up and saw him, at least before there was a chance to raise the alarm. Successful or no, he was counting on a swift dive towards Hampstead (about five miles to the northwest) to hide himself in the railway interchange tunnel, either to vent a victory cry or for a quick rethink. As plans went, it was about as subtle as a brick thrown through a window, but needs must and all that. If he could grab the king, grab the damn horn around his neck . . .

Speed was key. With a snap of his tail, he thrust himself upward, seeking what cover he could in the shredded clouds, following the aerial convoy as silent as a shark. Du Sang, muttering to himself, pressed closer to Ben's scales, shielding himself from the blasting air. If a stray gust caught him, it could blow him away like a paper bag, rags, bones and all. In Ben's grip, Caliburn, the Sword of Albion, hummed with power, but remained otherwise silent.

Six hundred feet above Westminster Abbey, the grand old building swallowed by thorns, he watched Arthur, his knights and the troop of goblins flit over the top of the barricade. The shadow of wings slipped over the wall, a quarter-mile stretch of evil-looking barbs with only darkness between them. Fall in there and one would become the proverbial needle in a haystack, Ben thought with a shudder, skewered on branches like spears. If he read some irony in the fact that the Houses of Parliament was now as full of pricks in reality as it had been metaphorically, he refrained from venting a snort and kept his sights fixed on his quarry.

He made ready to dive as the convoy coasted beyond the limits of the wall and over Broad Sanctuary, the patches of green between the government buildings where, on happier days, office workers would gather for lunch and tourists used to mill. Now the streets lay empty and silent, the shadow of the barrier stretching into St James's Park. The smoke, he saw, was coming from a series of small fires in amongst a ramshackle encampment set beside the lake, a huddle of caravans and tents dotted across the green in violation of every bylaw known to man. Not that anyone was around to enforce them. The scent of cooked meat and trash curdled in his nostrils as he approached, swooping through the pall. Too late, he noticed the artillery behind the sandbags at the edge of the park, loosely arrayed along the eastern end of Birdcage Walk. Even from a distance, the gun placements didn't strike him as modern, the weaponry an anachronistic gleam of brass handwheels, black iron mountings and barrels last seen, he surmised, sometime around World War I.

James Bennett

Someone's gone and raided the Imperial War Museum . . .

The thought prompted him to turn his attention to the road below. *Humans.* Thirty or more of them bearing rifles, machine guns and shell casings. At the sight of Arthur and the wyverns, a great cry went up and men hurried to wrestle with the machinery, pointing the muzzles skyward. But these weren't ordinary soldiers, Ben could see that. It wasn't the lack of khakis or their panicked movements that gave them away either. It was the leather jackets that each man wore. Ben drank in the sight with a grunt, the black tee shirts, jeans and boots. And the motorbikes that cluttered the encampment, the grass churned up by skid marks. In the rows of Harleys and Triumphs, he was sure he could make out steer horns and skulls . . . Lip curling, Ben realised that he was looking at a gang of dragon-slayers. A banner of Black Knights from House Fitzwarren. What the hell were they doing here?

Mounting an attack. Unbelievable.

He thought this and then he remembered the attempts on his life that Fulk after Fulk had made over the years, riding out on the hunt to answer the Mordiford Shame. Most recently – most *laughably* – a Fulk had tried to kill him on the slopes of Snowdon, the upstart with the old familiar sword. She'd babbled something or other about a prophet, the *lunewrought* allowing the girl to track him. In the events that had happened since, he'd barely given the encounter a second thought, and he didn't have the time now. A surge of admiration at the Fitzwarren courage took him by surprise, however, because he'd only regarded them as futile before, a medieval relic creaking into the modern age, along with a petty vendetta. *Spei est Vindicta.* All that crap. Seeing the knights here, focused on a target other than himself (and one that was no less formidable), struck him as somewhat disorientating. In countless clashes across eight hundred years, he never imagined he'd see the Black Knights as allies.

These musings exploded in shrapnel as gunfire burst from the road below. Alarmed, Ben saw one of the wyverns blasted from the sky, the beast shooting up to the same height as him and clawing at the heavens, a cargo of goblins spilling from its back. The looks on their wart-ridden faces almost made the pain in his eardrums worthwhile. Then the beast was spinning down to crash into the thorn wall, screeching and trailing a spiral of smoke. A handful of goblins tumbled into the trees below, one splattering in a bloody green star in the middle of the road.

But there were other wyverns and other goblins. At a signal from the king, the beasts dropped as one into a dive, Arthur leading the creatures in a low pass over the road and the park beyond. Machine guns barked and people screamed as the wyverns snatched at tarp and metal, dislodging a couple of the tents and the gun placements in a shower of earth and mud. Ben forced himself to look as several of the wyverns returned to the sky with figures struggling in their claws, blood painting the air as the beasts tore off head and limb, viscera splashing down into the lake. Then and only then did he close his eyes, his guts churning. In a matter of seconds, two things had become horribly clear. One, the banner of knights was ill-equipped and outnumbered. Two, so was he.

All the same, as the convoy wheeled over Pall Mall and back towards the park, Ben growled and drew in his wings, meeting the wyverns at the head of the flock with a blustering plume of flame. Two of the beasts went up with a whoosh, leathery pinions reduced to flakes of ash in the blast, joining the drifting smoke. The rest of the flight ignored him, however, eyes fixed on the human target. With cold grace, the corpse king yanked at his reins, the wyvern he rode upon veering sharply to his right and down, dropping to strafe the encampment again. The other wyverns, squawking in glee, followed in a rollercoaster of scales and wings, the goblins astride them swinging axes and swords.

Bullets rattled in response, thudding into serpentine flesh. The knights rolled and dived across tarmac, trying to dodge the aerial assault. Nevertheless, a blade split an undefended skull. A cudgel knocked teeth from jaw. As the wyverns shot back into the sky, the mangled remains of motorbikes and caravans dribbling from their claws, one of the beasts spat out gobbets of blood before crashing headlong into the park, gouging a furrow in the turf. Riddled with bullets, the creature croaked, shuddered and lay still. The next moment, a troop of goblins came pouring from its back, straightening their helmets and swinging their weapons into the fray. Some of the knights turned, their guns raised, firing wildly into the chaos.

Another shell burst beside Ben, smacking him around the ears and flinging him towards Horse Guards, the thorn wall rising from the Parade, dividing the broad white square. Grunting, he regained control of his wings, narrowly preventing himself from crashing into the briar, impaling himself on the thorns. With a snort of smoke, he flexed his muscles, ready for another sally. Wings spread, tail weaving, he flashed to the top of the barricade, just in time to meet the wyverns that were circling around again, his lungs ballooning, his jaws flowering with heat. This time, he lunged at the convoy side on, his claws splayed (one claw gripping Caliburn, a chill prize), following up his barrage of fire. He gave a roar as wings flurried around him, a section of the convoy breaking apart, hurled in all directions. Screeches rang in his ears, the wyverns snapping at him, their fangs splintering on crimson scales.

Any satisfaction that Ben might've felt evaporated as he watched the king swerve away from him, plummeting to sweep along Birdcage Walk, his mount plucking artillery and knights from the road. *Slippery bastard.* He made to follow, shaking off the scattered flock, when he felt an added weight on the back of his neck and heard du Sang cry out, some French profanity lost to the wind. Someone, a goblin most likely, had leapt from one of the passing wyverns and onto his back. In a second, the Vicomte found himself unhorsed, a bundle of rags and bone flung from the saddle, his limbs flailing. With a curse of his own, Ben turned from the sight of du Sang tumbling toward the rooftops below, but his concern wasn't for the vampire. Pain shuddered down his spine as steel sliced under his scales, hacking at the flesh of his withers.

Acting on instinct alone, Ben rolled in mid-air, a necklace of blood showering around him. He barked in delight as the one who sought to straddle him lost his footing and spun out into the air. *Smart move, numbskull.* And *numbskull* was right. Grizzled he was, this pale, dead thing in his blood-red armour, his eyes squirming with maggots, empty of conscious intent. Even as he fell, the corpse knight swung out his double-headed axe, an echo of skill from long ago and long since swallowed by the grave. In response, Ben shot out a claw and grabbed his assailant. Snarling, he squeezed, reducing the knight to splinters of bone, scraps of metal and fading blue light. Dead things, he reckoned, should stick to the tomb, where they belonged.

With flakes of dry flesh drifting around him, Ben turned his attention back to the battle. Completing another pass, the wyverns had left little standing of the Fitzwarren encampment. A couple of tents remained intact, albeit leaning to one side, but most lay flat on the grass, torn to shreds by passing claws. Across the sward, the knights were fighting it out with the goblins, their rifles raised to parry blows from axe and sword. Other men used the trees to hide behind, darting around the trunks now and then to shoot into the rabble. Along the road, the gun placements had fallen silent, abandoned and unmanned. Bullets sparked off helmets and clipped shields, and goblins fell left and right, but even a glance told him that the knights couldn't hope to win this battle. On the back of every jacket, he caught flashes of the Fitzwarren coat of arms, as wearily familiar to him as his view of the grudge: the hawk of perseverance on a field of gules. Well, perseverance was the last thing he could fault the knights for, but black leather was no match against wyvern teeth and a hundred swords. Soon, the ammo would run out while the dead king wheeled above.

As the convoy swooped away, rising from the park in a wicked murmuration over the streets beyond, Ben traced the battle up to the lakeshore. There, by the bridge, he saw the spark of steel meeting steel and he let out a gruff breath of recognition. Lord knows how long she must've searched the valley, travelling from Whittington to scour the slopes of Snowdon. Rather that, he guessed, than face the fury of the patriarchs. She held the old claymore with both hands, swinging the charred blade at the goblins as further troops swarmed across the bridge. He wanted to put her success down to the length of the sword rather than skill, but he had to admit that she wasn't entirely untrained. What Black Knight was? That didn't account for her presence here, all the same.

Fool of a girl . . .

A decapitated head, the size and colour of a watermelon, sailed through the air as if to confirm his assessment. And when she took a hand off the hilt, letting the blade thud into the ground while she fumbled for the pistol in her belt, he grunted in respect as she shot an approaching goblin in the face.

Cade. Annis Cade. That was her name.

At least she'd dispensed with the spiked helmet. Considering his mood, the sight of the Lambton Armour wouldn't help him any. She'd found a new jacket from somewhere, he saw, the heraldic hawk painted on the back, but it hung a little loose on her. In daylight, her hair looked vaguely medieval, her shorn black bob swinging in time with her sword. *Squire chic.* The Fitzwarren family, he knew, was never going to win any fashion awards.

Cursing, he dived towards the bridge, his draconic proportions dwindling as he plunged through the trees, the branches thrashing around him. He landed in a swirl of leaves, his feet leaving claw marks in the turf moments before they shrank to pink and five-toed size. A second of concentration and his scales ceased slipping into human skin, a layer retained to cover his nakedness, the meditation easier now, the conjured shape of his suit held at the back of his mind. At his ankles, wrists and neck, his scales blended smoothly into his flesh, his face the usual illusion of scars, sneer and green eyes. On his head, his hair stuck up like an out-of-hand fire, the ends crackling with absorbed heat.

With Caliburn thrumming in his grip, he lumbered up to the girl by the bridge.

"Thought I told you to keep out of my face," he said, shaking the sword at her. "What do you hope to achieve with this crap?"

"I'm in *your* face?" she shot back without looking at him, slashing at the oncoming horde. "I don't remember asking for your help."

A goblin ran up wheeling an axe. Ben dodged the blow and

punched the creature in the head, his would-be assailant slumping to the ground.

"It's your funeral," he told her. "It just so happens to be the funeral of every man out here as well. There's no way you can win this."

Annis glanced at him, her light brown face pulled into a sneer, but she couldn't hide the fear in her eyes.

"Then we'll die with honour." The claymore swung down, chopping off a green-skinned arm and the short sword on the end of it. Blood sprayed, the colour of the grass they stood upon. "The banner rallied to my call. London is under attack." She nodded at the sky, at the wyverns overhead. "Some of us won't sit back and watch."

"Thirty-odd men 'rallied to your call'," he said. *And why?* he wondered. *What's so special about you? Sure, you're related to a chosen knight, but . . .* "Drop the Prince Valiant act. This looks pretty desperate to me. And I'm guessing your patriarchs didn't approve of it either." He remembered her on the mountainside, whining about some past injustice, a drowned boy and a forbidden knighthood. Ben wasn't a big fan of tradition – he'd been on the sticky end of it one too many times – but he knew how this stuff worked. No daughter of House Fitzwarren had ever got to play slayer. Not till now, anyway. "You're a rebel, Annis Cade. Trying to win brownie points, am I right? Well, your *honour* is about to get you killed."

"Get with the times, dino breath. This isn't twelve fif—"

Dino . . . ? Patience running out, Ben stepped up to the bridge. He twirled the sword, a hum of energy through the air, and struck out at the goblins charging across the span. He hissed through his teeth as the sword slashed back and forth.

"I . . . don't . . . have . . . time for this shit."

With a sweep of the blade, the scene shuddered around him, vibrating with power. The jewel-studded weapon felt light in his grip, lighter than any sword had a right to be, and as *lunewrought* bit into Remnant flesh, his skull once more spun with images, echoes of an earlier time.

He saw the sword protruding from an anvil in a broad paved square, a man in armour heaving at the hilt, his brow slick with sweat. Then the image rippled, and a boy replaced the man, a gangling, sandy-haired squire in threadbare tunic and hose. With a cry, the boy pulled the blade free and Ben knew that he was looking at Arthur, a young Arthur before he'd stepped up to his destiny, ascending to the throne as the Once and Future King. Runes, blue as sapphires, shot out from the anvil in a great arc as the king drew Caliburn for the first time, the radiance blinding to look at, a mile-wide beam of light shooting across the rooftops of Dark Age London . . .

A Fay circle of protection, triggered by the sword . . .

Ben blinked, the light and the knowledge shivering through him. Time quivered, a web releasing him, thrusting him rudely back into the present.

The goblins had stopped charging across the bridge and lay in a heap at his feet.

Dead. All dead.

Bewildered, he let Caliburn fall, the tip of the sword sinking to the ground with a deep thrum of satisfaction. When his vision cleared, he could see the park again, obscured by light only for a moment, a few seconds out of time. The glyphs, however, continued to glow, riddling out from the ground at his feet. Astonished, he traced the symbols into the trees, the huge, il-legible markings dancing over the lake – *under* the lake – and off into the city. Did the glyphs seem brighter than before? *Yeah. Just like in Barcelona.* Their sour glow was ripening to silver, sparkling with returning health, he saw . . . It was strange to pick the glyphs out in daylight. Even as he stared, the circle shone to a near blinding degree, sparked, ignited by the magic of the sword. Of that he had no doubt.

Then, in a flash, it was gone. The circle had vanished.

What does this mean? What the hell are you trying to tell me?

Before he could ask Caliburn, Annis let out her breath with an awed profanity. When Ben snapped his head around to look at her, he found the girl staggering backwards, her sword scraping along the ground. At first, he thought she'd noticed the glyphs too. From the way that her gaze stayed fixed on the bridge, however, he realised that she couldn't see the Fay circle of protection. Presumably, the *lunewrought* manacle she'd carried wouldn't have had an effect on her, human as she was. No. The vision was his alone.

Frowning, he looked at the bridge. Or what was left of it.

A mangled lump of concrete and metal hung over the lake, a good ten feet of the span shattered and fallen into the water. Goblins swarmed along the twisted railings, spitting and snarling on the broken edge, unable to reach them. A single sweep of the blade had reduced the bankside section of the bridge to rubble.

Impressive.

"Perks," the sword said, as if in answer to Ben's thoughts.

Grinding his teeth, Ben jabbed a finger at the would-be slayer. It was time to put an end to this nonsense, send the girl home.

"Look, sweetheart—"

Annis flinched, but too late, he realised that it wasn't due to him. The trees thrashed around him, the wind rising, howling in his ears. He spun on his heel in time to see one of the wyverns dropping from the sky, the embattled knights diving to the left and right as the beast came sweeping across the park. On the wyvern's back, the corpse king sat and grinned, his eyes shining like the blue blazes.

The next moment, a slab of scaled flesh smacked into Ben, a claw snatching him up off the ground, bearing him aloft. One by one, he felt his ribs crack, the sword flying from his grasp with the impact. Caliburn spun through the air and clanged across the path below, wheeling once, twice, and then thudding point-first into concrete, the jewelled hilt quivering.

Ben caught the sword's comment as he soared skyward, faint, but no less bitter.

"Typical," it said.

Biting down on the pain in his chest, Ben tried to focus, exert a practised flash of will.

You're punching above your weight, newt face.

Spurred by innate magic and rage, his scales blossomed around his expanding girth, his face stretching into a yards-long snout of yellow fangs. His tail burst from his spine in a chain of muscle and horns, the arrowhead tip lashing back and forth. His humanoid limbs swelled into forelegs and haunches, each one ending in unsheathed claws. Like a bloodstain on the sky, his unfolding wings dwarfed the wyvern that clutched him, the creature left scrabbling at his breast, alarm warbling from its throat.

Ben grinned. Closing a claw around the wyvern's tail, he drew in his wings and relaxed, allowing gravity to do its work. A few seconds later, seven tons of draconic flesh smashed down into St James's Park lake, dragging the wyvern and the dead king with it.

The surface seethed, billows of steam hissing off the water.

A minute passed. Then Ben emerged from the bubbling muck. Red-scaled, horned and spitting out weeds, he clambered up onto the bank, ignoring Annis's slack-jawed stare and limping towards the sword sticking out of the ground. If Caliburn could do that to a bridge, imagine what it could do to old bones and rotten—

"Look out!"

Arthur, still mounted, burst from the lake behind Ben. Mud dripped from his naked skull, weeds straggling in his beard. His crown, dragon-shaped and much like a torque, gleamed with beads of water. The relic around his neck, the Horn of Twrch Trwyth, sparkled and shone, an impossibly dangling carrot. *I've got to get my claws on it somehow* . . . The wyvern shrieked, scattering Ben's thoughts. Thrusting itself forward, the beast lashed out its tail, tearing up a wall of leaves and dirt.

Ben's breath flew from his lungs, his forelegs lifting off the ground, the wyvern's tail smacking into him. A knot of limbs, he flew across the narrow stretch of water and crashed down into Duck Island Cottage, tiles, feathers and bird shit flying. Shaking himself, he rose from the rubble, the roofbeams sliding off his head. He vented a curse, a growl of *wyrm tongue*, but it had barely hissed between his fangs when spread wings and a bone-white grin eclipsed the sun. The wyvern was smaller, granted, but the beast had caught him off guard. Once again, claws outstretched and screeching downward, the wyvern plucked his stunned form from the ruins and flung him into the air.

As he tumbled, his shoulder caught the edge of the Guards Memorial, chipping the Rudyard Kipling inscription. Chunks of granite bearing words like *God* and *Glory* went scattering across Horse Guards Road. When Ben climbed to his feet, groaning and crawling towards the Parade, all he could see was a cloud of dust and broken stone. All he could taste was blood. It dribbled from his snout, speckling the gravel under him.

212

Directly ahead, the barricade loomed, a monstrous wall of thorns. He'd find no shelter in its jagged hollows. The briar had swallowed the turrets of the Admiralty and the Cavalry Museum, soaring hundreds of feet into the sky. To his right, Lord Mountbatten clutched his binoculars atop his plinth and observed Ben's position with bronze-eyed solemnity.

Limping, Ben turned to watch Arthur land, the wyvern alighting on the edge of the Parade, its wings throwing up dust. The beast cackled deep in its throat, its gaze reptilian and dumb, but its hunger was nothing compared to that of the king, who fixed his prey with a look of cold and unfathomable triumph.

There was nowhere to go. Beyond Arthur, out on the park, the cries were fading, the odd machine gun stuttering, but gradually falling still, the skirmish obviously quelled. Ben swallowed, his heart sinking. What the hell had the Black Knights hoped to do here? Would the goblins round up the few surviving men or kill them where they stood? He spared a thought for Annis Cade and her ill-advised heroism. Would she find ending up as fast food for the horde an honourable death? he wondered. He had no way of knowing these things. As the wyverns circled overhead, cutting off his escape route, all he knew was the old familiar taste of his failure.

He spat a star of blood on the ground. The king had him cornered. He was out of breath, his lungs aching, seconds away from summoning heat. If he was to meet his maker here, then at least he'd do so in true form. Perhaps he'd give Arthur something to think about as the looming thicket went up in flames. His ribs screamed, encompassing the girth of his heart. Rearing up on hindlegs, he spread his wings, a scarlet cloak thrown over the briar. His jaws parted, embers coiling in his throat.

High in his saddle, Arthur opened his fist. In his palm lay a sprig, some kind of cutting from a tree. Looking down on the wyvern, Ben strained to make out the object in the king's hand. It was hawthorn, he thought, stripped of blossoms. A hard, sharp twig, black as the thorns strangling the city.

Puzzled, he tipped his head. The king was chanting something, soft and sweet, the incantation lost to the distance and the fire rumbling in his breast.

Mumbo jumbo. I'll be damned if I give you time to—

A vice around his throat choked off his ire. With a bark of shock, the flames went thundering back down his throat, smoke puffing from his nostrils. As the heat dispersed, absorbed by his serpentine lungs, a fresh web of pain riddled his body.

Fuck. Struggling, he felt further bonds snaking around him, the coils tightening around his hindlegs, his belly, his snout.

What the fuck? Thrashing against his bonds, he wrenched his gaze downward to see a questing branch, as slender as birch, spear through the membrane of one wing, the emerging thorns slick with blood. Then he grunted and flinched, a prong shooting over his brow, narrowly missing his eye. Yet more thorns writhed over his claws and looped around his tail, binding him in a sharp embrace.

No. Brambles crushed his other wing, lacerating the skin between his pinions, the strips dripping with blood. The pain mounted, the spellbound briar quickening. Thorns pierced him, the sensation like a thousand blades sliding under his scales. Knives of living wood punctured his spine, stabbing muscle, scraping off bone. Blood pooled on the ground under him, spreading in a steaming tide across the Parade as, slowly but surely, his struggles grew weaker, the thorns tighter. The sky became faint, a gyre of wyverns, cawing in distant requiem. Numbness burned his chest, his back. A prison of thorns closed in a ball around him, fanged and black.

Ben screamed. Pain tore through him, drowning all thought. All he could see was the corpse king straddling the wyvern below, his palm raised, his skull turned to the wall of thorns and the great red dragon impaled upon it.

And his eyes, those burning blue hells.

Arthur, the Once and Future King.

Arthur, *dragon-slayer.*

FOURTEEN

Dusk. All Hallows' Eve.

At an unspoken signal from the king, the goblins climbed the thorn wall. In a tide as thick as ivy, the creatures made short work of the briar, hacking with axe and sword. By the time the wyverns plucked Ben free, from where he'd hung mounted on the branches like some fabulous trophy in a feasting hall, he was slipping in and out of consciousness. Loss of blood and fatigue conspired to weigh him down like lead. The thorns, each one a yard long, remained lodged in his body, pinning any chance of recovery. Heat tingled around his wounds, his flesh slick, raw and feverish in countless places, but the thorns neither withered nor withdrew once severed from the thicket and, unable to move, he had no way to eject them. Nor could he risk changing into human form, using his dwindling size to slip out of the snare. For one thing, he'd seen the king manipulate the briar for himself (*hawthorn, a sprig in his hand*) and he suspected that his bonds would shrink along with him if he made the attempt. For another, his present bulk stood a better chance of keeping the thorns away from his heart. Arthur meant to slay him – he didn't kid himself otherwise – but if he'd learnt anything at all about knightly conquests, then the king would want to make a show of it, dead or no.

What residual instinct echoes in your brain? Ben mused as the wyverns clutched his horns, drawing his heavy-lidded gaze up to the bearded skull above him, the king sat high in the saddle. *Do the worms chew on your chivalry, Arthur? You'd weep to see yourself. There's nothing left of you but blue light and ruin* . . .

The Dead and Buried King had no answer. Six or more wyverns had borne Ben aloft and, wings flapping overtime, carried his limp and bleeding body up and over the top of the barrier, rudely depositing him on the other side, onto the flagstones of Trafalgar Square. The square lay in shadow, dwarfed by the wall of thorns, but it was far from empty. A mighty roar went up at the sight of him, clubbing his stunned and wheeling brain. Filth and sweat stung his nostrils. Some of it, he noted, *human.*

Groaning, he looked down on the rabble, his gathered audience, welcoming him to the arena of his defeat. From the steps of the National Gallery to the four bronze lions crouched around the base of Nelson's Column, the horde spread out in a bristling carpet. Goblins hollered and bashed their swords against wooden shields. Greenteeth cackled, dragging their hunched, bony forms up to the inside edge of the fountains, the grand Victorian cascades silent, the waters stagnant, black with weeds, blood and shit. Bugbears looked up with round yellow eyes and open beaks, their ursine bodies aquiver. Ghouls, gargoyles and shucks slinked at the eastern limits of the square, eyes glinting from the shadows of the wall. A pair of hounds, skeletal, frost-eyed, barked and howled to see their master return. The throng parted, a jubilant sea, as the king descended with his prize.

For a time, there was darkness, but no dreams.

When Ben opened his eyes again, he found himself sprawled between the fountains, bound in thorns. The first thing he heard were the screams, a shrill reminder that no one was coming to help him. It wasn't the most pleasant of waking thoughts, but there it was, grim and undeniable. Pain shuddered through him, his wounds pricking him to semi alertness. Where were the other Remnants? The chosen leaders of the British tribes, untouched by the Sleep and protected by the Pact? Delvin Blain and Bolgoth Clave, for starters, though he realised that the former was an accountant and the latter a racketeer. Both would've fled if they had any sense.

Just like the Old Lands, you're over.

He knew it was true. The Old Lands were precisely that. Old. A polite way of saying *dead and gone*. As for Von Hart . . . Well, it seemed that the envoy had been right all along. Magic was souring and so was the Sleep. He couldn't afford to doubt it any more, afford the luxury of denial. Even as Arthur sounded his horn to summon forth the Remnants from their disenchanted graves, how many others lay grey and rotting beneath the earth? Dragons. Unicorns. Dwarves. How many fabulous beings and beasts would this world never see the likes of again?

A worm gnaws at the heart of things . . .

What was that worm? he wondered. Betrayal? Grief? Time? *No . . .*

For a moment, it felt as though the thorns had reached his heart, piercing the core of him, because an unexpected sadness gripped him. Here, at the end, he was on his own.

Aren't we all?

A deeper notion followed this, like a chiming clock in a cold hall.

I'm dying. And he didn't just mean from blood loss, his extraordinary healing abilities checked by the cage around him. *I've been dying for a very long time.*

Yes. Fulk had told him two years ago. The modern age held no place for him. For a while, he'd been able to pretend. Maud.

Rose. A thousand women in between. He'd sought comfort in their arms, hiding from the truth. And the Lore had given him structure, a vital role as the Sola Ignis, some kind of code to live by. These ingredients had nourished him over the years, given him a reason to go on. But time had stripped him of his illusions, dispelling the fairy tales he'd once held so dear. Lying here, with blood in his mouth and his breath running short, reality didn't feel like a happy ending.

Another chorus of screams drew his eyes up to the plinth before him, flanked by the figures of four black lions. From the great pedestal, the Corinthian pillar loomed, 160 feet high. Cast in stone, Lord Nelson stood at the top, surveying a battle two hundred years gone.

How humans love to celebrate bloodshed. His sluggish brain had no room for compassion. *Monuments in place of sunken ships, cannon fire and thousands dead . . .*

Judging by the effigy above him, the wooden giant propped against Nelson's Column, he couldn't think any better of the Remnants. The looming structure, constructed entirely from timber and lashed rope, hid a full two thirds of the pillar from view. It resembled the figure of a man, his latticed arms parallel to his body, his stubby legs parted on the plinth. The effigy – which Ben recognised as a god, recalling tales of the Old Lands – had a boxy torso and square shoulders, the structure crowned by a head of tightly meshed branches and leaves. As he focused, his flesh prickling, he could see the ogres in their fur-trimmed cloaks and powdered wigs hacking and sawing at the logs piled up at the foot of the steps, the trees presumably felled along the Mall and dragged here for construction. Chunks of wood clopped to the flagstones, the sawdust at odds with the creatures' fine buckled shoes, their hooked nails bursting from the leather toes.

But the wicker man was complete, Ben saw, and the ogres weren't chopping wood to build him any higher.

Oh, Jesus Christ! No!

He'd heard about such things before. Back in the Old Lands, when the era that the humans would call the Iron Age had mingled freely with the magic of another world, the druids had held many a ceremony on hilltop and in forest glade, making offerings to the gods like the one above him. Taranis, the Celtic god of thunder, if memory served. Taranis, the fire in the skies. With flowers of flame, the tree priests had appeased the Great Forest that had covered most of Albion in those days, begging for protection from wolves, witches and worse. Holding to an oral tradition, the druids had never written down their secrets, and the whispers about the nature of their offerings came solely from the Romans, who'd looked on British shores with jealous eyes. And along those shores, the druids had fought to repel the legions time and again, raising mist and sea winds, summoning storms to wreck trireme and skiff, frustrating Julius Caesar himself. But eventually, Albion – Britannia – had fallen. In revenge, a succession of emperors had struck the druids from the annals of history and Ben didn't know whether he was seeing a historical reenactment or a mocking defilement. So much around him stank of corruption, he suspected the latter.

It didn't matter. What mattered was the people. Humans, a thousand or more, crammed into the towering effigy. The sight stung him like no thorn ever could, row upon row of ragged, filthy people. Men, women and children packed into the prison so tightly that their arms and legs stuck out between the bars and their faces pressed, dull and fearful, against the lashed branches. Amid the press, Ben realised, some squirmed and struggled for air, crushed by the surrounding people. Screams and shouts issued from the captives, a ceaseless chorus in the dusk, the sun heedless, low and red as it sank behind the thorn wall. But the noise struck him as oddly muted, an exhausted, melancholy blare, and the silence beneath it seemed louder. Up and up Taranis soared, his bones hard and unyielding, his body stuffed with flesh. Sweat and shit sullied the air, the pervasive odour of terror. Of certain doom. Here, Ben made out a fair-haired child clutching a ragged doll, the both of them black with soot. There, an elderly woman stared down with wet, milky eyes, taking in the rabble with a look he recognised as weary belief. Like himself, these poor souls had had incredulity ripped from them. In horn, claw and fang, the humans above him had come to see the truth of the world, rudely unveiled with goblin whips that cracked back and forth, driving them back to the city to fuel the dead king's hecatomb.

Ben couldn't know the purpose of such a massacre. He didn't *want* to know. The wooden god struck him as a manifestation of everything that had gone wrong, the long oppression of the Pact hiding the truth of the world, a wound that had festered over centuries, finally exposed to the harsh light of day. Arthur was the embodiment of the chaos, he knew, a living symbol reborn, albeit one perverted and sour. *How long does the fruit stay ripe when cut from the branch?* Small wonder that the king should command such a ritual, beseeching long-dead gods in the destruction.

Gods. Or . . .

Alas, we are not what we were . . .

Like it or not, he couldn't shake the fact that he was looking at the result of magic. The king with his wintry gaze. The harp and the broken Sleep. The decaying circles and the Remnants gathered in the square . . . All of it had one source.

The Fallen Ones. The Fay.

And where there was a king, there was often a queen. Arthur and the Lady had history, didn't they? A history woven on the loom of time, the very fabric of Britain. Why should *now* be any different? The Lady wanted the sword. And how Ben empathised, itching for the weapon. Caliburn, he reckoned, would make short work of his bonds.

He was thinking this when the smell of smoke spiralled to his nostrils, joining the pall of jubilation and despair. This was a ritual, all right, and he was part of it. He looked up and saw the ogres chucking torches onto the pyre stacked around the wicker man's feet and it was painfully clear that one of the last things he was going to see was a human inferno. Hell, he'd probably wind up on the barbecue himself, ending his days as a draconic version of filet mignon for Arthur's army.

That's why you're not dead yet. He wants you to see this.

Arthur. Or . . . whatever force drove him.

He heard a shout, carrying his name, and craning his neck, he noticed the leather-clad figures locked in the effigy's head. *Black knights. The few who survived the battle, anyway.* Squinting, he located the source of the cry, the girl stretching her arms out between the bars, looking down and begging him to help her, to help them. *Annis Cade. The last Fulk.* Considering the scene around him, the conquered state of London, he had a feeling he was right about that – at least, she was the last slayer *he'd* ever face. But she looked anything but triumphant. Taking in her expression, he let out a groan, his snout sinking to the flagstones. Her desperation was as futile as his own, his cage spellbound, invulnerable. Still, he acknowledged a grudging pang of respect as the reason for her presence here dawned on him.

The gun placements in the park. It was a rescue mission, wasn't it? You wanted to save the captives. Instead, you've ended up joining them . . .

Annis was a fool. They had that much in common. But the last thing he wanted was to see her pay the price for her attack, her cropped hair and scrawny frame going up in flames. For all that, the would-be slayer had brought this on herself. There was nothing he could do for her.

You and the rest of Logres, honey.

His thoughts were sluggish, addled by pain. A fresh chorus of screams snapped him back to alertness, letting him know that the humans in the lower part of the effigy's torso had seen the smoke too – and felt the flames licking up around its legs. How many minutes did he have until the fire took hold, crisping an old woman's hair, devouring a ragged doll? Ben could feel time slipping through the hourglass of his fear. He struggled in his bonds, his tail thumping against the side of a fountain, but it was no use. The thorns gripped him, sinking further into his flesh. He only succeeded in smearing blood across the flagstones. His head swam as the branches grew tighter around his neck, preventing the chance of mustering his own inferno. Did he even have the energy?

Straining against his bonds, he noticed Arthur emerge from around the plinth, standing below the bronze lion to Ben's right. The king appeared to have no fear of the flames at his back, even as the ogres withdrew, their task complete, one or two patting embers from their cloaks. Armour rippling in the rising heat, Arthur merely gazed at Ben, his eyes a cold mirror to the flames. His grin related blind triumph.

Catching Ben's gaze, the king raised his hand, opening his palm as if to say, *Look. Look upon my works . . .* He was close enough for Ben to see the sprig of hawthorn, black against his

223

enervated flesh. His serpentine vision spared him nothing. He could even see the beads of blood on Arthur's skin, congealed and dull. And he felt the thorns around him pulse in response to the gesture, loosening a small degree, enough to draw the stakes that pierced him inches out of his body, his anguished roar joining the orchestra of dread above him. Such a little sprig, the evident fetish to a spell that had bound London and brought down its guardian dragon.

He wants you to know that you've failed . . .

Ben didn't need a reminder. He glared at the king, defiant. Then he blinked, some mote flickering across his eye. At first, he thought he was looking at a flake of ash, drifting from the effigy. *Those screams. The soundtrack to my downfall.* But the flake moved too erratically for that, jerking its way across Taranis's knees and dipping in a series of aerial steps toward the lion where Arthur stood. Squinting, Ben made out wings, tiny and black, and heard faint squeaks as the creature made its awkward dive. He realised then that he was looking at a bat – a fucking *bat* – come flapping out of the dusk from gods knew where. He groaned again, this time inwardly, even as his heart thumped with renewed hope.

Seriously?

The dead king hadn't noticed the bat. Maybe it was the roar of the flames or his pride over the vanquished dragon in the square, but his reaction came too late. Sailing on a hot draught, the bat made its final approach, fluttering down into Arthur's face. Caught off guard, Arthur staggered back, his eyes flaring, but when he made a grab for the creature, his fingers only closed on air. And the bat, squeaking in an oddly sardonic manner, twitched upwards and away, once again flapping towards the wicker man's legs. Ben watched as the creature dropped something from its claws, a small black object falling into the flames at the foot of the effigy. The next moment, pain went searing through him from snout to tail, a heat that had nothing to do with his inner gases and everything, he guessed, to do with the sprig of hawthorn that the bat had snatched from the dead king's hand.

Snatched and burned.

Hissing as the yard-long thorns in his body shrivelled and disintegrated, Ben looked up to see the bat change. There was no ripple of transformation, no muscular expansion from chiropteran to human form. A pop of air, a puff of dust, and the Vicomte Lambert du Sang was standing on the plinth between the two lions. The young man was naked, balls and all, his grin revealing his sharp white teeth and exactly how pleased he was with himself. Gone was the withered half-corpse of before. Du Sang appeared in the peak of health, his brown locks curling, his lips full, pursed with pride. In his eyes, malachite glinted, a hue that continued into his skin, Ben noticed, his face and body tinged a shade of green.

Goblins. It's the goblin blood.

Ben grunted, smoke spilling from his snout at the sight of his unlikely saviour.

"Get up!" du Sang said, wheeling an arm as the ogres, seeing him on the plinth, came lumbering up the steps toward him. "Get up, you witless wyrm!"

Easier said than done. With an effort worthy of Samson, Ben hauled himself up on his forelegs and haunches, his wounds screaming. Smoke plumed from his nostrils, wreathing the square. Blood splashed the flagstones, but it ran slower than before, he reckoned, his healing abilities kicking in, eager to restore him now that the pyre had dispelled his cage. Nevertheless, he was weak. It took a great deal to lash out his tail, swiping an approaching babble of goblins from the ground, their helmets and weapons clanging off stone. His wings sagged like peeling billboards, sweeping over the fountains, raking through muck and slime, the greenteeth hissing in retreat. Above, he heard wyverns shriek, responding to some unseen signal from the king. He had no time, no time, the flames roaring up before him. But du Sang hadn't risked all this for his health. Ben had to get out of here and recover the sword. If he failed, then everything was lost.

But first things first.

Neck rearing, horns piercing the haze, Ben vented a roar. The echoes thundered across the square, the ground shaking, throwing bugbears and hounds from their feet as they lurched towards him. Most of the horde cowered, vague shapes in the corner of his eyes, edging back into the shadow of the thorn wall. Most were perfectly aware of the damage a dragon could do, especially when unleashed and in a pissed-off mood. Ben was happy to prove them right. Embers glowed in his belly, still too weak to muster flame. But flame wasn't what he needed here. Taranis had seen to that.

Eyes narrowed on the towering idol, Ben pushed himself forward and up the steps to the plinth, a red-scaled battering ram. Horns lowered, he crashed headlong into the fire. *Whoomph!* The column shuddered and cracked, the impact travelling up yards of stone and shaking Lord Nelson on the top. Cinders exploded around him, the stacked logs flying to all sides, trailing sparks and billows of smoke. The ogres, preparing to attack, cringed instead, but whether their concern was for their clothes or their safety, Ben couldn't tell. Untouched by the heat, he shifted his bulk around in a half-circle, his claws flattening the blaze into heaps of charcoal and ash, his tail lashing out at the foundations. With a snarl of satisfaction, he felt the effigy budge above him, the great wooden structure, lashed together as it was, losing shape and stability. Vision rippling with flames and fatigue, Ben stretched out his legs, forcing himself upwards, his ridge of horns smashing through the trunks of the old god's legs. Through the fire, he heard an uproar above, a crescendo of screams that told him Taranis was giving way.

The plan was far from perfect; it was a long way to the ground. All the same, he had limited options. This way, at least, some of the captives stood a chance. All he could do was spread his wings as the wicker man fell, spilling broken wood and prisoners, a makeshift safety net. In a hard rain, men, women and children dropped and bounced on his pinions, weighing him down. Fifty or sixty of them, Ben reckoned, falling and sliding off his wings, then stumbling away across the plinth, off into the surrounding streets. Most of the prisoners picked themselves up and ran south, heading, no doubt, for the shelter of Charing Cross underground station. For the moment, the horde in the square was too busy scattering to give chase, climbing over each other in their bid to escape the collapsing effigy.

It's something.

But the element of surprise wouldn't last long. And even as some fled, he heard others scream, tumbling through the smoke, their cries cut off as flesh met stone. Here and there, the pyre flared up, fuelled by clothing, hair and flesh. Like it or not, hundreds were going to die here tonight. There was no escaping it. All Hallows would have its feast either way, the dark half of the year anointed with blood. He'd count himself lucky if even half the captives managed to get away. He looked up, navigating his wings to catch the greater part of the falling god, timber smashing apart on his head and shoulder blades. More people rolled and slid off his wings, a handful of them, he saw, clad in black leather.

Fitzwarrens. Rescued. Never thought I'd see the day . . .

On second thought, this had been the running theme of the past two years, hadn't it? His whole world flipping upside down. At this point, it shouldn't surprise him. Nor could he deny the bravery of these men, despite its foolhardy nature. After all, the slayers had gone after a dragon for centuries with nothing but a grudge and a rusty sword. As soon as they'd regained their feet, the Black Knights were shouting into the chaos, herding the survivors beyond the column and towards the tube station. The best chance these people had was to hide before the rabble recovered from Ben's attack.

"Ben! Look out!"

As if the thought was an omen, he saw Annis through the drifting smoke. The girl was waving at him from further along the plinth, her gangly limbs unbroken by the fall. Ash streaked her face and clothes, her hair resembling a chimneysweep's brush. She'd managed to grab a weapon from somewhere, an axe dropped by the fleeing goblins, but he didn't fancy her chances if she hung around much longer. He drew a breath to roar at her, tell her to run with the others, when he realised the reason for her warning, shrill and fevered in the chaos.

Arthur. Climbing the steps to the pedestal.

The corpse king bore no weapons; his legendary sword had refused his touch and he'd taken up no other. *He isn't Arthur. Not in the truest sense of the word,* Ben reminded himself, recalling Caliburn's warning. Did the wight that had taken his place imagine the crown on his skull was enough to make Ben quail and bend the knee? That his breastplate, silver and dull, could

228

withstand dragon claws? Or did he simply rely on the light in his eyes, illuminating his beard and teeth, to fill his foes with crippling fear?

Good luck with that.

Lungs swelling, Ben reared up as the king approached, coming to a halt between the bronze lions at the top of the steps. Arthur spared Annis a look, enough to make her take a step back and raise her axe, but the distance wasn't enough to assure Ben of her safety. *Curse her.* Even among the dispersing flames, he couldn't risk an inferno. He may not have been able to save all the victims from the wicker man, but he wasn't about to make some of his own. Not human ones, anyway.

He snorted, the king and the rebel knight shimmering below him. As the smoke cleared, he watched Arthur raise his hand again, his palm bearing a fresh sprig of hawthorn. *Fuck. He'll have a sackful of the stuff.* And he couldn't see du Sang anywhere. If he had any sense, the Vicomte would've gotten clear of the flames. He could see the wall of thorns, however. The barrier, he judged, was a couple of hundred feet away, rising from the roof of the National Gallery, but he'd seen how fast the briar could move with Arthur's help and he didn't fancy another thorny embrace. Could he detect movement over there, the shifting of timber and glass as the branches started to writhe? Yeah. He thought so. It was time to make a departure from this shitshow.

Exit stage left.

To that end, he spread out a wing, growling at Annis. The girl hesitated, then appeared to catch his intent. *Last flight. All aboard for survival.* Squaring her shoulders, Annis stepped towards him – then darted around in a half-circle, swinging her axe at the king.

No!

Metal met metal with a tooth-jarring clang. The echoes seemed to slow, events playing out in drawn-out seconds of shock. Ben watched as the girl let go of the axe handle and staggered away from the impact, her limbs shaking. She may as well have swung the axe into a tree trunk, the way that the blade protruded from Arthur's breastplate, stuck in his mouldering flesh. A fetor filled the air, a cloud of dust puffing from his chest, a breath from the tomb. Blood, as black as oil, oozed from the cleft in his armour. Arthur remained on his feet, however, swaying a little. Slowly, he turned his gaze on his assailant, his skeletal face unreadable.

Annis cried out as the king strode towards her. The Fitzwarren knights were gone now, vanished into the streets and the underground station. And the goblins, growing aware of the confrontation on the pedestal, were steadily creeping forward, a closing circle of green faces and bared fangs. Above, the wyverns circled – daunted, Ben thought, by the scattered flames and the dragon among them, but looking for their chance.

In the chaos, a glint of gold. The Horn of Twrch Trwyth, he noticed, had flown from around Arthur's neck. Clumsy, reckless as her swing had been, Annis had managed to sever the thong it hung upon, the ivory relic falling to the flagstones. In the flames of whatever went through his mind, the king hadn't marked its loss, his eyes solely for the girl. As he reached out, his bony fingertips protruding from his gauntlets, Annis shrieked. The next moment, the king fell upon her, clawing at her face. There was a hiss as he touched her, a web of frost crackling across her skin, the dead laying hands on the living. A spray of blood peppered the air. Arthur, ever grinning, drew a nail down the girl's brow, across her eye and the bridge of her nose, a ragged, bloody scratch.

Ben made his move. Red-scaled flesh eclipsed the king, a

giant claw closing around him, wrenching him from the girl. Clutching her face, Annis rolled away, groaning and kicking her legs. Ben felt her boots tapping against his scales as he reached out with his other claw, securing her in his grasp. Rearing, he thrashed out his wings, the blast sending goblins and ogres tumbling back down the steps to the pedestal, buying him seconds. Haunches bulging, he made to leap forward, meaning to snatch up the horn in his jaws and leave the rabble eating his dust. Before he could do so, a pain in his fist arrested him. A numbness was spreading there, quick, sharp and cold, riddling out from his knuckles and up his foreleg. Looking down, he saw frost covering his limb, a white tide crackling over his scales, chased by sapphire light.

No prizes for guessing its source. *Arthur. The touch of the dead.* Like the inverse version of a hot coal, Arthur was burning him, burning him up, the spectral force that empowered him emanating from his scaly prison. With a bark of alarm, Ben tried to open his claw, hurl the threat away from him, but the rime was thickening by the second, icicles dangling from his elbow joint, the cold seeping into the muscles underneath. If he didn't act soon, the frost would climb to his shoulder, reach his chest, twisting for his heart...

His bellow was part anger, part pain. Flames rushed from his jaws, fighting the creeping frost. Snout curling, he watched the inferno bluster from his lungs to meet the deathly chill that gripped him – and then roared in agony as his foreleg blackened and cracked, his flesh shattering like glass. The corpse king, instantly released, dropped to the ground in a smouldering cascade of scales, talons and blood.

Howling, Ben flung himself in retreat, crashing against the base of Nelson's Column, the edifice booming. As his spine struck stone, knocking the wind from him, his remaining foreclaw flew wide, dispensing Annis into the maze of burning wood. Groggily, coughing, the girl climbed onto her hands and knees. Shielding her mouth with her jacket, she peered through the flames at Arthur, the dead king rising unscathed from the chaos. Then she looked up at Ben, her face frantic.

Do something.

Tongue thick, senses frayed, he forced out the words, urging her to move with his great golden eyes. Annis shook her head. What was *wyrm tongue* to her? A growl through the smoke, unintelligible, strange. All the same, she seemed to catch his panic. She frowned, straining to understand, even as he crooked out a claw, jabbing a talon into the mess.

Don't look at me. Look over there.

She didn't wait for further instruction. The girl slipped away as Arthur came striding out of the flames, making another grab for her. Leaping over fallen timber, she sprinted and then slid onto her knees as she made for the object in the space between the bronze lions. *Bingo!* Rolling onto her back, Annis held up the Horn of Twrch Trwyth, a questioning expression on her face that resolved into pride as Ben snorted and nodded his snout, the gesture shaking the pedestal.

Arthur continued towards the girl, his eye sockets trailing light, his hands white with frost. Clutching the relic to her breast, Annis pushed herself to her feet, her head swinging this way and that, searching for an escape route. There wasn't one. At her back, the goblin horde was recovering again, approaching the pedestal steps. Before her, the flames and the dead king. She couldn't defend herself against either. If she lingered a moment longer, then she would die.

With a thump, Ben's tail swept across the flagstones, barrelling into the king. Arthur's crown flew from his head, a spinning coin in the dusk, but he didn't cry out as he followed it, tumbling through the air. In a jumble of armour, blue light and old bones, the dead king smashed down into the square, landing at the bottom of the steps. At once, the horde gathered around him, bugbears and greenteeth hooting and cursing, but Ben only spared them a moment's glance. For now, the king lay sprawled and unmoving. But Ben had met the dead before and he knew that the situation wouldn't last.

Groaning, he hauled himself up, onto his claws. Nursing his severed limb, he limped away from the column. Blood hissed on the stone under him, but no trace of frost, the murderous magic dispelled. *Amputated.* Lowering one wing, he saw Annis stagger her way through the flames, covered in soot from head to toe. *Again.* Her eyes, however, were bright beads, shining with desperate triumph.

This time, she grasped his meaning plainly enough. Spluttering, her face half hidden by the lapel of her jacket, the girl climbed the ladder of his extended wing and up onto his back. *Buckle up* . . . Dazed, his wounds screaming, he lumbered across the pedestal, crunching over the ruined pyre. With the last of his strength, he thrust himself into the air, leaping from the mess of Trafalgar Square.

Venting a plume of flame, he burst through the circling ring of wyverns, the smaller beasts shrieking as his wake tossed them from his path. Then up and up into the clouds, his tail snaking, Annis straddling his withers.

His blood fell from the heavens like red rain.

He didn't get far. Twenty minutes later, with the thorn wall forty miles behind him and the sun sinking behind the Chiltern Hills, wings, midnight black, were fluttering at the edges of his vision. As he flew across the patchwork of fields and farms, his body was trying to heal, his nerves tingling with inherent magic, a warm balm. But his wounds were deep and his blood loss considerable. With each passing mile, his breath grew more and more laboured. In the gathering darkness, he could feel himself drifting, drifting further towards the earth, the villages below, twinkling in the dusk, heedless of his presence.

But not of my existence, he thought, oddly resigned. *Not any more.*

And the girl on his back – *Anne? Alice?* – well, she may have shouted something, a warning into the wind, but he couldn't quite catch the sense of it and her words couldn't keep him from the shadows.

Not far from Christmas Common, the treetops were whipping against Ben's chest and belly. With a sigh that sounded like surrender, his wings crumpled, and his breast ploughed into a dense tract of woodland. His snout gouged a furrow in a hillside as he slid, grunting, into darkness.

FIFTEEN

The dragon dreamed in darkness.

But when Ben opened his eyes and found himself sprawled face-down on the ground, he spat out the notion of *dreams* along with a mouthful of grass. Climbing to his feet, he surveyed the state of himself before checking his surroundings, gasping with the realisation that he lived. *A close thing. But* . . . His skin looked unbroken, his flesh twinging with a familiar burning sensation. His wounds were healing, lending weight to his suspicions.

You wish *you were dreaming, mate.*

Somewhere, his body was struggling to mend itself, sure. In this place, he was naked, in human form, sans injury and scales. Frowning down at himself, he couldn't even see any bruises on his arms and legs, his flesh taut with sinew, pale and smooth. There was the usual web of scars, the map of his age-old mask weaving down to the crimson patch of hair between his legs, but that was it. Considering what he'd been through, he acknowledged a slight doubt about his situation, a grumble rising in his throat as he absorbed his location.

Here in the Orchard of Worlds time moves differently than on the terrestrial plane, if it moves at all . . .

He was *between* again, wasn't he? Deep in the nether. A glance through the rows of trees, each one crooked and pregnant with fruit, confirmed the fact as he spied the shimmering walls, the crystalline palace in the distance. In soft, radiant pink, the battlements, turrets and spires speared into the dark. That darkness, he'd come to learn, was as infinite as it was cold, an orchard sown with worlds that hung on the branches of the cosmos like ripe fruit. Branches? No. *Leys. Weaving like vines.* Worlds that the gods had seeded, tended by the creatures that survived them. *Replaced* them. The Fallen Ones. The Fay. And at least one of those worlds – his own – was growing more withered by the hour. With the souring, Earth had found itself haunted, hounded by an army of hungry ghosts.

Benjurigan. Welcome . . .

Ben curled his lip.

"Are we really going to do the whole theatrics thing again?" he said, nervous all the same. "I know you're here, my lady. Might as well show yourself."

Laughter answered him, somewhere off in the trees. Laughter that sounded much like bells. The echoes faded around him, spilling over the bluff at his back like the brook he'd seen before, trickling out into nothing, out over the glittering knot-world.

Avalon. I'm standing in the gardens of the High House of Avalon. And for some reason, I don't like the smell of it . . .

Rolling his shoulders, he traipsed into the trees, clover and yarrow brushing his feet. Blossoms shook from the branches as he went, a white storm swirling around him, and he tried his best not to look at the dangling fruit, these plump metaphors of Creation. It was bad enough being a Remnant, something different, other and strange, without dwelling on the fact that even his *planet* wasn't unique. *How small can a wyrm feel?* More than this, his discomfort centred, as ever, on his mistrust of the Fay. Whatever passed for air in the orchard – even that was sly and capricious. He wouldn't let himself forget the nature of the woman – the creature *shaped* like a woman – who played host to him in this nowhere place. Under the guise of granting enlightenment, Our Lady of the Barrows had drawn him here, summoning him in a waking dream. She'd shown him the supposed truth of the universe and then pressed her lips to his, a taste of need that lingered. Sweet. But cold. Nimue wanted something. Where it came to the Fay, there was always a price. Over time, the understanding had grown as deep as his instinct. One thing was for sure, she hadn't dragged him here for tea and biscuits.

Where the hell are you? What game is this now?

Thinking this, he looked through the trees and caught a flash of blue silk, whisking out of sight behind a gnarled trunk. Flapping blossoms from his face, Ben lumbered in that direction, drawn on by the laughter, the bells, the sound bringing colour to his cheeks in annoyance. Another whirl of silk, the hint of an arm, willowy and brown, led him down another row and across another, the Lady keeping ahead of him, a few seconds out of sight. Leaping around a bush, he saw her hair through the branches, her snow-white braids coiled high on her head, and he made in that direction, running now, a curse held behind his teeth.

Clod-footed in this delicate place, he crashed through a briar and into a glade, a storm of dragonflies, bees and small flickering creatures exploding all around him. For a moment, the miasma mingled with the blossoms hanging in the air, forming a figure, pale and tall. Ben caught the hint of long white hair, bony limbs spread in supplication – no, in embrace. As the insects, blossoms and whatever the little winged beings were (he didn't want to think about it) cleared, he made out the Lady standing a few yards away in the shelter of the trees, a ghost under the boughs. The strange cloud slipped from her, the floating figure drifting apart, evaporating in her arms. Even in the gloom, he noticed her pursed lips, her tilted neck, the echo of some long-ago kiss fading with the vision. When she turned to look at him, her eyes held sadness in their depths, shadows in violet. For a second, she didn't seem to see him. Then she turned fully, her robes swirling as though underwater, and offered him her usual indecipherable smile.

"And what of love, Benjurigan?" she asked him. "Will love alone save your world?"

Ben coughed, ashamed by his intrusion, though he understood that nothing here was happening by chance. If he'd caught this otherworldly queen in some kind of clinch, then it was because she *wanted* to be caught. He was long past the point of thinking otherwise.

"I used to think so," he told her. Then shrugged. "Guess I woke up. Or got old."

"You are yet young," she said. "And you cannot hide the truth from us. You love the humans with a fire as fierce as the one that burns in your belly. But your love stems from more than mere pity. You are bound to them. Part of them."

"You make it sound so romantic," he replied. "Try losing a limb now and then. Then get back to me."

"You were born of their dreams, Benjurigan. Yet you refuse to fade from them, when that is the easiest path."

"I swore to protect them."

Nimue gave a tut. "We both know that the Lore is over. Your continued loyalty is your own affair. Unshaken, even when you have lost everything. Admirable – in its folly, perhaps."

"So now you're my Agony Aunt? My lady, why am I here?"

The Lady regarded him for a moment, tracing an emotion that he wasn't sure he felt. Then she held out an arm.

"Come. Walk with us. Walk with your queen."

Ben curled his lip, discomforted. He disliked the fact that she had plucked him here, even out of pain, and that apparently, she could do so whenever she wished. But he wanted answers, more than anything, and who else but the Lady could provide them? Besides, something in her regal gesture and unwavering gaze made her command hard to refuse. Puffing out his cheeks, he lumbered across the space and offered her his elbow. Her arm slipped around his bicep as light and cool as an autumn leaf.

Arm in arm, she led him down the avenue of trees.

"You are not alone in your solitude," she said, her head turned slightly away from him, looking up at the arching branches. Careless of the paradox. "Once, I walked here with my consort, the King of all the Fay. What dreams we conjured in the garden! What golden hopes. Together, we shone our power into the darkness and embarked on the greatest undertaking. The evolution of Man. An Example to lead all into the light."

"Yeah. You said."

"With magic, with the Old Science, we brought our immortal seeding to your world and deigned to shape human dreams in flesh."

Ben took a moment to digest this.

Then, "Wait a minute. You mean . . . " He stole a breath, trying to calm his galloping heart. "The Remnants—"

The Lady pointed into the trees. "Look."

He looked. At first, he wasn't sure what he was seeing, a hint of movement in the shadows under the boughs, the gloom churning like smoke. A rustle of leaves drew his attention to the trees, along with the soft creak of wood, the bark there moving, rippling around the trunks. Squinting, he made out forms in the gloom, moving in the trees, bodies shaped by knot, vine and bole, writhing in moss-clad skin. Drawing to a halt, the Lady in watchful silence beside him, Ben felt colour climb into his cheeks as the coiling figures grew clear.

Here, a pointed ear. There, a willowy leg. Then a breast, wrinkled and sylvan within the trunk, but bare and human nevertheless, the nipple a rounded bud. The rise and fall of buttocks, thrusting between parted legs, moulded by the starlight falling on a pale, stripped part of the wood. The next moment, he discerned a man's face, his mouth open in ecstasy. In a shimmer of sap, he caught sight of a shivering branch, tendril-veined, that resembled a phallus as it plunged once again into the riddle, into the seething orgy of bark . . .

Reminded of a similar sight in the Fay crypt deep under London, the bacchanalian scene carved in the marble tomb, he looked away, down at his feet. Despite himself, there was an ache in his breast and between his legs, a sudden stab of longing, and he grumbled under his breath.

Tree porn. Fantastic.

To the Lady, he said, "If you're trying to embarrass me . . ."

He expected Nimue to laugh in that way of hers, but she didn't.

"Come now. You're far from prudish, surely. Not now. Not after all the—"

"Look, do we have to talk about this?" he said. "Just get to the point. Immortal seeding. Dreams in flesh. Fancy words, but I get what you're saying. You're saying that the Fay . . . that you . . . " *bumped uglies with the humans*, "had *relations* with the humans."

"Are we not flesh, Benjurigan?" the Lady said. "Alas, our godly provenance lingers in spirit alone. Like you, like them, we

240

are corporeal, creatures of blood and bone, albeit infused with magic. Creatures of love and hope. Of desire . . . "

"I get the picture. Am I meant to be shocked? Lady, I'm the last person to—"

He cut himself off, the gist of what she was telling him settling on his shoulders like a stack of bricks. Catching his breath, he released her, stumbling away across the grass, his head and body shaking.

"No. It can't be. It's . . . it's outrageous."

Now the Lady did laugh, although it was a sad sound, a whisper between the trees.

"When has the truth ever tasted sweet? You of all creatures must know that." She stepped toward him, her eyes adding to the weight on him. "Admittedly, our early experiments were . . . primitive, rudimentary. And did we not feel our own shame, such a sublime race, fallen to rut like beasts in the mud? In time, our quest to shape dreams took on a more scientific aspect. Alembics, potions, that kind of thing. But thus, we made you, Benjurigan. Witch, giant and dragon. We made you all. And when I said you were part of them, I did not lie."

"No."

"The Remnants are the children of the Fay. But you had earthly parents too."

"Shut up. Just . . . stop talking."

"Our endless magic runs in your veins. But your flesh? Your flesh was born solely of *their* dreams."

Somehow, Ben was on his knees, sinking into the turf. Blood pounded in his head, his skull threatening to burst with the knowledge, a thorn of truth that jagged down to his heart. The Lady's confession resounded in the depths of him, words he couldn't deny. Because somehow, he'd known this, hadn't he?

He'd known it all along. His empathy with humans, his restlessness with his draconic self. His need to feel close to them, to protect them. His love for Maud. For . . . *Rose. Oh God. Rose.* Thought of her almost floored him, the realisation that judgement was beyond him, that in the run of things, he'd committed the same act, echoed the seeding like a mirror of the past . . .

He spluttered, choking back a sob. He couldn't think about that now. Here he was, a Remnant, abandoned by the Fay and denied by humans. An orphan of both worlds. He drew a breath, shuddering, trying to shackle his emotions. To quell the anger bubbling inside him. It wouldn't serve him here. Gasping, he damped down the fire within, opening himself to the truth. Harsh as it was, the Lady had answered his question. And with the answering, left only one of his own.

"Why?" he spat, unable to look at her. "Why did you do this?"

He didn't hear the Lady approach, her feet a whisper over the grass. But he felt her shadow fall over him, as cold as the darkness above, the deeper darkness that the glow of the palace couldn't penetrate. Unlike her words, which frosted his heart.

"Why, to make them believe, of course," she said. "To make them see that dreams were possible and thereby inspire the Example. Magic, Ben. The power to change worlds. That was the gift we gave them. Human hearts, however, are weak, and belief is a tenuous thing, fleeting like mist at the first shadow of a doubt. You live in that doubt, do you not? Over time, it has become a prison. Your suffocating Pact . . ." He could sense her shaking her snow-white head. "Once, when the Old Lands were young, belief in magic, in dreams, shone like a beacon in the darkness. Belief fuelled the circles of protection. And the Earth thrived, a golden fruit in the orchard. But belief has withered and died. And so the Earth follows."

A worm gnaws at the heart of things . . .

He remembered Von Hart's fear last winter, booming from a maw of ghosts somewhere in this very gulf. Since then, Ben had puzzled over the envoy's words, wondering if he'd put a name to his own treachery or whether he simply meant the passage of time, the corrosive effect that the Lore – the lie – had had on the Remnants.

Now the Lady disabused him of the notion. The worm was disbelief. Human disbelief.

It made sense. A horrible kind of sense. In fact, the Remnants he'd encountered in this shitshow had been telling him all along. He just hadn't wanted to hear it.

Here we are: endangered species. Refugees. Fugitives from our own power . . .

The Pact is no truce at all, merely a cell where you wait for extinction . . .

Your compromise is false. A war of attrition, just as the Curia Occultus intended . . .

The magic of the Fay is growing old. The circles of protection are souring . . . And the stench of their corruption draws the Lurkers to its source.

A worm gnaws at the heart of things . . .

The memory of denial fluttered around his head like ravens in a cavern, arriving too late to warn him. All the same, he had a doubt of his own.

"That can't . . . that can't be the whole story."

"It is not," Nimue conceded. "Are you prepared to forsake your heart's desire and hear the bitterest truth?"

My heart's desire? For a moment, he thought that the Lady meant Rose. Then he realised she was talking about his faith in humans, his loyalty to the Lore. His need to believe in hope. In something.

"Do I have any choice?"

"Not if you wish to endure."

Ben growled deep in his throat. "I know this story, sweetheart. I know how it works. You're about to ask me for something."

"Oh, Ben," she said, and she sounded genuinely moved. "There is always a price."

"Name it!" The grass between his knuckles crisped to black in the heat from his throat. She didn't need to tell him the cost; he had seen Jia Jing pay in full, falling to an endless death. "I want to hear you say *please*."

"Bring us the sword. Bring Caliburn to us. Only with the blade can I reignite the circles and restore your world. Bring us the sword. Then you will have your answer." He could feel her stiffen at his back, the ice in her voice as she forced out the word. "Please."

Why? He had to know why. All the same, the temptation to refuse smouldered in his chest, a hot coal. Sarcasm bubbled behind his teeth, a breath he never got to use, as the Lady spoke again.

"If you will not do it for your queen, then do it for love." But there was no kiss this time; her words were plea enough. "Love, Benjurigan. The love with which we shaped you."

If he'd wanted the ground to swallow him, because after everything, after all his longing and loss, he was, in some way, part human, then he got his wish. Before he had a chance to pull away, to wrench himself to his feet and confront the Lady, the grass was weaving through his fingers and around his wrists, pulling him towards the ground, an inexorable embrace. Veins popping to burst out of his neck, he let out a protracted growl as the turf sucked him in. Slick green ropes lashed his torso, his legs, binding his struggling form. The trees were singing,

singing, joining with the blood in his head, a symphony of unwelcome revelation.

Then the earth opened under him, a starless void, and closed over his head like a grave.

SIXTEEN

Ben awoke, from darkness into light. Out of the fire, he rose, from the dregs of a memory, a great wooden god and billowing smoke. Thorns surrounding him, *binding* him. A grinning skull, gold-crowned. Then, the flicker of a dream, something about the Lady, souring fruit and a sword . . . all of it lost as he groaned his way to the surface of consciousness.

He lay sprawled on his back in a bed. A four-poster by the look of it. The kind of ornately carved berth where he used to tumble damsels back in the day, flitting in through this turret window or that, drunk on mead and about to get drunker. Usually on some baron or other's prime stock. Welcomed in by one bored lady after another, who tended to have a taste for . . . well, the exotic. Such things had amused him once, when he was young, self-absorbed and embittered, before the ages turned and showed him that he didn't have that luxury, not really. And lately, he'd changed. He recognised that now. He wasn't the same dragon that had set off for Cairo two years ago, looking to save a woman who didn't need saving. His adventures had shattered his illusions. Many of his enemies were dead. Many of his friends were friends no longer. His world had fallen apart. That was the price of his awakening.

Still, he lay under an eiderdown quilt with a cloud of pillows propping up his head. It wasn't much in the way of comfort, considering, but he'd take it. The bed meant that he was alive, and that particular realisation, he knew, would never get old. Sunlight streamed through the arched windows, illuminating the fine tracery and clear panels of glass, falling on his naked and human form.

How did I get here? The thought was sleepy, confused. He was pretty sure he'd been in dragon form when he'd made his escape from London. *Did they winch me into the back of a truck or what? Do I even want to know?*

The room around him brought to mind another house, presently lying in ruins near Hampstead Heath, thanks to the White Dog. This looked like another medieval throwback that a series of architects had put through the wringer of Tudor and Edwardian before ending up with a ramshackle mess, all under a sagging roof. Wooden panels lined the chamber. In one corner, an armchair sat like a portly madam in threadbare green velvet. A shield hung on one wall. A hawk, he noted, on a field of gules. The sight made him feel old.

Everything in the room smelled of polish and dust, a hint of dried flowers and old embers. And blood, of course. He could see patches of the stuff on his arms and chest, seeping through his bandages as his flesh struggled to heal. Blood had marked the sheets too, dark blossoms staining the linen. But surely, he should've healed by now? If it was the next day. If he was breathing, then . . .

All Saints' Day. Must be. Not that I'm gonna thank any myself.

He tried to sit up and he got his answer. A flash of silver, a faint burst of song in his skull – a phantom melody, he knew, an echo that lingered beyond the instrument on which a Fay hand had strummed it, enduring after the harp's destruction. *A song to circle the globe. Terrific.* The tingle of ice around his wrist

247

was enough to make him snarl, his teeth jagging into fangs at the restrictive power of *lunewrought*.

"For fuck's sake—!"

And someone said, "Please, Mr Garston. Relax. You're not in any danger here."

"Oh yeah?" Sulkily, Ben pushed himself up on his elbows, wincing at the man who stood at the foot of the bed. "That'll make a change. Who the fuck are you? And where the fuck is *here*, exactly?"

He already had some idea. There were nicer ways to wake up, he thought.

"I'm Lord Rulf Fitzwarren, Head Patriarch of the Last Pavilion," the man said, "which is where you find yourself. A pleasant, but admittedly neglected mansion in the Shropshire marshes. I realise this won't sound like good news to you."

"You realise correct. Now you're gonna tell me what I'm doing here before I rip this museum apart."

The man called Rulf spread his hands as if to show he wasn't holding a knife.

"Must we joust with words like this?" he asked. "Perhaps you'll feel more at ease if I remind you that we could've chopped off your head at any point during the night."

"You have a funny idea of reassurance, knight. But that isn't an answer."

Lord Rulf nodded, conceding the point. The silver in his beard caught the afternoon sun slanting through the windows, revealing his age despite his steely gaze and solid stance. He was a man edging sixty, Ben reckoned. Distinguished-looking in his smart burgundy suit. *And this is hard for him. I can see that. He's conflicted, deep down.* Ben gave an inward grunt. *No prizes for guessing why.* Rulf's shoulders, however, revealed the hardened muscles of most trained killers, and coupled with Ben's location and the manacle around his wrist, he guessed that it probably wasn't wise to make good on his threat.

Besides, how much more damage can I do to them? It's over.

Further silver tumbled from the patriarch's head in a loose knot of curls, bound at the base of his neck. Wrinkles lined the edges of his mouth, sanguine and patient through his beard, yet no scars marked his skin. No shiny patches of old burns, which made Ben think that this particular son of House Fitzwarren had never taken up a sword against him, notched and black, at any point in the past. And there was the name, of course. Rulf, not Fulk. Ben wished he could feel relieved. Evidently, the man before him wasn't a Black Knight, a slayer chosen to take up the family's singular purpose: to see his head hang on a wall in Whittington Castle, their long-lost noble seat.

No. He was a lord. A kingpin of slayers. Even better.

"*Spei est Vindicta*," Ben said. "'Hope is Vengeance', isn't that right? You might want to explain why I'm still alive. I can't promise that I'd treat you the same. How many has it been now, anyway, Rulf?" He pretended to count on his fingers, then gave a hollow little chuckle. "Wow. As many as that? Some might say that vengeance is blind."

Sir Rulf gave him a pained look.

"We have all lost much in the course of our grievance," he said.

"*I lost the woman I loved!*" Ben hadn't meant to shout, but the words flew from him before he could stop them, his roar shaking the walls. Silver answered him, glittering behind his eyes, the manacle forcing him back against the pillows. "You started this," he growled through the sickening light. "You and your

249

bastard king. You should've left me well alone in Mordiford. Left *us* alone."

He squeezed his eyes shut, forbidding tears. He wasn't about to cry in front of this man, show any sign of weakness, disadvantaged as he was. Nevertheless, Maud danced in his mind's eye, reaching up to kiss him in a moonlit glade, centuries ago, but not so far from here. Her spluttering face as she choked on poison. Dancing in the flames . . .

"It was a long time ago," Rulf told him. "Over eight hundred years, in fact. The stuff of our storybooks these days, I'm afraid. And I am not my ancestors."

"Fuck you. You lot are all the same." Ben remembered one of those storybooks from an underground car park in London, a faded little classic of revisionist history, designed to taunt him as the latest Fulk peeled scales from his flesh. "Like most fanatics, you think your stories give you an excuse."

Lord Rulf pinched the bridge of his nose.

"Mr Garston, we don't have time for this," he said. "I'm sure I don't need to tell you that the world has gone to hell. The Lore is over. A wall of thorns surrounds London. A Remnant army has taken the city – and that's just England. We've been watching the news closely – what few channels remain up and running, that is. Tokeloshe run amok in Johannesburg. A sea serpent attacked San Francisco. And bunyips rose from the Murray River and are currently feasting on Adelaide. You'll forgive me if my concern rests on the present."

"Forgive you?" Ben could've laughed. "Correct me if I'm wrong, but didn't your little conspiracy with the CROWS cause the breach in the Lore in the first place? And for what? A crumbling pile of bricks. For your precious honour, even though anyone with any sense had forgotten the name *Fitzwarren* centuries ago. For a rusty suit of armour and an old dragon's head." Now Ben did laugh, a bitter-sounding bark. "Shit, I'm surprised you haven't put the Lambton junk in the corner of this room, for added bullshit."

Lord Rulf glared, but he couldn't hold Ben's gaze. His jaw rippled, swallowing rage, and when he spoke, the words seethed between his teeth.

"If I told you we've made mistakes, would you confess your own? Or are you going to lie there and pretend you've upheld your side of the bargain? That in your mad dash to save one woman, you neglected to warn the Guild of the coming peril? And after Cairo, in fact, you ran away, allowing the mnemonic harp to fall into the hands of Mauntgraul, the White Dog? Hundreds died as a result. What was it they used to call you, beast? Sola Ignis, that was it. The Lone Fire, standing guard. But you are just as remiss in your duties as this house. And as such, you will not upbraid me."

For a moment, neither of them spoke, quietly boiling inside. Ben wanted to argue, blast his grudge upon the man before him, the constant trial of living under threat for simply existing and the treasures that the Black Knight had helped to steal from him. *Maud. Rose. Almost my life* . . . But a deeper part of him, the honest part, could only hear Fulk Fitzwarren sneer in his head, a couple of years back in New York. The words were as undeniable as ever.

You're asleep, Red Ben. You've been asleep for centuries.

It only seemed natural to find someone to blame.

"Von Hart . . ."

At the sound of this name, Lord Rulf appeared to get a grip of himself. He spoke quietly, wearily, letting his breath carry away his anger.

"We are both betrayed, dragon. Remnant and human alike. The envoy offered us a gift and we were stupid enough to take it. He promised us our home, a return to status, to glory. Tell me, what did he promise you?"

Ben mulled it over for a minute. When it came down to it, and after all the envoy's riddles and misdirection, there was only one thing he could think of.

Magic is souring. The Sleep is failing. The Remnants will die.

"Nothing," he said. "Nothing but death, anyway."

"Then he was honest with you," Rulf said. "Because death is what's coming. For all of us."

Ben pulled a face. "Whatever gives you that idea?" Rulf tutted at his sarcasm, but Ben went on regardless. "Look, what is this, knight? Why am I here? If you're gonna hold some fancy trial or other before you kill me, then at least make it quick. I'm a little tired of guessing games."

"As I said, you're not in any danger. I merely wish to parley."

"Now? You're eight hundred years too late."

"I'm asking you to trust me. If not now, then when?"

Ben laughed, a roll of thunder deep in his belly. Then he looked at the man at the foot of the bed and saw that he was serious. Exasperation rode on his shock, sobering him. His eyes narrowed into green slits.

"Never," he said, low and fierce. "Is never good for you?"

"Mr Garston—"

"Cut the formalities. I wouldn't trust you as far as I could throw you, my *lord*, which, ironically, is pretty damn far. But you have me at a disadvantage, don't you?" He lifted his arm, biting back the pain, the manacle glimmering around his wrist. "Is it considered polite to restrain one's guests? If you want to talk, we'll talk. But you're gonna have to release me first."

Rulf stared for a moment, uncertain. Then he shook himself and came around to the side of the bed. Keeping a safe distance, Ben noted. A wise distance.

"My apologies. The *lunewrought* was simply a practical measure. We couldn't exactly haul seven tons of dragon a hundred-odd miles across Oxfordshire."

Ben gave a grunt. "Fair enough." *Makes sense. But.* "Do you mind telling me where you got—?"

A screech interrupted him, cutting through the sunlight in the room, the dust scattering.

"*Idiota!* I wouldn't do that if I were you."

Rulf spun on his heel, then took a step back as a figure crept through the doorway, little more than a hunched shadow. The knight couldn't hide a shudder, which Ben noticed ran through his body from his silvery curls to the toes of his leather shoes. In the space between them, Ben saw the newcomer hobble into the room, leaning on a wooden cane. At first, he couldn't make out whether the intrusion was a man or a woman. The nondescript robes could belong to anyone, as could the strands of hair that straggled onto those crooked shoulders, as grey as the clothes. A gnarled hand gripped the cane, attached to an arm just as bony, an emaciated body under the rags.

The other hand, trembling, pointed at him, a finger curled out in blame.

"*Drago,*" the figure croaked, soft and harsh, her voice announcing her sex. "Demon. Destroyer. A blight in the eyes of the saints."

Ben suppressed the urge to draw back on the bed, pull the duvet over his head. The woman lurched closer, as though her outstretched hand was a lodestone, drawing her to the source of her disgust. Through the curtain of her hair, Ben caught the glint of spectacles and the spark behind them, the feverish light in her eyes. He caught the hint of a hooked nose and palsied flesh, her lips drooping, wet with the spittle of damnation. Recognition didn't bring him any sense of ease. The last time he'd seen this woman – this *creature* – he'd been far from here, up in the Alps last winter. She'd stood high in a lectern holding a fragment of the harp, bleating about Lucifer and glory and a holy scourge, overseeing his imminent execution. Well, things hadn't exactly worked out for her. The Invisible Church had fallen, reduced to rubble by the White Dog. Up until now, he'd suspected that the woman before him was dead. No. *Hoped.* Instead, he found her here. Here and singing from the same old song sheet.

"De Gori," he said. *The Cardinal of the Whispering Chapter.* "And they say I turn up like a bad penny."

"Lore-breaker," De Gori said in reply. "Traitor. Ab—"

"Abomination. Yeah. I heard you the first time." Ben poured weariness into his voice, covering his alarm. "Haven't you heard? The Lore is over. You've got no authority here."

The Cardinal screeched again and lunged towards him. Well, she hobbled as fast as she could for the bed. Before she could reach him, Lord Rulf snapped out an arm, preventing her charge. The knight hadn't meant to hurt her, Ben was sure, but the woman was no more than a collection of bones and she dropped to her knees on the floor, her cane clattering away from her. De Gori gave a wail, a thin, wet sound, and then covered her face with her hands, her shoulders heaving, her sobs threatening to shake her apart.

A flicker of pity touched Ben's heart. Then he remembered Jia, her cuts and bruises as the guards had returned her to her cell up in the mountains. The beaten, hollow look of her . . .

Why won't you let me help you? he'd asked her, but she had turned away.

He glared through his ghosts up at Rulf, a question in his eyes.

"The Cardinal came to us a couple of months ago," the knight said, by way of explanation. "And yes, we realised who she was. Or rather, who she used to be. I'm afraid that Evangelista is the . . . *doyenne* no more. The fall of the Chapter . . . it was hard on her."

"I can see that."

"Devils," De Gori muttered on the floor. "Devils with angels' wings, white as snow."

Ben clenched his jaw. "It's the *lunewrought*," he said. "Not that she was *compos mentis* before. The harp screwed with anyone who touched it." *Including me?* he wondered, but didn't say. "But I have to tell you, Rulf, you aren't exactly filling me with confidence."

"De Gori can't hurt you now."

Ben stared at the woman on the floor and he guessed that it was true. The state of her, as ruined as the monastery on the mountainside, didn't present an active threat. The brimstone lingered, of course, but the fire had gone out. Like everything else, the Curia Occultus, the Sleep and his love life, the Chapter was over. Ancient history. Wherever he stood now, it was on new ground. Uncharted territory. The normal rules no longer applied.

Still . . .

"Tell that to the brat who jumped me on Snowdon," he said. "Claimed she was a Black Knight, can you believe it? She knew where to find me too. And now I know how."

It was the *lunewrought*, all right. The Fay metal was all of a piece, wasn't that what they said? Contact with the stuff had tainted him, stained him with its magic. It had tainted the Cardinal too, of that he had no doubt. If the old woman had brought the remaining manacles to the Last Pavilion, the residual magic able to bind him, then chances were that she knew how to trace him too – or at least to point the "Black Knight" in the right direction, hoping for a last-minute assassination. Her idea of justice. But the girl, Annis, had told him that she'd stolen the manacle and gone after him herself, a foolhardy quest if ever there was one. And Caliburn bore a blade forged from *lunewrought*, as the damn sword liked to boast. Had Arthur's awakening helped the girl to find him, strengthening the signal, drawing her to the mountain? It seemed likely . . .

Lord Rulf looked at the ceiling. "Annis," he said. "She hasn't been the same since her brother drowned last year. She begged the patriarchs to hand the duty to her, the Fitzwarren vendetta. Of course, we refused. Not only was she too young, the collapse of the Lore gave us reason for pause . . ." And he did pause, looking back at Ben with the same dilemma in his eyes, the same doubt. "In the interests of transparency, I should tell you that this house has yet to reach an agreement over the matter of your slaying."

"That's nice," Ben said. "Why don't you tell me what's really going on here?"

Rulf opened his mouth to speak. Before he could do so, footsteps echoed down the corridor outside. In a flurry of cropped hair, red cheeks and baggy leather jacket, the would-be knight in question came bounding through the bedroom door. Annis collected herself, wiping the joy from her face at the sight of Ben, bloody bandages, bruises and all. She frowned at the weeping woman on the floor. Then up at the patriarch.

256

A little shyly, she said to Ben, "You're alive." Typically, she masked her obvious pleasure with teenage ambivalence.

He took in the welt across her face, running from her brow, across one eye and the bridge of her nose. It would make quite the scar; Annis wasn't going to forget the dead king in a hurry.

When he spoke, it was through a pang of guilt.

"Just about. I'd feel a lot better if someone would take this damn thing off my wrist."

De Gori wailed behind her hands.

"Lucifer unleashed," she said. "Inferno. Hellfire. Monsters walking the earth."

Annis puffed out her cheeks. She stared at Lord Rulf for a moment, watching him hesitate, then rolled her eyes.

"Father, do as he says. He saved us, didn't he? He could've just let us all burn."

Ben grunted. *So that was it.* Taking in the man and the girl by the bed, he could see the family resemblance for himself, mostly in their eyes, that icy determination. Some Indian heritage had softened Rulf's features in his daughter, lending her dark hair and brown skin in place of his pale flesh. Between them, some unspoken challenge hung in the air, a hint of grief, both recent and older, mixed with a quiet resentment. Ben had seen enough of his own to recognise the sense of it. It struck him then that perhaps a son and a brother wasn't all that these people had lost, the mother absent too, an echo of her in Annis. Ben didn't like to pry – he of all people respected privacy – but he guessed that this was the issue that Lord Rulf, the patriarch, found hard to refuse. With a shrug, he stepped past De Gori to the bedside, reached in his pocket and retrieved a little key. As Annis looked on and the former Cardinal sobbed and muttered, Rulf bent and unlocked the manacle around Ben's wrist, sliding the *lunewrought* into his jacket.

At once, Ben felt the tingling sensation ebb and fade, the chiming in his head silenced. Warmth crept into his bones, washing away the coldness of his binding. His nerve endings shivered like sun-kissed branches and he could feel his flesh begin to knit anew, his bruises sinking under his skin. He stretched, allowing a thin carapace of scales, red as blood, to slide over his nakedness, forming his mentally conjured suit. Sans symbol. Then he swung out his legs and, a little unsteadily, stood up, not entirely disliking the way that De Gori cringed or the way he towered over Lord Rulf. The latter took a step backwards, the old enmity stifled between them, embers not quite cooled. But then the knight gathered himself and he met Ben's gaze with the same steely resolve.

"Ben Garston, consider yourself our honoured guest," he said. "You have the thanks of House Fitzwarren. And as for myself . . ." he tipped his head at Annis, forcing the words out, "I owe you a personal debt of gratitude. As I said, I request a truce. A day for us to parley. I ask that you escort me to our hall and speak with the council assembled there. I don't need to tell you that we're up against it. I believe it's time to discuss a new understanding. A new . . ." again, the hesitation, "pact. And to seek a way in which to answer the present crisis. With your fire and our swords. Together."

Ben glared down at the patriarch for a moment. Then he looked at De Gori and at Annis, who was practically hopping from foot to foot in anticipation. Finally, he looked out of the window, at the autumn trees and the sky beyond, offering him something that these people never could. He could've laughed. After all his trials, living in the shadows over the years, he stood here among his mortal enemies, the Chapter and House Fitzwarren. Where the Guild of the Broken Lance had suffered his existence, these bodies never had, both calling for his head. How small they looked now. How insignificant. Their schemes, their rules, their power in tatters. Now it was their turn to feel endangered. Alien. Unwanted. Obsolete in a changed world.

But the realisation only made him sad. Once again, Jia sprang to mind, her eyes reaching for him much like her fingertips, brushing his own before she fell into the gulf, forever lost. She'd reached him with the truth too, and once enlightened, he'd never forget it.

"The Lore was a lie," he said, speaking to the ones in the room, but also to himself, letting the air carry the weight of his decision. "And lies are like poison, corroding everything they touch. Seems to me that's why we're in this mess. The Lore was just another name for oppression. For hiding the truth of the world. You see, others walk among you. Remnants. Creatures from the Old Lands." He sighed, wishing that the sunlight outside could reach his heart. "Shit. Even Von Hart realised he'd made a mistake. It's staring us all in the face. We'd have been better off fighting to the death back then. Instead, we denied our own existence. We're cowards. All of us."

"Or we could've made peace, yes," Lord Rulf said. "My ancestors may have failed to understand that, but that's what I'm offering you now. A last alliance to—"

Ben turned to look at him.

"No," he said. "No more councils. No more Pacts." *No more sleep.* "I'm done with all that. It didn't work. It won't work."

Rulf swallowed at this, then spoke in measured tones, obviously trying to quell his anger.

"Then what do you suggest, Mr Garston? That we simply lay down and die?"

Ben jabbed a finger at the knight. "You know what? You can do what you like. For better or worse, I'm heading back to London. I can't leave them. The city . . . I can't leave them like that." He squared his shoulders, testing his muscles, his returning strength. "Besides, I left something behind. I get the feeling I'm going to need it."

Only with the blade can I reignite the circles and restore your world. Bring us the sword. Then you will have your answer.

The dream was still with him, in all its shimmering weirdness. All its suspect insistence and claims. The Lady had offered him some truth of her own, but he realised that it wasn't the whole story. And if he knew the Fay at all, then he probably wasn't going to like the rest of it. Still, he knew who he was now, didn't he? *What* he was. He'd decided to meet his fate on his own terms. That meant letting everyone else do the same, Remnant and knight alike, whether it served him or not.

We're all bound up in this, he wanted to tell the knight. *The Pact we made. This is our mess. But the humans out there, left in the city . . .*

He held his tongue. If House Fitzwarren was ready to acquit him and take measures to save this land, then the knights would have to prove it first. In recent years, he'd been on the sticky end of too much betrayal. Bardolfe. Jia. Von Hart. People he'd trusted once. In light of that, he would ask nothing of no one. He didn't want the responsibility. Not any more. Too many had paid the price on his watch.

He saw Lord Rulf's shoulders fall, his disappointment plain.

"Fair enough," the knight said, his tone belying his words. "Then you leave the Last Pavilion in a quandary. But before

260

you go, I'll ask of you one more thing. Kindly remove that ghastly creature from the Fitzwarren family tomb."

Annis, still breathless, still bruised, caught up with him as he strode across the lawn. He was heading for the large stone edifice under the trees, the turf cool under his feet. The tomb was an ugly thing, a building in itself, flanked by pillars and graven knights. Who knew how many coffins lay inside? Lots, if memory served. Hundreds of Fitzwarren sons. And almost one of their daughters . . .

Afternoon was fading, the shadows slipping between the trees, the eager grip of the coming winter. He'd stayed here too long already and he didn't turn around as the girl ran up behind him.

"Aren't you forgetting something?"

Grim-faced, he slowed, letting her keep pace with him, a reluctant concession. Instead, she ran around in front of him, halting his steps.

He growled at her, but Annis didn't budge.

"If you're going to try and change my mind, I'm—"

She waved his refusal away, meeting his gaze with the same frustrating resolve.

"I don't blame you for going back. Someone has to take a stand. We'll go down fighting one way or another," she said, and he knew it was true. "But the sword isn't all you need."

With this, she reached into her jacket and brought out the relic she'd recovered in Trafalgar Square, in the ruins of the wooden giant. The Horn of Twrch Trwyth glittered in the sunlight, all ivory and gold, carved centuries ago from the tusk of the monstrous boar. Here it was, plucked straight out of legend, and Ben couldn't suppress a gasp at the sight. In his flight from

London, his dream-that-was-no-dream and his subsequent chat with the patriarch, he had forgotten all about it. *Dummkopf* . . . It was humbling; his bold words in the bedroom sounded a little hollow now. All the same, the memory of the dead king on the shores of Lake Bala came winging back to him, sounding the horn and summoning Remnants, raising an army to invade London.

The girl held the horn out to him, the relic offering its own desperate suggestion.

"I know you're not taking me with you," she said. "I won't even ask. Still, you'd be a fool to go back to the city alone."

He let out his breath, finding himself unable to argue with this. He found the scar on her face hard to look at and he wanted to say something, but the words escaped him. Likewise, he wanted to warn her. To tell her to stay away. Find somewhere safe until this was over. *One way or another.* But he couldn't muster that either. He'd made his decision and set out on his own course, leaving this House to do the same. There was no Pact. No Lore between them. He had no right to tell her anything at all.

With a grunt, he took the horn from her. He hung it around his neck.

"Take care of yourself, Annis Cade," he said.

Then he stepped past her and left her to watch his retreating back as he strode for the tomb, for the moss-covered knights guarding the entrance. As he approached, the deep gloom behind its broken door caught and echoed his call.

"Rise and shine, du Sang. We've got a war to fight."

And somewhere in the darkness, he heard a weary groan.

SEVENTEEN

And so, after everything, it comes to this.

Red Ben Garston stood on the bluff of White Horse Hill, looking down on the Manger, a deep vale sweeping through the heart of the ancient site. A few yards above him, the prehistoric figure of the so-called horse, carved in chalk and cantering over the rise for all to see for miles around. Below, the flat-topped mound of Dragon Hill, where the scarred summit spoke of legend and myth, the ground forever stained by wyrm's blood, or so the story went. Beyond, the great flat valley, a patchwork of twilight fields and farms, cut by a railway line and wind turbines in the distance. In the air, the smell of wildflowers, bramble and chaff, joining the spice of his sweat. At this hour, Manger, hill and valley floated in the evening mist, ships cast adrift from another time.

Like me. Like us.

In the distance, the village of Uffington lay dark and still, abandoned to the autumn night.

It comes to this. Full circle.

No one had noticed Ben alight on the rise, a dragon returned after many long years. *Eight hundred odd, if truth be told.* His claws made scars of their own as he'd landed, wings folding, tail thumping the earth, snout pluming smoke. He scanned the gloom with golden eyes, picking out the leap of rabbits miles away, the tentative wheeling of birds. Nature, as ever, went on, despite the upheaval in the land. The warping of all that was good and true. For how much longer, he couldn't say.

Some of that upheaval, he could see first-hand. The shattered ridge of a nearby hill, a fissure running up the slope to the summit. Much of the earth had fallen back in, choking the mouth of the cave, but the scale of the wound made it clear where Cormoran had risen, before striding east across the Downs for London. Not that he needed a reminder, the sight made him think of the Remnants who'd come to the Manger on that long-lost midsummer night, a thousand strong or more, united in their plea for answers. For survival. Things might've turned ugly if not for the harp, strummed far away in Westminster Palace, the music already rippling out across the land.

Guilt aside, that was the reason he was here.

Perhaps out of courtesy, he dwindled into human form, thinking that this hill belonged to one beast alone. The one etched in chalk above him. Many around here claimed that the figure was a horse, whereas a handful of others knew better. Ben knew better.

The Vicomte Lambert du Sang rolled from his shrinking shoulders with a sharp Gallic curse, but made no other sound as he fell, the grass muffling his enervated frame. Then, all rag and bone (*he's hungry again*, Ben thought. *And for more than just goblin blood*), the boy brushed himself off and joined his companion, slinking into his reluctant and grim-faced shadow. Together, the two of them stood gazing down into the valley. Into the bones of the Old Lands.

"If you do this, *mon ami*," du Sang told him, "there is no going back."

Ben paid him no mind. He'd waited, the November wind

ruffling his hair, until the sun had slipped into the west, sinking under a tree-lined ridge like embers behind a grate. Until the darkness poured in, streaked with gold. Blood on velveteen. Until his heart slowed, thudding in his chest with a desperate resolve. He didn't need to explain himself to the creature beside him, the *vampyr* who, for all his apparent redemption, remained as murderous as ever. Indeed, who was only here for personal gain, the promise of fire and death. All the same, du Sang had helped him, flying in the face of his enemies, facilitating his escape. And as he stood here, on this ancient ground where his duty had first begun, it was impossible to blame him for wanting an end.

Perhaps it is our turn again . . .

Von Hart whispered to him through the heather, a sigh under the stars. Ben drew no comfort from the notion of a return to power; time had shown him that this was a lie. The envoy had wanted to undo the Sleep, he'd claimed, and summon the Fay to save the Earth. Restore the failing circles, whatever. The Lady had told him much the same. Ben knew he had every reason to doubt them. He had seen the light in Arthur's eyes, the corruption of the dead king. He'd seen the Remnant army, enthralled by the horn and marching on London. He'd learnt the source of all these things, the experiments of the Fay, and yet, somehow, he still felt responsible. He'd pledged his loyalty to humans long ago and in this very place, leaning over a table in the vale below to sign the king's scroll. The Pact. The foundation of the Lore. Overseen by knights (each one in armour, evidence of their distrust), he had turned his back on his own kind. In the name of preservation. Survival. A way to end the war and break the ground for peace, some dreaming day in the future. Or so he had thought at the time.

All that had fallen apart. Von Hart was right, damn him. It had all been a mistake. That didn't change the fact that Remnants and humans had failed to reach an accord. A decent one anyway, the former trapped in enchanted slumber, the latter stripped of magic.

To banish magic forbids the world its very nature . . . We'll snuff out the soul of the world. All will fall into darkness . . .

In the end, the Pact had been the first drop of poison, souring the Earth entire. And much as it scared him, his present course, he could easily have told du Sang that there had never been any going back. Not from the moment he'd put quill to parchment, eight hundred years ago . . .

The truth was he had no choice. If he wanted to save them, to save London, then Annis was right – he couldn't do so alone. As much as it pained him to use magic, to compel others to come to his aid, the only other option was to accept defeat. Time was short. In his bones, he knew he should recover the sword and go after the envoy. He could feel each grain of sand running through the hourglass, stealing away his chance of the truth. Of revenge.

One day. I'll give it one day, fairy. And then I'm coming for you.

But it was more than that. If the world was to end and take them all with it, then he'd see out his oath beforehand. At least that. His last mission. His final quest. He'd go to his death knowing that he'd fulfilled his promise.

So he said nothing to du Sang. Instead, he looked down on the Manger and let the wind cool him, match the chill of his fears. Then, trying not to think of the skeletal teeth that had last met the gilded mouthpiece, he lifted the relic to his lips.

He let the night fill his lungs. Then he blew the Horn of Twrch Trwyth.

Its sounding rolled out over the valley, a haunted peal, a blast that shook the hillside under his feet. Mournful, deep, the horn pressed its demand upon the sky. Upon the earth. In his peripheral vision, he saw du Sang stagger back, his wail lost in the echoes. The birds overhead dived for their nests, a breaking wave of black. Rabbits froze, stunned in the hedgerows. Trees creaked, bending in a force beyond the wind. Far away, the bell tower of St Mary's Church, Uffington, gave a lonely toll, struck by the shuddering air, a widening pool of resonance flooding over the shadowed land.

Then, silence. Ben lowered the horn, peering into the dusk. After a second or two, he glanced at du Sang, who simply shrugged. *Nothing.* Ben opened his mouth to speak, to vent a profane or caustic phrase, when another uproar answered him, riding on the waves of the first. Like a thunderclap, snatched from the clouds and buried underground, the surface of the Manger rippled and cracked, a rumpling carpet of green. In a heartbeat, a fissure zigzagged up to the empty road, swallowing trees and fences, the odd abandoned car.

For a breathless minute, Ben gazed into the maw, tracing the glitter of obsidian walls, molten, rippling, catching the starlight. The night throbbed around him, alive with residual power. *A song of the Old Lands. A song of summoning.* The moon and the stars shone down, ever cold, ever watchful. The night fell still, as though measuring the force of the accelerant spell, this spurring of the shattered Sleep.

And then – one by one, at first, and then in greater numbers – they came.

Wide-eyed, the horn trembling at his side, Ben watched the Remnants return.

The gnomes roused first, clambering from the earthen wound

in muttering, ragged bunches. Their tiny, wizened forms shuffled into the meadow, brushing off dust with a tinkle of bells, their tall, colourful caps shaking.

Then came the green men, their leafy faces rustling in the wind, their vine-clad arms stretching, throwing off the slumber of ages.

Next, Ben watched the ettin climb from the chasm. Their grey, boulder-like shapes had easily passed for standing stone and barrow back in the Old Lands, changing whenever a traveller drew near. The shy creatures, strong as ogres and just as large, blinked with hollow eyes in the gloom, looking about themselves with sleepy, yet mesmerised purpose.

The dwarves followed them, a grumbling lot, readjusting their helmets and smoothing beards rumpled by sleep. Axes and pikes clattered on shields as they gathered on the sward. Will-o'-the-wisp danced among them, bright silvery balls of gas, lighting the mist draping the valley.

With an ache in his breast – part longing, part awe – Ben watched the Sleepers rise. A hundred of them quickly swelled to five hundred and more, the earth offering up its hidden bounty, swallowed and subdued by the lullaby over eight centuries ago. In amongst the gathering throng, he saw tiddy mun, the marsh guardians, and reynardine, the tawny were-foxes of yore. He saw hedley kow, blue caps and hunky punks, the little gnarled keepers of river, rock and tree.

Then, bursting from the smouldering crack, a flurry of feathers filled the air. Sleek hides flexed with muscle. Claws spread. Beaks opened in an awakening cry. Strong they were, and golden, these winged warriors of old. The griffins swept across the face of the moon, high above the bluff on which Ben stood, his heart leaping at the sight. A flicker of white soon joined them, wreathing the bellowing gyre. Pale shreds of cloth streamed behind them as the women rode the wind, singing, singing with unfettered voices, hurled from the earth to the sky.

As the emerging creatures slowed, the fissure belching forth dust and Remnants, Ben looked down on the mob and his joy at their revival waned somewhat. He saw no giants and no dragons. The absence of the *wyrm-weir*, the old guardians, the keepers of a thousand treasures, sat like a stone in his chest, an unbidden and unanswered yearning. But for all his disappointment, his wish to add the might of these beasts to his ranks, he knew that such creatures slept as they dreamed. The deepest of all. Deep in the darkness under the earth.

Tears stinging his eyes, he clung on to hope.

This is just the beginning. The beginning of the end, maybe. But still a beginning . . .

For all his rapture at the view, the roaring above, the clamour in the Manger and du Sang's gasp, he couldn't ignore the sorry state of them. The hunched shape of once-proud forms. The blunt weapons and the broken swords. The patchy feathers and limping gait. The tattered ears and dull eyes. Their decline. Their *decay.*

They're all dead. Or dying.

Wasn't that what Jinx had told him, moments before the manticore went up in flames? And here, he knew, was the proof of Von Hart's claim, made months ago in the nether, resounding from the maw of the Ghost Emperor.

Magic is souring. The Sleep is failing. The Remnants will die.

Here was the fire of Jia's mission, her desire to steal the *Cwyth*, the mnemonic harp, and bring it to her master.

I can save them . . .

And here was the reason for her sacrifice.

He blinked away tears. He couldn't think about that now. He had no way to undo the past. He'd come here on the business of the future. Whatever he could salvage from it anyway. Whatever good he could do. The legacy of the last dragon, wakeful and walking the earth . . .

Surveying the Remnants in the Manger, a shadow of guilt touched his heart. Not one of them, he knew, was free from enchantment. Even though he'd released them from the Sleep, broken, unravelling as it was, there wasn't a creature down there, awake or no, who didn't have good reason to rebuke him. Punish, kill him even, for choosing to side with the humans and for signing the king's damnable Pact. The griffins, the women wheeling in the sky, had more than enough to hold him to account. To blame him for their spellbound and stolen lives. What could he tell them? How could he press his reasons upon them, make them accept his ancient mistake, his selfish need to survive? Would they care? Would they listen before they tore him apart?

He doubted it. The truth was he held the Remnants enthralled. Bound. Enslaved by the horn. Was he any better than Arthur? He'd simply replaced one enchantment with another, dragging them out of the earth.

Silently, he begged their forgiveness.

I need you. Albion needs you . . .

But much like councils and pacts, this was no time for speeches. And as every eye in the meadow turned towards him, a flame-haired figure on the bluff, he met the roar that went up with a weary hand.

He raised ivory and gold to the moon, calling the Remnants to war.

London

Astride a wyvern, Arthur, the Once and Future King, swooped high above Bloomsbury. Carrying a twelve-strong contingent of goblins, the green-winged squadron shadowed the thorn wall below, a dark and tangled boundary in the pre-dawn chill. The king wasn't best pleased, not that his grin conveyed the matter. Or rather, the power that steered him, making of him a puppet of bones, rankled at the present calamity. Only the light in his eyes, blue and unextinguished, flared with the ire that drove him, magic as fierce as it was sour.

Time is running out.

Caliburn, his sword, had refused him. Taranis, his beacon, had collapsed, the dragon and the knights escaping, his hecatomb undone. *We are in the dark.* And he had lost the Horn of Twrch Trwyth. *In the dark. But still, we come . . .* How long these idiot creatures, with their dented helmets and hunger for flesh, would stay bound and loyal to him was anyone's guess. He had promised them a feast to end all feasts. Instead, they had ash in their mouths. Once sounded, the horn spoke to whatever lay in the hearts of the Remnants who heard it. In this case cruelty, savagery and greed, wrenching the creatures from the broken Sleep and pressing them into his deathly service. Soon, the echoes of enchantment would dissipate completely, of that he had no doubt. And, craven, mercenary at best, every goblin, ogre, greentooth, bugbear, gargoyle, grim and ghoul would break rank to go in search of easier prey, out there in the wilds of Britain.

The hour had come to strike. If he couldn't capture the humans, enough to send a chorus of screaming souls into the sky, then he would bring the hecatomb to them, decimate resistance where it stood. Thanks to the viewing platform of the Shard, he'd gained a perfect bead on the enemy, watching the smoking encampments on Hampstead Heath, the regiments of tanks, the jeeps and artillery, the camouflaged soldiers milling around them. To the east, he'd seen the black shapes of gunboats and the strange, submerged ships, now and then bobbing to the surface of the Thames, tall glass eyes glinting in the sun. And he had seen the swift metal birds, both winged and with rotors, zipping and chugging over the city, their quiver of rockets primed. The human armies gathered, recovering after the shock of attack, consolidating, waiting. But they would not wait for long. With fire, with rage, the troops would force their way through the thorn wall and meet with their king in battle. Arthur couldn't risk their triumph. This time, his reign must endure.

Come sunset, all will kneel to the throne.

He'd meant this sortie for closer surveillance, to check the boundaries of the thorn wall for infiltration, the planting of bombs and such, while his troops mobilised on the ground. Commanding half of the horde to spread out to key points around the inner circumference of the briar, the king had mounted his steed and taken flight into the west, where he deemed the greater threat lay. Let them look up and see him in the distance, the Pendragon reborn! Let them shiver in their boots, clench their sphincters and turn to each other with ashen faces. Let them witness his gauntlet thrown and know that soon all would join him in death.

Yet he'd misjudged them. A memory tugged at him, a maggot twisting in the muck of his brain, nudging an emotion from his previous life. A life long lost by a lake between snow-capped mountains, far from here in Wales. Once, he'd been a warrior. A man himself, yes, elevated by a wizard, a sword and fate to the throne of Logres. Despite the code of the Round Table, despite wooing damsels and prancing after cups, he had always remained a fighter at heart, clad in armour, his justice often coming at the point of a sword. But in Sleep, in death, it seemed he'd forgotten an important matter. Human intuition. The prescience of fear. The scent of approaching destruction.

The sight of the jets in the distance, the helicopters droning behind them, served to remind him. Sunlight peeped through the thorn-shadowed ruins of Canary Wharf and the masts of the Millennium Dome, speaking of blood to come.

The humans came to make war.

The squadron roared towards him, vapour trailing in its wake. Six steel birds, he counted, spear-like missiles under their wings. The jets shot over the misty expanse of Regent's Park and the empty streets around it.

And so it begins . . .

Arthur signalled to his troops. No sooner had he raised his hand than the jets opened fire. Bullets zipped through the air, shattering the morning calm with tracers of ammunition, bright streaks riddling over the top of the thorn wall. Sharply, he banked, dodging the fusillade, the sky ripped apart inches to his right. And more than the sky. With a squawk, he watched one of the wyverns burst into pieces, become a scattering cloud of blood, the unhorsed goblins shrieking and tumbling into the briar below. The jets shot past, the wyverns flapping up a storm in their wake. The goblins clung on, crouching low in the saddle. The planes were fast. Too fast, Arthur reckoned, for a focused attack on a slower and smaller target, and he barked at his troops to spread out. Yanking at the reins, he rose again on an updraught, veering to watch the jets boom past him. The squadron wheeled over the city, preparing for another pass.

Let them come . . .

That left the helicopters, bringing up the rear-guard. Again, he counted six, an opening salvo to spark the battle. Six slender, wasp-like machines with rotors spinning, gun barrels whirring with grease-smoke and fire. The sky shuddered as the king rose, his steed swift enough to evade the bullets thudding all around him, hitting nothing but air. The troops followed his lead, the wyverns thrusting for the heights. In response, the human pilots leaned back in their seats, punching at controls and steering to join them, reclaim the aerial advantage.

But it was too late. As the king's arm fell, the goblins above him gave a unified cry. The next moment, they released the rope-bound bundles that ran alongside the wyvern saddles, each long and lumpy sack coiled upon a green-scaled flank. With a rattle and a clank, a torrent of chains, studded with bones, nails and hooks, came raining from above. Most of the chains snaked earthward, missing the enemy by yards, lost to the thorns and the streets below. Some, however, struck home, smashing into two of the helicopters, quickly reeled in by the rotor blades, smoke coughing into the dawn.

Spinning, growling, one of the vehicles juddered earthward like a sycamore seed. Its tail met the other stricken craft and

tangled in mid-air, metal splintering high above the city. In a
billowing plume of smoke, the helicopters tumbled behind the
briar, a scream of engines and a loud crash reverberating between
the office blocks of Euston Square. As the echoes faded, the
shrieks of the wyverns eddied back in, blooded, gleeful and wild.

Then the squadron went grumbling past, the remaining helicopters heading east, random gunfire opening a path before
them, the wyverns scattering. Another of the beasts gave a screech,
a shell thudding into its neck, a spray of blood and frantic wings
whirling through the smoke. Arthur watched the craft lose altitude over Angel, sinking into the cover of the thorn wall. A
glance into the distance told him that the jets were coming back,
however, roaring between the cracked dome of St Paul's Cathedral
and the brickwork heights of the Barbican. Taking cover struck
the king as wise. With fist held high, the other gripping the
reins, he steered his mount to follow the helicopters, sweeping
down into the shadow of the briar, his troops falling in behind
him.

The choppers were fast, angular shapes zipping along the inner
wall of thorns. Hot in pursuit, the king and the goblins swooped
after them. The distance between the two squadrons was growing
by the second. There was no way that the wyverns, for all their
strength, could outpace the flying machines. Smoke from the
choppers' engines wafted in Arthur's face, a flag promising defeat.
But the dead king was not dissuaded. Looking down, he glimpsed
activity below, tanks grumbling along New Road for Hoxton, the
soldiers busying on the bridge over the canal. They were setting
up a barricade that bristled with gun placements, he saw, the
ordnance levelled on the hedge. The king knew that the soldiers
had nothing left to lose. Desperation had made them bold. And
he pictured similar scenes taking place at other points around

the barrier. The concrete arteries that fed London would be rumbling with troops, vehicles and artillery, surely. With rocket launchers, with bombs, the human army prepared to enter the city, to breach the thorn wall with fire.

Let them come. Let them come . . .

Now the aim of the attack became clear. Drawing level with the ground troops beyond the wall, the choppers released a volley of munitions at the briar. The bombs burst apart as they struck the barrier, a series of smaller explosions showering the perimeter, gobbets of flame deep in the knotted depths. In no time at all, streaks of fire painted the towering face of the thorn wall, devouring the dry and tangled branches. Tunnels of embers and pluming ash riddled their way towards the ground. In this way, the humans sought to weaken the wall. It might take hours to blaze a trail through a quarter-mile of thicket, but still they came. The king couldn't help but admire them, the warrior in him unable to deny the bravery of this assault, even as he focused on a suitable reprisal.

At some unspoken signal, the barrier ahead broke apart. And with more than smoke and flame. In a grey-skinned tide, a flock of gargoyles poured forth from the wall, taking flight from perches in the briar, where, silent, sinewy and cold, they had waited for battle. Each creature weighed several tons and had no logical capacity for flight; it was the magic in their veins that bore them aloft. The Horn of Twrch Trwyth had peeled the gargoyles from the gables of mansion, monument and church, dragging their wakened horror to London. The magic, however sour, bound the Remnants to the king, and his horde moved as one, shackled to his will. The goblins cheered at the sight of the gargoyles. Fifty or more of the beasts filled the sky. Horns, claws and teeth. A palisade of snarling, spellbound granite.

Arthur grinned – as he always grinned – watching the obstacle dawn on the helicopters. Locked into a bombing run, there was only time for the pilot at the rear to react, breaking formation to veer away, awkward and chugging over the streets below. The remaining craft crashed headlong into the flock of gargoyles, metal meeting stone with a sound to shatter the sky. Snapped rotors, splintering claws and fire rained down on the city. The king looked on, satisfied, as one of the choppers, whining and bleeding smoke, smashed into a high-rise at the edge of Shoreditch Park, glass and steel glittering in the sun. With a boom, the aerial wreckage hit the earth, gouging up greasy black furrows, splashing the surrounding green with fire. Another helicopter twirled directly onwards into the thorn wall, detonating in flowers of flame, adding to the spreading inferno.

As one, the king led the wyverns up and away from the blaze, an arrow of fangs, swords and scales climbing through the smoke. In the distance, the Shard glimmered, a sword held high in challenge.

Arthur drew no breath from the clearer air, his lungs long withered to rags. He felt neither fury nor fear as he levelled his gaze on the returning jets, winged death spearing towards him. In a burst of gunfire, two of the wyverns squawked and exploded, blood painting the sky at his back. Goblins screamed, torn green guts joining the miasma.

But as the planes came on, the surviving gargoyles were rising, rising from the thorn wall. Yellow eyes, chipped claws and cracked wings raced for the space between the king and the jets. Let granite meet the glass-fronted cockpits and steel wings. Let gravel choke the engines. The gargoyles, enthralled by the horn, gave no thought to their personal safety as, shrouded by smoke, they rose to collide with the squadron.

Arthur maintained his position, straddled upon the air, bullets whipping around him. Breastplate proud, crown gleaming in the sun, he sat as a decoy, watching the planes approach. In a minute or so, all would be shattering stone and death.

Your machines are no match for magic . . .

But this conceit, it seemed, was premature. The first inkling that things were amiss came from a subtle twist in the atmosphere. The king sensed it. An ill wind up his spine. Then another cry went up from the goblins. This time in fear. A wyvern shrieked in unmistakable dismay. With a hiss, Arthur turned in his saddle, just in time to see a feathery tide descending on the beasts behind him, a squall of wings and muscled flanks. Beaks open, sharp and black, the intruders vented a ferocious battle cry. Attention fixed on the choppers and jets, Arthur had neglected to notice the flock of griffins sneaking through the clouds above, now falling like holy fire upon his airborne troops.

No! In mute alarm, the king could do nothing but watch as, with outstretched claws, griffins plucked several of his soldiers from their mounts and flung them out into the air, a scatter of helmets and swords over Hoxton. Then, in a snarl of limbs, green thrashing against gold, the griffins and the wyverns were spiralling downwards, blood and feathers flying around them like windswept leaves.

The jets came on, shooting over the wall and into the arena of London. The noise of their approach snapped the king's attention back to them, seconds away now, and then to the gargoyles, ascending below. Again, he took no pleasure in the sight, his black heart quailing. The sky down there was full of white, a confusion of rags and streaming hair that took him a second to place.

No! No! A host of women were swooping up from the shadow

of the thorn wall, where no doubt they'd hovered, unseen and silent, waiting for their chance. Helpless, Arthur watched as the flight of witches, each woman riding a broom, shot into the ranks of gargoyles, intercepting the assault. There must have been thirty or more of them, each one bare-limbed and pale, a vanguard to challenge the stony flock.

Free. The king would've frowned if he could. *Free of the Sleep. Yet not by my hand . . .*

The coven, the sisters of forest, river and standing stone – the guardians of nature back in the Old Lands – wasted no time getting to work. White fire fizzled below, released from raised and open palms, the muttered spells crackling through the air with righteous fury, lightning without a storm. Wherever the light touched, striking into granite flank and maw, dust showered in place of blood. Cracks appeared in the gargoyles' bodies, in their haunches, torso and wings. The spells spoke to the magic of the beasts, the king realised. Unbinding. Undoing. Asserting the natural weight of stone. Arthur watched the gargoyles thrash their wings, fighting sudden gravity, an anchor dragging them down. As the flock broke apart, their retaliation checked, the witches raised their voices in song, a shrill chant of power and reproach sending the beasts into frenzy. Hair and hands weaving, the women darted among the creatures, chasing them down with fire and song. A dispersing gyre, a torrent of stones, scattered over the city.

It's the horn. The stolen horn. In cold alarm, the king grasped his peril. *An army summoned to defy me.*

The jets zipped through the sky, heading directly for him. His eyes flared, seeing one of the planes release a rocket from under its wings, firing into the fray. The humans, he knew, would make no distinction between wyvern and griffin, gargoyle and witch.

Or a skull-faced king, his legend, his right to the throne unknown. Like it or not, it was time to retreat. From this particular skirmish at least. He had seen this kind of combat before, far from here, in the shadow of walls not thorny, but white. The besieged ramparts of Camelot. The griffins would make short work of the wyverns. And the gargoyles, granite or no, couldn't withstand a barrage of spells. All of them were in danger now, the human war machines a clear and present threat. To the north, the thorn wall was aflame, coils of smoke staining the sky. Soon, the tanks and the soldiers would come, fighting through the blaze to bring their vengeance home.

Yet the hour is late. The king grinned, gripping the reins. *Too late now. I have drawn your gaze while we come, riding through the dark . . .*

With this thought – one not his own – the king in the mountain, Once and Future and now deceased, dug in his spurs. At once, his steed dived for the city below, narrowly evading a fresh burst of bullets. As the jets roared overhead, buffeting his wyvern's wings, Arthur abandoned the attack and circled down to the sprawling streets, keen to join the horde on the ground.

The battle for London had begun.

EIGHTEEN

Five goblins and an ogre were heaving away in St James's Park when Ben Garston landed – softly, for a seven-ton dragon – on the sward behind them. To his left, the twisted remains of the bridge, the lake wreathed in mist at this hour. Overhead, somewhere to the east, the sky resounded with gunfire and shrieks, the echoes of aerial battle. At dawn, he'd sent the griffins and the witches ahead, an opening strike to make his presence known.

I'm coming for you, worm brain.

The briar shadowed the park, a cold cloak that didn't quite reach the embers in his blood at the sight of the creatures. Why the goblins and the ogre should be here, and not with the rest of the horde behind the thorn wall, he could only guess. Had Arthur sent them to recover the sword? Although, in his present state, the king couldn't touch it . . . Perhaps with Ben's acquisition of the horn, presently clutched in one claw, the grip of its magic was loosening, releasing the Remnants to their natural self-interest. In this case, their lust for *lunewrought* and jewels. He could empathise with that, even if it was a slender hope.

The creatures had found a chain somewhere, presumably recovered from the ruins of the Fitzwarren encampment. They had looped it around the hilt of the sword, sticking out of the path a few yards ahead of him. In a combined effort, the ogre at the head, the goblins grunted and heaved at the chain, veins sticking out of their faces and necks. Their boots slipped on the wet ground, the chain stretched taut. The ogre's teeth protruded over his upper lip, his velvet cloak dragging through puddles, the feather on his cap dangling, dancing with his laboured breaths. So intent were the creatures on the tug-of-war, none of them noticed Ben's shadow falling over them, his wings folding into crossed arms as he changed, dwindling into human form.

The sword, of course, didn't budge. The blade, carved with glyphs and shiny as a mirror, didn't even quiver. The chain strained, however, fit to break. Ben could've told the goblins that they were wasting their time. Destiny had bestowed the sword to one hand alone, a scruffy squire, according to legend, who'd pulled the blasted thing from a stone. And then ascended to the throne, uniting the tribes of Logres in the golden age that some liked to call the Old Lands.

Much like the Fay, Ben knew that one couldn't rely on legend. *Hardly.* Legend was a capricious beast, tricky, slippery at best. Recently, he'd seen for himself that destiny alone hadn't bound the blade. In fact, the sword appeared to retain the right of choosing its bearer itself. Ben was living proof of that. He was many things, but none of them came close to *king*.

From a distance, the diamonds on Caliburn's crossguard regarded Ben with cool irritation.

"Punctual as ever," it said. "Thank heavens there isn't a war on."

Ben grunted in greeting. The ogre and the goblins hadn't batted an eye when the sword spoke – no doubt it'd been cheerfully berating them all morning – but they certainly did when Ben replied.

"Oh. Is this a bad time? I can always come back later."

As one, the creatures froze, looking up at him. Then the chain clanked to the ground. The ogre straightened his shoulders while the goblins flinched, their beady eyes taking in the newcomer, openly sizing him up. Red-scaled suit. Red hair. Green eyes and all.

Yeah, you know my name, all right. "Incineration" is my middle one.

The ogre swept the feather from his face and snarled, a buckled shoe splashing through a puddle as he took a step towards Ben, his fists clenched. Then the Remnant hesitated, his eyes straying over Ben's shoulder and off into the trees, his cheeks drooping. He glanced behind him, looking for reassurance from the goblins, but found that his cohorts were already fleeing, scattering across the park. Dragon or no, six against one was one thing. But as the ogre took in the rabble at Ben's back, a mist-shrouded throng rumbling up the sward, he appeared to change his mind, his fat lips quivering.

Ben grinned. Then he held out his hand, palm crooked at the ogre.

Be my guest.

The ogre seemed to think better of it. Shoes slipping in the mud, cap flying from his head, the creature turned and ran, lumbering across the grass with only a porcine squeal in his wake.

Ben watched him go. Then he walked up to the sword, cricked his neck and closed his fingers around the hilt. Again, a shiver of silver worked its way through him, *lunewrought* thrumming through his bones. In his mind, the sense of a gulf yawning around him, dark and deep. Endless. Thankfully, there were no visions. No Lady high on the palace walls gazing into the nether. *Searching* . . . No worlds upon worlds, a cosmic orchard dangling on the leys of Creation. And at his feet, only the faintest shimmer, a flicker of blue, the circle fading as he tugged at the sword. All the same, he felt no relief. It was bad enough knowing that the circles were there. There and souring . . .

Blinking, he found himself looking at the sword. Wrenched free from the ground and light in his grip. He gazed at his reflection in the blade, the scarred, careworn look of him. The mask he'd worn for so long. A mask torn from him by the times, a pale, redundant rag. But his face, he'd learnt, was more than illusion, reminding him of the bond that he shared with the humans, those trapped beyond the wall. The humans he had come here to save.

"No grand speech?" Caliburn said. "No glorious call to battle?"

Ben clenched his jaw. "Speeches are so 1215."

"A shame. Arthur was rather fond of them. Stirring the blood. Galloping off into the fray."

"Yeah? How did that work out for him?"

"You arsehole," the sword said.

With the horn around his neck and sword in hand, Ben led the Remnants onto the Mall. Behind them, at the end of the long, tree-lined boulevard, Buckingham Palace shone in the morning sun, her flag limp, her halls empty. The Queen had surrendered her seat to a royal bag of bones.

And the Remnants came, a ragged tide eclipsing the building, the ground rumbling under their feet. Gnome, dwarf, green men, ettin, will-o'-the-wisp, tiddy mun, reynardine, hedley kow, blue caps and hunky punks spilled through the trees and onto tarmac for the first time. In his once-fine suit, now filthy and torn at the elbows, the Vicomte Lambert du Sang crept at the head of the army, a withered, reluctant lieutenant. Of course, Ben knew that the "youth" only wanted to feed – had no *choice* but to feed – and to eventually earn his reward, a long-awaited fiery death. It was a promise that Ben had made and one he intended to keep; the grim fact had no hold on his emotions.

The Remnants, however, were a different story. Spellbound, entranced as they were, he couldn't suppress a pang of guilt every time he looked at them. His makeshift army. Free of the spell, he wondered what he'd do in their place – join the fight for the city or seek vengeance against the ones who'd remained, awake and unfettered upon the earth. *The Chosen and the Sleepers. Divided and conquered.* For most of these creatures, the harp had stolen the chance from them, forcing them down into the dark. Into history, forgotten myth. And here, with magic – with bloody *hoodoo*, of all things – he held them still, chained by ivory and gold to his will. This was the grist of his remorse, troubling his thoughts. But in his heart, he realised that the Remnants' freedom could prove short-lived. He was probably leading them all to their death.

They're dying anyway. He didn't need the envoy to jog his memory; he could see it for himself. *Another year, maybe two, and myths are all they will be.*

Still, it didn't make it all right.

He swallowed the thought. The last thing he needed was doubt, not when desperation, more than courage, drove him. He gripped the sword and moved on, striding ahead up the Mall, his army marching behind him. Rusty weapons clattered on shields, bells tinkled, leaves rustled, stone crunched, tails swished, helmets sat low over haunted, mesmerised eyes. It seemed wise to head for the section of the briar, clawing at the sky at the edge of the park, which had suffered the touch of fire. The fall of Taranis in the square beyond must've weakened the barrier. It would be a simple thing for him to assume dragon form and fly over the wall, but he couldn't waste time transporting five-hundred-odd Remnants into the city and hope to stand a chance against the king's horde. Time was of the essence. Double the danger lurked behind the thorns. He'd seen the jets above, the streaking bullets and bombs. He could hear the explosions somewhere to the north of him, booming off the sky. The humans were coming, tanks, missiles and all, to make a last stand. From bitter experience, he knew that the troops, as desperate as him, wouldn't make a distinction between a goblin and a gnome, an ogre and a dwarf. A dragon and a dead king.

He grunted. At least he'd had the luxury of the truth, brutal as it was.

Your fairy tales have all come true. Ben couldn't know the shock of such a thing, the realisation that myths were real, dreams made flesh. *Dreams. And nightmares . . .*

He'd almost reached the Guards Memorial, an obelisk flanked by bronze soldiers, when he drew to a halt, hearing the approaching growl of engines. He raised Caliburn, his ragtag army halting behind him. He scanned the park and the road for the source of the noise, his shoulders bristling with horns as he tensed for an ambush. If need be, he'd command the Remnants into the trees and take to the sky, find a way to divert the jets and the choppers with as few casualties as possible. *If only I could reach them, let them know that we're on the same side . . .* But he also knew that better creatures than him had tried and failed. Centuries ago, granted, yet the prejudice went deep. The first thing the humans would do at the appearance of a diplomat dragon was open fire, perhaps with a rocket launcher or two. Panic would render them blind to a truce, he could feel it in his bones. His white flag would go up in flames. Eight hundred years or no, human nature hadn't changed.

But not all *humans.*

His shoulders fell as the newcomers rode into view, grumbling in a loose convoy up Horse Guards Road. Brow drawn, he'd counted about sixty of the bikes by the time the first one reached him, skidding to a halt a few feet from where he stood. The gang must've ridden half the night, down the stalled, traffic-choked stretch of the M40, before roaring into London. The bikes came on, a black wave washing up the road. A legion of Triumphs and Harley Davidsons slowed to a halt, an array of leather jackets, machine guns and exhaust smoke in the shadow of the thorn wall.

The lead rider wasn't wearing a helmet, he saw. But then there was no law to stop her. And no Lore to prevent her alliance.

Fool of a girl.

"I told you—"

"That we could do what we liked," Annis reminded him, ignoring his outstretched finger, her face scarred yet defiant. "House Fitzwarren chooses to help you. Whether you like it or not."

Knights.

Stymied by his own words, he puffed out his cheeks, conveying his annoyance.

"It isn't a funfair in there, honey. I can't be responsible—"

Again, she cut him off. "This is our fight too. Some of us prefer to die on our feet."

He recalled Lord Rulf in the Last Pavilion, the barely veiled desolation in his eyes. What would the patriarch say if he knew that his daughter was here, preparing to lead a charge into London? Ben guessed that he already knew. That things had come to that. That when the chips were down, when destruction loomed, Rulf had faced her rebellious spirit and found that he had nothing to say.

Ben found the same. The fact was he'd been through fire and back with the ill-made knight and he had no reason to doubt her. And he realised then, standing there in the road, exactly what he was looking at. What he was seeing in her smooth-skinned face, her stubborn gaze. Not fear alone, no. Not just folly. Loyalty, perhaps, but more than that too. She represented something much greater, something larger than them all, Remnant and human alike. But it was too soon to put a name to it.

Instead, he lifted the sword.

"Then take this," he said. "Loath as I am to part with it." He gave a little cough. "I guess it belongs in human hands."

And you'll need it, he thought but didn't say. *Magic won't run out like ammo.*

Even in the gloom thrown by the briar, the blade gleamed, drinking in the morning. The gems on the crossguard sparkled as Annis reached for the hilt, with anything but cheery accord.

"Excuse me," Caliburn said. "Am I a spare umbrella kept in the hall? I'll have you know that I was forged in *lunewrought* and—"

"Shut the fuck up," Ben replied.

Red Ben stood before the thorn wall. In the settling silence, he took off the horn from around his neck, holding the relic tightly in his fist. With a flicker of will, his ribcage swelled, a ladder of scales rippling from groin to neck. His haunches bulged, rhino-sized, a growing shadow in the gloom. His splayed talons gouged furrows in tarmac. An unfolding chain, his tail snaked out behind him, the arrowhead tip reaching the vanguard of his troops, waiting at his back. Horns danced along his lengthening spine, travelling from snout to rump. He spread his wings, as red as the heat in his belly, his lungs swirling with gas.

He grinned, his fangs parting.

Time to open the gates of Hell.

With a deafening roar, he blasted a flood of fire at the thorn wall.

NINETEEN

For the rest of that day, in fire, magic and blood, the Battle of London played out.

At zero nine hundred hours, the Royal Artillery opened fire on New Road, a bombardment of rockets and shells hissing into the thorn wall, the briar bursting into flame. Explosions boomed off statue, parkland and reinforced glass, threatening to shake the hedge-swathed buildings apart, most of them riddled by monstrous roots. The thicket supported high-rises, office blocks and houses, the flames releasing the sagging structures in a crumple of girders and bricks. Trucks and cars, borne aloft by the brambles, shifted and fell, crashing into the road. The blaze lit the surrounding streets, shadows weaving across the Canonbury rooftops, rippling over the surface of Hoxton Canal. As the tangled branches writhed and split, charred wood caving inwards in the heat, the tanks crawled forward over the bridge, wolfhounds and panthers grumbling beside them, the armoured vehicles entering the breach. Down a corridor of swirling ash, the vanguard crept, pausing on occasion to refresh the fusillade, open the path ahead.

Above, helicopters had wheeled and buzzed, strafing the barrier with rockets, pillars of fire bleeding through the thorns. With a crash of sparks, the dense vegetation shrivelled and fell, dark clouds shrouding the sun. Here and there, soldiers rappelled from the circling choppers, zipping down ropes to land in clusters on the rooftops of shopping malls and car parks. Gas masks winked, bug-eyed in the haze. Soldiers held machine guns and rifles close, the weapons loaded and ready. On the ground, through the manmade eclipse, the troops had come on, headlights blazing, barrels raised, forcing a passage to the other side, the empty borough beyond.

It took time, but the flames worked swiftly, devouring the briar. For all its sorcerous provenance, the hedge remained simply a hedge, a mass of dry and knotted wood. The barrier may have bought the enemy time, a seemingly impenetrable obstacle, but these were not the Dark Ages, and Challengers, Apaches and Typhoons weren't knights on horses with pincushion swords. Within an hour, the tanks and the armoured vehicles had broken through into Shoreditch and were roaring down the road for Old Street roundabout. In the distance, the Leadenhall Building rippled like a fountain in a mirage. Behind them, the advance guard, marines in aluminised helmets and suits, had managed to cross the canal. Silver boots shuffling through ash, flame-throwers belching, they picked their way through the breach. With burning thorns looming on either side, every man and woman among them believed that they'd entered the jaws of Hell.

Goblins were waiting for them.

At the roundabout, in the shadow of the office blocks, under the hoardings in the middle of the junction, the scattered divisions of the armies met. Behind overturned buses and cars, the goblins shrilled and hurled projectiles, rocks and trash bouncing off the tanks and the grated windshields of the wolfhounds, unable to make a dent. Gunfire tore through the day in answer, pinging off metal and tarmac, green blood splattering the scene.

A rocket launcher popped, a stray rocket spinning through the air and detonating against a billboard, some sunny televised holiday prize exploding in glass and flame.

The tanks advanced, crunching over the debris. Confident that the primitive state of the enemy was no match for a modern military force, the human soldiers had neglected to scan the surrounding buildings. They failed to notice the beasts, hackles raised, that lurked in shadowed porches, waiting. As the vehicles grumbled forward, the black shucks snarled and pounced, fifty or more of the coal-eyed beasts leaping into the approaching ranks. Fangs met throats and limbs in the blood haze, random bullets peppering the day. Men and women screamed, wrestling with savage balls of fur, flailing on the ground, then falling still. A tank rolled over one of the beasts with a groan of steel and a muffled whine, rumbling on towards the roundabout, keen to meet the screeching horde.

Faced with goblins alone, the advancing troops may have stood a chance. But these creatures had long ago learnt the art of slyness. Nearby, on Great Eastern Street, a gaggle of greenteeth poured from the medieval mouth of St Agnes Well, climbing from the ruins and the sewers below, the slick-skinned hags dripping with wastewater and shit. Beady eyes glittering with hunger, the greenteeth crawled in a swampy, stinking mass toward the junction of Old Street, their hands, knees and breasts dragging on the ground.

Above, gargoyles swooped, dropping like boulders into the fray.

Meanwhile, the Remnant army, led by Ben, had broken through the thorn wall and charged into Trafalgar Square. With a mighty roar, the dwarves went barrelling through the smoke, axes swinging, to meet the rabble on the other side. Ogres, their furred cloaks no longer so fine, their hose torn and blackened, had come lurching down the steps of Nelson's Column, knives and clubs in hand. Between the bonfires that littered the square, the creatures had clashed, helmets, shields and teeth splintering, bloodied beards cracked in grins, feathered caps flying. Gnomes leapt from armoured shoulders, tearing at hair and poking at eyeballs, teeth nipping at the lobes of grotesque ears. Here and there, the smoke condensed and took on equine form, shagfoal galloping out of the brume, their eyes flaming, leaving heaps of trampled bodies in the stampede. In the wreckage of the fallen idol, the thorn wall a smouldering mouth, Remnant met Remnant with bellows and screams. As though no time had passed at all, the fabulous beings and beasts resumed the battle of centuries ago, on the gore-soaked fields of Camlann.

Gradually, faced with such a force, Arthur's horde began to fall back, spilling into the surrounding streets, dispersing into tight knots of conflict. On Shaftesbury Avenue, shop windows exploded, the black knights roaring out of the smoke, guns blazing, driving the goblins back. Soho became a warren of smoke, bullets and blood. Bugbears lurched behind the crumpled stalls, stalked by green men in the brume, the two creatures clashing on occasion, leaves and fur flying. At Waterloo, a witch came spinning down from the skies. Aflame with some backfired spell, she went crashing into a petrol station, an explosion blossoming on York Road.

At dusk, the battle came to a head on London Bridge.

Ben swept over the city, his wings shredding the clouds of smoke, a widow's veil over the sunset. Tucked behind his plated breast, the Horn of Twrch Trwyth felt cold against his skin, the touchpaper to the terror in the streets. The relic had dragged the Remnants from the Sleep and plunged them headfirst into the whirlwind, the storm of violence below. Others, free of enchantment and the quickening spell, had come, armed to the teeth and ready, desperate to liberate London.

The thorn wall was truly ablaze now, ignited by the crashed aircraft (wyverns, griffins, gargoyles and witches still wheeling and screeching between the smouldering spires and rooftops) and the British squadrons that arrived on all sides, spurred on by the chaos in the city, the stirring call of war. From above, Ben could see them, the rows of tanks, trucks and soldiers marching down the shrouded arteries into London. The A23 to the south. The M4 to the west. He tried and failed to push the image of a conveyer belt from his mind, fresh meat rolling towards a grinder. Or perhaps an oven. This conflict, it seemed, was no place for humans. *But what choice do they have?* He could only admire their courage, while curling his snout at the price of the attack. An ocean, a waste of blood. The smell of it hung rank in the air, a pall as thick as the smoke.

Is this really our nature? Us and them? he wondered, his mind shrinking from the truth. *To kill or be killed? After all this time, is this the world we've made . . . ?*

To the east, down the winding length of the Thames, a submarine bobbed to the surface to launch a missile, sections of the briar hissing down into the river in giant flaming burrs.

At various sites across the capital, pillars of smoke coiled into the sky, joining the general miasma. Coasting on the sweltering wind, scales greased with ash, Ben followed the arc of the Embankment, searching for Annis and the Black Knights, lost somewhere in the fray. Somewhere, oil blazed, stinging his nostrils, spiced with the stench of burnt fur and flesh. Big Ben and the Eye danced and shimmered, uncertain silhouettes in the haze. Every window of Somerset House was aglow, an audience of cracked glass raging at the ruin. The river reflected its tears of flame. Cleopatra's Needle rose from the smog, a reminder of recent trials, when he'd imagined that an undead priest, a goddess reborn and a breach in the Lore were the worst of his troubles. Back when he could still afford hope. Believed he could restore the balance of his world, lonely, oppressed as it was.

Under this, dark wings smothered his heart. Carrion crows, the harbingers of doom, went fluttering through his soul. *Things change.* That's what the witch had told him, a year ago on the Brooklyn Bridge. Such a seemingly mundane prophecy, at odds with the catastrophe since. For hundreds of years, this had been his city, his home. Hidden in the depths, the Fay burrows under St John's Wood, he'd scratched out a life, of sorts. Over time, as the Great Forest fell, replaced by a jungle of concrete, steel and glass, he had slipped into her majestic shadow, a ghost of a long-forgotten land. *That it should come to this* . . . The devastation below, over which he swept like a visiting demon, only served to compound his despair. He'd sworn to protect this city and its people. And he had failed both.

Shouts, gunfire and the clash of steel shook him from his remorse, drawing his gaze to the river, oily and red in the deepening twilight. Through the centuries, a number of bridges had spanned the Thames. One of them had fallen in 1212, devoured by dragon fire, the houses upon it reduced to ash along with the people inside them. Thanks to him, Rakegoyle had fallen too, her wings smouldering, the river boiling around her bones. Once again, Ben shuddered at the synchronicity of fate, returning him to the site of his struggle with the old bitch. A struggle that had sparked the human panic in the first place, driving a king to press his seal to the Pact . . .

This latest bridge was also aglow, he saw, lit by machine-gun fire and the flash of swords. Goblins and ogres swarmed along the concrete span, bullets sparking off makeshift shields, which even from above, Ben could see were nothing more than manhole covers and torn-off car doors. Enough to withstand the volleys of the Black Knights, who were retreating along the bridge towards King William Street, some on motorbikes, some not, many of the vehicles left lying abandoned in the road. *They're running out of petrol,* he realised, his heart in his throat. *And ammo.* With rising dread, he heard the fading roar of gunfire and he couldn't ignore the diminished numbers of the knights. He had no way of knowing how many of them fought elsewhere in the city and how many had fallen since he'd blazed his way through the thorn wall, but this loose banner of a hundred or so wouldn't present much challenge to the horde when the last trigger clicked on empty.

Worse, he could see the horrors to the north, a throng of bugbears, ghouls and greenteeth gathered around the foot of the Monument, the bronze crown atop the stone column ruddy in the flames and the sunset. Blood running cold, Ben watched as the troops rumbled as one away from the square, a tide of owl-like eyes, beaks, claws and flesh both pallid and green pouring into the narrow stretch of Fish Street Hill. Siphoned between the shattered façade of pub, restaurant and corner shop, the troops lurched in a hushed, grotesque mass, preparing to cut off the Fitzwarren retreat. Caught between the converging hordes, the Black Knights looked set to be the jam in a deadly sandwich.

His eyes like lamps, the scene on the ground filled Ben's vision with unwanted, but necessary detail. Drawing closer, he made out du Sang, the boy's face streaked with gore, his curls lush in the half-light, the vampire gorged on Remnant blood. The Vicomte had little to fear from the oncoming troops. Perhaps he even welcomed them, embracing the chance of a lucky death.

Du Sang appeared to rally the knights, calling to them with words beyond Ben's hearing.

Near to him stood Annis Cade, her bike discarded, her blade raised. Caliburn drank in the flames, the burning buildings along the river caught in silver. The two of them, one young and one not so young, might offer some in the horde a bloody end, but fangs and *lunewrought* would never be enough, Ben knew, to counter the attack entirely. Soon, the rabble at their back would come, pouring like tar onto the bridge, and the tide would carry them away, crashing over the remaining knights and ending all resistance. In fire and blood, the horde would see the nightfall in triumph, flames roaring to rub out the stars, a throne secured for a long-dead king.

The armies met with a crunch of leather, steel and wart-ridden flesh. Du Sang bared his teeth, a red portcullis falling on a goblin's skull, muck splashing from shattered bone. Knights were firing at close quarters or kicking and punching at the swarming mass. Bodies dropped to the ground, the troops trampling them underfoot.

There came a burst of silver, as blinding as lightning. Annis was swinging the sword, severed limbs blooming from the bridge. Caliburn took out a good portion of the vanguard, thirty or more goblins hurled into the sky. But the Remnant horde was great in number, victory so close now they could probably taste it. On and on the goblins came, the troops an ugly, gibbering mess, a cloud of weapons at the end of the bridge, the span shuddering with battle. And wherever Annis swung the sword, Caliburn thrummed with magical force. Silver flashed, bright in the mob, clusters of goblins flying.

It isn't enough. It'll never be enough.

Ben drew in his wings, preparing to dive, when he noticed

the king, a smear of gold and blue, dropping like a stone from above. Out of the smoke, the squawk of aerial battle, Arthur leaned back in his saddle and descended, his wyvern shooting earthwards. Here then came the killing blow, the wyvern's claws outstretched, aiming for the rear-guard of the knights with all the precision of a hawk.

It was too late to stop him, the distance between them too great. Ben forced himself to watch as Arthur dived, some of the knights looking up with drawn faces and slack jaws, a shadow falling over them. With a deafening shriek, the wyvern raked its way through their ranks, flinging clawfuls of knights this way and that. Machine guns rattled, bullets thudding off scales. The dead king yanked at the reins, steering the beast skyward once more. He circled above the bridge, ready for another pass.

Ben snapped in his wings, a spear thrown at the chaos below. He let gravity pull him down, down towards the battle, every minute spelling death. As he did so, Arthur returned, blood peppering his beard, wyvern claws ploughing into the frontline of knights. A furrow of blood and broken limbs parted along the length of the bridge, leading to the spot where Annis stood, wide-eyed and breathless, sword in hand. Ben cursed, loathing the distance between them. *No.* Wings eclipsed her tiny form, the king bearing down on her, determined to crush her, tear her from the bridge.

Another death. Another death on your hands . . .

A bolt of silver struck the sky, the echoes slapping off the river. Ben blinked, momentarily blinded, the clash of magic and leathery flesh boxing his ears. Even through the noise, he heard a roar go up below, human and elated. When his vision cleared, he saw the wyvern spinning away, its tail whipping over the water, a ribbon of guts in its wake.

Annis lay on her back on the bridge. Caliburn had flown from her grip, lying several feet away. The girl was bloody, but whole, Ben saw, his heart swelling at the sight. She looked stunned and exhausted, but he could see that she still breathed. And the sword, it seemed, had opened up the wyvern's belly. The beast wailed, flapping awkwardly over the Embankment, framed by fire and the night. High in the saddle, Arthur was wrenching at the reins, his spurs digging in. Crown askew, he pressed for speed, dragging the bucking beast around for a final pass.

Fallen, disarmed, Annis watched the king descend, a bone angel come to claim her.

Ben chose his moment. Roaring, he barrelled through the smoke, smashing into the wyvern's spine. Scale met scale with a fang-jarring thud, claws tearing at flesh. Together, dragon and wyvern tumbled through the air, crashing into the middle of the bridge. *Boom.* The span shuddered with the impact, a wave of grit hitting both banks. Girders groaned under the sudden weight. Dust showered from the bridge struts, sugaring the water. Concrete buckled, cracks fanning out from a broad crater. Wings and tail flailing, Ben rolled with the smaller beast in his claws, barging his way through the mob. Under them, a carpet of crushed ogres and goblins, a slick of ermine and blood. In the face of the juggernaut, some of the creatures dropped their weapons and leapt out of the way, jumping with hands on caps into the river. Through the air, a crown spun, the last of the sunlight winking on gold. Then it clattered down on tarmac.

When Ben came to a halt, the wyvern was still, limp in his grip. Panting, he let the beast go, his talons sliding out of its neck. A sack of scales and broken bones slumped to the ground. Unfolding his wings, casting Remnants away from him like roaches from a table, his head swung around, horns high above the rabble. Through the haze, he made out Annis, climbing to her feet. Limping, she headed for the sword, a hand raised to signal that she was all right, her eyes filled with smoke and confusion.

It would have to do. If anything, Ben had only bought the girl some time. If he could clear the southern end of the bridge, scatter the horde, the remaining knights might stand a chance of crossing the river, escaping the throng of bugbears at their back.

And what then? The truth bit at him, a knife under his ribs. *Hide in the shadows? Live in the dark? Yeah, you'll get to know just what it feels like . . .*

The thought gave him no sense of justice. In the end, the Remnants and the humans – some of them at least – had found themselves forced into kinship, a desperate alliance. If he drew hope from the fact, it was like the last glimmer of sunlight, slipping behind the rooftops.

We're the same, aren't we? The Lady had shown him in the Orchard of Worlds. *I'm part of you. Made of your dreams.*

To the south, the Shard glimmered, lit by the burning city, the spreading inferno of London. The towering building of steel and glass shone like a blade, steeped in the blood of Britain.

On the bridge ahead, beyond the carcass of the wyvern, King Arthur, the Once and Future Corpse, rose to his feet. Pale he was, a small figure in dented armour, a mess of broken bone. Still, he grinned. Still, the light danced, a promise of winter in hollow eyes. He was ruin, Ben knew, and *ruined*, his torso bent over crushed ribs, his right shoulder up by his chin, jammed there by his battered frame. No viscera dripped from him. No guts coiled between his legs. His flesh had congealed long ago, a nest of maggots and worms. Whatever muck comprised his brain held no sense to move him. Only light, blue and spectral, made him animate. The energy of magic.

But that energy had to come from somewhere.

A certain failsafe, a certain spell, has triggered to signal our return. Arthur, the Once and Future King, has risen. He recalled how the Lady had looked off into the trees, betraying her shame. Her fear. *Or . . . a corrupted version of him.*

Yeah. Fear. *And something else . . .* In his mind, the shift of silk in the orchard. *Something you don't want to think about.*

Ben had seen masks before. He was pretty sure he was looking at one now. Arthur was a tool, nothing more. An instrument of the High House, playing out the course of a mouldering spell.

And some say that he shall come again, when the realm faces its direst threat . . .

Prophecies whirled in his skull. Promises of return. Of revival. The dangling carrot of the Sleep, compelling the Remnant leaders to agree to the enchantment, allaying their fears. An illusion. A lie in which they had longed to believe.

Well, here he stood, this feted king, ravaged yet defiant before him. Along with his suspicions, Ben got the feeling that he wasn't looking at the real threat, only a storm cloud come to the city, raising Remnants and a wooden idol to devour a feast of souls. *And for what? To throw the country into panic? To draw our eyes from . . .* He caught his breath, his scales cooling despite the embers in his belly. Earlier this year, he'd come to learn the taste of the truth, bitter and cruel as it was. Whatever was coming, Arthur's work here was done. His hecatomb roared around him regardless, claiming innumerable lives . . . Ben had seen enough rituals to curl his snout at the smell, wondering what powers the king had summoned. To which gods he paid tribute.

Gods?

Once, perhaps. The First-Born had their day. Now she is merely a queen . . .

Caliburn. Damn you. Ben spat out the notion in gobbets of blood, scraps of flame. This had all started with the Fay, and with the Fay he guessed that it would end. In fact, he'd learned that things went even further back, back into the darkness before Creation and the womb of myths. Back when the earth was golden and new, a ripe fruit on the branch.

Before everything had gone to shit.

Arthur's jaw hung loose, his grin missing a handful of teeth. The king shuffled forward, dragging one leg behind him, his body mangled by his fall. Ben suppressed a surge of pity, curdling with his disgust. The man that the king had once been, bringing Logres to its most glorious hour, had nothing to do with the horror before him, that was clear. The awakening charm had usurped his glory, perverted his legend, the cruel alchemy of gold into shit. And wasn't that the nub of the matter? The Old Lands debased, crushed by the modern world? *Christ.* Arthur was nothing less than he'd ever been, Ben realised then, bruised and aching on the bridge. A metaphor. A living symbol, mirroring the health of his realm.

The king's spurs scraped on the ground, setting Ben's teeth on edge. His breath made a mirage of the space between them.

You're a plague. Ben drew himself up, his haunches tensing. *You were meant to be an Example.* His tail swished back and forth. *And in the end, that's what you'll be.*

Claws splayed, he bounded over the wyvern, rushing at the king. Flame swirled in his throat, mustered to turn flesh into ash. As his jaws stretched wide, a plume of heat flooded from his lungs, blackening the road.

The king was waiting for him. Arthur threw out an arm,

releasing fire in response, a jag of blue light crackling through the air. The force of it smacked into Ben, his breath scattering in sparks and smoke. Frost splashed across his breast, cold as the horn tucked behind his scales, hissing against his heat. He bellowed, the sorcerous volley as fierce as a burn, pricking tears from his eyes. All the same, he couldn't stop. *Wouldn't* stop. Roaring, he let his momentum carry him forward, a red-scaled boulder along the bridge. He met the king with claw outstretched, snatching him up in his grip.

Between his talons, the light blazed and sang, blue, flickering shafts. Magic hammered in his skull, thrashing at focused thought. Grimacing, Ben watched his claw turn from red to pink, frost crackling over his scales, up his foreleg. *Fire and ice. Death versus life.* The notion skittered through his brain, its meaning evading him. He had to move fast. Or, for all his strength, he'd find himself frozen on the bridge. Breathless, empty of life.

With a howl, he snapped out his wings and leapt into the sky, a spark shooting from the city. Through the smoke he soared, the clouds churning in black rags, the night yawning beyond. The air burned through his under-wing gills, pulling him into the heights. Frost was spreading across his shoulder now, biting at his muscles, sinking into flesh. In no time at all, his grip was weakening, the king a blizzard between his claws, trying to fight his way free.

As Ben rose over the city, the streets bleeding like magma below, he could feel winter gnawing at his heart. The Horn of Twrch Trwyth met with the floe, a deepening core of cold. Leaden, encased in ice, his foreleg was growing as heavy as stone. Snarling, he fought against the creeping magic. Brow knotted, he focused his will, pushing ever skyward.

Then, with a snap of his wings, he came to a halt in the air, suspended high above the river. Between his talons, he made out eyes, blazing at him in fury. The dead king grinned at his handiwork. In moments, that grin said, this fight would be over. And the dragon would fall.

But you'll fall with me. This is my city. Mine.

With this, Ben reached his destination, his bulk reflected in panels of glass. Tail thrashing, its arrowhead tip slicing the dark, he'd soared his way up the face of the building. Roaring, he forced open his claw, his scales cracking and spinning away from him, shards of ice and frozen flesh. The next moment, his foreleg shattered, releasing the king from his grasp.

As he tumbled through the air, triumph blazed in Arthur's eyes, his beard weaving in the wind. Then, with a resounding crunch, the summit of the Shard speared through his back. The tip of one steel and glass blade pierced his armour, snapping his spine like a twig. In a plume of bone and dust, his ribcage burst along with his heart. Somewhere, wyverns shrieked, a distant dirge. Flames danced, cackling below.

Ben barely heard them, his gaze fixed on the king. Silently, Arthur slid a foot or two down the panel, the glass shuddering, but holding true. He hung there, impaled and struggling, his limbs thrashing at nothing. Then he slumped, falling still, the fire in his skull snuffed out.

Once. Future. And no more . . .

Ben could only trust to that. Frost binding him, his strength ran out, leaving him hanging, a deadweight in the sky. His wings, limp in the wind, covered his bulk like a shroud as he fell. Unconsciousness claimed him, the air screaming in his ears.

He crashed down into the Thames, the waters hissing over his head.

PART THREE

Golden Age

Then fell on Merlin a great melancholy;
He walked with dreams and darkness, and he found
A doom that ever poised itself to fall,
An ever-moaning battle in the mist,
World-war of dying flesh against the life,
Death in all life and lying in all love,
The meanest having power upon the highest,
And the high purpose broken by the worm.

Tennyson, Idylls of the King

TWENTY

Benjurigan . . .

Around him, darkness yawned, filling his dreaming eyes as he opened them on the sward. The strict rows of trees swam into view, marching off into the gloom like stooped hags. Elsewhere, he had a sense of himself thrashing underwater, bubbles raging around him, the Thames swirling in embrace. The notion was fleeting, an echo fading with returning awareness. Or the uneasy insight of a fugue.

London was far away now, his pain, his grief, clutched like a postcard in his heart, the edges burnt. *The dragon city. My city . . .* Here, in the orchard, he found himself whole and man-shaped, washed up on the infinite shore. Avalon shimmered, a helix far below.

The Isle of the Apples. The Font of All Worlds.

As he heard his name whisper through his head, Ben detected something wrong with the light. Once silver, lit by the core of a cracked moon, the leys spiralling through the gulf, the scene before him had drastically dimmed. Everything held a familiar hue. Familiar and unwelcome.

And it was *cold*. The chill of the nether pressed upon him, prickling across his suit. His body, encased in crimson armour, couldn't quite withstand its touch, a troubling sensation, to say the least. Somewhere, he guessed, the ice was melting from his

307

flesh, and here, he found its mirror, the breath of the abyss kissing the orchard. The meadow, suspended like a leaf on a tree, could no longer keep out the chill.

Nursing his inner heat, he climbed to his feet. As though in defiance, he stretched out his limbs, checking that he still lived. There was no way of knowing for sure, of course. In this place, he could breathe and move, free of injury, but he grasped his circumstance well enough, for all its discomfort. Only his soul tarried here, plucked from the material plane by the queen, Our Lady of the Barrows, and spooled in across the endless gulf, caught on a string of dreams.

She's your creator, of sorts. She can do that.

But this was no dream. It was an *audience*. The knowledge irked him, making him rankle at the thought, a leash around his neck. Whenever he passed out, when he drew close to death, it seemed that the Lady could reach him, call him at whim. *Great.* He'd come to find Nimue's whims questionable, to put it mildly. An extension of his feelings about Von Hart, the pale-faced, absent traitor. Having drawn the eyes of the High House, summoning the Fay to Earth, the envoy had greeted his success with triumph. With blind hope. His ambition had overridden the grief that he should've felt. His reluctant sacrifice. The loss of Jia Jing. The envoy's plan had worked, all the same, and then some. The first time Ben had come to the garden, the Lady had told him the consequences. And he hadn't liked the sound of it then.

Even as we speak, a company of Fay rides across the nether, bound for the gate to your world.

After all he'd been through, to China and back, he wished he could share Von Hart's enthusiasm. The fairy's eyes in the crypt, bright with longing, the loneliness of ages, would stay with Ben for as long as he lived. Which, all things considered, might not be long.

The light and the chill were one thing, the stench quite another. As he stood, he pulled a face, his lips curling in revulsion. *Ugh.* The scent, sickly and sweet, coiled in his nostrils, the breath of a thousand graves. Queasily, he looked around him, seeking the source of the pall, mentally bracing for the sight of a corpse. Despite the surrounding vegetation, the smell was meaty somehow. Rotten. A glance over his shoulder revealed the little brook, once bubbling like laughter, diamonds spilling over the edge of the sward. Now it ran sluggish and black, choked by weeds and scum. Slop dripped into the gulf with all the lustre of shit.

Not good. On further inspection, Ben taking hesitant steps into the nearest row of trees, he found the truth of the matter. The ground squelched under his feet, mulch oozing between his toes, forcing him to put a hand to his mouth, his eyes watering. It was the fruit, carpeting the ground. *All* of the fruit. Withered, dull, the strange apples formed a pebblelike road into the gloom, the ground soft with putrescence. As far as he could see, the branches around him stretched gnarled and bare, devoid of their glimmering bounty. Instead, it appeared that a storm had swept through the orchard, destroying the cosmic crop.

Cosmic, yeah. When Ben recalled the seeded metaphor of worlds on worlds, he couldn't suppress a shiver, looking upon the failed harvest with a stab of fear.

But there was worse. Glancing up through the trees, he spied the palace, the walls looming in the distance, the towering battlements and spires. Crystalline and pink, that's how he remembered them, a fairy castle (of sorts) in the clouds, a jewel in the immensity. No. It was more than that: a spindle of realities, of countless worlds, cultivated by the Fallen Ones, the void-travelling Fay.

Not so now. The palace rose as black, as dull as the nether

around it, reminding him of a certain mirror, an octagon of unmarked wood framing a bottomless pit. And there he'd strayed, through the door of Creation, into the province of ghosts . . . The palace looked haunted, all right. Its chambers empty, stripped of the echoes of long-ago laughter, lost in time and forgotten. Whatever glory, whatever beauty it once held, it had long since decayed, presumably stricken by the same blight that had ravaged the orchard. Imagining its abandoned halls, the wind singing around a cobwebbed throne, he felt the coals snuff out in his belly, plunging him into dread.

A worm gnaws at the heart of things . . .

This had become his mantra. A silent lament. And he'd come to suspect the nature of the worm too, invisible and ravenous. Not time, he reckoned, although that was part of it. Not time, but something else. Something more . . . intimate.

Magic is souring . . .

Ben had seen masks before. He'd seen illusions, both in physical form and in the mind, the belief in a comfortable lie. Jia had shown him the truth and, a ghost, a revenant, the *sin-you* haunted him still. Like the glass of the Eight Hand Mirror, the illusion had shattered, the scattering shards carrying away his world. The Lore. The Sleep. His ancient heart. And what had the Lady shown him, the first time he'd walked here? A garden. A dream, no doubt. A thriving hub of magic. Eternal. Bright.

A *memory?*

He'd seen King Arthur, a puppet of bones, dancing on strings of blue light. The circles of protection, the indecipherable glyphs fading. Winking out in a valley. Across the sea. In a city park. Here he saw the same corruption, the same pestilent glow, the flesh of magic rotting away. The *real* state of the place. He didn't know what it meant. Couldn't quite grasp the sense of it. That the souring of the earth should reach even here, into the depths of the nether. Lapping at Avalon's shores . . .

One thing was for sure. The sight sat at odds with everything the Lady had told him.

We are lost. Fallen . . .

Her voice led him on, between the trees. Every step he took refreshed the stink around him, fruit splitting under his feet. Despite his unease, he was almost relieved to see her, this fairy lady from another world. *Nimue* . . . He found her in a glade, kneeling upon the ground. With her back turned to him, her braids coiled high and pale in the dark, he traced the line of her spine, her trembles betraying her tears.

Hands covering her face, the Lady fell silent as he drew near, clutching at dignity. Or so it seemed. Like the last time he'd come here, the wondrous visions and her confessions, he wondered how much of this was for show, designed to secure his allegiance. To spur him on to bring her the sword, the prize she so desperately wanted.

Only with the blade can I reignite the circles and restore your world.

That's what she'd told him. Nevertheless, by her own admission that wasn't the whole of it. And the light around him, inky and dim, shared the same shade as her gown. The same shade as the failing circles. The same shade as a dead king's eyes. It was all connected, he got that now. The magic was a plague that had taken them all, perverting everything good and pure.

"Arthur is dead," he told her, then grunted, shrugging off his portentous tone. "Again."

"Yes. We sensed his passing," she said. "The flames of a city. The screams. A beacon in the dark. Guiding us to the earth."

Ben swallowed, her words sinking in. When he thought of the

311

scale of it, the dead king, the towering thorn wall, the wooden idol in Trafalgar Square, the hundreds, if not thousands who had died, his fingertips bit into his palms. It was her casual tone, however, that floored him.

"Typical," he said, hating the ache in his voice. And in a way, he wasn't surprised, having doubted her from the start. Well, she was Fay, wasn't she? And Camlann was a long time ago. Von Hart, he realised then, wasn't the only one who'd changed. "You're as fucked up and twisted as your magic. The king wasn't triggered by some kind of *failsafe*. You raised him, didn't you? You raised Arthur to buy you time."

"The way is long. And long forgotten," she said, as if that served as an answer. "We could trace the echoes of the harp, of course, but time was of the essence. We required a beacon, leading us on. And we would turn the eyes of the world away as we travelled through the dark. So yes, we reached out to our dead son. Our dead Example, deep in the mountain. What else could we do? We lack the maps and the power of old. Only one gate leads to your world, dragon. One road, tangled with all the others. And it was broken."

Was? He didn't much like the sound of that either.

"Forgotten," he shot back. "Like you forgot us. Your children."

And in the time since this race had left the earth, it seemed that the Remnants were not the only ones to have dwindled and declined, changed, warped by the ages. The souring had reached the High House too. The fact of it was all around him, in the dark palace walls and the rotten orchard. In the stench in the air. As his gorge rose in his throat, sickened by the revelation, Ben felt another crack in his heart, a lingering hope evaporating. That one day the Fay would return. That the Queen's Troth would come true. That, even after all, Remnants and humans would learn to live in peace and get their happy ending. Begin a new golden age. Even after all, he'd still believed. Somewhere deep down in his soul.

No more.

You fool.

Instead, there was only an end. He knew that now. Somehow, he'd always known. Recent trials had forced him to look, rubbing his face in the fact. Having half-slept his way through the centuries, he was more awake than ever. Awake and stranded in a nightmare.

The Lady's confession left him with a question.

"Why, then?" he asked, taking another step, the ground giving a little beneath his feet, slick and rank. "Why bother to return? I thought you said that you were out there, seeding worlds or whatever." *All worlds hold the power, the potential to become something more.* He remembered her words only too well, the measureless scope of them, prompting further fears. He funnelled them into his confusion, pressing his anguish upon her. "Why not just leave us to die?"

Her hands fell into her lap, but she didn't turn around. Perhaps she couldn't face him, or so he longed to believe. The cold in his veins, his galloping heart, told him otherwise, of course. What was she keeping from him?

"Oh, we have already told you, Benjurigan," she said. "Not that you would listen. Long ago, in the history of history, the First-Born walked as gods, unchained and bright in the cosmos. We shaped worlds. Breathed life into the void. And yet our ambition destroyed us. There was . . . a storm. A silence in heaven. And we were cast down. We became the Fallen. Shadows of our former selves."

The Fay. Yeah, I've heard this part. But . . .

"Perhaps we were angels once," she said. "And echoes of our glory remained. For a while, at least. Alone, adrift, we sailed the void, following the map of our shattered magic, the silver veins of Creation. Mighty, we came through the dark, visiting worlds we'd made and forgotten, trying to recover our vanished art. Our *power*. In great cities under the sea. On mountaintops that speared the moon. In deserts of glass and forests of gold, travelling ever onwards. We were desperate. Searching, searching . . . And in time, we came to your world."

"Your precious Example," Ben said. "In the end, it was all about you."

The Lady had told him, yes. All about golden dreams and noble aspirations. The grand evolution of Man. The white walls of Camelot. A legendary king, a mortal paragon to lead all into the light. How could he forget the Fay crypt in the caverns under London, the marble figures entwined, locked in warped copulation? The carnal experiments of long ago, melding human with alien flesh, giving birth to the Remnants. How Nimue's words stung him now, ringing with the bells of untruth.

Are we not flesh, Benjurigan? Alas, our godly provenance lingers in spirit alone. Like you, like them, we are corporeal, creatures of blood and bone, albeit infused with magic. Creatures of love and hope. Of desire . . .

"Poor beast," the Lady said. "Did you honestly imagine that you were so special? A lizard granted human shape, filled with hunger and fire?" She shook her head, but despite her sympathetic tone, he could tell that she was laughing at him. At his pain. "Did you think that the Remnants were the height of our experiments? It wounds us to tell you that you were but one of many. Orchard upon orchard. World upon world."

Fingers growing sharp, blood dripped from Ben's fists, unseen flowers blooming on the ground.

He'd been here before. "I know this one. You weren't just seeding worlds. You were harvesting them. And what were you hoping to find? Let me take a wild guess."

"Redemption. Ascension. *Revival*," she said, without a beat. A shred of shame. "Is that not the ambition of all who fall? Do not all gods long to return, craving worship, the fuel of belief? You've seen it yourself. A goddess. A ghost. Risen from the grave."

Ben had a mental image of playing cards fluttering around the envoy, liquid in the gloom of Club Zauber. In Berlin, a couple of years back.

The Long Sleep is simply a human term for a universal fact. All myths have their season, and in their time, pass. Dreams, monsters, ghosts, gods . . .

This was all one. All part of the same story.

"You . . . the First-Born created her. A serpent who became something . . . more."

"Atiya was one who showed us the way. That a return was indeed possible. Alas, she was destroyed, centuries ago. Only a memory remains." Ben, who'd felt the sting of that memory, in black claws and lightning, begged to differ. But the Lady went on. "Later experiments came close to our goal, but we did not count on human pride. At the last, we were refused. Arthur chose war. He shattered the harp. We lost everything. Years of toil, of magical endeavour. In his folly, he cursed your world to remain base. Animal. Enslaved by emotion. Blighted by disbelief. Doomed to wither and die." *By the turn of the ages. By the lie. The Lore.* He knew this part too. "And so we departed. We . . . moved on."

Now Ben recalled the painting hanging in du Sang's tomb, the blazing black sun on the rise, the ghostly forms moving towards it. The Eight Hand Mirror, the last door of Creation, sealed by a charm and yet left intact. Von Hart standing with the fragments at his feet, the shattered *Cwyth* in the snow. There was a secret here, he was sure of it. Another hidden truth. But the shape of it escaped him.

He spoke with embers in his throat. "To some other poor sod of a world, I guess. Did you abandon that one too?"

"Oh, we have reaped *thousands*," she said, in the same dismissive manner. "The God-seed, once planted, is hard to tend. Too easily, the scions become tainted. Unstable. With the Pendragon, we came so close to its highest expression, preparing to distil the juice of dreams, drink and make the climb to the heavens, back into the light." She looked up, gazing at some imagined star, perhaps, a place that Ben couldn't see. "We failed. In the end, all we birthed were monsters. Divinity evaded us."

Remnants.

Here, then, was her offered truth. Ben couldn't know where her experiments would lead her, what essence the Fay had hoped to squeeze from the process, the mix of magic with human flesh. He didn't *want* to know, the fire inside him devouring curiosity, leaving only disgust. After all he'd suffered, the long, lonely years . . . and here she was, this otherworldly Lady, this queen, telling him that he was nothing. Less than nothing. A discarded scrap of a cosmos-spanning soup.

The wisdom weighed him down, a stone in his chest.

"You still haven't answered my question." He kept his voice low, tamping down rage in his quest for understanding. "You're saying that your Troth was bullshit. That you never promised to return, isn't that right? But you also told me that you left your gate behind. One of your doors. Locked, sure, but unbroken."

The fact didn't make sense. It was a contradiction. A mystery. "Why?"

At this, she stood, her gown swishing, the silk drenched by muck. With a shudder, she let out her breath, speaking into the dark.

"We told you," she said again. "Oh, we were younger then. Foolish. Caught up in the dream, the light that shone on all Logres. Can a queen not love her king? We are *Fallen*, Benjurigan. And we were not untouched by desire. By hope in an impossible future. Yes, we should've destroyed the gate, made our peace with our failure. But what are the Fay if not one? Much like *lunewrought*, all of a piece. Not all in the High House agreed to embark, ride with us into the dark. We have told you, dragon. We didn't have the heart."

She'd said this before. And it had remained a riddle . . . Until now, when he grasped some sense to it, slippery, unwelcome in his mind.

"Wait. What are you saying? You—"

"We are not what we were," she continued. "Like power, like glory, love has long since flown from us. The feel of it, the taste . . . Perhaps we tarried too long in your world, became stained by human need. In time, we have come to see our error, small as it at first seemed. How long does the fruit stay ripe when cut from the branch? Yet the branch remains, does it not? It's the branch, it seems, that wounds us, winding across the gulfs of time, spreading rot to the shores of Avalon itself. And so we return. Summoned by our broken harp. Reminded of our lapse in judgement. Enlightened to the source of our decline."

Ben's breath rushed from him, a scatter of sparks in the gloom. He fought to stay on his feet, the stench of the fruit as

James Bennett

he staggered to one side pouring over him. Keeping him upright, clinging to a mast of shock.

"You're not coming to save us at all," he said. "You're coming to . . . to . . ."

But he couldn't put it into words, the scope of it making him dizzy, twisting his tongue.

"What becomes of gods when no one believes in them?" the Lady said. "What becomes of magic when faith grows sour? All it takes is one bad apple to spoil the crop entire. The rot has crept along the leys, spreading from all we left behind. It took us too long to learn of it. Your world is a canker. Nothing more."

"No. It can't be. It *can't* be."

But in the pit of his stomach, the core of his soul, he knew it was so.

"You will bring us the sword," Nimue told him. "You will bring it, or I promise you, we will make of your world a hell before the end. A blazing hecatomb from shore to shore. An ocean, a sky full of screams. Bring us the sword. Bring us Caliburn. Let us sever the rot from the branch. In return, we shall grant you a painless death."

He'd like to think she meant him alone, but he didn't flatter himself. She meant all of humanity. All of the Remnants. Everything that lived. All the same, in the cold, in the dark, it sounded oddly appealing. An end to his troubles. To betrayal. To fighting. To the sight of his world falling apart. To loneliness and hiding in the shadows. To fear.

An ending. A return to dreams, perhaps. The dreams from which the first dragons had sprung.

But he'd made a promise. A choice.

And thinking of Von Hart, the hope on his face, he realised then that he wasn't the only one.

Together, we'll go into the dark.

"He doesn't know, does he? Your envoy. He believes in the Troth. That's why he did all of this. He thinks that you can save us."

Memories raced through Ben's skull, a picture trying to form. The conspiracy of the CROWS, bringing about a breach in the Lore, making all of this possible. Into the weakened magic, Von Hart had played his hand, using Jia to see the truth. To shatter the glass. Open the way . . . For a moment, Ben experienced a pang of sympathy for his one-time ally, the envoy extraordinary.

Lord Blaise of the Leaping White Hart. I've never known you. Not really.

If never exactly a friend, the fairy had saved his life on at least two occasions, muttering about some future task, something that Ben wouldn't like. And in all the confusion, Arthur coming to London, Ben hadn't stopped to question it, distracted by the chaos. Now, standing here in the Orchard of Worlds – the cosmos in decay under his feet – the intricacy of it almost overwhelmed him, the centuries that the envoy had required to spin his plan, his redress of an ancient mistake. The way he'd kept an ace up his sleeve, playing the odds, hoping that Ben could save his servant, his pupil . . .

Let me fall.

In all of that, would Von Hart honestly have forgotten the prize in question? The relic, jewelled and silver, that the Lady so desperately craved? Under London, Ben had resisted the fairy's spell, tearing at the suit. He'd refused to help recover the Eight Hand Mirror and almost breathed his last in a spreading pool of blood. What challenge had he presented then? What threat? Von Hart had no one left to face in the crypt and yet he'd departed empty-handed, neglecting the task of centuries.

The envoy had left him the sword.

"What becomes of gods, Benjurigan?" the Lady asked him, bringing him back to the here and now. "When the gods fall. When Creation unravels. When the hunger is all that remains."

She turned to face him, a whisper of silk on the sward. She was crying, he saw, tears rolling like gems down her cheek, silver on brown. Her eyes, violet and sharp, revealed only coldness, her concern simply for herself. For the destiny she'd wrought. Corrupted. Deadly. The slow venom of greed.

But here, all masks fell. In a heartbeat, he noticed that something was wrong with her face. Her braids, coiled high, were seething, dislodged by a sudden fluidity of bone. Her cheek looked swollen, as if she was chewing on something large and bitter, unable to spit it out. Then, as the cold snaked into his extremities, a delta of fear, he watched Nimue's body convulse, her flesh rippling. A shimmer passed through her like static. A flash of fire, white as snow.

What the hell?

Under her skin, her bones surged, a sharp crackling in the air. Wincing at the sound, Ben wasn't sure whether he was shrinking at first, his gaze glued to the Lady, the trees around him a blur. Leaves swirled, her transforming bulk breaking through the branches, her spreading shadow freezing him to the spot. Up she rose, her legs stretching, impossibly long, throwing off her humanoid shape. Sinews strained, creaking and popping, into a blanched, bony tarsus. There came a snap of ribs, sharp as a pistol in the gloom. Ben watched, breathless, as her back ballooned outward, bulging into an egg-shaped abdomen, milky and striated with markings. Dwarfed, he choked, gagging in shock. For all her shifting, swelling presence, he could see that a part of her remained. Her right arm, breast and leg merged with the front of the creature's head like a rag doll hanging from its jaws. As eight eyes, burning with ghostly light, settled upon him, one of them, he saw, still shone violet, pressing a warning upon him. A *need*.

We are Fallen. And falling still . . .

As Nimue's words shuddered through his skull, he grasped the full horror before him, the curtain of the dark rising on a nightmare. In her fangs, her quivering pedipalps, the skeletal legs bursting from her body, the sight of the monster barrelled into him, threatening to snuff out his mind. The rot wasn't only around him, infecting the orchard, the palace walls. It was in her too, eating away at her essence, the ancient, alien life of her. The Lady was dying, yes, but worse than that, her decline was distorting her, revealing a terrifying truth.

What becomes of gods . . . ?

He'd seen masks before. And what hid behind them. Nimue, Our Lady of the Barrows, was a *Lurker*. Or on her way to fast becoming one. A phantom, a ghost of a withering power. With a bellow, a bark of dismay, memories went spiralling through Ben's brain. His encounters with the ghost-beasts iced his veins even as their manifest queen crowded his vision, rising into the dark.

Lurkers. The Walkers between the Worlds, drifting through the gulfs of the nether, mindless and blind – or so he'd believed. No one could say where the creatures had come from, these spectral watchdogs of Creation. These silent guardians, feeding on an excess of magical force, drawn to the souring of the earth.

Now he had an idea.

There are more of them now. Again, he pictured Von Hart in Club Zauber, his chest heaving under star-spangled silk. His hair hanging like gold in his face. *They gather like . . . flies on shit.*

And Ben had wondered where the ghost-beasts had got to lately. The last time he'd seen the phantoms, they'd been in the guise of an Emperor, converged on the bait of a living source. Despite the sorcery, the spells, wreaking havoc on London and the world, the Lurkers had been absent from recent events, a fact that struck him as strange.

You don't know. Panic fluttered in his breast, his fear moot, unable to reach the envoy. *You don't know what has become of them.*

A chill fist closed around his heart, the sight of the Lady making a terrible kind of sense. The pale amoebae, circling ravenous, drifting in the dark, were nothing less than the vestiges of gods. The putrefaction of fallen powers. The degeneration of the Fay.

We are not what we were.

No shit. Ben turned and ran. He ran with his lungs raw and his eyes closed, trying not to hear the crashing through the trees, the Lady – the *hunger* that she had become – lurching after him.

The Lurkers are coming. They always were. Trying to return . . .

With all the sluggishness of a dream, his feet pummelled the fruit, sweet and foul. On the back of his neck, her breath like winter, hissing through the thrashing branches, heavy with desire. He cried out, slipping down a slope and splashing through muck, the stagnant brook sucking at his knees, his thighs. Grunting, gasping, he wrenched himself free, pulling himself up on the opposite bank.

Chancing a look over his shoulder, he saw fangs descend, pale, slick with ichor. When he turned again, nothingness filled his eyes, his mind, as he ran out of ground.

Screaming, he tumbled headfirst into the dark.

TWENTY-ONE

Coughing, spluttering, Ben dragged himself from the river, up onto the stony shore.

In human form, he sprawled on his back, shivering with the chill of the water and the kiss of near death. And dreams – or something much like them – their clarity fading, leaving only a vague sense of horror and the sting of the truth. The First-Born had fallen. And the Fay had never *stopped* falling, poisoned, warped by their souring magic. The rot had spread across centuries. Across worlds. The knowledge shuddered through him, the scales of his suit thickening, hoarding warmth. The dead king was no more than a harbinger, an evil sent to prepare the way. They were coming, this debased race. These half-ghosts. These *Lurkers.* Coming to destroy the earth.

Not on my watch. Not if I can help it.

He grimaced, scoffing at his own bravado. Nothing, he knew, would ever be the same. He was alive, that was something, but his world was already over. As he lay there on the bank, the pebbles needling his spine (*Get up. Get up, you bastard*), he knew that there was no going back. Who among humans could deny the truth now, the fact of fabulous beings and beasts in their midst? All the prophecies had come true, after a fashion. But the future, he feared, belonged only to war.

In his hand, he clutched the horn, the ivory relic cold in

323

his grip. With the same sense of guilt, he remembered he had command of an army. That a battle played out somewhere above him, along the banks of the Thames. All he could hear, however, was the roar of the flames. The collapse of buildings. The distant surrender of wood, glass and stone. *The dragon city. Devoured* . . . He couldn't hear any choppers or planes. No doubt the inferno had pushed the squadrons back to the suburbs, the sky claimed by smoke. No shriek of wyverns harried the air. No whistle of brooms. No gunfire, no clash of swords. He wondered how long he'd been out for, the time slipping, out of sync, between worlds. Through his dismay, a spike of relief. He couldn't hear any screams either. It was short-lived. A false hope, all the same. The people trapped in the city had either managed to flee or met their end in this Hell.

He sat up, jarred by the thought. The ice had gone from him, Arthur's touch dispelled by the embrace of the Thames. He remained a mess of cuts and bruises, and he winced as he moved. But his muscles were tingling too, busy with magical needles, stitching him back together. *One last time. You can do this* . . . Swaying, he climbed to his feet. *Not like you have a choice.* To the left of him, the bridge struts loomed in the dark, concrete giants catching the light from the city, reflecting off the water. Nearer to him, a ramshackle jetty, driftwood steps leading up to the Embankment. Ash coiled across the sky, the ruin mixing with the charred wall of thorns, stray sparks flickering like fireflies. There was no going back. No time to *look* back either. The king in the mountain had fallen, his corpse hanging up there in the dark, broken and empty on the summit of the Shard.

There was only one thing left to do.

*Even as we speak, a company of Fay rides across the nether, bound
for the gate to your world. The envoy will meet us there, Benjurigan.*
One thing alone.

He found them at the north end of the bridge, a huddled, ash-
streaked band of knights. Around them, he made out shapes in
the dark, some leather-clad, some furred and beaked, the bodies
of the slain. *Too many. Way too many.* Motorbikes lay abandoned
in the road, their wheels like the makeshift markers of graves.
Pools of oil and blood glimmered here and there, catching the
enveloping glow. The few who remained, thirty or more, were
sitting on the pavement nursing their wounds, their heads bowed
and silent, or shuffling blank-faced through the piled-up mass,
calling for their dead. The battle, it seemed, had moved on,
leaving a mournful lull. He didn't kid himself that it was over.

As Ben emerged from the smoke, a flame-haired figure staggering into view, one by one, the knights stood, a hush falling
over the scene. Then a cheer went up, weary and hollow, but a
cheer nevertheless. He raised a hand, heavy as lead, to wave
away their regard.

I'm not your champion, he wanted to tell them. *Hardly.*

As much as he longed to absorb their hope, draw on each
expectant face like a flower in the sun, he knew that he'd failed
them, every man and woman here. Downriver, Tower Bridge
sailed through the smoke, torn black sails to the wind. The
outline of St Dunstan-in-the-East, the old church spire, scratched
at the billowing night. The Walkie Talkie building, its meshed
windows, a thousand or more, rippling with unchecked flame.
These sights supported the fact of the matter, a deadweight on
his heart. These people were merely temporary survivors; he'd
only saved them for the end. This fight, he might've said, was

just the beginning. A greater threat rode towards them through the dark. Bringing cataclysm. Bringing death to all.

He opened his mouth to offer them this, or perhaps an apology, feeble on his lips, when his breath went out of him. A scrawny figure ran from the throng and flew into his arms.

"You're alive! You're alive!" Defeated or no, he couldn't help but welcome her warmth, her head on his chest, a tousled ball of black. But her words, joyful as they were, thrummed sadness into his bones. He'd never be what she believed him to be. "We saw you from the bridge, snatching up the king . . ." She spoke in a breathless rush, a touch of hysteria through her fatigue. "He's dead, isn't he? Arthur? Tell me he's dead."

And over the top of her head, he found himself looking into malachite eyes, du Sang on his feet, watching him in silence. Blood soaked the front of the Vicomte's suit, at odds with his luxuriant curls and smooth skin, his arrested youth in full, bone-white bloom. Of everyone assembled here, the vampire perhaps grasped the gravity of the situation. Du Sang gave him a nod. An acknowledgment of his survival, nothing more.

"He died centuries ago," Ben told the girl. *And the world along with him.* Gently, he put his hands on her shoulders, pushing her away. "Annis, what happened here?"

The Black Knight appeared to remember where she was, exhaling and straightening. As she looked up at him, he took in the scar across her face, the welt showing white under the soot. No one around him remained unscathed for long, it seemed, and he could've cursed, but he didn't, for her sake. Sensing his scrutiny, she glanced down at the road, between her boots.

"We fought," she said simply. "The goblins scattered when you grabbed the king. The bugbears came up on our rear . . . greenteeth, ghouls . . . it wasn't pretty." Remembered fear trembled on her breath. "There were so many of them. We were seriously outnumbered. But then, for some reason, they . . . Well, the horde fell back, retreating into the streets. Perhaps because of the fire. Or the sword, I don't know." Caliburn, sheathed through her belt, gleamed, but stayed thankfully silent. *Satiated*, perhaps. For now. "And the goblins never returned."

"It was the horn," Ben said, holding up the relic in question, flames dancing in gold. "The spell. It was only going to last for so long. When Arthur – or whatever he was – met his maker, I guess his minions lost heart."

None of the summoned creatures, from goblin to ogre to wyvern, had ever been fond of a fair fight. *Shit, du Sang wouldn't be here if we hadn't struck our little bargain.* Few of them, he reckoned, would've rallied beneath a banner of war under their own steam, not without dragons and giants to help them. Even then, it was unlikely, when faced with the British Army, let alone the risk of Remnant retaliation. And in the Old Lands, at Camlann, Ben had read that the Usurper, Mordred, had employed a similar charm, beguiling all foul and craven hearts. A charm that the Lady had sought to counter, with harpsong and magical slumber . . . Not that he placed much faith in fairy tales. Not any more. He'd closed the book on that particular dream.

News of the horde's retreat didn't cheer him. These Remnants still presented a threat, whether hiding in sewers to prey on humans or taking their chances out in the open, in the shell-shocked counties of Britain. There was nothing to stop them now, no way to send them back into the Sleep. And no Lore to hold them to account or an official body to uphold it. The Anarchy had returned, grown fat and deadly on the ages. In that moment, every long, lonesome second of them felt like a massive waste of time.

Old Lands. Dead Lands. At this hour, they were much the same.

Annis read his misgiving, plain on his face, and did her best to encourage him.

"Well, it isn't *all* bad," she said. "You still have the horn, don't you? There's an army down there, in case you hadn't noticed. Waiting on your call."

Ben followed her outstretched arm to the side of the road, the girl pointing west, upriver. Reluctantly, unmoved by her optimism – but glad to slip away from du Sang's patient gaze – he strode over to the railings. Down there stretched a riverside path, a broad open area wreathed in shadows cast by the water. In the drifting smoke, he couldn't see anything at first, picking out the hazy silhouettes of bankside piers, tugboats and darkened restaurants, the cross-Thames railway and Southwark Bridge beyond. As he stood there, it began to rain, gently at first and then harder, hissing through the smothering pall. He looked up, quietly thankful, and when he peered down again, the downpour had washed the ash from his eyes.

He saw them, gathered in the dark. Two hundred or so Remnants filling the space, packed in ranks between the Thames and the bankside office buildings, the troops stretching off into the gloom. The tall, colourful caps of the gnomes, the creatures sat on the stone shoulders of ettin or clinging to the gnarled backs of the green men. Dwarves shuffled at the front of the crowd, their helmets dented, beards bloody. He picked out tiddy mun, reynardine, hedley kow, blue caps and hunky punks, dotted throughout the restless throng.

A fluttering drew his gaze up to the Victorian towers that flanked the Cannon Street railway bridge, the twin spires retaining grandeur despite the blaze. Against the skyline, he made out griffins perched on the ledges, proud-chested and visibly impatient. Witches leant against the weathervanes, their robes like flags in the haze, though despite their pale shade, he knew that these women would never surrender, would rather die than admit defeat.

Christ knew that many of them had. Even in the murk, he could see for himself their dwindled numbers, along with the wounded state of them. A dwarf, struggling to stay upright. An ettin, chipped and blackened by fire. A green man with a sword protruding from his neck. His army. And, taking in the sea of upturned faces, expressionless, expectant in the glow, he knew, with a pain in his chest, that he couldn't really think of them as *his*. Like Arthur's horde, few of these creatures would've fought by his side of their own volition, whatever the peril befalling Britain. That was why he'd spared them the speeches. He was no general. Nor even a soldier. If anything, he was a mercenary, throwing in his lot with a medieval king for the simple profit of survival. Most of these Remnants would view him as such and worse, turning their minds to justice, even recompense, instead of allegiance. Few would see him as the *Lone Fire*, that was for sure, standing guard over their beds. Some might try to kill him. No one would thank him for his leadership, not when he'd escaped the Long Sleep, remaining awake and free upon the earth.

And these Remnants weren't free, having simply exchanged one prison for another. Here he stood, holding the key.

In his mind, ghosts stirred, whispering over old scars.

A witch on a bridge. *A bard's song to bind the bestiary. It could never contain the likes of us.*

A goddess on a mountain. *The Pact is no truce at all, merely a cell where you wait for extinction . . .*

A warrior in the dark. *My master chose me for that very purpose . . . To pave the road to our freedom.*

Prophets, all.

Annis said, "They aren't many, I know. But enough to—"

"No."

Ben turned to face her, the flames at his back. She probably couldn't see his face, but his voice checked any argument she might've made, her mouth closing, chewing on an unspoken retort.

A little more gently, he said, "I'm afraid I'm going to have to ask for your sword."

"Eh?" Caliburn said, stirring at her belt with a jolt. "Oh, for heaven's sake. Never a moment's peace."

They both ignored it, caught up in the question between them. Annis screwed up her lips, conviction and doubt warring inside her. For a breath, she merely stared at his outstretched hand. Then she seemed to sense that she was never going to persuade him otherwise, her shoulders falling. After all they'd been through in the past few days, she wasn't about to refuse him. With a sigh that let him know exactly what she thought about it, she drew the sword from her belt and, gingerly, turned it pommel first towards him. The jewels glittered, irate.

Ben took the weapon, testing its weight. It was a big decision. A dangerous choice. His actions now could easily make matters worse, but the heat washing off the water, the charcoal sky and the heaped bodies along the bridge told him that the time for such doubts was over. A *choice*, yes – but then, he knew he had one. The Remnants in his thrall did not. And, with a breath that held a fair share of regret, he accepted that his long service was done, his duty defunct, an oath built on sand. He was the Sola Ignis no more. As such, he had no right to lead them, this wounded, sorry host. To drag them into further peril, further suffering, bound by the horn. He shrugged off the responsibility. The choice must be their own. They must face the end like him, free to meet death on their own terms.

With a degree of ceremony, he placed the Horn of Twrch Trwyth on the flat top of the bridge railings. Tensing his shoulders, he raised the sword, the inferno dancing in silver. Caliburn thrummed in his grip, the cold sensation of hunger.

Annis, fidgeting behind him, seemed to think better of it.

"Wait—!"

The sword cut her off, its descent scaling into a scream. In a burst of light, *lunewrought* met ivory and gold, the gilded tusk of the ancient boar splintering into shards.

In the echoes, in the afterglow, Ben lowered the blade and faced her again, the last slayer, speaking low and deliberately into her shock. He found that he could put a name to it now, what he saw in her face, her expression wrestling with resentment and alarm. *The time has come.* He could pass on the burden, at last. It saddened him to realise that was all it was. All it had ever been.

"You're the future now. Do you understand?" Lord, but he was damning her. For all her passion, she wouldn't thank him for it. "Your father was right, in his own way. There has to be order. A compromise of some kind. When the fire dies down – and it will – when only embers remain, you're going to have to talk to them, Remnants and humans both." *But no Pact,* he might've told her, *no Lore, is going to make the world forget this. Still* . . . "It's the only way out of this mess. If there's a mess left to get out of. Tell me you understand."

Unlikely as it was, he had to try. For all their sakes.

Annis bowed her head. Then this scarred young woman, who

was really no fool at all, nodded to herself, accepting the weight of it. When she looked back up at him, however, her lips trembled and tears shone in her eyes.

"You're leaving again, aren't you?" she said. "And you're not coming back."

Awkwardly, he reached out and gave her shoulder a squeeze. What more could he tell her? It was too late to explain, the hours running short. *Let her face the end with a shred of hope, at least* . . . Every second he tarried here, the Fay drew closer, riding through the nether . . . If the Lady wasn't already here, that was, bringing her promised pain, her promised doom. There was nothing left to do but bring her the sword, although not in the way she was probably expecting. This had started with the Fay and with the Fay it would end. Von Hart was waiting for him, he believed, somewhere up ahead.

Annis was right. This was a farewell. To this city. To Britain. To the past. He was going to seek redemption, if he could, even if it meant going down in flames. He was heading to a place where she couldn't follow.

We must all make sacrifices.

He offered her a smile, kind in its way. Bearing the sword, he moved off down the bridge, away from the bodies and the bikes and the sorrow on her face.

At some unseen signal, du Sang slipped after him, dwarfed by his flourishing shadow.

TWENTY-TWO

Into the north. Into ice . . .

Wings spread, the Vicomte saddled high in his withers, Red Ben Garston soared across the North Sea, heading ever onwards. By dawn, he'd left the Scottish coast behind, reluctant, yet thankful, to depart the land he'd loved and lost. That he'd salvage, if he could. *The green lawns of Logres, once again blazing with war . . .* He saw no aeroplanes and the ships down there looked scarce, most of them called to shore by the catastrophe. *Or sunk.* He tried not to think about it, but it did no good. *Wrapped in tentacles, dragged into the depths . . .* With a shudder, he took his bearings from the strewn steppingstones of Shetland and veered east for Norway, the aerial pathway etched in his head. Cloaked by clouds, he kept the hills and the fjords in the corner of his eye, grey and misty in the distance. There were memories down there. Of broken bridges. Harpsong and drinking. The long months of his wandering, when he should've been seeking the Guild, warning them, helping them resist the rise of the Chapter. *Well, that's hindsight for you. Always 20/20 . . .* It was only out over the open sea, a golden expanse below, that the last dregs of smoke seemed to trail from him, chased away by the wind and the cold, if not by actual relief. *What good would it have done?*

Reading the compass of the sun, a milky orb low to the

horizon, he drew on the restless heat in his belly, spearing into the blue. The air rushed through his gills, skirling with frost. Fangs locked, his snout cut through the sky, leaves of flame fanning from his nostrils, melting the ice that formed on his flanks. In his claw, Caliburn tingled with a force that his warmth couldn't touch, pulsing stronger with each passing hour, the brief day dawning and dwindling, swallowed by the miles. He spared no concern for du Sang. The Vicomte had little to fear from the altitude, his veins long since cooled, his breath a redundant affair. Likely frozen, du Sang sat silent and still, a fact that Ben was grateful for. With only his pounding heart and the wind for company, he could focus on the task at hand, following the route his passenger had given him.

Up there.

All the same, as Norway gave way to the Barents Sea (which, Ben recalled, used to be known as the Murman Sea, on account of the creatures that once swam here, along the shallow coral shelf), it became clear that he no longer needed the Vicomte's guidance, regardless of their bargain. In his grip, the sword practically sang with energy, rattling against the scales of his palm, silver rays beaming between his claws. He'd felt this before, this magnetism, *lunewrought* calling to *lunewrought*. But the envoy extraordinary had broken the harp and the manacles lay two thousand miles behind him, in the care of the Last Pavilion. He sensed, somehow, that Caliburn wasn't responding to the Fay metal, not exactly, but something larger, some unseen beacon up ahead.

Only one gate leads to your world, dragon.

The Eight Hand Mirror, or whatever was left of it. It had to be. The glass may have shattered, the door unlocked, and a temple may have fallen, burying the artefact, but despite all that, the hole in the world remained intact. Judging by the scale of Von Hart's scheme, the web he'd woven, Ben knew that it wouldn't have taken much for him to move it, relocating the mirror to these chilly climes. *Together, we'll go into the dark . . .* Ben feared that the envoy's words would become a prophecy in their own right. And he didn't kid himself that Von Hart needed him for such an endeavour. If a dragon refused to play packhorse, there were plenty of Remnants who would, beguiled by the fairy, in cahoots with him or otherwise. No, Von Hart, he suspected, had used him in another way entirely – was probably using him now. A wild card hidden up his star-spangled sleeve.

This is what you wanted, isn't it? Ben cursed his wits, even as he shivered with the prospect of pain. *Why did you save me? Why did you spare me? I could've stopped you before. In Egypt. In China . . .* But no. The envoy might've played him for a fool, but he wasn't stupid enough to believe his own bravado, leaving him only with questions. *Why did you forget the sword? If you didn't want me to follow you here . . .* Presumably, the envoy had brought the gate north to greet the Lady, welcome his people back to the Earth, heedless of their decline, their debasement.

Or refusing to see it, more like. The harp, the lunewrought, has it driven you mad?

The north spread out before him, filled with ice and silence. In his grip, Caliburn, thrumming with power, eager, anxious, leading him on. This, of course, raised another question. Like the ocean ahead, jewelled with icebergs and the ever-rising headland of Svalbard. The island, with its glacial cliffs, its mountains streaked with cold black rock, was a fist holding mystery. Holding threat.

Along with the light, the temperature was falling, sinking into perpetual dusk, the grip of the Arctic winter. Any further and du Sang might freeze completely, his old bones cracking apart, splintered by the wind. Would he tumble from his back, Ben wondered, shrugged off like a sloughed scale and sinking into the depths? Even that, he realised, probably wouldn't be enough. *You rot, but you endure.* That's what du Sang had told him. Years might pass, centuries even, the tides shifting the vampire's remains, flotsam on the waves. But if Ben knew him at all, du Sang would eventually wash up somewhere, the worst of all bad pennies, hungry and grey on some luckless shore.

He was thinking this, his jaw clenched, when the throbbing of the sword merged with the atmosphere. A strange condensation, a thickening pressure pooled out around him, eddying under his wings. In his peripheral vision, a flicker of light drew his gaze down to the sea, to the phosphorescence dancing there. An aurora lit the whitecaps from beneath, the foam forming patterns. Catching his breath, he traced the arc, the sapphire band glimmering through the water. East to west he traced it, the sight a mile wide or more, alive with the swirl of arcane symbols.

One of the circles, triggered by the sword . . .

But no, he wasn't sure about that. Taking in the breadth of the vision, he suspected a phenomenon he'd strayed upon rather than sparked.

This isn't like London. This circle was alight before, ignited by . . .
Yeah. Take a lucky guess.

From this height, he could almost describe the entire circle of protection. A good half of it curved out across the waves, stretching into the Greenland Sea and off, off into the north. Into the Arctic Ocean, hazy and dark on the horizon. The circles, he'd learned, were nothing less than the brandings of the Fay, the Fallen Ones, their power, their wisdom lost. Designed to shield the Earth, the circles were heading the same way, their magic souring, failing, leaving Creation – or at least this corner of it – doomed and undefended. He watched, expecting to see the circle waver as the others had done before, the sigils fading, fizzling out one by one. Yet this one didn't, retaining its gleam, fuelled by some uncanny source below . . .

The sight pricked Ben with unbidden sadness. If the Fay had wanted to ward off the ghosts of the nether, using the earth for their precious Example, then they had only courted disaster. In time, the Fallen Ones had met the same fate, the souring magic gnawing on their essence, a plague spreading across worlds. In the end, the dreams of Avalon had made no difference. The Lurkers had come to sup on the stuff of the *real*.

It's a circle, all right. Ben grasped the nub of it now. *From the stars right down to the gutter.*

And here he was where the circle met, the spindle of time coming around, crushing all that it had spun. It didn't take a genius to see that Svalbard, the shattered islands below, rested in the middle of the circle. A forsaken, frozen heart.

There was a darkness down there between the peaks, radiating menace. An area where the dusk ran out, as though sucked in on itself. A space at odds with the mountains around it. One less substantial, less real. Ben had encountered that blackness before, had come to know it well, the kiss of the nether. Even though he couldn't make out any details from above, he could feel the subtle *pulling* in the air, the lodestone to which the sword responded, humming in his grip.

Are you here, old friend? He slowed on the airstream, shadowing the coast. *Waiting for the end?*

With this cheery thought, Ben folded his wings, drew in a breath and descended towards the crumbling cliffs, his nebulous destination. Down there, who knew what horrors he'd face, pitched against the fairy and his spells? But he had no choice. Not if he wanted to make good on his oath, die with a shred of honour. He'd come full circle himself, a lone sentinel standing guard. The only one who stood between the world and ruin.

But first, he had made a promise.

"You're not the same creature that I found in that hole. Under the cemetery in Paris."

It had taken some time – time that Ben didn't have – for the Vicomte to thaw, held gently in an open claw, the heat of his breath washing over him. Then, as old bones creaked and pale flesh stretched, du Sang had blinked up at him with sleepy eyes. Ben had set the youth-who-was-far-from-young down on the escarpment, a snowy rise overlooking the tundra. A mile or so ahead, the lake stretched, a broad plain of ice in the twilight, up to the mountains that fanged the far shore.

Between the peaks, the darkness loomed. A slice of night, cupped by rock. There was light down there too, vague through the drifting snow. A radiance that Ben might've taken for an outpost or a town if not for its cold blue shade. Framed by the glow, the Vicomte stood with back turned, searching the half-light, awed by the scale of the abyss ahead.

"*Non*. Perhaps not," he said. "Nevertheless, I wish I could say it had given me reason to live."

"Du Sang—"

"Please, Ben. Don't. I know what you're going to say." He turned then, and even in the gloom, Ben made out the glimmer of tears, cold as dew on a grave. "My mind was made up a century ago. I . . . I mourn for the boy I used to be, long ago in the Age of Light. If only I could reach back then and cuff

338

myself around the head. Turn my eyes from those old occult books. My promises to the dark . . . To be forever young!" He sighed. "Oh, and how the dark answered me. The Families . . ." He seemed to run out of breath, weighed down by the memory. "For a while, we had fun. Didn't we?"

Ben tipped his snout, implying that this was a questionable point. He found that he had little to say. He couldn't say that they had all made mistakes, when the creature before him had betrayed him and worse. Still, du Sang was a Remnant. Even though the friendship between them had long since drowned in the wine fogs of Versailles, serial murder and the passing of ages, he had to respect the Vicomte's help, no matter the price of it. In the end, he settled on the same words he'd uttered months ago, in the shadows of the tombs.

"The past is the past."

Du Sang was quick to challenge him. "Are you sure about that?" he said. And then, more softly, "You know, I meant what I said. Before. I could tell you where she is, even now. Call it . . . a parting gift."

Ben looked away at the towering cliffs. The sweeps of snow, ashen in the dark. This time, he took no offence, hearing the vampire's sincerity. *To find Rose. Find my child . . . Tell them I'm sorry . . .* But Rose had asked him one last thing. Another promise, of sorts. He had nothing to indicate she'd changed her mind and the truth was he'd only ever brought her trouble. What made him think that would change? Besides, the Lady had played the worst kind of oracle, damning him with the truth. Words that he couldn't refute, that he'd somehow known all along. *You'll never see Rose McBriar again. Not while you live.* All he could do was focus on the present, the threat to the world entire, and hope, in this way, he could save them.

339

After a while, he looked back at du Sang.

"No. I'm . . . grateful. It's enough to know that they're alive."

The Vicomte nodded, expecting this answer, and then he flung out his arms.

"Life. So fragile. So precious," he said. "And death, so over-rated." He gave a little laugh, no joy in the sound. "Look at this world, Ben. Look what it's come to. Even this ice is fleeting, melting under our feet. For a while there, I thought we had a chance. That we could go on and build something better. But no, we're all slaves to desire, selfish to the last. Gold, power, blood . . ." He shook his head. "So much blood. We are all of us monsters, are we not?"

"Yes."

The Vicomte shuddered, letting out a frosty breath. He looked up at the stars, twinkling like pearls on satin above.

"Tell me, what do you think is out there? What awaits a creature like me? Heaven? Hell? Nothingness . . . ?" He turned the last word into a sigh, betraying his hope. "A true ending, free of sorrow and pain."

Ben grunted, aware of the minutes bleeding out, stealing the chance of salvation. And he'd never been fond of goodbyes.

"I don't know," he said. "Du Sang . . ."

The Vicomte smiled up at him, his fangs white in the dark.

"Very well. I won't keep you. Let's make this quick."

With this, Ben pushed regret from his mind, drawing himself up. *A promise is a promise.* He stretched out his neck, a rising diadem of horns, a furnace glowing behind his teeth. Through the heat haze around his snout, he looked down to see du Sang waving his arms.

"*Mon dieu!* It will not do!"

For a moment, Ben thought that the vampire had changed

his mind, opting to face destruction like the rest of them, at the hands of the Fay. But no. He remembered the Vicomte's words on the top of the Arc de Triomf, Barcelona, the flames swirling at his back.

Even dragon fire wasn't enough, quelle surprise . . .

With a heavy breath, he shrugged off dragon form, his body dwindling, folding inwards on the rise. In no time at all, a red-haired man in a scaled suit stood barefoot on the snow, his features pained. He stood before du Sang, Caliburn in hand.

One strike. One strike and you'd turn me to dust . . . The Fay metal is a bane to our kind.

"*Bonne nuit,*" the sword said.

And the Vicomte, closing his eyes, replied.

"Goodbye."

Ben raised the sword, a flash of silver in the dark.

When the sword fell, there was only ash, drifting with the snow on the wind.

TWENTY-THREE

A speck before the dark, Ben fleeted over the lake. He couldn't look back now; the time for looking back was done. Hell, Du Sang had got what he wanted, which was more than he could say for himself. He only wished he would meet such a merciful end. *Good luck with that.* Flat, long and blue, the glacier stretched out under him, narrowing to meet the bordering mountains, the jaws of the future awaiting him.

Between the peaks, the maw loomed, a starless, wavering mouth. There was no way he was looking at the Eight Hand Mirror – he'd even seen that from afar, up on the precipice. He didn't know what had happened to the frame, but the void it once held had far exceeded it, released from the earthly bounds of old yet unremarkable wood.

Blast you, fairy. What have you done?

Cupped by the snowbound slopes, a frayed nothingness clawed into the air, gnawing at the dusk, devouring the stars. Three thousand feet high or more, he judged, his shadow sweeping over the ice, heading for a vaguely triangular rent in the sky that made him feel like a mote in comparison.

Here, reality met with its antipode, the torn gateway of the nether. The Dark Frontier.

As he drew closer, Ben could see, with a chill to his marrow, exactly what was shredding the portal, rending and chewing on its edges, the fissure widening, a gradually opening wound. The clamour of mastication echoed across the tundra, rebounding off ice and rock, off the stricken dome of the sky. It was a hollow drum inside his skull, beating out fearful recognition. *Lurkers!* Hundreds of the bastards, edging the breach on all sides, a seething, pale boundary. From this angle, it was like looking down on a nest of termites, a swarm devouring a fruit from the inside out, the perspective dizzying, sickening. Picking out their busying shapes, he winced at the sight of them, the glassy, ravenous ghosts. Pincer, mandible and claw were working overtime, ripping at the physical plane. Tentacles, slick with ichor, lashed at the egress, lacerating the sky. Bulbous eyes gleamed in the gloom, fixed on the borderland banquet.

Despite his horror, Ben prayed that they would stay that way, his approach unmarked, an overlooked morsel. Gorge rising, he grasped what he was seeing, the knowledge a fist in his guts. Piece by piece, the phantoms were feasting on the fabric of Creation, stuffing its unravelling essence into jaw, proboscis and beak, and down their ethereal throats. He had seen such a frenzy before, of course, in car park walls, in a gathered, unified mass, but never on this scale. And if he'd wondered about the absence of the ghosts, oddly missing from the battle befalling Britain with all its unleashed and ruinous magic, here he found his answer. Von Hart must've come here, mirror in tow, and punched this hole in the cosmos. Somehow, he'd expanded the gate, granting the creatures their aeons-long wish, to dine on the dying earth.

Nice one.

It made sense. Before, in the guise of the Ghost Emperor, Von Hart had managed to distract the ghost-beasts, giving Jia time to steal the fragments of the harp. For all the havoc the envoy had wreaked, there was method in his madness, not that the insight, Ben conceded with a growl, was going to help him any. There was no end to the Lurkers' appetite. Give it a week, a month, and what would remain of Svalbard? A black hole, nothing more, growing ever wider, the ocean rushing in . . .

Did Von Hart know what he'd summoned? The origin of these freaks? Ben doubted it. The envoy was a latter-day Pandora, opening a deadly box. His longing to reunite with his people had blinded him to the truth. A fact, considering his efforts, which struck Ben as bitterly ironic. Even cruel. But then why should the anarchy spare the fairy when everyone else had suffered, caught up in the end of the illusion, many of them destroyed? *I thought . . . I thought you could save her . . .* A grim thought followed this one, but Ben allowed it. A shiver of satisfaction ran up his spine as he pictured facing the envoy, looking into his violet eyes and telling him that he was wrong.

The Fay are already here, he'd say. *Do they look golden to you?*

Under this, the hint of revelation, the pieces of the puzzle clicking together, insinuations of a deeper purpose. A desperate, dangerous need . . .

Are we not flesh, Benjurigan?

These suspicions drew him on, shooting over the lake. Drew him on like the tides in the air, the slow, gravitational pull of the portal, sucking up the distance. A mile or so from the mountains, he found that he could resist that pull, shove it off with muscle and scale, as though rejecting questing hands. Any closer, however, and he sensed that resistance would weaken, the inverse mass of the nether swallowing him like a spider down a plughole. That's if the Lurkers didn't swallow him first.

Turning his attention to the light, the foxfire igniting the shore, he angled his wings, slowing and decreasing lift. He had little choice; the pressure in the air was curdling with an earth-bound force, rippling and pulsing below. It wasn't hard to see where it was coming from. The confluence warred above the lake, an unseen maelstrom in the sky. The emanations threatened to tear off his wings, urging him to land. Sword in claw, Ben banked, veering around the scene. The radiance, foggy as it was, hurt his eyes. Squeezed his brain. Electricity fizzed in his nostrils, the spice of occult interference.

Magic. Open sesame. All that shit.

In a faint rosette that stretched off in all directions, the energy leapt and crackled. Light flickered along sapphire veins, the elaborate, knotted pattern carved in the ice. *The spell. The summoning. Whatever.* He'd seen symbols like this before. Sun wheels and pentagrams. Udjats and all-seeing eyes. Last time, the glyphs had shone in Day-Glo paint, protecting the walls of Club Zauber, keeping the Lurkers out. Here, etched in the lake, he guessed that they served the same purpose, shielding their architect's efforts in case the gate wasn't distraction enough, its disintegrating limits drawing the spectral threat. Atop the slope on the far shore, the threshold touched down in a jet-black spindle, absorbing the rock, a mere hundred yards from the edge of the circle.

And in the middle of the circle – surely, the hub of a much greater one, spreading out across seas, across continents – the architect stood, a tall, thin figure on the ice. Arms spread, Von Hart, the envoy extraordinary, was directing the streams of light like a pale puppeteer, the energy bursting and crackling off his fingers. Rivers of blue snapped across the ice, converging on the edge of the spell. Like a lightning rod, the fairy drew on the magic around him, channelling the flailing loops and thrusting them up at the darkness above. In the pull of the nether, the force dragging at the gate, his robes – red, silk, star-spangled – fluttered around him like wings yearning for flight. His white-gold hair shone in the radiance, a beacon in itself. It was too bright for Ben to see his face, though he could envision the strain upon it. The concentration. The *need*.

That need was all around him, threading through the atmosphere, as sour as the light. On the ionised air, a smell like sweat drifted to Ben's nose, rank with urgency. In that moment, he was grateful that the light spared him the envoy's expression, knowing he'd see the same thing he'd seen in the White Dog's eyes. In De Gori's. In Jia's. The same desperate longing. *Lunewrought.* The touch of madness. But it was more than that, he reckoned. The Fay metal spoke to a hunger that was already present. Hidden. Cradled in the heart. Hadn't he seen the same thing in the mirror for years, the threadbare hope in his gaze? He thought so. He thought he'd see the same thing in all Remnants and without looking too hard. In that moment, with the wind usurped by the abyss and the ache of his trials in his bones, it was hard to feel anything but sympathy for the creature below. His onetime ally, Blaise Von Hart.

But sympathy wouldn't serve him here. The envoy was indeed the architect of all these things. The shattering of the harp. The opening of the gate. And whatever his reasons, his *weakness* in doing so, Ben had only come here to stop him.

I'll face you, old friend. One last time.

He couldn't rely on the strength of the ice and so, with a blink of will, he changed in mid-air, his bulk shrinking inward. He landed, with a grunt, on the lake. Frost crackled, melted by the soles of his feet, the heat in his flesh. The static in the atmosphere plucked at him, teasing his hair into flamelike tufts. In human form, the surrounding pressure felt even greater, bearing down on his shoulders and back. Soupy and cold, the air buffeted around him, and he moved forward as if wading through water, shielding his eyes from the blazing circle. As he raised the sword, the boundary danced in silver, the hilt throbbing in his grip.

You forgot something, fairy. You may live to regret it . . .

On ground level, through the capering light, Ben could see what the envoy was about, the reason for all the symbols. He'd seen enough now to guess at the science, the equation unfolding around him. Conducting the beams, Von Hart was spooling the power in his hands and pouring it toward the shore. The ice there split and twisted, the rock melting, flowing upwards in bubbling, abstract shapes. Ben caught sight of the rainbow shimmer deep in the mix, absorbing, reflecting the envoy's magic, a prism he'd come to know. Like liquid glass, the ice fused and surged skyward, ten yards across and twice as thick, arching, glistening, into the dark.

The bridge. The ley. He's repairing it . . .

The thought drew Ben's eyes to the fissure, tracing the stretching span. It arced up to the point where the light ran out, consumed by the void. Squinting, he noticed the gleam up there, a silver streak dwindling into the black. It was the severed end of the ley, snapped months ago by the harp and left hanging, suspended, over nothing. But he got it now. He understood. For years – centuries – the silver ley had linked the earth to Avalon, the Font of All Worlds. In time, the rot had set in, creeping through the dark to the High House itself, into an orchard and up palace walls, at least according to the Lady. Broken or no, the fall of the bridge had come too late to stop it. Too late to sever the worlds completely.

The memory, the dream, was a knife in his skull.

James Bennett

Your world is a canker. Nothing more . . .

No. It was the gate, he realised then. The door of Creation. Sealed after the Battle of Camlann when the Fay – except one, that was – had left this world, abandoning the failed Example and departing into the nether. A gate recently opened by Jia Jing, the *sin-you* breaking the charm. It was the *gate* that linked the Earth to the nether, just as much as the road, the Silver Ley, stretching off to God knows where. *To Avalon, the Isle of the Bad Apples . . .* As long as the door remained open, the canker would continue to spread, the connected worlds bound by plague as much as fate. The doom of the dying magic.

Unseen, veiled by centuries, the plague had festered, the Fay withering behind closed doors. For those same centuries, the Remnants had either been asleep or preoccupied with the business of survival. Civilisation had rumbled on. Cities rose that blackened the sky. Poisoned the seas. Melted the icecaps. The humans forgot the magic in their midst, reducing the truth to fable, to myth. *Remnants of belief.* No one had noticed the tumour until it was too late. The worm, gnawing away at the heart of things.

O Rose thou art sick . . .

But the Fay were returning. The echoes of the lullaby had called to them, ringing out across the gulf. And some doors, Ben had learnt, should always stay shut. In this case, the breach drawing all to the wound, the rotten core of the chaos.

But how to close the damn thing? How?

As if the notion mocked him, the vision in the deep became clear, a distant disturbance along the ley. Like a baleful star, a cloud, silvery, ghostly, was approaching through the dark, the fracturing rays betraying great speed. Holding his breath, he made out a faint rumbling. It sounded uncomfortably like hooves. Hundreds of them, pounding in his head.

348

Riders. A company of Fay. Bound for the gate.

The thought chilled him in a way that no ice could.

He turned his attention back to Von Hart, the envoy rippling in the light. *If I can reach him somehow. Tell him the truth . . .* He might not be able to save the earth, but he was pretty sure that he could throw a spanner in the works. At least stall the disaster, prevent the Fay from alighting. He didn't hold out much hope, but what else could he do? What other way to break the spell, stop the bridge from mending?

And in his heart, a darker, more desperate idea, prickling under his scales.

Kill him.

With this, Ben stepped into the circle. The effect was immediate and anguished, the light shrieking at his intrusion. Caliburn, he noticed, took the brunt of it, the eldritch force homing in on the blade, magnetised by *lunewrought*. The runes along its fuller shone, blue as the surrounding ice. On its crossguard, the jewelled quillons sparkled and shone, liquid in the brilliance. *Aware.* In his grip, the hilt grew colder. Needles sank into his flesh, freezing his fingers, binding him to the sword in pain. Gritting his teeth, Ben pressed on, crossing the outer ring. The blade, he believed, could withstand the barrage – withstand *anything*, according to the weapon. He doubted that he'd have made it this far alone. Caliburn was drawing the fire.

The proof of this came as he reached the second ring, pushing himself through the light, glyphs beaming under his feet. A bolt of energy, sharp as fangs, bit into him, spearing through him from chest to rump. Jaw locked, spine straight, he spasmed, slipping on the ice, the sword a blur before him. In the dissonance, he couldn't hear himself scream, his throat raw. White fire filled his skull, bursting with untold heat.

Still, he pushed on, forcing himself through his shock, the bolt passing, crackling away over the circle. At once, his bulk swelled. Horns sprouted up on his shoulders. Scales rippled up and down his neck. Rhino-sized and snarling, he thrust himself forward, tendrils of light clinging to his legs. Burning with cold, he crossed the boundary, heading for the inner ring.

Von Hart, curse you . . . Sparks played in his hair. Danced between his teeth. Veins stood out on his neck, ripe with determination. The energy clawed at him, his transformation stymied. He grew and dwindled, grew and dwindled, snared by the light. He felt the scales on his back peeling away, prompting another howl. The stench of scorched flesh rose in his nostrils, sickeningly sweet. His shoulder blades ached, unable to summon wings. A sting at the bottom of his spine informed him of the danger. The magic, it seemed, was wrenching at his essence, finding its echo in his bones, eager to soak it up. Another bolt, another misstep, and the spellbound circle might consume him completely, unravel the stuff of his making. *Our endless magic runs in your veins. But your flesh? Your flesh was born solely of their dreams.* Divided, the dragon ripped from him; he'd reach the envoy merely as a man, naked and exposed to the elements, breathing his last in the snow . . .

Biting back pain, his mind clinging to his body like a cloak in a high wind, he staggered, smouldering, across the ice. And he reached the edge of the inner circle.

Veiled in silk and rainbow light, Von Hart noticed him then, throwing a glance in his direction. Eyes bright, the envoy hissed at him between his teeth.

"*Stop!* Come no closer!" he said. "Don't break the circle."

That's the least of your worries, old friend.

"Fairy," Ben growled through the maelstrom of light. "I'm gonna break your neck."

"You stand here . . . at the heart of the world . . ." The envoy's effort threaded through his words, a song of yearning and strain. "The knot that binds all together. The Cardinal Locus. Undo the spell and all is lost. Stay back. For your own sake!"

Right.

Through the brilliance, Ben could see the sense of this, all the same. Framed by the inner ring, the envoy stood inside a burning core. A heart, in fact, a few feet wide in diameter, carved into the ice. Under his boots, the light cavorted and flashed, beating with power. All the same, there was something unhealthy about the sight. The rhythm seemed off, a galloping pace. No doubt scaling to a kind of magical . . . cardiac arrest. *Cataclysm.* Symbols, faint, hung in the air, spilling from the envoy's lips. One by one, they winked out as he paused, the prism dimming, the ice on the shore slowing. The bridge, as yet, unforged.

Again, he looked over at Ben, this time with narrow eyes. It only took Ben a moment to realise that Von Hart wasn't interested in him.

"Caliburn," the envoy said, and he couldn't hide his satisfaction, drinking in the length of the blade. "World-cleaver. Demon-slayer. Harp-breaker."

And the sword said, "My king."

Ben curled his lip, its obeisance, for all its weary scorn, sinking in.

Of course. The insight should've shocked him more than it did, coming as it did on the heels of his suspicions. *I'm a sword, not a subject.* That's what Caliburn had told him, back in the chamber under the mountain, all jewelled and steely arrogance. And in the cavern under London, the sword had sounded anything but, chastising the envoy for his meddling. *You've been busy, hexenmeister . . .* It struck him now that the blade, forged long ago in Avalon and bestowed upon an earthly ruler, had aimed its disdain at Arthur. Perhaps at all humans, its provenance springing from other hands entirely, alien and afar. The harp. The horn. The sword. The Fay had made all these things, hadn't they? Shaping their magic in *lunewrought* and placing them in mortal hands. Tools with which to toy with the world, advance the cause of the Example. *Sleep, enchanted. Binding. And severance.* A trinity of intervention, left discarded on the earth. Relics of failure. Of doom . . .

The knowledge shuddered through him, an ache in his skull.

And what of love, Benjurigan? He remembered the Orchard of Worlds, the blossoms in the air, forming a figure, pale and tall. The hint of hair, white as snow. Arms spread. The vision drifting apart in the Lady's embrace.

Once, I walked here with my consort, the King of all the Fay. What dreams we conjured in the garden!

Ben gasped, the memory hitting home. He hadn't just interrupted a reunion, the envoy summoning his people. He'd interrupted an aeons-long tryst.

"You think I'm stupid," he said to Von Hart, forcing his words through the storm, thin and razor-sharp. "*Dummkopf*, wasn't it? But all this . . ." He nodded at the blazing circle. At the breach in the Lore. The shattered mirror. Absent ghosts. "The lengths you've gone to . . . Fairy, you've shown your hand. You loved her, didn't you? The Lady. Nimue. You were the one who started all this, back in the . . . God knows. You were her fucking *king*."

Von Hart straightened at this, unable to hide his surprise. Perhaps he'd imagined himself so clever, hiding the crux of his plans, the desire that had driven him to risk all. *I made a mistake* . . . Betraying the Lore he'd founded. The Sleep he'd brought about. Sacrificing his student. His friend. *I asked you to catch her. To let me fall.* But there was a deeper devotion here. A deeper need. Ben had seen it in the envoy's eyes, back in the crypt under London. And he was seeing it again as Von Hart sighed and hung his head, his hands falling limp at his sides. At once, the light flickered out completely. The rainbow faded, swallowed by the dark. Up on the shore, the ice stopped flowing, the bridge, for the moment, arrested. Its glistening arc had stalled in the mouth of the gate.

Even in the gloom, Ben couldn't mistake it. The envoy looked sick, he thought. His cheekbones were gaunt, holding a sallow sheen. Threads of gold clung to his brow, plastered by cold and sweat. The effort of the spell reeked on him, that was plain. As was his fatigue, perhaps the weight of his ages-long scheme. It was coming to fruition here, out on the ice. Ben's chest grew tight as he took in the envoy's expression, the sorrow in his eyes. He'd known enough of it himself, a burden that he'd carried for years, to recognise it on sight.

The wound of a long-lost love.

"We believed once," Von Hart told him, simply. "We struck a sword into stone and challenged this world to aspire. To reach its highest expression. We believed that we could shine our light upon all. Climb our way back to the stars. Back to . . ." *Godhood.* Ben had heard this part. It didn't surprise him that the envoy left the thought hanging, a silent admission of guilt. "We believed that we could make *them* believe. The humans. With magic. With dreams made flesh. *Remnants,* Ben. The *erlscion.*" He smiled, as though seeing a younger version of himself in the surface of the lake. "And on their belief, the *power* of it, we believed that we could build a ladder, restoring us to glory."

"Things didn't work out that way," Ben said. *Understatement of the year.*

"No," Von Hart said. Then he gave a tut, frowning. "The Example failed. We remained Fallen. The Fay turned their backs on this world, marching off into the nether. Yet she promised to return . . ."

One shining day, when Remnants and humans learn to live in blah blah . . .

"I hate to break it to you, but the Queen's Troth . . ." Ben hesitated. Why was his voice trembling, the words like thorns in his heart? He'd looked forward to this moment, avenging himself on the envoy with the truth. Instead, all he felt was pain. "That's all bullshit. Whatever state the Fay were in when they left the earth, all shiny and whatever, that doesn't describe them now. I've *seen* her, Von Hart. The Lady. In visions. In dreams." *Or something much like them.* "The Fay are dying like we are. The souring of magic has spread across the leys, polluting Avalon. They're not just Fallen. They're *fucked*. Your precious people are corrupted. Twisted. They're turning into Lurkers."

The envoy shot him a look, a stab of violet in the dark.

"You have to put an end to all this," Ben went on, waving an arm at the circle. The gate. "You have to shut this shit down."

Von Hart held his gaze, desire and shock warring in his eyes. Then his face resolved into a pleading look. Ben caught his breath, realising what he was seeing. The fairy *wanted* him to say it wasn't so. He wanted to reject the revelation, cling on to hope. But the grip of *lunewrought*, of longing, clearly wasn't strong enough to thwart the truth, now that the envoy heard it. Ben had expected denial. Fire, even, blasting him away across the ice. He'd expected death.

Instead, Von Hart sank to his knees, his robes spilling around him, dark as blood.

"*Ja*. Typical," he said in a murmur. "Here we stand at the heart of all belief, watching the last hope fade."

Ben wasn't quite sure what he meant, but there was no time. "Von Hart. Damn you—"

To his surprise, the envoy gave a sob. The sound skittered away across the lake, rebounding between the mountains. Cradling himself, his head sank towards the frozen surface, and when he spoke, it was through bitter teeth.

"It was all for nothing. Nothing." He shivered like a leaf in the chill. In that moment, he looked old and frail, a sight that shocked Ben more than his grief. "I thought that we could go on. I thought I could find a way. I thought—"

"A decent master looks after his pets," Ben said, summing up the maths of his doubt, the penny dropping. He could see it now. The full scope of the envoy's scheme, fraught with danger and stretching back years. Centuries. Back into the Old Lands. *And beyond* . . . "That's what you told me, back in Berlin." *And recently, under London.* "Is that . . ." He could barely bring himself to say it. "Is that why you stayed behind?"

All along, the envoy had been trying to tell him, his riddles threaded with the seeds of a greater truth. Perhaps it was the magic in the air, or the fairy's sorrow, that pricked the realisation from him, the puzzle at last clicking together. Clicking together like the fragments of a harp, shattered by the sword at the Battle of Camlann, the pieces left lying in the snow. In du Sang's tomb, Ben had seen the painting on the wall, the blazing black sun on the rise. And the envoy, watching his people depart . . .

Until now, it had never occurred to him that Von Hart's role of ambassador, of envoy, wasn't a position appointed by the Fay, the High House, but one that he had chosen himself.

His mistake.

"I was tired, Ben," the envoy said. "Tired of the endeavour. The harvesting of worlds. And with the Remnants, we had come so *close*." He looked up then, tears crystallising on his cheeks. "I had . . . changed. You're not the only one who feels kinship with humans. Who learnt to love their fragility. Their fleeting nature. The power of their dreams. And you were our *children*. Our greatest achievement. How could I leave you? Leave you to die. Alone in the dark. When the moment came, I found that I could not."

Ben sagged, his shoulders falling. Steam eddied from his mouth, swirling with hurt. The sword tip sank to the ice. It was all he could do to stay on his feet. For the past two years, from conspiracy to catastrophe, he'd come to see Von Hart as a traitor. A knife in the back. His worst enemy. A creature of deceit, his cruelty unfolding in innocent blood and the end of the world. And while this was true, after a fashion, he realised then that he'd misjudged the fairy. That really, here at the end, he was simply seeing the envoy's despair, a surrender to an inevitable doom, and a longing to see his people again. His queen again. His love.

And then, another echo. Another memory.

Oh, we were younger then. Foolish . . . Can a queen not love her king?

Yeah. The Lady had told him. This ancient romance – treacherous, disastrous as it had proven to be – had cut both ways.

"The Eight Hand Mirror," Ben said. "The last gate. She . . ." He recalled Nimue's sadness in the garden, the memory stinging his eyes. *In our pain, we did not see . . . One by one, we destroyed the gates, closing the roads through the nether. One alone, we left intact, although locked and bound by a charm, because . . .* "She couldn't bring herself to do it either, could she? To leave you behind forever. Like you, she thought there was still a chance. Because—"

And above him, in the wound of the world, a voice echoed from the darkness.

"Yes. Because we didn't have the Hart."

TWENTY-FOUR

Nimue, Our Lady of the Barrows, stood on the brink of the broken bridge. When Ben turned, her words resounding in his skull, the perspective clawed at him, his guts churning. It was as though he stood on the lip of a chasm, albeit one that had cracked the heavens apart. Ice prickled up his spine, a chill that had nothing to do with the surface he was standing on. The gate was wider now, he saw, its fraying edges lapping against the mountains. The snowbound slopes were losing solidity, swallowed by an abject, insatiable darkness. By *Lurkers*, who swarmed on all sides, nibbling, pecking, gorging on reality, the fabric of the material plane. The arrested spell hadn't stalled them; the guests were already at the feast. Even the stars seemed to quail, unable to withstand the onslaught, winking out like candles. Looking at the gate, Ben knew only too well that to fall into the nether was to fall forever, spinning and spinning until his breath ran out, and then spinning still. But if he had to follow Jia to stop this disaster – this *invasion* – then so be it. What did he have to live for, anyway? Everything was gone.

But I'll go down in flames like I promised. The Lone Fire. Snuffed out.

The Lady, however, didn't look bothered either way. Summoned by the breaking of the harp, she had followed the road through the void, back to this forgotten place. This long ago rejected fruit. Rotten. Sour. Left hanging on a withering branch in some nowhere corner of the cosmos.

And she hasn't come alone. Dear God.

At her back, beyond her slender, blue-gowned figure, Ben took in the length of the ley, wide as a highway where it reached the gate. It was a silver beam that dwindled into the distance, devoured by the deep. The cloud out there was closer now, as was the rumbling in his ears, the tidings of a coming storm. *A company of riders*, the Lady had told him. But fresh from the Battle of London (not to mention the trials of the past), it didn't take a genius to see that it was an army. A narrow vanguard roared and creaked down the last road, out of the Dark Frontier. *The High House of Avalon, brought low.* Cursing his extraordinary vision, he was sure he could make out the flash of swords. The flurry of hooves. The gleam of strange and alien machinery. Siege engines, towering, bristling with spikes. Great mangonels, armoured like seashells, their flanks a silvery whorl. Jewelled cannons, no doubt loaded with munitions, blasting all in a magical barrage . . . And reluctant as the insight was, he couldn't mistake the aura around the galloping ranks. A cold, milky glow enveloped the vanguard, trailing scum and ghost-light. If he looked closer, he reckoned he'd see a claw here, an antenna there. An array of blank, compound eyes, all wrestling inside elegant armour, squirming to get out . . . To *feed.* Instead, he looked away, the view too much for him, threatening to usurp his reason, turn his fire into stone.

Safer to look at the Lady. Nimue on the edge of the bridge. How she'd got here so fast, he couldn't know, although she had said something about the nature of time, how it moved differently in the nether, if at all. In a way, she had *always* been here, carried in his head, in his heart, in the dreams of all Remnants, merely waiting for her moment. Or an invitation. A way back to the lands she'd sown, ripe with ruin and regret . . .

For all her debasement, she showed none of it now. She'd restored her mask, her glamour, the illusion shimmering in silk and long brown limbs, her hair coiled high on her head, white as the mountains she stood between. With eyes as violet as dusk, she peered across the gulf, the ice clawing from the lakeshore into the maw. Then, with obvious disdain, she looked down at the edge of the broken span, tapering out a few yards from her toes.

Ben found himself thankful for that gulf, although he couldn't quite trust it – couldn't trust a thing about these creatures. He disliked the smile that haunted her lips, faint, yet darkly amused. In the poise of her neck, her folded hands, he could read her scorn for this paltry latter-day summons. In her eyes, there lingered the gleam of a greater art. A half-remembered power. A lost divinity. All of it eclipsed by hunger.

Nevertheless, Von Hart said, "My queen." And then, softer, through tears, "My love."

Across the distance, the Lady frowned, troubled. She blinked and gave a twitch of her head, as if to shake off a discomforting thought. And when she replied, a gentleness threaded through her voice, at odds with the fathomless dark. The reason for her arrival.

"My Lord Blaise," she said, and bobbed in the shadow of a curtsey. "The Leaping White Hart of Camelot. Consort of the High House. How long has it been since we walked in the garden? Arm and arm and dreaming of the future? Dreaming these worlds anew? Tell us."

"Many, many years, Your Majesty." In the centre of the circle, the envoy bowed his head. "Too many. Beyond count."

"And Merlin," the Lady said. "Your student. How do our subjects fare?"

Merlin? As Nimue's eyes settled upon him, Ben didn't know what to expect. Her usual greeting, ambiguous, teasing, or a show of drooling fangs, rendering him a morsel in eight eyes, a tool that had served its purpose. *Bring us the sword.* But he realised then that he was less than that, a minor presence in her regard. A Remnant. A failed experiment. A beast and nothing more.

Did you honestly imagine that you were so special?

No. When all was said and done, he accepted that he wasn't. To some, he may have played guardian. To others a pet. Or a lie, an illusion of human love. But she hadn't directed her question at him, only at the weapon he held.

Caliburn.

"My lady," the sword said, thrumming. "I'm afraid I remain exactly where you put me, all those years ago. In a prison that is sometimes a blasted oak and sometimes a tower of glass. And sometimes, of late, a sword, forged in *lunewrought* and star-studded, tempered in the ice of Avalon and spun across worlds to the hand of a king."

"What the hell?" Ben growled, his breath steaming. "You kept that quiet."

But Caliburn – *Merlin* – ignored him and the Lady was speaking again.

"As it should be, old cambion," she said. "As it will always be. Ah, how you inspired us, wizard. The son of a devil and a nun. And how you failed us. With your temptation. Your lust. How mortal, how weak, you remained."

361

"In my soul, you bound the fate of this world, great lady," the sword replied. "Yet that was my choice, was it not? In the end, there were some who refused you. Arthur. Even your consort, Lord—"

"Fools all," the Lady said, her smile fading. "And that choice was your last. The sealing of your tomb. Indeed, you remain our prisoner. Your fate in our hands. And you will not refuse us now."

So saying, Nimue raised a hand, a delicate twist of fingers in the dark. Instinctively, Ben tightened his grip on the weapon, feeling the force eddying around it, tugging at the blade. But it was no use. A burst of silver, pokers in his head, rewarded him for his efforts. A bolt of energy shot through him, arching his spine, locking his teeth in pain. Through screwed-up eyes, he looked down at the sword, the dragon-shaped hilt, the graven, indecipherable runes. On the crossguard, the jewelled quillons sparkled in the glare, appearing to stare up at him. And with that gleaming, pointed look, images scattered, refracting in his skull.

A blazing black sun on a rise. A woman – no, the Lady – turning. Turning her back on the battle below, on human folly and weakness. On the one who stood there in star-spangled robes, his hair like milk poured down his back. And then the envoy, running, running and weeping up the slope, leaving no footprints in the snow. His hand reaching out, reaching for her shoulder . . . And his fingertips meeting glass . . .

It was only a moment. Then it was gone. Gone like the fire, dispersing around him. Gone like the sword in his hand.

Cursing, Ben staggered backwards, shaking off its sting. *Fuck.* He spat on the ice, the surface hissing. With wounded eyes, he looked up at the bridge where the Lady stood, suspended, waiting, over nothing. But she wasn't looking at him, his presence already forgotten. With open triumph, her gaze rested solely on the sword.

She held it up, admiring the blade, and then she looked down at the envoy, Von Hart.

"What of love, Lord Blaise?" she asked him. "What of it? It is a memory. An echo swallowed by the deep. We are not what we were and love alone cannot save your world. You were unwise to ever think otherwise. A pale fool who spurned his throne to crawl in the muck and the shit, under the boot of talking apes. Cradling our misbegotten spawn through the ages, thinking to nurse their ragged forms and finding only dust spilling through your fingers. Oh, we have learnt of your efforts, my faithless lord. Compromises and devil's bargains. Threadbare spells and broken relics. Pacts and promises and lies. And love!" She barked a laugh, quick as a bee sting. "You dare to kneel before us with that word on your lips, when all is air and darkness. Tell us, what has love brought you? Your attempt to fulfil my Troth? A worm gnaws at the heart of things. The worm of disbelief."

Ben straightened, breathing hard. It hurt him to hear it, the lesson he'd learnt. To put his finger on the stove of his fears, burnt by the brutal fact of them. The worm, invisible, ravenous, had eaten away at the Old Lands. At the circles of protection. The soul of the earth. The worm wasn't time, no, though that was part of it. The road along which it crawled, growing fat over the years, the centuries that had thrown up cities and smoke, the Remnants falling into their shadow . . . Not time, but a loss of faith. The slow poison of doubt, corrupting all. A festering wound that became a scar, old and unremembered. Until truth became myth and myth became lie. A story, a fiction, no more.

And over the ages, the magic soured, fed by the drying stream. The dismissal of dreams. The denial of ghosts. The death of fairies. The worm, the destroyer, had a name: human disbelief.

Von Hart looked up at her and said, "I know."

The Lady laughed, devoid of humour or mercy.

"This audience is at an end," she said. "And so is this world."

With this, the Lady spread her wings. Against the shuddering darkness, her gown whipped up around her limbs, tossed by an inexplicable wind, the dynamism of magic. The fabric stretched and swelled, fluid in the air, fanning out on either side of her. Her pennons made her look like a butterfly, her body small and dark between them. The gap, Ben realised, the broken span, wouldn't stop a power like hers, now that she was here. And here, he knew, he'd indeed witnessed a chrysalis, bound in illusion, the guise of a lost and beautiful queen. His gorge rose, dread flooding him. He had no desire to see her transformation again, the monstrosity breaking free.

Nimue took a step, and another, reaching the torn lip of the bridge.

Von Hart answered her then. He looked up, tears on his cheeks like rivers in snow. As he spoke, symbols dripped from his lips, a vague prism in the air. Ben couldn't make out his words, the language unknown to him, belonging to another time. Another world. Still, he caught the sense of them, the spell stirring his blood, flickering around the edge of the circle.

Summer days, gold and endless. Nights where the moon never waned or set. Kisses, soft, in leafy bowers. And castle walls, high and white. Alien hands on pale flesh, shaping, moulding, revelling in the mortal clay. The sensation, brief, of life. And then sadness. Great sadness, carried on the wind. Carried with the scent of blossoms and blood. A song of farewell . . .

All these things Von Hart said to her, his scorned and fallen queen. And Ben could see what he was doing, how he was trying to reach her, remind her of a million yesterdays, crushed under the heel of time. For a breathless moment, he thought it might even work. The Lady hesitated on the brink, her head tipped, listening. Light washed around her, spiralling through the murk. Her aura, blue, brightened to silver, throwing off the touch of the ages, the creep of her long decay.

But then she pursed her lips, a bitter seed. She raised the sword, slashing at the air. With a whine of *lunewrought*, the symbols scattered, the prism dispelled, the envoy's words denied. Blue seeped back into her wings, riddling down the gossamer veins, winding around her transfiguring body. With a crack of bone and a surge of flesh, the Lady grew, her legs stretching into slender spines, white, translucent, incorporeal. One questing limb broke from her shoulder, a glistening, quivering sprig, while her torso bubbled and bulged, tearing her gown into shreds. Gasping, Ben watched her abdomen swell. A glassy, striated orb eclipsed the ley behind her, eclipsed the cloud of the oncoming horde. Eyes, eight of them, burst from her skull, a bloom of mushrooms in a murky wood, ballooning to grotesque size. And just as before, dangling from the maw of this arachnid beast, a part of the Lady remained. A bared breast. A violet eye. An arm clutching the sword.

Wings, skeletal leaves, rustled against the sky. Thrusting her legs against the bridge, the Lady shrieked and took to the air.

No!

Without thinking, Ben flung himself forward, launching into his own transformation, unravelling from the ice. Scales broke from his flesh, rippling around his burgeoning bulk. Wings sprang from his shoulders, their leathery span bearing him aloft. Horns popped up along his lengthening spine, a row of caltrops, sixty feet long. His tail whipped out, the arrowhead tip jerking on the end of it, taut with the speed of his passage. Snout extending, he spread his claws as he reached for the Lady, reached for her spectral flesh.

Too late, he realised his error, the heat of his intervention. Flame blustered from his jaws, illuminating the space between them. But through the inferno she came, too large, too cold for burning. With a cry, her bristling body filled his vision. The Lady smacked into him in mid-air, thunder across the lake. Fangs sinking into flesh, the creature that had once been Nimue bore him down, smashing him into the ice.

His breath went out of him, a gust of sparks and smoke. The surface of the lake hissed, buckling under the combined weight of dragon and queen, the stymied heat of him. In his ears, a popping sound, joining the Lady's teeth-jarring scream. Cracks went riddling across the ice, a widening web with him at its heart, the ghost-spider thrashing above him. The sky wheeled, a carousel of emptiness and stars, swallowed by the mouth of the gate. Wider, ever wider . . . There was no way to shut the breach now. Upside down, wings flailing, Ben bucked and squirmed, tearing at her face, her underbelly. Pearly scraps of ooze and bone scattered all around him, evaporating in mist. It did him no good. A pincer closed around his leg, forcing him against the ground. Then another, and another, his claws trapped, snared by her glut of limbs. With a vice closing around his neck, colder than the wind, he vented a roar. It was quickly silenced, a manus squeezing his throat.

With fangs, with *lunewrought*, the Lady tore at him, silver splitting the sky. In his nostrils, the smell of blood, hot and rank, and he knew it was his own. The blade was shredding him, viscera painting the ice. The sword was beyond cold, slicing through scales as if they were paper, bringing pain that he'd never known. Its steely kiss shattered his fury, usurping it with fear. Like twigs, his ribs cracked, giving way under the Lady's weight, her relentless, vicious assault. In a horrified flash, he grasped what was happening, even as he struggled against her, resisting her with his dwindling strength, pinned against the ground. This wasn't merely a physical attack, a clash of draconic and spectral brawn. The sword was cutting away at his *essence*, carrying the Lady's intent. Here he lay, one of her abandoned children, the spawn of egg upon egg. But his origin, he knew, was entirely down to her, bound long ago in spells. And like a mother chiding a brat, Nimue was taking him to task, reminding him of her authority. How *dare* he challenge her? Her, Queen of Phantoms. Harvester of Worlds. The Doom of Wizards and Kings!

Howling, Ben realised that he was shrinking, his mauled body hoarding his heat. But this was no ordinary transformation, the familiar thump of himself coiling back in, the dragon locked in his heart, an ancient, ever-glowing coal. Instead, it was as if thorns snagged at him, his flesh a cloak caught in a briar, the Lady wrenching at his core. In his mind, a cold fire, the ghost-spider searching for him. For the dreams. The hopes. The sentience that held him together.

An egg abandoned in a deep wood, the shell cracked like stone. Fire and smoke. A girl in a cave. The sound of sobs that he knew as his own. A cool, white hand on his shoulder, promising him purpose, a reason to go on. A moonlit meadow under the stars. Knights stood around a table, watching him bend with quill in hand . . .

With an effort of will, Ben clutched at the threads of his being. He was desperate to save the sense of himself, his inherent magic, from her snapping scrutiny. In this, only his diminishing size helped him, allowing him to slip from the Lady's claws. Again, her fangs darted down, this time striking the ice. Groaning, he rolled, blood smearing his naked skin, painting the lake. *It's cold. So cold* . . . Hands on his belly, he pressed on his wounds. The deepest of them chugged, red between his fingers. His flesh tingled, his heat uncertain, his healing abilities checked somehow. The gash remained open, wet and raw.

Not good.

Shadows fluttered in his skull. *Damn.* He was losing consciousness. Blearily, from miles away, he could hear the envoy shouting. Words that might mean anything, useless to him now. By degrees, the chill was slipping from him, the storm of violence receding. Leaving him to die.

The Lady, distracted, shifted her bulk. Then she turned and scuttled away across the ice.

Grimacing, broken, Ben managed to roll onto his stomach. The blood in his hair crackled, already freezing in the still. He peered across the surface of the lake, seeing Von Hart climbing to his feet, his arms spread in welcome. In the gloom, he looked small, a bony figure in a ridiculous robe. His face, a mask of white, turned to the creature bearing down on him. From the ghost-spider's maw, the hominid remains of the Lady hung, her arm raising the sword.

No.

Across the distance, the envoy extraordinary, King of the Fay, stood in the heart of the circle. Its light was dim now. Doused in darkness. Shrouded by snow. Arms falling to his sides, he simply hung his head. And waited.

A shadow fell over him, hissing with rage. Despite that, the fairy smiled. A sadness, a surrender on his lips. When he spoke, it was barely a whisper, a sigh stolen by the wind. But Ben heard him clearly enough, a tinkle of bells in his head.

"I thought that I could save them," he said.

Then silver flooded the scene, *lunewrought* slashing down.

With a sweep of the sword, Nimue, Our Lady of the Barrows, chopped off the envoy's head.

TWENTY-FIVE

Ben was too tired, too cold, to cry out. All he could do was let out a breath, a hollow puff in the still. Fighting the shadows, he closed his eyes, ice crackling down his cheeks.

Lost. He's lost.

The fact slammed into him. For all Von Hart's cunning, his scheme had failed, his futile endeavour, spanning years. *The envoy extraordinary. Lost.* His mistake remained just that, one he'd never undo. Conspiracies and spiked armour. Broken harps and shattered glass. What good had it done?

Ben summed up his despair in a single, remembered name.

Jia. She died for nothing. Nothing . . .

The gate stood open, a black rent between the mountains. It grew wider with every second, a threshold devoured by ghosts. Down its throat, the vanguard came on, rumbling ever closer out of the dark. In a matter of minutes, the Fay would alight, all shining swords, strange engines and ghost-light, on the rotting soil of the Earth.

And what then? What then? The world was dying, withering on the branch. He tried and failed not to think about its last days. A tyranny of evil, of mad queens and ravenous beasts. Stampeding giants, dragons and war. The gate, he knew, would grow and grow, until it yawned in an endless gulf. Sucking up deserts and seas. Cities and plains. Gulping down Creation. He spared a thought for the people, the humans – his damn *family* – the ones he had failed to protect. He'd hoped beyond hope to stop all of this, to build a bridge to the future. But even Annis Cade, that bright, bright spark, flickered and waned, extinguished in his thoughts.

The ice he lay upon, stained a deep red, crawled into his ravaged flesh, his broken bones. The last of his heat was unable to thwart it. The *lunewrought* blade, Caliburn – Merlin, whatever – had made good on its promise, felling him like a tree. The wound in his guts wasn't healing, he could tell. Sprawled on the ice, he was bleeding out, as good as a naked man cast adrift on the tundra. Along with the world, he was dying. The last waking dragon, sinking into his final sleep.

Yes. There was only darkness now. Darkness and death. *Welcome death.*

As if to mock him, light filtered through the gloom, stinging his eyes.

No. Let me rest. Let me go . . .

Grudgingly, he squinted through the glare at its source, the Lady in the middle of the circle. The Cardinal Locus. Her legs, eight of them, scuttled like giant pins around the carved heart, her equal number of eyes fixed on its smouldering hub. The circle, it seemed, was responding to her presence, however monstrous and warped. *And why wouldn't it?* Ben thought, distantly. *Why not?* After all, aeons ago, the Fay had been the ones to carve these circles, branding their sigils into the earth, or so the story went. *The myths of myths. Lost as the magic.* Perhaps the ancient binding remembered her. Remembered the goddess she used to be, even if she'd long since fallen, forgetful in her decline.

As he thought this, he realised his error. The Lady, clearly, was experiencing some difficulty, skittering around the inner ring. Her abdomen bobbed and bulged, the striations fluid in the light, shafts of blue through her legs. She lowered herself, drool splattering the ice, then straightened, venting a curse. As she turned, Ben made out her fangs, opening and closing, whickering in annoyance. Her skeletal wings flapped uselessly. She didn't crave the sky, but the ground.

Dangling from her maw, the rags of her humanoid form, trapped, embedded in spectral bone. Her arm swung, clutching the sword. The bloodied blade flashed with jewels, striving for the ground. At first, Ben wondered, his mind dull, what she wanted with the corpse between her legs. A headless heap of star-spangled silk, pooling with the blood on the ice. *He's gone.* And why couldn't she resume earthly form? Apparently, the changing art had been stripped from her, the Lurker, the rot taking hold. Then, as the circle brightened, the sword dipping towards its core, a residual heat shivered through him, sparking every nerve, bright with the understanding.

Only with the blade can I reignite the circles and restore your world. Bring us the sword. Then you will have your answer.

One could never trust the Fay, and in her case, it was no different. Everything she'd told him was a mirror. An inverted prophecy, or a spoiled one, going the same way as the magic. Going to Hell along with everything else.

Your Troth is tainted. A promise of death. That's your answer.

The Lady hadn't come to restore the circle. She'd come to destroy it.

In that moment, the truth struck him. Nothing he was seeing here had happened by accident. Von Hart had drawn the Lady to the heart of the circle, the Locus, choosing this remote and frozen place to welcome her return. Perhaps he'd really believed that he could reason with her, remind his queen of love and persuade her to heal the world. Even when the envoy learnt of her decay, he'd pressed on, trying to reach her. *What else could he do? He had nothing left* . . . All the same, his blindness had cost him dearly. Cost them all so dearly.

But Von Hart had forgotten the sword. *Neglected* it. Caliburn had fallen into Ben's hands, unlikely, clumsy as they were. And Ben had followed the ravens to the mountain, answering the ancient summons, taking up a task meant for another, meant for the envoy alone. Had that been an accident too?

You knew all along, didn't you?

He remembered the envoy on the desert sands, looking back with a smile over his shoulder. And as for Jia . . . *Catch her. Let me fall.* He'd wondered all along why Von Hart had kept him around, tangled up at the edges of his schemes. Blundering, chasing riddles and ghosts, Ben had turned over the cards one by one, their faces spelling catastrophe. And much as the thought rankled him, the envoy had obviously known that one washed-up dragon couldn't stop him, simply serve as damage limitation. Not that it had exactly worked out . . .

And what else? Ben knew he'd never be a hero, no. Not the saviour that anyone wanted. He'd let too much slip for that, even turned his back on his own kind, choosing survival instead. *And Maud. Rose. Jia. You couldn't save them* . . . He couldn't deny his part in all this. His long, waking sleep had enabled the destruction. The gate that yawned above, hungry and black. But it struck him that he was here for a reason. The envoy wouldn't have left anything to chance, particularly the presence of a seven-ton dragon, here at the crux of his plans.

It's the sword. He wanted to bargain with the sword.

This prompted another thought. Another faint shiver of heat.

Here we stand at the heart of all belief, watching the last hope fade . . .

And it was the *sword*, he saw, not the Lady, that the circle was seeking to answer. As Nimue once again lowered herself, her legs locked, her joints meeting with a glassy click, keeping her belly from the ice. She was an ill-formed thing. A ghost from the dark, never meant for this world. As such, the arm that stretched from her maw couldn't quite reach the heart of the circle, the tip of the sword a foot or so from it. The circle shone, the light uncertain, responding to *lunewrought*, eager for connection.

Yes! All of this, the Example, the war, had started with the damn sword. The blade had been thrust into anvil and stone, waiting to spark a tragic destiny. When Ben's hand had closed around the hilt, he'd seen it. As he'd seen the sword used like a key, unlocking a mountainside, the chamber deep under Snowdon. In Barcelona, in London, he'd seen how the sword triggered the circles of protection and wondered what it was trying to show him.

Now he understood.

With our spells and the hope in our heart, we bound the fate of your world to the blade.

The Lady, of course, had lost hope long ago, descending into madness. And her spells had soured, infecting all. *The Earth. The leys. The Isle of the Apples, wilting in the orchard* . . . Nimue, for all her promise, hadn't returned to save them at all, to reignite the failing magic. No. She had come to cut the rot from the branch, and for that, she needed the sword. As soon as he thought it, Ben grasped the sense of it, the things he'd seen on his journey – his *battle* – rising to the surface of his pain. The sword, never one to resist an insult, had told him from the start.

374

I'm right in front of you, numbskull.

Ben groaned, his stomach burning, a dark sun dawning on him. He might not have trusted Von Hart, but Von Hart had trusted *him*. At least, trusted his love of humans, his unshakeable sense of duty. Maybe even his need for answers, the conviction that Ben would follow him. And why not? He'd chased Atiya all the way from London to Cairo. And Jia from the Alps into China. The envoy had wanted to greet his returning queen, that much was clear. Perhaps to bargain with her. To plead . . . though it seemed he'd been quite aware of the gamble he was taking and so, in typical fashion, he'd left the sword out of the picture. Somewhere that the Lady couldn't reach it. Across the gulf of the nether. The gulf of earthly dreams. In this way, Von Hart had kept an ace up his sleeve, a bargaining chip in case his plan, his entreaty, went wrong. If Ben had been his escape route, then the sword was his get-out clause.

But Caliburn was more than that. The full weight of Ben's position landed on his shoulders. The envoy hadn't just placed a sword in his hands, but the fate of the world. The Lady wanted to stick the blade through the heart of the circle and, in darkness, in death, fulfil it.

The heart of the spell. She can't reach it.

Thinking this, he looked across the surface of the lake. He squinted at the sword, weaving, useless, in the air. *One thing. One thing left to do . . .* And there, in silver, in *lunewrought*, he saw himself reflected. To all intents and purposes a naked, bloody figure on the ice, a man who had never been a man. The onetime Sola Ignis. Benjurigan. Guardian dragon of the west. Flame-haired, pale and wounded, his embers dying out, pooling all around him.

Get up. Get up, you oaf.

Muscles screaming, Ben stretched out a hand. With an effort of will that threatened to break him, he extended a trembling claw. Talons splayed where his fingers had been, scrabbling at the ice. Teeth gritted, he dragged himself forward, one claw over another. A red carpet smeared the frozen surface as he crept for the circle.

The Lady, focused on her efforts, didn't notice him approach. The seconds crystallised around him, the chance trickling out. Trickling out like the stuff in his veins, an hourglass of blood. *There's no time*. How long until the vanguard arrived, screaming out of the nether? *No time*. Silently cursing, he reached the inner ring and hauled himself under her, under her quivering belly, crawling between her legs. Only then, as the sword slashed down, did she vent a shriek. Over the thrumming of the blade, her outrage shook the sky. Ben looked up, seeing himself reflected in eight eyes, furious at his intrusion. And behind her rage, the understanding that she was too late to stop him.

I am not . . . nothing . . .

With the last of his strength, a blink of will, Ben forced draconic brawn into his body. He rose, an awkward mass of scales and horns, from the graven ice. Half-formed, a rhino-sized brute, he reached out for the pendulum blade, his claw closing around the crossguard. And with a grunt, a blast of ash, he wrenched Caliburn from her grip.

Closing his eyes, he thrust the sword into the ice. Into the heart of the circle.

The effect was immediate and dazzling. The sky boomed. A cannonade of magic. Wild. Unleashed. *The last of it. The last.* As Caliburn stabbed the surface of the lake, half of its length embedded, a web of cracks went riddling out, the ground rumbling. With it went light, loops and arcs of power, lit by the legendary blade. The glyphs shone, rippling out in blazing rings, a bright rosette with Ben at the centre, clinging onto the hilt.

Somewhere above him, the Lady shrieked, her fear plain. As the light intensified, the sour blue brightening to silver, she hunkered over him, reaching for the sword. The radiance washed out the night, the lake, the mountains and the gate. All was swallowed by white.

In the glare, he caught her intent. Her alien thirst. Her hunger. With magic, with *lunewrought*, she would suck up the soul of the world, draw the last of the magic into herself and leave the Earth to die . . .

But another intention, draconic, mortal, had stolen her chance, curdling with her ambition.

You're too late, my lady. Your story was already over.

In Ben's skull, memories wheeled, visions sparked by the blade.

Who are you? What are you?

In his head, he heard Rose. Or rather saw her. She was staring at him in Central Park, a hand to her mouth, shocked by his inhuman strength.

Then, high in the Alps, he saw a cable car dangling by a thread, the passengers wide-eyed and screaming, taking in the dragon in the sky.

This was followed by the boom of shells, pounding in his ears. The tanks in Cairo, firing on a monster that burst from the roof of a shattered museum. A beast that shouldn't be.

In China, he saw people running and screaming. Dragons locked in battle – impossible battle – thundering across Tiananmen Square.

In newspapers. On radio waves. On TV screens. The news of him had spread like fire.

And in London, his city – the dragon *city – how many eyes had turned to the heavens, watching him snake through the ash and smoke, a creature from the pages of myth?*

Hundreds. Thousands of them.

All these things, the Pact had forbidden. The Lore had served to prevent.

And the Lore was over.

It was only a moment, nothing more, but in the whirl of images, the blinding light, he grasped its meaning.

Somewhere in the glare, Caliburn said, "Now. Now you see."

He did see. Because his journeys had exposed him to the world, blowing the lid off an eight-hundred-year-old secret. But with the collapse of everything he knew, everything he'd tried to protect, the humans hadn't greeted his presence with fear alone. He realised that now, the sword pressing the wisdom upon him.

Not with fear alone. No. Also with *belief.*

It was in him, this belief. Like the touch of *lunewrought*, he was stained by it, tainted with credulity. Gripping the sword, he forced his memories into the blade, this bright catalyst, and into the heart of the circle.

The Lady screamed. Fangs bared, she tore at him, trying to wrench him from the sword. Pincers raked his spine, sparking off scale and horn. Shrieking, wailing – the light was *hurting* her, he realised, spearing into her deformed shape, the diseased, murderous core of her. In a blast of silver, Nimue released him, relinquishing her claim. The radiance was too much for her, driving her away from the Locus. She scuttled away over the ice, spurned by the arcane energy. Steaming, hissing, the light ripped into her, finding her presence foul, at odds with the kindled spell. Here, at the heart of the world, Caliburn, the Sword of Albion, world-cleaver, demon-slayer, harp-breaker, ignited the circle of protection, fuelled by the fire of belief.

And the circle, branded in the earth by forgotten gods, designed to protect Creation from the dark, shuddered and did its work.

Everything was silver now. The lake. The mountains. The sky. Glittering veins fanned out from the rings, exceeding the bounds of the circle. The radiance snaked over the ice. Onto the shore. Up into the peaks. The stars fled from its touch. On a shimmering disc, Ben lay, a spinning coin in the emptiness, the ocean of splintering light. With an understanding beyond his own, universal, vast in scope, he realised what was happening. The rivers, he thought, these streams of faith, would go rippling out from the sword, shooting through the bedrock, over the seas, setting fire to the other circles. The sword would restore the ancient spells.

I can hope. I can hope that at the end . . .

In his grip, the sword burned, growing molten. The blazing core was devouring the blade. The gilded dragons bubbled on the hilt, losing their shape. The runes, indecipherable, sank into the fuller, rubbed out. Runnels of gold bled through his fingers, searing his scales, his flesh. Then the *lunewrought* warped, the blade bending. Liquid beads spilled into the circle, feeding its beating heart. Gems popped from the melting quillons, glimmering, a little sadly, on the ice. Then they too were gone. Inhaled. Eaten by the light.

Even the gate, the hole in the world, couldn't withstand the brilliance, the rejuvenated magic. With a rush of air, a blast that tore snow, trees and rock from the surrounding slopes, the fissure in the sky twisted and churned, a black spindle, shuddering in the glare. The gate throbbed, once, twice, unreality fighting reasserted mass. Fighting *belief*. And then, with an indrawn breath, a rumble of hooves and the echo of screams, the gate boomed shut, a wound sealing in the air.

The door of Creation had closed.

For long moments, the lake blazed. The circle spun, silver and aflame. Ben clung onto the heart, aching, groaning, the light squeezing his brain. Nausea raged in his guts, and he vomited, hot on the snow. Blood fanned out around him. So much blood. Too much...

And then, silence. Silence and snow. The night swept in, strewn with stars, the circle fading under the sky. The mountains, black, drank in the echoes, the retreating tide of magic. Darkness lay between them, but it was only darkness, deep, yet earthly. The wind whistled out of the north – a little peevishly, Ben thought, keen to reclaim its reign in these lands. Somewhere, the sea roared, crashing against the cliffs. Ice shifted and cracked, a slow, ceaseless dance. In the distance, a bird squawked, as though challenging the still.

Ben lay on the ice, the shadows folding around him. Soft, dark wings. Partly scaled, partly naked, he curled in an ungainly heap, looking up at the heavens. His breath swirled in front of his face. Passing clouds, growing thinner by the second. Bruised and broken, he lay, embracing the gradual creep of sleep. He was numb now, the wound in his belly rimed with frost, the heat slipping out of him. If only he could focus, draw on a flickering flame of will, staunch the flow of blood. It was still there, the magic. Still there. He could feel it in his bones. The Lady hadn't stripped him of it, for all her violence. The circle around him blazed on, hidden deep in the earth. Would it take that much to reach for it? Reach for the light, beg for its power in this lost and frozen place . . .

But he was tired. Too tired. And so cold. So very cold. The last ember winked in the hearth and he couldn't stoke himself to act.

Nimue, Our Lady of the Barrows, was gone. Just like the envoy. *Gone.* He couldn't see her on the ice, but even if he managed to turn his head, he somehow knew that he wouldn't see her. No charred carcass on the lake, her legs curled in the air. She'd been a ghost, nothing more. No, a fairy tale. She'd never truly belonged to this world. None of them had. The Fay.

He looked up at a shooting star, arcing through the darkness, and he made a wish. Didn't they say you could do that? Well, he could hardly trust to legends. Legends were given to change and unreliable, full of fancy and wild ideas. But he could hope. He could hope, sure. The Long Sleep was undone and the Remnants would be stirring, rousing in the deep. Dragons. Giants. And worse. There was no way that he could stop that now. Whatever remained of the fabulous beings and beasts, the children of the Fay, they would find themselves blinking in the light of the modern world – a *woken* world – with no Pact, no Lore to guide them.

Would there be war? Certainly. Chaos, magic and fire? Grand schemes to rule the world? Yes. Without doubt. It gave him a strange kind of comfort. Because the world would go on. In the end, the world would go on.

Red Ben Garston smiled in the darkness, the shadows enfolding him.

There would always be stories, he knew. He might have laughed, accepting the truth of the matter. There had always been a king in the mountain. Swords in stones and sleeping gods. And giants in the earth, in those days and this. As long as there were tongues to tell them, there would always be stories. Once upon a time and happy ever after.

All myths have their season. And in time, even dragons have their ending.

Acknowledgements

I wrote *Burning Ashes* for Britain, drawing on the rich mythology of my homeland and with a mind to the authors who inspired a kid in countless libraries across the land. Those books, I believe, became the thread on the loom of my imagination. The visions of T. H. White, J. R. R. Tolkien, C. S. Lewis, Mary Stewart, Alan Garner and Susan Cooper, then as now, certainly filled my mind during the writing of this novel. In some ways, *Burning Ashes* serves as a love letter to a golden age, or perhaps the dream of one, and its childhood remembrance.

But those who deserve my thanks for their kindness and assistance as I travelled and wrote are as scattered as the four winds, proving yet again that stories belong to everywhere and to everyone.

Firstly, and once again, I'd like to thank agent extraordinaire John Jarrold for his unflagging support and encouragement. A good agent is worth their weight in gold, and believe me, Mr Jarrold is the Fort Knox of agents.

Thanks to Anna Jackson, Joanna Kramer, Lindsay Hall and Sarah Guan, my editors on both sides of the pond. And to all the Orbit team, Tim Holman, Brit Elisabet Hvide Busse, James Long, Emily Byron and Naz. And not forgetting Tracey Winwood for another fabulous book cover. I'm so grateful for your support, artistry, insights and patience.

James Bennett

Thanks go out to a whole slew of bloggers and reviewers for picking up these books, the most notable of whom I'll mention here. Ed Fortune of *Starburst Magazine*, Theresa Derwin of *Terror Tree*, Paul of *The Eloquent Page*, Aoife Lawlor of *Storyful*, Claire of *Brizzlelass Books* and Michael Grunier of *Kickstand Sound*. Thank you for reading and for having my back.

Special thanks to Danie Ware, genre-bending author, doyenne of Forbidden Planet and, most importantly, friend, for all her help with my launches and events. Thanks to Julie "lizard queen" Hutchings, Ian the Beer Colonel and J. B. Rockwell for the arm punches and props.

Ditto to Adele Wearing of Fox Spirit Books, my feral and furry knight gallant and all-round champ. Hugs to everyone involved with that bushiest of bushy indie publishers.

Thanks to Sarah Pinborough, Lavie Tidhar and Elizabeth Chadwick for the retweets, kind words and chuckles.

On a personal note, I'd like to thank Anne-Mhairi Simpson for her generosity and Greg Smith for the online pep talks.

Much love to all my family, as ever. I realise I travel far and wide, but you are often in my thoughts. I owe so much to your belief in me. Thanks to Ben and Karl for giving me shelter when I most needed it.

Last but not least, a big thanks to all the unexpected angels I met on the road as I wrote this novel. Eduardo and Lucia in Valencia and Bratislava respectively. Bernat and Tony of Plata Bar, Barcelona. Liz and Khalid in London (hi, Kiyana!). Mike in Hanoi. Edward in Puerto Rico. Andrew of Canada. You all kept me smiling and pushing forward, and you will always have my friendship.

And thank you, Britain, for the dreams you gave me.

extras

orbit

www.orbitbooks.net

extras

about the author

James Bennett is a British writer raised in Sussex and South Africa. His travels have furnished him with an abiding love of different cultures, history and mythology. His short fiction has appeared internationally and the acclaimed *Chasing Embers* was his debut fantasy novel. James lives in London and sees dragon bones in the Thames whenever he crosses a bridge.

Find out more about James Bennett and other Orbit authors by registering for the free monthly newsletter at www.orbitbooks.net.

if you enjoyed
BURNING ASHES
look out for
STRANGE PRACTICE
by
Vivian Shaw

Meet Greta Helsing, doctor to the undead.

After inheriting a highly specialised, and highly peculiar, medical practice, Dr Helsing spends her days treating London's undead for a host of ills: vocal strain in banshees, arthritis in barrow-wights and entropy in mummies. Although barely making ends meet, this is just the quiet, supernatural-adjacent life Greta's dreamed of since childhood.

But when a sect of murderous monks emerges, killing human undead alike, Greta must use all her unusual skills to keep her supernatural clients – and the rest of London – safe.

CHAPTER 1

The sky was fading to ultramarine in the east over the Victoria Embankment when a battered Mini pulled in to the curb, not far from Blackfriars Bridge. Here and there in the maples lining the riverside walk, the morning's first sparrows had begun to sing.

A woman got out of the car and shut the door, swore, put down her bags, and shut the door again with more applied force; some fellow motorist had bashed into the panel at some time in the past and bent it sufficiently to make this a production every damn time. The Mini really needed to be replaced, but even with her inherited Harley Street consulting rooms Greta Helsing was not exactly drowning in cash.

She glowered at the car and then at the world in general, glancing around to make sure no one was watching her from the shadows. Satisfied, she picked up her black working bag and the shapeless oversize monster that was her current handbag and went to ring the doorbell. It was time to replace the handbag, too. The leather on this one was holding up but the lining was beginning to go, and Greta had limited patience regarding the retrieval of items from the mysterious dimension behind the lining itself.

The house to which she had been summoned was one of a row of magnificent old buildings separating Temple Gardens from the Embankment, mostly taken over by lawyers and publishing firms these days. It was a testament to this particular homeowner's rather special powers of persuasion that nobody had succeeded in buying the house out from under him and turning it into offices for overpriced attorneys, she thought, and then had to smile at the idea of anybody dislodging Edmund Ruthven from the lair he'd inhabited these two hundred years or more. He was as much a fixture of London as Lord Nelson on his pillar, albeit less encrusted with birdlime.

"Greta," said the fixture, opening the door. "Thanks for coming out on a Sunday. I know it's late."

She was just about as tall as he was, five foot five and a bit, which made it easy to look right into his eyes and be struck every single time by the fact that they were very large, so pale a grey they looked silver-white except for the dark ring at the edge of the iris, and fringed with heavy soot-black lashes of the sort you saw in advertisements for mascara. He looked tired, she thought. Tired, and older than the fortyish he usually appeared. The extreme pallor was normal, vivid against the pure slicked-back black of his hair, but the worried line between his eyebrows was not.

"It's not Sunday night, it's Monday morning," she said. "No worries, Ruthven. Tell me everything; I know you didn't go into lots of detail on the phone."

"Of course." He offered to take her coat. "I'll make you some coffee."

The entryway of the Embankment house was floored in black-and-white-checkered marble, and a large bronze ibis stood on a little side table where the mail and car keys and shopping lists were to be found. The mirror behind this reflected Greta dimly and greenly, like a woman underwater; she peered into it, making a face at herself, and tucked back her hair. It was pale Scandinavian blonde and cut like Liszt's in an off-the-shoulder bob, fine enough to slither free of whatever she used to pull it back; today it was in the process of escaping from a thoroughly childish headband. She kept meaning to have it all chopped off and be done with it but never seemed to find the time.

Greta Helsing was thirty-four, unmarried, and had taken over her late father's specialized medical practice after a brief stint as an internist at King's College Hospital. For the past five years she had run a bare-bones clinic out of Wilfert Helsing's old rooms in Harley Street, treating a patient base that to the majority of the population did not, technically, when you got right down to it, exist. It was a family thing.

There had never been much doubt which subspecialty of medicine she would pursue, once she began her training: treating the differently alive was not only more interesting than catering to the ordinary human population, it was in many ways a great deal more rewarding. She took a lot of satisfaction in being able to provide help to particularly underserved clients.

Greta's patients could largely be classified under the heading of *monstrous*—in its descriptive, rather than pejorative, sense: vampires, were-creatures, mummies, banshees, ghouls, bogeymen, the occasional arthritic barrow-wight. She herself was solidly and entirely human, with no noticeable eldritch qualities or powers whatsoever, not even a flicker of metaphysical sensitivity. Some of her patients found it difficult to trust a human physician at first, but Greta had built up an extremely good reputation over the five years she had been practicing supernatural medicine, largely by word of mouth: *Go to Helsing, she's reliable.*

And *discreet.* That was the first and fundamental tenet, after all. Keeping her patients safe meant keeping them secret, and Greta was good with secrets. She made sure the magical wards around her doorway in Harley Street were kept up properly, protecting anyone who approached from prying eyes.

Ruthven appeared in the kitchen doorway, outlined by

light spilling warm over the black-and-white marble. "Greta?" he said, and she straightened up, realizing she'd been staring into the mirror without really seeing it for several minutes now. It really *was* late. Fatigue lapped heavily at the pilings of her mind.

"Sorry," she said, coming to join him, and a little of that heaviness lifted as they passed through into the familiar warmth and brightness of the kitchen. It was all blue tile and blond wood, the cheerful rose-gold of polished copper pots and pans balancing the sleek chill of stainless steel, and right now it was also full of the scent of really *good* coffee. Ruthven's espresso machine was a La Cimbali, and it was serious business.

He handed her a large pottery mug. She recognized it as one of the set he generally used for blood, and had to smile a little, looking down at the contents—and then abruptly had to clamp down on a wave of thoroughly inconvenient emotion. There was no reason that Ruthven doing goddamn *latte art* for her at half-past four in the morning should make her want to cry.

He was *good* at it, too, which was a little infuriating; then again she supposed that with as much free time on her hands as he had on his, and as much disposable income, she might find herself learning and polishing new skills simply to stave off the encroaching spectre of boredom. Ruthven didn't go in for your standard-variety vampire angst, which was refreshing, but Greta knew very well he had bouts of something not unlike depression—especially in the winter—and he needed things to *do*.

She, however, *had* things to do, Greta reminded herself, taking a sip of the latte and closing her eyes for a moment. This was coffee that actually tasted as good as, if not better than, it smelled. *Focus,* she thought. This was not a social call. The lack of urgency in Ruthven's manner led her to believe that the situation was not immediately dire, but she was nonetheless here to do her job.

Greta licked coffee foam from her upper lip. "So," she said. "Tell me what happened."

"I was—"

Ruthven sighed, leaning against the counter with his arms folded. "To be honest I was sitting around twiddling my thumbs and writing nasty letters to the *Times* about how much I loathe these execrable skyscrapers somebody keeps allowing vandals to build all over the city. I'd got to a particularly cutting phrase about the one that sets people's cars on fire, when somebody knocked on the door."

The passive-aggressive-letter stage tended to indicate that his levels of ennui were reaching critical intensity. Greta just nodded, watching him.

"I don't know if you've ever read an ancient penny-dreadful called *Varney the Vampyre, or The Feast of Blood*," he went on.

"Ages ago," she said. She'd read practically all the horror classics, well-known and otherwise, for research purposes rather than to enjoy their literary merit. Most of them were to some extent entertainingly wrong about the individuals they claimed to depict. "It was quite a lot funnier than your unofficial biography, but I'm not sure it was *meant* to be."

Ruthven made a face. John Polidori's *The Vampyre* was, he insisted, mostly libel—the very mention of the book was sufficient to bring on indignant protestations that he and the Lord Ruthven featured in the narrative shared little more than a name. "At least the authors got the spelling right, unlike bloody Polidori," he said. "I think probably *Feast of Blood* is about as historically accurate as *The Vampyre*, which is to say *not very*, but it does have the taxonomy right. Varney, unlike me, *is* a vampyre with a *y*."

"A lunar sensitive? I haven't actually met one before," she said, clinical interest surfacing through the fatigue. The vampires she knew were all classic draculines, like Ruthven himself and the handful of others in London. Lunar sensitives were rarer than the draculine vampires for a couple of reasons, chief among which was the fact that they were violently—and inconveniently—allergic to the blood of anyone but virgins. They did have the handy characteristic of being resurrected by moonlight every time they got themselves killed, which presumably came as some small comfort in the process of succumbing to violent throes of gastric distress brought on by dietary indiscretion.

"Well," Ruthven said, "now's your chance. He showed up on my doorstep, completely unannounced, looking like thirty kinds of warmed-over hell, and collapsed in the hallway. He is at the moment sleeping on the drawing room sofa, and I want you to look at him for me. I don't *think* there's any real danger, but he's been hurt—some maniacs apparently attacked him with a knife—and I'd feel better if you had a look."

Ruthven had lit a fire, despite the relative mildness of the evening, and the creature lying on the sofa was covered with two blankets. Greta glanced from him to Ruthven, who shrugged a little, that line of worry between his eyebrows very visible.

According to him, Sir Francis Varney, title and all, had come out of his faint quite quickly and perked up after some first aid and the administration of a nice hot mug of suitable and brandy-laced blood. Ruthven kept a selection of the stuff in his expensive fridge and freezer, stocked by Greta via fairly illegal supply chain management—she knew someone who knew someone who worked in a blood bank and was not above rescuing rejected units from the biohazard incinerator.

Sir Francis had drunk the whole of the mug's contents with every evidence of satisfaction and promptly gone to sleep as soon as Ruthven let him, whereupon Ruthven had called Greta and requested a house call. "I don't really like the look of him," he said now, standing in the doorway with uncharacteristic awkwardness. "He was bleeding a little—the wound's in his left shoulder. I cleaned it up and put a dressing on, but it was still sort of oozing. Which isn't like us."

"No," Greta agreed, "it's not. It's possible that lunar sensitives and draculines respond differently to tissue trauma, but even so, I would have expected him to have mostly finished healing already. You were right to call me."

"Do you need anything?" he asked, still standing in the doorway as Greta pulled over a chair and sat down beside the sofa.

"Possibly more coffee. Go on, Ruthven. I've got this; go and finish your unkind letter to the editor."

When he had gone, she tucked back her hair and leaned over to examine her patient. He took up the entire length of the sofa, head pillowed on one armrest and one narrow foot resting on the other, half-exposed where the blankets had fallen away. She did a bit of rough calculation and guessed he must be at least six inches taller than Ruthven, possibly more.

His hair was tangled, streaky-grey, worn dramatically long—that was aging-rock-frontman hair if Greta had ever seen it, but nothing *else* about him seemed to fit with the Jagger aesthetic. An old-fashioned face, almost Puritan: long, narrow nose, deeply hooded eyes under intense eyebrows, thin mouth bracketed with habitual lines of disapproval.

Or pain, she thought. *That could be pain.*

The shifting of a log in the fireplace behind Greta made her jump a little, and she regathered the wandering edges of her concentration. With a nasty little flicker of surprise she noticed that there was a faint sheen of sweat on Varney's visible skin. That *really* wasn't right.

"Sir Francis?" she said, gently, and leaned over to touch his shoulder through the blankets—and a moment later had retreated halfway across the room, heart racing: Varney had gone from uneasy sleep to *sitting up and snarling viciously* in less than a second.

It was not unheard-of for Greta's patients to threaten her, especially when they were in considerable pain, and on the whole she probably should have thought this out a little better. She'd only got a glimpse before her own instincts had kicked in and got her the hell out of range of those teeth, but it would be a while before she could forget that pattern of dentition, or those mad tin-colored eyes.

He covered his face with his hands, shoulders slumping, and instead of menace was now giving off an air of intense embarrassment.

Greta came back over to the sofa. "I'm sorry," she said, tentatively, "I didn't mean to startle you—"

"I most devoutly apologize," he said, without taking his hands away. "I do *try* not to do that, but I am not quite at my best just now—forgive me, I don't believe we have been introduced."

He was looking at her from behind his fingers, and the eyes really *were* metallic. Even partly hidden she could see the room's reflection in his irises. She wondered if that was a peculiarity of his species, or an individual phenomenon.

"It's all right," she said, and sat down on the edge of the sofa, judging that he wasn't actually about to tear her throat out just at the moment. "My name's Greta. I'm a doctor; Ruthven called me to come and take a look at you."

When Varney finally took his hands away from his face,

pushing the damp silvering hair back, his color was frankly terrible. He *was* sweating. That was not something she'd ever seen in sanguivores under any circumstance.

"A doctor?" he asked, blinking at her. "Are you sure?" She was spared having to answer that. A moment later he squeezed his eyes shut, very faint color coming and going high on each cheek. "I really am sorry," he said. "What a remarkably stupid question. It's just—I tend to think of doctors as looking rather different than you."

"I left my pinstripe trousers and pocket-watch at home," she said drily. "But I've got my black bag, if that helps. Ruthven said you'd been hurt—attacked by somebody with a knife. May I take a look?"

He glanced up at her and then away again, and nodded once, leaning back against the sofa cushions, and Greta reached into her bag for the exam gloves.

The wound was in his left shoulder, as Ruthven had said, about two and a half inches south of the collarbone. It wasn't large—she had seen much nastier injuries from street fights, although in rather different species—but it was undoubtedly the *strangest* wound she'd ever come across.

"What made this?" she asked, looking closer, her gloved fingers careful on his skin. Varney hissed and turned his face away, and she could feel a thrumming tension under her touch. "I've never seen anything like it. The wound is . . . *cross*-shaped."

It was. Instead of just the narrow entry mark of a knife, or the bruised puncture of something clumsier, Varney's wound appeared to have been made by something flanged. Not just two but four sharp edges, leaving a hole shaped like an X—or a cross.

"It was a spike," he said, between his teeth. "I didn't get a very good look at it. They had—broken into my flat, with garlic. Garlic was everywhere. Smeared on the walls, scattered all over the floor. I was—taken by surprise, and the fumes—I could hardly see or breathe."

"I'm not surprised," said Greta, sitting up. "It's extremely nasty stuff. Are you having any chest pain or trouble breathing now?"

A lot of the organic compounds in *Allium sativum* triggered a severe allergic response in vampires, varying in intensity based on amount and type of exposure. This wasn't garlic shock, or not *just* garlic shock, though. He was definitely running a fever, and the hole in his shoulder should have healed to a shiny pink memory within an hour or so after it happened. Right now it was purple-black and . . . oozing.

"No," Varney said, "just—the wound is, ah, really rather painful." He sounded apologetic. "As I said, I didn't get a close look at the spike, but it was short and pointed like a rondel dagger, with a round pommel. There were three people there, I don't know if they all had knives, but . . . well, as it turned out, all they needed was one."

This was so very much not her division. "Did—do you have any idea why they attacked you?" Or why they'd broken into his flat and poisoned it with garlic. That was a pretty specialized tactic, after all. Greta shivered in sudden unease.

"They were chanting, or . . . reciting something," he said, his odd eyes drifting shut. "I couldn't make out much of it, just that it sounded sort of ecclesiastical."

He had a remarkably beautiful voice, she noticed. The rest of him wasn't tremendously prepossessing, particularly those eyes, but his voice was *lovely*: sweet and warm and clear. It contrasted oddly with the actual content of what he was saying. "Something about . . . *unclean*," he continued, "*unclean* and wicked, *wickedness*, foulness, and . . . *demons*. Creatures of darkness."

He still had his eyes half-closed, and Greta frowned and bent over him again. "Sir Francis?"

"Hurts," he murmured, sounding very far away. "They were dressed . . . strangely."

She rested two fingers against the pulse in his throat: much too fast, and he couldn't have spiked *that* much in the minutes she had been with him, but he felt noticeably warmer to her touch. She reached into the bag for her thermometer and the BP cuff. "Strangely how?"

"Like . . . monks," he said, and blinked up at her, hazy and confused. "In . . . brown robes. With crosses round their necks. Like *monks*."

His eyes rolled back slightly, slipping closed, and he gave a little terrible sigh; when Greta took him by the shoulders and gave him a shake he did not rouse at all, head rolling limp against the cushions. *What the hell,* she thought, *what the actual hell is going on here, there's no way a wound like this should be affecting him so badly, this is—it looks like systemic inflammatory response but the garlic should have worn off by now, there's nothing to* cause *it, unless—*

Unless there had been something on the blade. Something *left behind.*

That flicker of visceral unease was much stronger now. She leaned closer, gently drawing apart the edges of the wound— the tissue was swollen, red, warmer than the surrounding skin—and was surprised to notice a faint but present smell. Not the characteristic smell of infection, but something sharper, almost metallic, with a sulfurous edge on it like silver tarnish. It was strangely familiar, but she couldn't seem to place it.

Greta was rather glad he was unconscious just at the moment, because what she was about to do would be quite remarkably painful. She stretched the wound open a little wider, wishing she had her penlight to get a better view, and he shifted a little, his breath catching; as he moved she caught a glimpse of something reflective half-obscured by dark blood.

There *was* something still in there. Something that needed to come out right now.

"Ruthven," she called, sitting up. "Ruthven, I need you."

He emerged from the kitchen, looking anxious. "What is it?

"Get the green leather instrument case out of my bag," she said, "and put a pan of water on to boil. There's a foreign body in here I need to extract."

Without a word Ruthven took the instrument case and disappeared again. Greta turned her attention back to her patient, noticing for the first time that the pale skin of his chest was crisscrossed by old scarring—*very* old, she thought, looking at the silvery laddered marks of long-healed injuries. She had seen Ruthven without his shirt on, and he had a pretty good collection of scars from four centuries' worth of misadventure, but Varney put him to shame. *A lot of duels,* she thought. *A lot of . . .* lost *duels.*

Greta wondered how much of *Feast of Blood* was actually based on historical events. He had died at least once in the part of it that she remembered, and had spent a lot of time running away from various pitchfork-wielding mobs. None of *them* had been dressed up in monastic drag, as far as she knew, but they had certainly demonstrated the same intent as whoever had hurt Varney tonight.

A cold flicker of something close to fear slipped down her spine, and she turned abruptly to look over her shoulder at the empty room, pushing away a sudden and irrational sensation of being watched.

Don't be ridiculous, she told herself, *and do your damn job.* She was a little grateful for the business of wrapping the BP cuff around his arm, and less pleased by what it told her. Not critical, but certainly a long way from what she considered normal for sanguivores. She didn't know what was going on in there, but she didn't like it one bit.

When Ruthven returned carrying a tea tray, she felt irrationally relieved to see him—and then had to raise an eyebrow at the contents of the tray. Her probes and forceps and retractors lay on a metal dish Greta recognized after a moment as the one that normally went under the toast rack, dish and instruments steaming gently from the boiling water— and beside them was an empty basin with a clean tea towel draped over it. Everything was very, very neat, as if he had done it many times before. As if he'd had practice.

"Since when are *you* a scrub nurse?" she asked, nodding for him to set the tray down. "I mean—thank you, this is exactly what I need, I appreciate it, and if you could hold the light for me I'd appreciate that even more."

"*De rien*," said Ruthven, and went to fetch her penlight.

A few minutes later, Greta held her breath as she carefully, carefully withdrew her forceps from Varney's shoulder. Held between the steel tips was a piece of something hard and angular, about the size of a pea. That metallic, sharp smell was much stronger now, much more noticeable.

She turned to the tray on the table beside her, dropped the thing into the china basin with a little *rat-tat* sound, and straightened up. The wound was bleeding again; she pressed a gauze pad over it. The blood looked *brighter* now, somehow, which made no sense at all.

Ruthven clicked off the penlight, swallowing hard, and Greta looked up at him. "What *is* that thing?" he asked, nodding to the basin.

"I've no idea," she told him. "I'll have a look at it after I'm happier with him. He's pushing eighty-five degrees and his pulse rate is approaching low human baseline—"

Greta cut herself off and felt the vein in Varney's throat again. "That's strange," she said. "That's *very* strange. It's already coming down."

The beat was noticeably slower. She had another look at his blood pressure; this time the reading was much more reasonable. "I'll be damned. In a human I'd be seriously alarmed at that rapid a transient, but all bets are off with regard to hemodynamic stability in sanguivores. It's as if that thing, whatever it is, was directly responsible for the acute inflammatory reaction."

"And now that it's gone, he's starting to recover?"

"Something like that. *Don't* touch it," Greta said sharply, as Ruthven reached for the basin. "Don't even go near it. I have no idea what it would do to you, and I don't want to have two patients on my hands."

Ruthven backed away a few steps. "You're quite right," he said. "Greta, something about this smells peculiar."

"In more than one sense," she said, checking the gauze. The bleeding had almost stopped. "Did he tell you how it happened?"

"Not really. Just that he'd been jumped by several people armed with a strange kind of knife."

"Mm. A very strange kind of knife. I've never seen anything like this wound. He didn't mention that these people were dressed up like monks, or that they were reciting something about unclean creatures of darkness?"

"No," said Ruthven, flopping into a chair. "He neglected to share that tidbit with me. Monks?"

"So he said," Greta told him. "Robes and hoods, big crosses round their necks, the whole bit. Monks. And some kind of stabby weapon. Remind you of anything?"

"The Ripper," said Ruthven, slowly. "You think this has something to do with the murders?"

"I think it's one hell of a coincidence if it *doesn't*," Greta said. That feeling of unease hadn't gone away with Varney's physical improvement. It really was impossible to ignore. She'd been too busy with the immediate work at hand to consider the similarities before, but now she couldn't help thinking about it.

There had been a series of unsolved murders in London over the past month and a half. Eight people dead, all apparently the work of the same individual, all stabbed to death, all *found with a cheap plastic rosary stuffed into their mouths*. Six of the victims had been prostitutes. The killer had, inevitably, been nicknamed the Rosary Ripper.

The MO didn't exactly match how Varney had described his attack—multiple assailants, a strange-shaped knife—but it was way the hell too close for Greta's taste. "Unless whoever got Varney was a copycat," she said. "Or maybe there isn't just one Ripper. Maybe it's a group of people running around stabbing unsuspecting citizens."

"There was nothing on the news about the murders that mentioned weird-shaped wounds," Ruthven said. "Although I suppose the police might be keeping that to themselves."

The police had not apparently been able to do much of *anything* about the murders, and as one victim followed another with no end in sight, the general confidence in Scotland Yard—never tremendously high—was plummeting. The entire city was both angry and frightened. Conspiracy theories abounded on the Internet, some less believable than others. This, however, was the first time Greta had heard anything about the Ripper branching out into *supernatural* victims. The garlic on the walls of Varney's flat bothered her a great deal.

Varney shifted a little, with a faint moan, and Greta returned her attention to her patient. There was visible improvement; his vitals were stabilizing, much more satisfactory than they had been before the extraction.

"He's beginning to come around," she said. "We should get him into a proper bed, but I think he's over the worst of this."

Ruthven didn't reply at once, and she looked over to see him tapping his fingers on the arm of his chair with a thoughtful expression. "What?" she asked.

"Nothing. Well, *maybe* nothing. I think I'll call Cranswell at the Museum, see if he can look a few things up for me. I will, however, wait until the morning is a little further advanced, because I am a kind man."

"What time *is* it?" Greta asked, stripping off her gloves.

"Getting on for six, I'm afraid."

"Jesus. I need to call in—there's no way I'm going to be able to do clinic hours today. Hopefully Anna or Nadezhda can take an extra shift if I do a bit of groveling."

"I have faith in your ability to grovel convincingly," Ruthven said. "Shall I go and make some more coffee?"

"Yes," she said. Both of them knew this wasn't over. "Yes, do precisely that thing, and you will earn my everlasting fealty."

"I earned your everlasting fealty last time I drove you to the airport," Ruthven said. "Or was it when I made you tiramisu a few weeks ago? I can't keep track."

He smiled, despite the line of worry still between his eyebrows, and Greta found herself smiling wearily in return.

Enter the monthly

Orbit sweepstakes at

www.orbitloot.com

With a different prize every month,
from advance copies of books by
your favourite authors to exclusive
merchandise packs,
**we think you'll find something
you love.**

facebook.com/OrbitBooksUK

@OrbitBooks

www.orbitbooks.net